MOTHER OF FIRE

Have a good ride on
this safari — journey.
Warmly,
Jean Davison

ALSO by Jean Davison

Voices From Mutira: Lives of Rural Gikuyu Women (1st Edition)

Voices From Mutira: Change in the Lives of Rural Gikuyu Women
(2nd Edition)

Gender, Lineage and Ethnicity in Southern Africa

The Ostrich Wakes: Struggles for Change in Highland Kenya

Mother Of Fire

An Iraqi Woman's Journey from Mosul to Malawi

Jean Davison, Ph.D.

KIRINYAGA
PUBLISHERS

Cover design by Valerie Gazaui
Map designs by Maureen Farr
Title page by Maureen Farr and Valerie Gazaui
Photographs courtesy of Sr. Lise Therrien, Archivist,
Fille de la Sagesse Order, Rome, Italy.
Plant illustrations by Jean Davison

Published in the United States of America by
Kirinyaga Publishers
www.kirinyagapublishers.com

This is a work of fiction based on the life and travels of an actual person.
The original name of the person, other characters, and incidents come from
the author's imagination or are used fictionally. The second half of the book
draws from the life of Sr. Marie Reine de Jesus, a Fille de la Sagesse sister,
and is based on archival material from the Order in Rome. The author is
indebted to the archivist, Sr. Lise Therrien, for the use of the materials. The
section on Malawi is fictional, but draws on archival data and the author's
own experiences living and working in that country.

Library of Congress Cataloging in Publication Data
Davison, Jean
    Mother of Fire: An Iraqi Woman's Journey from Mosul to Malawi
    /by Jean Davison
    p. cm.

    1. Iraq/Syria—History—Ottoman Empire, 1880-1889—Fiction,
2. Christians in the Middle East and France—History—Fiction.
3. Malawi (Nyasaland)—early Catholic missionaries—History.
4. Historical fiction I. Title

ISBN 0-9785150-1-3   (pbk.)

CONTENTS

PREFACE

The spark for this book came from a footnote. It referred to an Iraqi nun who had left Mosul for France in 1898, and ended up in Malawi, Africa in 1904. I was living and teaching in that country at the time. A former British colony, Malawi is sandwiched between Zambia and Mozambique. Arab traders penetrated its interior in the sixteenth century in search of slaves and ivory, and were followed by the British in the late nineteenth century. The woman I call Amina Rassam was one of the first Catholic sisters to enter largely Muslim Malawi. A few tempting threads set me on a ten-year quest to discover the identity of this tenacious Middle East woman who subsequently became Sister Marie Reine, a pharmacologist, then Mai Moto, Mother of Fire.

Jean Davison
Harborside, Maine

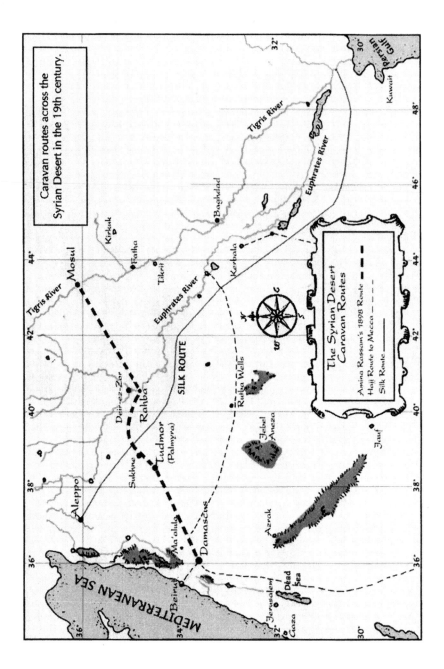

Caravan routes across the Syrian Desert in the 19th century.

The Syrian Desert
Caravan Routes

Amina Rassam's 1898 Route ▬ ▬ ▬
Hajj Route to Mecca — — —
Silk Route ————

MEDITERRANEAN SEA

Persian Gulf

Kuwait

Tigris River

Euphrates River

Mosul

Tigris River

Kirkuk

Fatha

Tikrit

Baghdad

Euphrates River

Karbala

Deir-ez-Zor

Rahba

SILK ROUTE

Rutba Wells

Jebel Anezu

Jauf

Azrak

Tudmor
(Palmyra)

Sukhne

Aleppo

Ma'alula

Damascus

Beirut

Jerusalem

Gaza

Dead Sea

N

CHAPTER 1

Desert Awakening

The moon was still up when Amina heard rustling outside the caravan tent she and Hanna shared. She held her breath and turned on her back, listening. There it was again. She froze. Something was rummaging in their canvas bag outside. She raised herself on her elbows and listened again. It sounded bigger than a rat.

The next instant, she saw in the moon's light the shiny edge of a knife slit through the tent flap.

Dear Lord, Mother Mary. She dared not breathe for fear of being discovered.

A hand reached in and felt around. It landed on their goatskin water bag and pulled it through the rip in the tent. *That's all the water we have,* she wanted to shout, but nothing came out.

"Hanna," she barked. "Wake up. There's someone outside. He stole our water bag." Startled, Hanna sat up stiffly. Her eyes widened. "Who's there?" she shouted in a gruff voice to cover the panic she felt rising.

Nothing.

Grabbing the lantern, Hanna struck a match on a stone. The scuffling outside ceased. She saw that the skin bag was missing. "We've been robbed. Help us. Someone, help us," she cried out in Syriac, reverting to her mother tongue.

Amina saw her putting on her boots and ducked deeper into her quilt. *Don't go, Hanna.*

Hanna got up and, leaning low, stamped to the entrance of the tent, looking for a hard object to wield. None.

"Be careful, Hanna," Amina found her voice.

Hanna untied the cloth straps and raised the tent flap quickly.

No one.

Shoving the lantern through, she pulled up her headscarf and stuck her head out cautiously, letting in cold air.

Amina shivered. Her heart beat like hard rain.

Hanna stood up quickly. "Help us," she shouted. "We've been robbed . . . Mustafa, help us." She heard a horse whinny in the distance.

"I just saw someone slinking away between the tents," she called to Amina. "Whoever it was knocked over the tent bag. There's a maze of footprints out here."

It was dead still for a minute then Hanna called again. "Amina. There's no lantern coming our way. All I can see is the light of the campfire. Where is Ahmed Mustafa?"

Amina heard her voice spark with anger.

Hanna opened the tent flap wide and, backing in, pulled the canvas bag inside. She shoved it behind the rolled up blankets she slept in. "There's nothing more precious than water out here. Who would do this?"

What are we going to do until we get to the Euphrates? Amina thought suddenly.

Retrieving the lantern, Hanna put it down and tied the tent straps tightly. She turned around and met Amina's terrified expression.

"Who was it?" Amina whispered. At eighteen, she was a year younger than Hanna, her lifelong maidservant, and felt vulnerable in a desert she knew could be hostile.

"I don't know. They tried to get something from the tent bag then snatched our goatskin. It's hard to believe that none of the men heard our cry."

Amina saw her cold fury rising and kept still.

"What kind of people are we traveling with?"

Amina shrank. "Maybe it was a Yezidi," she whispered, shifting in her quilt. "I'm sorry I didn't help. I was too scared."

"There was little you could have done," Hanna said. "I hope it wasn't one of the camel handlers. Anyway, he's gone now. But we do need a watchman. That's the least Mustafa can do."

"When we see him, I will insist on it." Then as an afterthought Amina added, "It's going to be hard to get back to sleep."

"Well, let's try. We have a long day—and night—ahead of us tomorrow." Hanna went and sat down beside her on the carpet. She began rubbing Amina's arm gently back and forth, back and forth . . . until her eyes began to close and her breathing sounded like the steady cooing of a dove.

Hanna blew out the lantern and rolled into her blankets, alert to every sound. The first two nights of the caravan and trouble had already found them. She didn't feel safe. Could they trust Mustafa, after this? What about Sheikh Hassan, the caravan's leader? She had promised Amina's father she would look after her, but this attack on them left her feeling shaken, unprepared for such a task . . . or the journey across the Syrian Desert.

She fell asleep just before the caravan men began their early morning prayers.

*   *   *

Amina heard the haunting voices when she woke. The camel handlers were saying the first of five daily prayers to Allah. *Where were they when we needed them last night?* She shuddered. They had camped in the shadow of a striated ridge that resembled the iron-red back of a dragon the second night of their journey. In the distance were the Sinjar Hills. "It is where the long-haired Yezidi live," Ahmed Mustafa, her father's friend, had told her.

He had approached Amina on his camel to see how she was doing on hers, and had related that the Yezidi were known to steal mares and trade goods. "And, they worship Satan, the Prince of Darkness," he'd added, rolling his eyes. Amina had no idea whether he was telling her the truth or teasing her. It hadn't eased her mind.

After she and Hanna had finished a cursory supper of dates and rice, they had left the campfire for their tent, feeling exhausted. They were still outside when Ahmed Mustafa appeared to check on them.

"I've brought you a skin of water." He'd put down a heavy goatskin bag next to the tent's entrance. "You must be careful the way you use it. We won't be stopping tomorrow night and water is scarce between here and the Euphrates. Keep the water bag inside your tent tonight," he had warned Amina in Arabic.

"*Shukran.* We will."

She'd told Hanna what he had said about the water. "We should drink only a little tomorrow so we won't have to stop." She had decided not to tell her what he'd said about the Yezidi. No sense in scaring her.

Hanna had crawled into her blankets. "I've heard. Good-night, Amina."

Amina had snuggled into her quilt. Turning toward the wall of the tent, she's noticed the moon had risen. Its penetrating brightness shone in their sleeping quarters giving her a sense of comfort. Her tired body had continued to sway with the rhythm of the camel's gait until she was asleep.

She had never expected the attack, but she was determined to confront Mustafa about it.

The men's prayers continued, reminding Amina of the soothing calls that came from the neighborhood mosque back in Mosul. Thinking of home, the anguished scene with her mother before her departure came flooding back, unbidden.

*   *   *

"We have an offer for your hand, Amina." Her mother had surprised her while she cared for Leila, her small sister. "It is from a merchant. You have met him. He attends our church."

Amina recalled a feeling of panic hearing the news as she struggled to put a diaper on Leila, who tossed on her mother's bed.

"Hold still." She pouted at the toddler. Leila was the youngest of Zakariya and Beta Rassam's six children, and the only other girl. Amina's hands were clammy. She shook her head at Leila to cover her anxiety. "There." The little girl sat up and crawled into her lap.

Their mother was lounging on raised cushions. Her knitting needles clicked a lively rhythm through wool threads in the process of becoming a blanket. Her round face had begun to crease along the edges and silver threads broke through her dark hair. She had a sweet disposition and a backbone of steel, as Amina had learned early in life.

Amina looked at her mother's calm demeanor. She felt ants in her stomach.

"Amina, we must talk about this marriage offer," her mother continued. "You have completed your education as your father wished. It's time you became someone's wife."

Amina's arms tightened around Leila. *I am not ready to talk about marriage.* Dropping her head quickly, she hid her face in Leila's curly hair. She knew that an arrangement for her marriage was possible—afterall she was seventeen—but she dreaded it. Now that she had made up her mind about what she wanted to do, it was unthinkable. Her heart pounded.

"Who is it, Mama?" she managed to ask, a sudden dryness in her throat.

"Michel Shaniss, the son of Yuhannas Shaniss. His sister is Mariam."

Amina paused, stricken. "I know him little. From what I remember, his face has pox marks and his hair is thinning. He is not so young, Mama." She saw displeasure written across her mother's face.

"But these are not reasons to reject him, I know." She sucked in her breath, and said a silent prayer.

"The real reason I cannot marry him is that I wish to do God's work . . . to take the vows of the *Filles de la Sagesse* in France. I learned about them from the Montfort brethren, the ones who stayed at the inn recently. The Daughters of Wisdom work along side the Montfort Brothers as missionaries administering to the poor. I feel I am being called, Mama, to work among the least fortunate of God's children." She could feel tears forming.

Her mother's needles dropped to her lap. She blanched.

At that moment, Leila struggled out of Amina's arms. She ran to their mother Beta, on shaky legs, her feet making a pattering sound on the polished marble floor. She put her head in her mother's lap and began sucking her thumb. Distractedly, Beta put aside her knitting, gathered the little girl to her. Unsnapping the front of her dress, she gave Leila her full breast.

"Amina ma, tell me," she said, "When did you start taking an interest in joining an order? It is such a . . . commitment."

"It is not something that came overnight, Mama. I've dreamed of the Virgin Mary for the last year. Her eyes reach out to me in the painting of her in St. Peter's Church. She seems to understand me. She gives me courage. I want to do something with my life, something to help others." Amina held her breath, full of dread.

Her mother was quiet for a moment. Then she smiled gently. "My daughter, don't you see that by making a good marriage and being a mother, you can do God's work?"

"You have shown me, with your own efforts, that this is possible, Mama. But I seek a different life, one that is spiritual. It is partly your own devotion that has inspired me."

Her mother looked grim. "I will talk with your father. Have you spoken to him?"

"No. Not yet. I wanted to wait to hear from the French brothers whether it is possible for someone like me, from Mesopotamia, to join the Daughters of Wisdom."

"And, what did they say?" Beads of perspiration had collected on Beta's upper lip.

"Yes." Amina looked down at her square, umber hands, and then up again. "They have told me it is possible to join the order."

Beta lowered her head to the baby sucking at her breast. Amina could tell she was angry. "Go now, Amina. We will talk about this later."

*   *   *

Beta Rassam sat in her sitting room, feeling numb. *How dare Amina betray her! The girl was abandoning her chances for marriage. And what about motherhood?* She tried to smother a feeling of mounting anxiety, but it overwhelmed her. She had assumed that Amina would want to marry, have a family. Instead, she had discovered that she was not like other girls her age . . . or her own mother. She wanted something else. It rankled Beta's sense of propriety and demeaned her feelings of worth as a mother. The set of Amina's chin and downturned lips haunted her. She could not reason with her daughter, now. Her mind was set.

*   *   *

Amina sat up in the tent and shook her head free of the memory of her mother's anger. It had upset her again. She knew Beta had not accepted her decision to leave Mosul. Never mind. She and Hanna were supposed to be up and packing their bedrolls by now. The next night of the journey promised to be difficult. They would be sleeping in their *haudaj* instead of a tent.

Amina looked at Hanna, still asleep.

"Hanna. Wake up."

Hanna woke with a jolt. "I meant to wake before you." She struggled out of her quilt and crawled over to the corner opening and untied the tent straps. Reaching out in the dark, she found the lantern and brought it inside. She lit it and turned up the wick. They quickly packed up their quilts, had a quick cup of tea, and were ready to mount their camels.

Amina looked for Mustafa to tell him about the attack, but he was nowhere in sight. She was angry with her father's friend for letting them down.

The caravan began traveling west along a broad plateau, in the direction of the Euphrates River. Ahead of them lay a parched landscape with nothing but flat, hard, stony sand. There were no hills, no striated ridges to break the monotony of the monochrome, sepia-tinted earth. It looked bleak, without life. The only animal Amina saw was the twisted carcass of a camel near the track. Thirsty flies clung to it. She grimaced. It seemed the desert made no exceptions in its claims to forgotten travelers—man or beast.

As the afternoon sun crept lower in the sky, Amina settled into the swaying rhythm of the camel's gait. She felt her eyelids drooping and almost fell asleep against the *haudaj's* cushions. Shaking herself, she called to Hanna, "Let's sing." She had heard their Bedouin guides, chanting together earlier as they made their way over the rutted, pebbled sand, keeping pace with one another and the camels.

She began singing a French song she remembered from her school days.

Eman and Salem, walking ahead, each leading a string of camels, turned with surprise. She could see amusement in their eyes. It was the first time she had seen a spark of light. *They smiled,* she sang to herself.

Hanna was silent. But when she saw the men turn around with laughing eyes beneath the swath of cloth they wore to protect themselves from the sun, she couldn't resist. *"Ding, dong, ding. Ding dong ding,"* she joined in. For the next hour or so, they overcame their boredom and entertained their Bedouin guides with songs they remembered from childhood.

When they had run out of songs, Amina rested. Her thoughts drifted back to the first time she met the Montfort brothers, who were to change her life.

CHAPTER 2

Mosul, Iraq, 1897

Amina adjusted her headscarf as she peeked through the heavy latticework shutters that hid her from the visitors. Two grizzled men in long gray robes stood in the inn's enclosed courtyard below. They were talking with her father. She studied them, one slightly shorter than the other, both with fringes of hair that ringed their shaven heads. "We have guests from France, Montfort brothers," Zakariya had explained earlier, as if Amina, at seventeen, should know of their importance.

She turned to Hanna, who had been her special companion since early childhood. Amina's father had taken in Hanna's widowed mother, Dina, and given her a job as the inn's cook when Hanna was a tentative toddler and Amina had just opened her eyes to the world. They had explored the inn together, ferreting out its secret hiding places and taunting each other to go past the kitchen and into the visitors' dining room when Hanna's mother was preoccupied with gutting a grouse or chicken. They made up plays using Beta's old chemises, scarves, and slippers. Amina's brothers were forced to become the audience. Then, when Amina began attending school at seven years and Hanna was left behind, their time together dwindled as Hanna's duties at the inn increased and more of Amina's time was devoted to her studies.

Watching the French visitors in the courtyard, Amina turned to Hanna. "I wonder what they're here for?"

"They've come to inspect the monasteries," Hanna said softly. "Mama says they will stay a fortnight." Her mother's position in the kitchen gave her an ear to everything newsworthy in the inn. Hanna detected the savory blend of cardamom, cumin, and mint wafting up from the kitchen where Dina was preparing mutton stew for the inn's guests. She knew she should go down to help, but paused to ask, "Why are you so interested in these foreigners, Amina?"

"I want to speak French with them . . . and Father says they have our safety at heart. Perhaps they would like to visit the Church of St. Peter, the one the Ottomans call Shamoun al-Safa. Did you know it was built over six hundred years ago?" She stopped, noticing the distracted look on Hanna's face.

"I've never been to it," Hanna said quickly.

"Father took me to see it once. It is ex-quis-ite." Amina drew out the word. "Especially the painting of the Virgin Mary."

Amina and her family belonged to an eastern Christian church that traced its roots to the first century. Later, to protect themselves against Muslim Arabs, Chaldean Christians had sought a haven in the Church of Rome while retaining some autonomy in Mesopotamia. Mass continued to be in the Eastern Syriac language, which took its roots from Aramaic, the language Jesus spoke.

Now, in the late nineteenth century, Amina and other Christians found themselves at the mercy of a Turkish Muslim Ottoman ruler. Her father's words, explaining that it was the support of European monastic orders that protected their churches in the East, came back to her. She had never heard of the Montfort Order, only the Dominicans. As she eyed the two men in the courtyard, she murmured to Hanna, "I wish I could hear what they are saying."

Hanna shrugged and pulled on Amina's arm. "Come. We need to go. I have too much work to do. And I wouldn't understand what they're saying, anyway. I have to help Mother. She will be threatening to whip me."

Amina closed the partially opened shutter. Picking up the edge of her long, rust silk dress she followed Hanna down the narrow rear staircase to the warm kitchen. It was filled with a medley of aromas: steaming mutton, mint, raisins, turmeric and garlic. Recognizing the look of concentration on Dina's face as she stirred a large pot of bubbling stew, Amina feared she had made Hanna late. She ducked out quickly, leaving her to her serving tasks, and hurried up to her own room to ponder the new visitors' intent.

After the French brothers had enjoyed their sumptuous feast of cold delicacies, followed by warmed dishes that were among Amina's favorites—steamed fish from the Tigris with cucumber dressing, mutton stew with squash, and other vegetable dishes—the two men moved to the inn's sitting room for coffee. Hanna served it from a samovar set on a table. As she poured the scalding liquid into cups, Zakariya appeared with Amina.

"We hope that you found the meal sufficient," he bowed.

"C'etait magnifique!" the older man said, hardly noticing Amina.

"That's good. May I take this opportunity to introduce my daughter Amina Marie?"

Amina bent her head as she stepped next to her father and watched Hanna pour a long stream of coffee into a cup.

"She speaks French quite well," her father continued. "If you have time, I'm sure she would like to learn something about your country."

With a fleeting smile to hide her embarrassment, Amina raised her head and greeted the two guests: *"Bonsoir, messieurs."*

Delighted, the two men returned her greeting and introduced themselves. Brother Herbert was the gray-haired one. Brother Philippe, his younger companion, wore spectacles that gave him the look of a scholar. Brother Herbert asked Amina where she had learned their language.

"Dans l' ecole. Les religieuses nous ensegnaient, " she replied.

"C'est bon. " Brother Herbert looked pleased, which made Amina feel more relaxed.

At this point, her father interrupted to explain that French Dominican nuns had come to Mosul shortly before Amina was born in 1880, and had set up a school where they taught girls reading and writing in French, Syriac, and Arabic. "I felt that, as my oldest child, Amina should have the same opportunities for education as her brothers," he smiled.

"Bon, " Brother Herbert exclaimed. "Girls need schooling, too."

His words encouraged Amina. She spoke up, hesitantly. "I was lucky. Many girls are not so fortunate." She thought of Hanna. "If you have time during your stay in Mosul, and with Baba's permission," she turned to her father, "I would be happy to show you one of the city's oldest churches. It is not far from here." She waited nervously, uncertain of either their response or her father's.

"I'm not sure these gentlemen will be able to manage that, Amina," her father interjected to cover her brashness.

The Montfort brothers looked at each other. *"Pourquoi pas?* Brother Herbert shrugged. He reminded Amina of a portly uncle. Brother Philippe was nodding his head in eager agreement.

Brother Herbert turned to her father, "Would you allow your daughter to accompany us for a visit to the church tomorrow?"

Amina lowered her head to hide her excitement then raised it, waiting for an answer.

Zakariya turned to his guests. "I would go myself, but I will be occupied tomorrow. My son Isaac and a servant will accompany you and Amina." He scowled at Amina.

Amina knew it was the only way she would be allowed to take the visitors to the church—with her brother as a chaperone. She wondered who the servant would be.

"We will meet Amina down here after breakfast," Brother Herbert said. "We've had a long day of travel. It's time we retired." The two men shook hands with Zakariya and made their way up the inn's main staircase to their rooms.

After they left, Amina said, "I know I spoke too boldly, Father." She hung her head. "Which of the servants will accompany us to St. Peter's tomorrow?"

Zakariya's eyes softened; he was uncertain whether to tease Amina or reveal the truth. He studied this daughter whose many questions and insistence on having her own way, he often found perplexing. He didn't deem her pretty; yet her lively eyes, a ready smile, and natural charm, were pleasing.

"I will release Hanna from her duties in the morning, but she must be back to serve the midday meal. Isaac will escort you."

"Merci, Baba. " Amina stood on tiptoes to give her father a hug. As she did so, she felt the roughness of his beard and smelled his acrid breath; she did not like the sour odor of tobacco that clung to his ample beard and clothes.

* * *

Amina had been born in 1880 a year after the territory including Mosul became a *wilaya,* one of the three provinces under the Ottoman Empire. The city in which she grew up flourished as a strategic crossroads for trade between Turkey, Europe, and the Orient. Her mother, Beta, was a *Moslawi,* a native of Mosul, and the daughter of a Chaldean merchant. She knew her way around the twisted streets where Christian neighborhoods had sprung up long before the Ottoman Turks took over the city. She remained a devote Chaldean Christian.

Zakariya's family came from southern Europe, but its roots were Arab. The family settled near a mountain village north of Mosul to farm and raise sheep. In the mid-nineteenth century, Zakariya had left home to find his fortune in Mosul. His father was distantly related to a prominent trading family, the Rassams. A branch of the family settled in Mosul where two brothers did a lively business in finished textiles. The Rassam's business acumen was a magnet for young Zakariya. He arrived in Mosul with a letter of introduction. Yuhannas Rassam, the older brother, took Zakariya in. He worked hard and the older man's affection for him grew. In time, Amina's father adopted the Rassam name. Within five years he had saved enough money to launch his own textile venture and negotiate a marriage with the daughter of a well-respected Chaldean Christian merchant.

Amina's father was doing reasonably well in textiles when Amina was born. But he became increasingly restless. He sold part of his business and purchased an inn soon after her mother gave birth to Isaac. Zakariya moved his family to the inn soon thereafter. Built in the seventeenth century, it was a tall, narrow building with a façade of intricately carved dark oak. Latticework shutters covered the upper windows, partially hidden behind small balconies from which guests, like the Montfort brothers, viewed the teeming life below. Tucked into a cobbled side street, the inn was not far from one of Mosul's busiest bazaars.

*   *   *

After the French clerics retired to their rooms, Amina dashed to the kitchen to tell Hanna about her encounter with the Frenchmen. "Father has arranged for Isaac and me to be their guides to St. Peter's tomorrow," she burst out. "And he says you are to accompany us."

"I wouldn't mind going," Hanna said, putting glasses away in a cupboard. "I have some news of the French visitors, too," she said gravely.

"What is it?" Hanna's expression alarmed Amina.

"I heard from Mama that the French brothers traveled via Aleppo. After they left there and the caravan entered the desert, it was attacked by Anazeh raiders."

"Are you sure?" A chill bit the back of Amina's neck.

"I wouldn't deceive you." Hanna pursed her lips.

"Was anyone killed?"

"None of the traders. But one of the Bedouin guides . . . disappeared."

The Anazeh were a troublesome Bedouin tribe. The girls knew that among caravan leaders, the Anazeh were feared. The tribe preyed on caravans, at times stealing camels, horses, and trade goods before travelers going east reached the Euphrates River. Sometimes lives were lost. At others, the caravan's leader was forced to pay a fee ensuring its safe passage. It was not unheard of for caravaneers to outrun the marauders. What Amina heard made her shiver.

"Imagine how terrified the Montfort brothers must have been," she gasped.

"I don't know what I would have done," Hanna said. "I'm sure they prayed hard."

Amina agreed with her. The Frenchmen were no ordinary men. They had survived a harrowing journey.

*   *   *

Remembering that scene, as their caravan traveled on across Mesopotamia, Amina realized that she and Hanna had survived their first encounter with desert thieves. She wished she had a chance to talk to Mustafa, but there was no rest break that afternoon. When hunger nagged, Amina nibbled on bread and sucked oranges Hanna's mother had carefully packed in their satchels. The fruit proved the only remedy for thirst as the desert heat intensified. The water in her canteen had become hotter than tea. She peeled an orange and ate it, one segment at a time, savoring the tart juice.

She remembered her mother once tellling her that she was born with a restless spirit. She thought about it, now, and wondered if she might have inherited it from her father. He'd told her that she showed a thirst for learning at a young age. "You constantly asked questions—about where the moon came from, why pidgeons roosted in the courtyard, and how many seeds there were in a pomegranate. You wanted to learn how to read and write. That's why I enrolled you in the Dominican school." She knew the real reason she had gone to the school was because her father didn't like the government schools run by the Ottomans. She recalled him heatedly discussing the Turkish occupiers' policy of osmanlik. "Under that law," he had hissed, "students get a heavy dose of Ottomanism: nationalism and loyalty to the Pasha. And, they're forced to learn Turkish Arabic." Amina shuddered hearing the anger in his voice. She had been happy to learn French and Arabic from the nuns.

Before she and Hanna had left Mosul, Amina had begun reading the city's Arabic newspaper. In it, she learned that her city held a strategic position in the Ottoman Sultan's control over Mesopotamia's northern front. Even though Mosul was smaller than Baghdad, it was a provincial capital that had been called Nineveh under the ancient Assyrians. It had a sense of history that grew with the coming of the Arabs and, later, the Ottoman Turks. The Ottomans had conquered the fertile land between the Tigris and Euphrates rivers in the sixteenth century. Mosul was home to Arabs, Kurds, Armenians, Greeks and Chaldeans. It was a trading hub known for its textiles and banking. Its proximity to Istanbul, from which the tentacles of the Ottoman Empire radiated, meant it was a vital link to the rest of the region.

"You know," her father reminded her shortly before she left, "Mosul's merchants play a vital role in provisioning the caravans that cross the Syrian Desert, not only between Mosul and Damascus, but Istanbul and Basra. It won't last forever. The freedom the caravan traders have enjoyed is threatened."

"Threatened?"

"Even today, you can see new French and German steam-powered ships on the Tigris. They move faster than camels."

"How can that be?" she'd asked, without really understanding how steam, which she knew from watching a pot boil, could push a ship. She had accepted what he'd told her, and stored it away for future use, but her skeptical expression must have betrayed her.

"It's true," he told her. "But it is expensive. Most people still come by caravan across the Syrian Desert, despite the risks."

CHAPTER 3

Amina's Quest

"Salaam alaykum, peace be with you," a bearded Arab merchant called to his neighbor over the clanging of a metal shutter.

"Alaykum alsalaam," the other man returned.

Amina and Isaac were taking the Frenchmen to see St. Peter's. Isaac, at 15, looked handsome in his tunic, even if the black stubble growing at his chin was a bit rakish. He took the lead. He escorted them through the narrow streets of their neighborhood where shopkeepers were rolling up large metal shutters that protected their stores at night.

As they entered a larger street, the sharp, earthy aroma of roasting coffee came from an open shop where traders gathered for a cup of the city's best Arabica.

"If you would like, we'll stop for a cup on our way back," Amina told the Montfort Brothers.

Down the street a spice merchant was beginning to roll out onto the front sidewalk barrels of dried raisins, black walnuts, hazelnuts, and almonds. A boy wearing an embroidered black skullcap emerged from the shop balancing a large tray with heaps of dried brown cumin, rust cinnamon sticks, cloves, and small red peppers. He set it down on an empty barrel as they walked by. A running child, not looking where he was going, collided with Amina, nearly knocking the tray over and eliciting an angry string of words from the spice merchant.

"Are you all right?" Isaac gave Amina a worried look.

"Yes." She smoothed down her long skirt.

Across from the spice seller, a baker whirled a large round of flat dough above his head then dropped it onto a sizzling-hot skillet. His assistant picked up the delicious-smelling baked rounds and put them on a long wood tray-table for sale. People crowded to the front of the table, eager to get bread while it was still warm. They traded greetings and news in a calliope of voices.

Brother Philippe stopped, entranced with the bakers. *"C'est magnifique!"* He exclaimed. "They are true artists."

Amina smiled. Living in such a neighborhood, she had taken much of it for granted.

Farther along, spying a row of shops and open stalls that specialized in silk fabrics from Baghdad, muslin manufactured locally, and bolts of wool and serge from Europe, Brother Herbert said with glee, "This is truly wonderful. You have everything here." He nodded toward a tailor bent over in his stall, transforming a piece of dark muslin into a long, loose *thobe,* the tunic that Mosul's men preferred.

"Muslin takes its name from our city," Amina told them proudly. "It's almost as important as our famous marble."

"Really?" Brother Herbert's eyes widened.

Traders of precious stones and goldsmiths had their own section. Mosul's Jews, who wore mustard-yellow *imama,* or turbans, dominated the jewelry trade, crafting beautiful gold and silver medallions, necklaces, earrings, and pocket watches to adorn the fashions of the wealthy. Apothecary shops, chemists, and herbalists had their niches in the medley of storefronts. Isaac made sure Amina, Hanna, and the men walked on the inside of the high walkways lest they fall into the knee-deep gutters filled with sewage that separated the cobbled streets from the sidewalks.

Leading them through an alleyway to save time, Isaac warned the visitors of night slops being hurled from overhead balconies. "Take care, *messieurs,*" he called, as the Frenchmen backed away from a bucketful of gray, malodorous liquid that splashed down on the cobblestones in front of them, scaring a wayward hen that ran off squawking indignantly.

At last, the maze of streets opened onto a square that fronted St. Peter's church. The old yellow stone building with its prominent dome seemed to hunker down into the street.

"Come, we'll go into the sanctuary first," Amina told the French brothers. "I want to show you the paintings of the Virgin Mary. They are exceptionally beautiful."

"Avec plaisir," Brother Herbert said. "The Montfort Order gives the Virgin a special place in our spiritual life."

"What do you mean?" Amina asked.

"Our order was founded in 1703 by a French nobleman, Louis-Marie Grignion de Montfort. As one of Our Lady's greatest apostles, he wrote a book, *Traite de la vraie devotion,* Treatise on the True Devotion to the Blessed Virgin. In it, he describes his conversion as a revelation. He explains why the Virgin, as the Mother of Christ, is so crucial to our beliefs and way of life."

Amina was stunned. "What is the place of Mary in your order?"

"Ah, *ma fille,*" Brother Herbert said, smiling. "Mary leads us to Jesus. She is always with him. It took a saint like de Montfort to recognize this. As Montfort brothers, we give our spiritual lives to Mary.

"Je vois." Amina mulled over Brother Herbert's explanation.

"That's why we are known as the *Montfort de la Compagnie de Marie,* the Montfort Order of the Company of Mary," Brother Philippe added.

"Quel nom! Amina grinned.

"Yes, it's quite a mouthful." Brother Philippe laughed. "De Montfort became a missionary, working with the poor and infirm. We've followed in his footsteps, working among the least advantaged, including women."

"What did your founder do for women?" Amina could see that Isaac was becoming bored, but she wanted to find out.

"He founded an order for them, too. They became the *Filles de la Sagesse.* They dedicated themselves to helping the poor and crippled, fashioning devices to assist them to walk. They showed them how to adapt to their environment, and also provided health care. The order set up institutions to teach impoverished, neglected children. It is still very active."

Amina listened intently to everything the Montfort brothers told her. She was stunned.

"Now, come. Let's go into the church and have a look at the painting of the Virgin you told us about," Father Herbert said.

Amina recovered her composure. "The original church is below street level. The city grew up around it," she told them. "We'll have to enter through the side door."

As they entered and stood in the weak light, Amina recognized the narrow stone steps that led to the sanctuary below.

An elderly man appeared with a lantern. He was dressed in a long, brown tunic. He turned out to be the warden. Isaac greeted him and told him of the visitors' desire to see the church. The warden welcomed them and led them to a darkened stairwell.

As they descended the stairs, lanterns placed at intervals along the sidewalls cast an eerie light on them. The place smelled moldy and damp. Their uneven footsteps echoed in the narrow passage. They emerged into a hall that was buttressed by low curving limestone arches. Tall open windows at each end of the hall that rose above the ground level allowed the morning light to stream in, making the place less gloomy. The warden took them to the heavy double doors of the sanctuary and opened one.

"I will be outside should you need me," he said.

Amina nodded, and thanked him.

Windows ran down both sides of the sanctuary. A simple but beautiful dome rose above the nave. Votive candles lighted the space at the back of the church. Lanterns were lit at intervals along the outer walls. The pews were made of unpainted oak, worn down to a polished sheen. Hanna dropped into one of the pews to rest.

The Montfort brothers genuflected and uttered a blessing. Amina led them slowly up the center aisle. A clean aroma of incense came from a place near the raised altar. When they reached the nave, Amina turned and drew them toward a large illuminated painting of the Virgin Mary.

She stopped before reaching it and fell to her knees, overcome with emotion. She looked up at the young Mary with a small adult-appearing Jesus balanced on the crook of her left arm. She was dressed in swaths of blue silk, her head covered with a veil of the same color, trimmed in gold braid. A single star shone on the veil above the center of Mary's forehead. Her right hand was extended toward her small son as if to catch him if he fell off her bent arm. The infant Jesus was fully dressed in a robe and long trousers. He stared straight ahead, a miniature young adult with his thin arm stretched toward his mother. Mary looked down at Amina and her visitors from half-closed black eyes outlined in kohl. She had a long, straight nose and small, grave mouth. She showed neither joy nor sadness, but seemed to be contemplating them while two angels watched over her from the upper corners.

"A lovely painting. I can see why you like it," Brother Herbert said.

"I would like to spend a little more time here, if it is all right with you," Amina said, coming to her feet. "I'll meet you outside in the hall."

Once they had wandered away, Amina fell to her knees again.

"Blessed Virgin," she pleaded, "I need your guidance. Today I have learned that I can serve you by taking vows of poverty and humility, by commiting myself to God's work." She paused, so moved that tears began to fill her eyes.

"My love for you is boundless as is your love for your son. When I look at you, I feel you understand me. Your faith inspires me with your divine spirit. It is the Montfort brothers, your servants, who opened a path for me. What should I do?" She felt tremulous. Her eyes reached up to Mary's.

The Virgin gazed down at her as if listening to her every word. The hand extending toward Jesus seemed to reach out to her, too, beckoning Amina to join her in community. Amina took it as a sign. She tried to blink back her tears. Then she crossed herself and rose to her feet. She took a deep breath and, with it, a feeling of peace came over her. Amina knew, then, that she wanted to join the *Filles de la Sagesse.*

When they returned to the coffee shop near her father's inn, Hanna left them. Amina begged Isaac to let her go with them for coffee, even though she knew few women entered coffee houses. Isaac relented. In the coffee house, he found seating around a square table on one of the carpeted platforms in the courtyard. It was a place where Amina would not be so visible. Amina folded her legs and sat down across from the Montfort brothers.

She had so many questions she wanted to ask Brother Herbert. *Where are the Daughters of Wisdom now? Are their members only from France? How does someone join the order? What kinds of training do the sisters receive in order to work with the infirm and the crippled? To teach among the poor?* With Isaac present, she knew she should not ask them. He might think her bold, and tell their father.

"How long are you staying in Mosul?" she said, instead.

"Two weeks," Brother Herbert told her.

Amina nodded her head, relieved. It would give her time to find the answers to her questions.

"Four coffees," Isaac told the waiter.

The man nodded, without looking at Amina, and disappeared.

Listening to the men's conversation, she felt at peace.

"What will you do now that you have completed your education?" Brother Herbert asked her.

Amina hadn't anticipated such a question. It flustered her. She looked at Isaac. "I don't know," she stammered and bent her head.

*   *   *

Now, as the camels plodded across the plain in the late afternoon heat, a shimmering mirage appeared, giving the bare landscape a mystical quality. Amina was entranced. She hadn't expected to find beauty in the desert. She fanned herself and thought about the two Montfort brothers. She wondered what had become of them. Being with them that day had crystalized her belief that becoming a Daughter of Wisdom was her destiny.

What had remained was to convince her father. She recalled approaching him with trepidation after her tense exchange with her mother.

CHAPTER 4

A Test of Wills

"Baba," Amina rounded the inn's reception desk. "I must see you. It is urgent. Can we meet this afternoon, after the midday meal?"

"What is it that can't wait until tomorrow?"

"It is a matter of the heart . . . of my future," she implored. She swallowed and did her best to remain calm.

"Ah ha," Zakariya smiled, thinking she had learned of the suitor who had recently visited the inn to express his interest in her. "If it is of such importance, we will talk while the guests are eating. We can meet near the fountain in the courtyard."

"Thank you." Amina backed out from behind the counter. She hurried up the steps to her room to collect her thoughts.

Rays of sun shimmered as they hit the spray of an ornamental fountain that graced a corner of the inn's garden courtyard. Marble paths divided the space into four flowerbeds, bordered by low hedges. The beds were a profusion of colors; reds, yellows, and fuchsia. Within each were carefully tended roses, cannas, lantana, and honeysuckle. Their fragrance offset the aromas of the kitchen. A voluptuous pomegranate tree stood in the center of one bed, its fruits hanging like small lanterns among the branches. Amina waited for her father near the fountain, hidden in the shadows of the tree. A starling darted down from the pomegranate and began pecking at the ground. Its antics distracted Amina, relieving some of her tension.

"There you are," her father's hearty voice broke in. "I'm free. Let's go over and sit, out of the sun." He led her to a marble bench under one eave; the overhang protected a veranda that marked the perimeter of the courtyard and provided shade from the blistering heat.

Amina followed her father, lifting her skirts slightly to protect them from picking up fallen petals on the path. Her father settled on the bench, leaning his back against a wall. He motioned her to sit beside him. For a moment, neither of them spoke, enjoying the peace and lushness of the garden.

"Now, Daughter. What is it you wish to tell me?" He looked at Amina's proud profile, the slight curve of her broad, aquiline nose, the veiled eyes framed by dark, expressive eyebrows—her best feature—and the generous mouth that softened her sometimes willful countenance. Small in stature, the energy she exuded made her appear larger. She had demonstrated on many occasions that she was not to be trifled with. One day soon, this daughter would leave them. He would miss her quick wit and discerning mind.

"Baba, for the last few months, I've had dreams. The Virgin Mary speaks to me in them, helping me to find . . . how I can serve God.

Her father appeared surprised, but said nothing.

She looked out over the garden and heard the fountain's steady murmur, like a soothing hand.

"I've learned through the French brethren that the Daughters of Wisdom look to our Blessed Virgin as their guide. The Montfort brothers and the Daughters of Wisdom are missionaries. They serve the poor, the diseased, and unfortunates who are crippled, some missing a leg or other limb. They help the deaf and mute. They assist children to improve their lives. They work with them physically to strenthen their limbs, and by educating them. They give the least of God's flock something to hope for," she told him.

Her father had not spoken.

"I want to join them in God's work . . . by taking the vows of the *Filles de la Sagesse.*" There. It was out. She had revealed her deepest wish. She held back tears and waited for her father to speak, not daring to look at him.

Zakariya stood up and began pacing.

A sense of foreboding assailed Amina as she watched him.

"This is not the news I was expecting, Amina," he said. "I thought that, perhaps, you were ready to marry. But I see, now, that you have other ideas." He sat down heavily.

Amina remained silent, while she weighed what to say.

Finally, she spoke: "I have spent much time and prayer over this decision, Baba. I know it means leaving you, our family, and Mosul. But I feel at peace with it." She turned to him, her eyes hopeful, as she held her breath.

"Your mother will be distraught by this turn of events. We were both looking forward to a joyful wedding. I guess we will have to wait for your brothers . . . if you're truly committed to becoming a nun."

"I am, Father. In my heart I know it is the right path for me." She spoke softly then smiled inwardly; what she had most feared was that he might force her to marry the merchant Michel Shannis. It was his right. She knew other girls whose fathers had insisted they marry the man chosen by them. Baba was not going to force her to marry. She felt a deep sense of relief. Her breath came more easily. She felt a quiet resolve rather than joy.

"Daughter, I would like you to take a little more time with this decision, to make absolutely sure it is what you want. In the meantime, I will talk further with the French brethren to learn if it is, indeed, possible for you to enter the Daughters of Wisdom Order, and what is expected of me in the way of a dowry.

That's a consideration. We will also need to think of how you might travel to France." He wiped away beads of perspiration collecting on his brow.

She was startled by his revelations. She had no idea that the order would require a dowry for her entry. Nor had she thought about how she might get there. Most of her journeys had been limited to trips outside Mosul, to the hot springs of Ain el Kibrit, the ruins of ancient Nineveh and, occasionally, to her grandparents' home in the mountains. Realizing, then, that it might mean a lengthy caravan trip across the desert, such as the one the Montfort brothers had taken, she cringed.

Her father turned to her. "You see, my beloved daughter, such a decision entails much more than your will to pursue it. And a journey across the Syrian Desert requires great stamina. Sleep on your decision. Give it more thought."

"I will, Baba. You have given me much to think about." She put her small, square hand over her father's large one. "What about Mama? I know she will be disappointed."

"I will talk to your mother tonight."

"Thank you, Baba." She threw her arms around him.

He winced, anticipating the impending loss of this eldest daughter.

*   *   *

After Amina had divulged her decision, Zakariya had gone through a welter of conflicting emotions: hurt that Amina had gone to the Monfort Brothers without his knowledge; anger over her choice of a religious order rather than marriage; a recurring stab of grief like a nagging toothache. At the same time, a feeling of admiration for his daughter's sense of social justice—of wanting to right the wrongs plaguing the least fortunate—emerged. It touched him, this caring for others. He had observed her tightly held body and mouth, her determination to pursue her destiny. Still, he felt an empty sensation in his gut at the thought of losing her to a religious order that was so far away. He ruminated over the decision, saddened by what she would miss by not marrying: *She would have no children to bring home. Was she really willing to forego family?*

Later, he had a chance to weigh Amina's decision in light of what he learned from relatives and friends with daughters her age. They told him it was not unusual for girls grappling with approaching adulthood to go through periods where they became intensely religious. Some were even drawn to mysticism. It was as if they were unsure of what they might become in the future and were not quite ready for the transformation. Usually, the ambivalence disappeared when a girl married and assumed the role of wife and mother. But, there were those who did not take easily to marriage, who seemed to rebel, for one reason or another. He recalled the daughter of a cousin who had been unhappy with her parents' choice of husband: after her marriage, her health had deteriorated and she eventually had gone mad. The idea frightened him. A few girls had rejected marriage, preferring a life of chastity and contemplation. These daughters were sent to convents in Baghdad.

Amina's devotion to the Virgin seemed to answer some need in her soul. Becoming a Daughter of Wisdom would provide her with a spiritual community. It would enable her to work among the world's most neglected people. Was that such a bad choice? He wrestled between his desire to see her married and living close by and her desire to explore a life that seemed austere and would take her far away from him.

He finally called her to him.

"Amina, I have talked with your mother. You know her feelings. If, in six months' time, you are still determined to join the Daughters of Wisdom, I will see to it that you and one of the servants have a place in the caravan of my treasured friend, Ahmed Mustafa. You have met him. He's the one who transports goods between Mosul and Damascus. Sometimes he takes travelers. I'll inquire if he has plans for a spring caravan. I trust him completely. He is a man of honor."

Amina smiled at her father's last statement. It was so like him—ever protective of her. "Six months is a long time, Baba, but I know you have my interests at heart."

She had agreed with the arrangement.

*   *   *

Over the next several months, especially during Christmastime, Amina attended the weddings of several childhood friends, girls she had known at church or at school. She witnessed their happiness in exchanging marriage vows. Each time, a feeling of melancholy had overtaken her. *I will never get to experience this. And I will never give birth to children.* Seeing small Leila so full of life didn't help. In such moments, she took courage in the thought that she would be joining a larger community dedicated to serving God and the needs of destitute children, even though they might not be her own. It carried her forward, sharpening her sense of devotion to becoming a healing or teaching sister.

Her father summoned her several times to see if her intention to join the Daughters of Wisdom had wavered. He'd heard from Mother Patrice, the Superior of the order, confirming that Amina would be welcome as a novice. Still, he wanted to make sure of her commitment. Each time, she had been resolute about her decision.

"My mind is made up, Baba," she informed him with finality, one day. "Now that I have been been granted a place among the *Filles de la Sagesse,* it is my duty to join them."

"What about the long journey across the desert? Are you prepared for that? It won't be easy. I recently heard about a convent just north of Damascus, in a village called Ma'alula. Perhaps you should stop and visit it before you continue all the way to France. You may decide that you have had enough travels by then. I will make the arrangements."

"I will, if you wish," she told him, "but do not change the plans with Mother Patrice for me to be met in Marseille." She knew he was trying to dissuade her from leaving. It made her feel uneasy. "I have thought about the desert crossing, Baba. At times, it frightens me. Then I pray for strength and protection." Amina shut her eyes then opened them. "I am ready for this journey, Baba."

*   *   *

Knowing in his heart that his daughter was not going to change her mind, and not wanting to run the risk of alienating her, in February 1898, Zakariya Rassam visited his friend Ahmed Mustafa with a proposal for the inclusion of his daughter and her maidservant, Hanna, in the trader's late spring caravan to Damascus. By then, the swollen rivers would have receded somewhat, and the fierce, penetrating heat of the desert was still ahead. He refused to let himself think about the other dangers that his daughter might encounter.

CHAPTER 5

Facing An Uncertain Future

Ahmed Mustafa was a large man with deep-set eyes that could be penetrating or playful, depending on his mood. He wore a long, flowing *thobe* that did nothing to hide his ample girth as he sat behind his cluttered desk, observing Zakariya. His office was crowded with boxes piled on top of one another, ready for shipping. Layers of dust clung to some. With no windows, the air was dense and smelled of dried grass used in packing.

"It's a risk, taking two young women that distance," Ahmed Mustafa told his old friend. "It will require additional protection." He would have to take precautions to see that they were safe, and had certain amenities required for the fairer sex. For one, *haudaj,* special wooden platforms with fortified grass-woven shelters fixed to their base and covered by canvas on all sides to protect the women from the elements, would have to be built. When the time came, they would be secured to the backs of two trusted camels, carefully selected to carry the Rassam daughter's party on its journey. In addition, there was the question of where the women would sleep when the caravan stopped for rest and to feed the camels. As the caravan leader's wife would not be coming, there was no possibility of the women sleeping in his tent. They would need their own tent and a guard. At times they would be forced to travel through the night to avoid the worst of the desert heat and tribal raiders who sometimes attacked under cover of darkness. Would the ladies be willing to sleep sitting up in their *haudaj?*

"Is the maidservant going all the way to France with your daughter?"

"No. No. She will go only as far as Damascus. She will come back with you on your return caravan, provided you can find a family for her to travel with."

"I see." Mustafa's face took on a worried look.

"I know my request is unusual and you are going beyond what is expected to accommodate Amina and her maidservant. I will make it worth your trouble. Name your price."

"For you, thirty-three thousand *paras,*" the wily trader said, stroking his long salt-and-pepper beard as he eyed Zakariya Rassam.

"I thought twenty-five thousand might be reasonable." Zakariya smiled.

"That would hardly pay for the camels and transport of your daughter's belongings. Will they bring any of their own food?"

"To cover the first week, and their bedding, too. We'll see to that."

"If I'm to take such a risk, transporting two young women for a journey that usually takes six weeks, I must be compensated accordingly. I will not take less than thirty-thousand *paras*." Mustafa pushed up his *keffiya*.

"I accept your offer, my friend. Give me four days to secure the funds."

The two men embraced and kissed one another on the cheek to seal the transaction.

The caravan would leave in two months.

*   *   *

Amina recalled weighing the realities of her decision to go to France, the possibility that she might never see her family again, and the hazards of the upcoming journey. It made her palms turn damp. She wondered, briefly, if she had the stamina to survive such a rigorous trip. She had turned eighteen in December, and had noticed that her parents were beginning to treat her with new respect. Her earlier anxieties about missing motherhood had receded. They had been replaced by growing excitement about the journey.

*   *   *

During the last week before her departure, Amina visited St. Peter's with her father to pray to the Virgin for strength to survive the caravan. By the time they left the church, the weather had turned foul. A cold, dripping fog had settled over the city. Amina pulled her gray serge cape more closely around her and lifted the hood to cover her head. Even the shopkeepers were hunkering down in the damp weather.

When they got home, she shed her cape and went upstairs. She rapped on her mother's door. She knew she was still upset over her decision to join the order in France.

"Who's there?"

"Amina."

"Come in."

Amina found Beta standing between two medium-sized black trunks, open and empty. They smelled of neglect. Her mother frowned at the trunks.

"These are your father's. It's been some time since he used them. It was kind of him, but I don't see how we are going to fit all of your things in these two boxes."

"Perhaps, I will have to leave some of my dresses at home," Amina said. "They will provide me with a habit once I enter the Mother House at St. Laurent."

Her mother pouted. "You *will* need outfits for the journey," she said. "It won't be easy mounting a camel each day. You'll need travel costumes with full, lightweight skirts. Your undergarments must be simple. And, my love, though it will cause you some embarrassment that I mention it, we must address the problem of your monthly flow. Imagine getting it on a camel. You'll have to take plenty of rags." Her voice had an edge to it.

Amina quickly put her hands up to cover her mouth, reddening over the prospects of this predicament. "I hadn't even thought of that."

"We'll have to buy you some boots for the desert, too."

Amina nodded. Her eyes drifted to the new striped settee her mother had recently purchased from a European trader. On it, her clothes were arranged in neat piles; folded chemises and petticoats in one, nightclothes in another, piles of soft, white rags in a box, long woolen stockings for cold weather, gloves, and two hats, one of canvas with a wide brim for the caravan. Her dresses, she noticed, were still hanging in her mother's armoire along with several capes and a new jacket. Though she felt she wouldn't need more than the one hat, she was glad her mother, with Hanna's help, had taken charge of her travel clothes.

Amina had noticed her mother becoming more withdrawn and tight-lipped since her father confirmed the caravan arrangements for her journey. She had tried to cheer her by spending more time with her, knitting and doing needle-point. However, as the month of April drew near, Beta became agitated, insisting they go shopping for some last minute items. It puzzled Amina but she acquiesced.

She wanted her last week with her family to be harmonious. Her brothers, except for the youngest, were away at school. They had said their *adieus* over the Christmas holidays. It remained for her to enjoy the last few days with her parents, her brother Simon, and Leila. She would miss Leila—her small joys and effervescent giggles, her eagerness to master new things, even her occasional tantrums—more than anyone in her family, other than her father. Though she adored her mother she felt unsettled about her. She knew that she would never live up to her mother's dreams for her. Amina also admitted to herself that the inn had become confining. What she needed was a place where she could learn new skills and ways of doing things in the embrace of a religious community.

*   *   *

"Wake up. We leave today. Your father is waiting." Hanna woke Amina by shining a lantern in her face. It was well before dawn. A light mist covered the city.

"Ouch. That's bright," Amina cried, then remembered the day.

"I've put out your clothes. Your trunks were taken last night to be loaded on the camels. I left a small satchel for your daily needs next to the door."

Hanna had not been around much the last few days; she had her own things to take care of in preparation for the trip.

"Thank you, Hanna," she raised her head. That Hanna was going with her on the caravan was reassuring.

"Get up," Hanna repeated, more stridently. She swung the lantern onto the bedside table.

Amina was savoring, for the last time, the sweet warmth of her cozy bed. She rubbed her eyes and sat on her bed.

"I'm up." She saw that Hanna wore a new, dark-gray travel outfit. It looked becoming on her. Her unwieldy, raven hair was hidden under a long midnight-blue scarf. "You look lovely," she told her.

Hanna blushed. "It's half past three and we have less than an hour to get to the camel post," she told her mistress. "Remember, it's out of town."

Amina threw off the quilts, sped to the marble basin and splashed cold water on her face. She hastily ran a brush through her hair and tied it into a knot at the back. She slipped into her new cotton chemise and drew a blouse over her head.

"Here. Let me help you with your skirt." Hanna held up a long brown skirt and dropped it over Amina's head and then fastened it at her waist. She handed her the matching jacket. After covering her head with a beige scarf and tying it securely around her neck, Amina sat down on a pile of cushions and pulled on long wool stockings while Hanna got the boots Amina and her mother had bought for the trip. Amina put her foot into one long boot and struggled to pull it up. She stopped and pulled some more, but the boot didn't budge. She finally let go, and looked at Hanna, exasperated.

Hanna hid a smile and, without a word, came to Amina's rescue. "These boots are stubborn things," she said, wiggling the boots back and forth until both were in place. "We're going to have to help each other with them." They laughed at the absurdity of the boots then collected the last of their things and descended the inn's front staircase.

At the bottom, Beta waited with a lantern to embrace them one last time. At the last minute, Hanna's mother, Dina, hastened from the kitchen to give them a careful inspection making sure they had forgotten nothing. She gave each girl a tearful hug.

"Good-bye, my daughter," Beta said. "We will miss you." She drew Amina to her, pulling her close, then released her and quickly wiped her eyes on a sleeve.

"Good-bye, Mama. Stay well until we meet again." Amina felt a mixture of anguish and guilt as she returned her mother's embrace. "I will send word when I arrive at the convent."

Amina turned to Hanna's mother. "Good-bye, *Omm* Hanna. Take care of Mother."

She turned abruptly, fearing tears, and followed Hanna through the front door of the inn.

Her father, who had left earlier to secure transport, waited outside in a black, horse-drawn cab. He was ready to escort the girls and their luggage to the caravan stage. Zakariya leaped out to help Amina, then Hanna, up into their seats. He joined them. The girls waved good-bye to their mothers who stood in the doorway with stiff smiles.

Amina was so torn by feelings of remorse that it was all she could do to stem the tears that threatened to engulf her.

Hanna was overcome by her own feelings of misery in saying good-bye to her mother.

When Amina felt she could speak again, she looked at her father with a smile to reassure him. "This is a fine beginning," she waved her arm to encompass the cab's interior as the carriage left the inn behind.

"A bit of an extravagance," her father said, "but it's much the quickest way to the caravan post."

Hanna, having been up most of the night making preparations, fell asleep against the side window of the cab once it fell into a steady pace. Amina, however, was fully awake.

"I wish I could see out," she told her father.

"There's not much to look at. The streets are empty at this time of night. There will be more to see when we get to the caravan post. And you've never eyed a camel up close. They are unique beasts of burden."

"What are they like, Baba? Tell me."

"You've seen them at a distance. They're cud-chewing animals. Constantly chewing. They're also stubborn, like donkeys."

"I hope their handlers know how to control them."

"Of course, they do. Camels can also go for days without water, though someone once told me they usually drink 200 liters of it a week. Amazing, isn't it?"

"Yes." Amina's attention was flagging.

Her father chatted softly with her for a while to keep her mind off the leave-taking they knew was ahead. Neither of them liked farewells. Amina wished Hanna would wake up. She wanted to talk to her. Just then, she felt the bumpy cobblestones beneath the cab turn to dirt.

They left the city and entered one of the outlying settlements that had sprung up around Mosul in the past decade as ever more people migrated to the city.

"Wake up, Hanna. We're nearly there." She shook her awake.

"Where are we?" Hanna righted herself and looked from Amina to her father with a sheepish smile—she had been caught sleeping.

"We're in sight of the caravan post," Zakariya told her.

They heard one of the horses drawing their cab neigh. A response from others followed as they drew to a halt.

Amina peeked out through the small window. She could see nothing but inky darkness. Her ears picked up the shouts of caravaneers, calling back and forth in Arabic. Then she heard the low gurgling and moaning sounds of a camel being lowered to the ground against its will so that baskets and leather containers full of cotton and silk textiles, clothing, silk slippers, and other trade goods, could be secured to its back. The animal's protests became a chant as other camels sounded their displeasure. The driver of the cab, with a lantern in hand, opened the door and Zakariya stepped down into the milling crowd of men and animals illuminated by torches stuck into the ground at intervals.

Amina took her father's hand and alighted, followed by Hanna. The two young women huddled together. The rank odor of camel urine and dung assailed their nostrils. It mingled with the smell of the handlers' sweat as they loaded the beasts. The camels' grunts grew in volume, some snorting, others rumbling and groaning in dissonant heated tones. A horse neighed from somewhere in the mist.

Ahmed Mustafa appeared on horseback with two men. "Greetings Rassam sahib," he said, dismounting, as did his companions.

"Greetings to you, my good man," Amina's father replied, eyeing the duo that accompanied him.

"Allow me to introduce two traders who will be making the journey to Damascus with us, Jamal Obaid and Yousif Hamid." Then he said, as an aside, "They've insisted on riding horses, which are much faster than camels. As for me, I enjoy a camel. Horses tend to tire easily and need more fodder." He looked over at Hanna and Amina with a rueful expression.

Amina stifled a giggle and took a quick look at the two traders. They were neither young nor old, close to her father's age. Both had iron-black beards. One wore an imama, a white length of cloth wrapped around his head and neck with the ends left free in the back. The other wore a white and black keffiya. Both had long trousers under their thobe and sturdy boots. Amina was glad they were traveling on horseback. They would probably ride at the front of the caravan with the leader, which meant that she and Hanna would see little of them.

Zakariya smiled at Ahmed Mustafa's comments and introduced Amina and her companion to the two Moslawi travelers. The latter appeared stunned by the revelation that two young women were traveling with the caravan. As if reading their minds, Zakariya told them, "My good friend Ahmed Mutstafa is in charge of their comforts and safety on the journey."

The two men nodded.

"Come with me, ladies," Mustafa turned to Amina and Hanna, "I want to show you how to mount your camels. Your two beasts are veterans of the desert road. They could make their way to Rahba blindfolded."

Zakariya followed them, a hint of skepticism on his lips.

"Where is Rahba?" Amina asked.

"It's on the Eurphrates River, where the caravan makes its crossing to the Syrian Desert. It will be the first real stop. Getting eighty camels across a river of that size takes time."

The two Moslawi traders remounted their horses and pranced off into the mist with an air of certitude.

Amina, her father, and Hanna followed Ahmed Mustafa between groups of camels. Some camels moaned and others puttered with nasal grunts while they were being loaded for the journey.

"Take care," Mustafa said, "some of the more ill-tempered of these brutes have a habit of spitting at anyone near them. It's to take revenge against their handlers. Give them ample berth."

Amina and Hanna, who were walking hand in hand to give each other courage, looked at one another, horror mirrored in their faces. Even with the camels' legs folded under them for loading, the beasts seemed huge and menacing.

"Here we are. These are your camels, ladies." Mustafa stopped. "The first one is a true veteran of the road." An impressive turmeric-brown camel stood in front of Amina and an equally large, dirty-white one stood near-by.

Amina's eyes grew wide as she gazed at the long, knobby brown legs in front of her that supported a sturdy, shaggy body. The animal's head, dominated by a scarred Roman nose and heavily-hooded black eyes with long lashes, was held steady by a thick lead rope that ran through one of its nostrils. A middle-aged, sturdy Bedouin handler in a long thobe controlled the twine. What surprised Amina most was the structure on the camel's back; it looked like a child's tent, supported by four corner poles, lashed to a sort of platform secured to the top of the animal's hump. Both beasts were outfitted similarly.

"You will be riding in the *haudaj*," Mustafa explained. "It is quite comfortable once you get used to the camel's gait."

To Amina, it looked like the howdah she had seen on an elephant's back in a book of Arabian tales her father had once read to her. She looked at Hanna, who appeared as dubious about this venture as she felt at the moment. "We will be riding together in one of those things, won't we?"

"It might be crowded." Mustafa said. "You each have your own camel." He failed to tell them that Bedouin women, with their children, squeezed into larger *haudaj* for travel.

Amina tried to hide her disappointment. Riding alone was not what she had expected. It would be lonely without a companion all day.

A series of steps on one side of a wooden platform stood between them and the camels. "Eman," the trader called to the first camel's handler, "Bring that beast over to the stage."

Turning to Amina, he took her leather satchel. "Eman will be in charge of your camel. Should you need to stop or have some trouble, call him. He knows these animals well and has made more than fifty trips across the desert. You can trust him."

Amina studied the Bedouin swathed in a brown turban that covered his head and face: only his dark eyes shone above the wrapped cloth. His demeanor was reserved. She noticed the leather sandals he wore sticking out beneath his beige *thobe* and wondered if they would last through the rough desert crossing.

"It's time to mount," Mustafa told Zakariya.

Amina's father moved to the bottom of the steps and took his daughter's hands in his. "May God protect you on this journey. We will miss you, Amina ma." He felt a searing pain somewhere between his throat and his gut, and quickly threw his arms around Amina before she had a chance to see his brimming eyes.

"Oh, Baba. I'll miss you, too." She buried her head against his chest. This was harder than she thought it would be. She finally had to force her face away from him. "I'll send word when I get to St. Laurent," she said in a flood of tears. Then she turned quickly and took Mustafa's extended hand, feeling shaken. He led her, with a certain chivalry, up the few steps to the platform.

"Take care of her, Hanna," Zakariya admonished.

"I will," she stammered, as the two of them watched Amina reach the top step.

"Mounting from here will make it easier the first time," the trader told Amina. "But once you are in the desert, Eman will have to find a rock or you'll mount the camel while he's on his knees."

Nodding her head, Amina studied the *haudaj* on the camel's back. In the light of Mustafa's lantern, she was relieved to see a small, grass-woven oval cab inside the square tent. It was nestled like an egg in a box.

Mustafa took her to the side of the camel. "Put your feet here," he nodded to her and put his broad hands, which were cupped to form a U, against the camel's flank. She placed her boots in his hands. "Now, grab the small rail at the front of the *haudaj* and hoist yourself up." He gave her a boost.

Amina did as she was told and scrambled into the *haudaj* just as the deep purple of tentative dawn began giving way to streaks of magenta in the eastern sky.

She found the seat was covered with several blankets and a quilt, folded in quarters. Pillows rested against them. She smiled down at her father and Hanna. "It has cushions." She held up a red one, and then straightened her skirt over her legs. She looked around her little nest and found it protected her on three sides, with only the front open to the elements.

The trader handed up her satchel.

"Shukran," she thanked him.

She was jolted as Eman led her camel away so that Hanna could mount hers.

Hanna was taller than Amina. It gave her an advantage in hoisting herself up to the seat in the *haudaj.* She had also learned something by watching Amina mount.

"Your camel's handler is Salem," Mustafa told Hanna. "If you need to stop, tell him." Salem was dressed similarly to Eman, but was taller and appeared younger from his slim stature and smooth face. His command of the camel impressed Hanna.

The two Bedouins led their charges toward the front of the caravan. Amina felt the camel's rocking motion, forward and back, forward and back. It was not unpleasant and had a soothing effect. She was reassured when she noticed that Eman and Salem would be leading their camels in a string of several owned by the chief of the caravan, the man responsible for the caravan's safe passage to Damascus.

Ahmed Mustafa introduced Zakariya to Sheikh Hassan, the caravan's leader. The man set the course for their crossing and his word went unchallenged en route. Now that the eighty camels had been loaded and their burdens secured, the caravaneers, each with a line of four to five animals tied one to another like beads on a string, led them to their places behind the caravan leader. He gave a series of shouts to signal their departure. Mustafa and the two Moslawi traders on horseback fell in behind him.

Strings of camels and their guides moved slowly in an undulating, uneven line that snaked across the plateau southwest of Mosul, away from the morning sky as it turned to shades of mauve, magenta, and gold. Remnants of mist, like wisps of wayward smoke, evaporated in the rising warmth of the encroaching desert sun as the caravan headed westward, into territory that Amina and Hanna had only heard was hostile.

In the wake of the caravan, a lonely figure stood silhouetted against the rising sun, watching the string of camels disappear and weeping for the daughter he might never see again.

CHAPTER 6
_____

The Trek to Rahba

Endless waves of dun-hued sand, pitted by rocks, stretched out like fans on either side of the plodding camels. Amina and Hanna were riding side by side. Their camel guides had drawn the two beasts parallel to one another; only the bulky *haudaj* on each animal's back kept the girls apart.

The caravan had gotten as far as Huwayah, a desert outpost, on the first night. They had arrived just before dark at a meager spring surrounded by a few date palms. Amina would never forget dismounting her camel that day. First, Eman had pulled her camel down on its knobby front knees. The motion had caused a sudden jarring slant in the *haudaj*. It had caused Amina to slam forward against the small front bar. Terrified, she had grabbed it with white knuckles to keep from sliding over the camel's neck and falling to the ground. She had barely recovered when, at a clicking command from Eman, the animal lowered his mighty rear legs to his haunches, throwing Amina against the rear of the *haudaj*. She'd sat up just as the camel further collapsed his front legs with his belly resting on the desert floor. The move had pitched Amina forward again. She'd never experienced anything so unsettling.

Eman had tied a sturdy rope twice around one of the camel's folded forelegs to hobble him so he couldn't rise. Only then, had she eased herself out of the *haudaj* onto to a wood stool that appeared. From there, she'd jumped to the ground. When she had tried to walk, she found she was wobbling like a drunk. It was as if she had been rolling back and forth for days.

"How do you feel, Hanna?" She'd asked her when she was safely on the ground.

"I didn't know these animals collapsed like that." Hanna looked ghostly pale.

Amina remembered laughing. "It jolted me, too. I need to walk to get the kinks out of my legs." She suggested going to find a place to relieve themselves before Mustafa arrived.

They had left the camp, searching for a clump of bushes while the camel guides set up a tent for them. The moon had not yet risen and in the semi-darkness, Amina and Hanna had stumbled down a small embankment of reeds into a dry riverbed.

"Yoo. I wish we'd brought a torch." Hanna said. "I guess this spot will have to do. You go first. I'll guard you." She had turned her back on Amina.

Amina recalled retreating into the reeds and nervously pulling up her long skirt.

They had taken turns, first Hanna acting as the watch, then Amina doing the same.

By the time they had returned to the campsite, a fire was burning. Eman, who had proved to be a capable handler, appeared with their satchels. He led them to their tent. It was a comfortable distance from where Ahmad Mustafa and the Moslawi traders had set up their tents. Eman bid them good night with a slight bow. The hardy Bedouin who looked after the camels, Amina noticed, did not have tents; they rolled themselves up in heavy blankets and slept in huddles, like sheep, near their camels.

Amina and Hanna had washed the desert grime from their faces in a small, metal basin of water that someone had left outside their tent. The tent was square with a center post forming a peak in the middle. The front flap of their shelter was secured at each corner with sturdy cloth ties to keep the dust and desert creatures out. Amina had untied the fastening and pulled back the flap. She'd peered into the interior delighted to see that a carpet covered the ground. Quilts and blankets were spread out on each side.

"Not much room, but it looks cozy," she'd told Hanna, who had crouched down beside her to have a look.

"We'll get used to it . . . living like the Bedouins," She stood up and circled the tent, inspecting the sandy ground around it. "I hope there aren't any rats or snakes here."

"Don't even think of it," Amina had told her.

They had walked back to the campfire, hand in hand, feeling closer after their excursion to the dry wash.

When they arrived, a young boy led them to a small carpet. It had been spread on the sand for them. They collapsed on it, grateful for the chance to sit down.

Ahmed Mustafa had appeared, at that point, with a giant of a man whose eyes were like onyx. Amina looked at his downturned lower lip and decided that he was a person who was perennially at war with the life he'd been given. The man wore an elaborate turban and a flowing white cotton *djellaba* with an embroidered vest. Silhouetted against the fire, he was an imposing figure.

Mustafa greeted them. Then he introduced the giant, Sheikh Nawal Mohammed Hassan, the leader of the caravan.

"Salaam alaykum," the man said in a deep, resonant voice.

"Alaykum alsalaam." Amina returned the greeting, keeping her eyes lowered.

"I hope you find the journey not too uncomfortable, ladies."

Amina nodded, afraid to look up.

Sheikh Hassan told them that the cook was preparing their tea and something to eat, "He will make tea each morning and a meal at night," he explained. "There will be no midday stops between here and Rahba. We leave before dawn. See that your belongings are outside your tent, ready for loading, when you hear the men saying their early morning prayers."

He told Mustafa that they would be camping the next night, but after that, they would travel through the night to get to Rahba by the Sabbath on Friday.

Mustafa nodded. He wished Hanna and Amina a peaceful sleep and handed a lantern to Hanna to take to their tent. Then they left, backtracking around the fire to the opposite side where the Moslawi traders sat.

After they had gone, Amina turned to Hanna, "That man scares me. I don't think he likes carrying women in his caravan.

"He's the kind of man who might have his daughter flogged if she crossed him," Hanna said, rolling her eyes.

At that moment, the young Bedouin boy approached them with half gourds of rice, fresh dates, and warm camel's milk with the froth still on it. The savory rice was enticing, but Amina hadn't been sure about the camel's milk—it tasted raw and had a slightly smoky flavor. The boy returned with a plate-size round of hot, sweet-smelling bread and cups of steaming tea. Amina bit into the bread and realized with a start that sand had found its way into it.

Once they finished and found their tent, they stood outside in the dark with cups of water to rinse out their mouths. Amina looked up at the tar-black sky and saw speckles of light thrown across it like sugar crystals. "I wish I knew the names of all these stars," she told Hanna.

They had crawled inside the tent that night and struggled to take off their boots and skirts, then rolled themselves into their quilts, little realizing what they would face the second night of their journey.

CHAPTER 7

The Euphrates Crossing

It took them two more long days and a night of travel before they saw the great Euphrates River. It seemed to Amina that they had been gone for weeks, rather than days. The Yezidi were behind them, thank God. She was happy to spend a night in the cramped space of her *haudaj*. Even though it was uncomfortable, she felt safer. The steady pace of the camel finally lulled her tired body into a restless sleep.

When she awoke in her *haudaj* the next morning, she saw that the caravan had come to a halt. Sheikh Hassan, the caravan leader, had called for a prayer stop.

Amina's bladder sent an urgent message. "Let's get down," she shouted over to Hanna. "It's our only chance."

She and Hanna shot behind a few scraggly bushes to relieve themselves. Walking back to their camels, they saw in the distance another caravan as large as theirs. It was traveling in the opposite direction.

"I wonder where it's headed?"

"Probably to Baghdad," Hanna said.

Amina asked Eman about the caravan as she began to mount her camel.

"Toward Baghdad," he said, helping her up into the *haudaj*.

"If it was later in the year, you'd see many caravans with pilgrims on their way to Mecca for the *hajj*. This is one of the main routes to Mecca from Damascus."

"It must be wonderful to see them."

"Sometimes there are over 3,000 camels in a single caravan. It's like a moving village," Eman said, his mustache twitching proudly as he handed Amina her satchel.

"We must be getting close to Rahba," she ventured, gazing at the string of camels disappearing into the eastern sunrise. Then there was a jolt, as the camel began his three-stage rising ritual, moaning and showing formidable teeth as he twisted his head to protest against Eman's pull on the rope that ran through his nostril. Amina hung on with clenched teeth, determined not to fall backwards as the animal got to his front feet.

Once the beast was standing, Eman gave her a friendly nod and said, "You're beginning to learn how to mount a camel."

Amina smiled with a warm sense of pleasure knowing she had mastered one skill.

"We won't be in Rahba until we've crossed the Euphrates," he told her. "It's on the other side."

"I see." She tried to hide her disappointment.

Eman turned her camel and pulled it by the lead rope to the other five in his string loaded with baggage and trade goods. He tied them in a line behind Amina's camel then led the group back into its place in the caravan. Salem followed with Hanna's mount and his string of provision-ladened camels.

The caravan was about to descend a rock-studded track that went from the plateau they had crossed during the night down to a dry valley that held the Euphrates like a green snake in its belly. It would take most of the day to get there.

Descending the steep, winding path that threaded its way between sheer cliffs proved to be treacherous for the camels. Although their wide, splayed feet were perfectly adapted for travel across flat endless deserts, in uneven rocky terrain they were less sure-footed, lacking the natural equipment of horses and donkeys whose hooves enable them to maneuver through scree. Amina slid against the bar at the front of the *haudaj* as Eman led her beast, grumbling audibly, down through the first set of boulders and rocks to a turn in the track that was barely wide enough for a single animal. She felt the weight of the rest of Eman's camels stumbling behind them, threatening to overtake her, and smelled the hot, fetid breath of a determined animal that had pushed forward until he was nearly crowding her camel off the path.

"Back. Get back, you brute," she yelled. "Eman. Do something."

The guide obliged by stopping the train and going back to push on the nose of the eager one, getting him back in line. "That one was a lead camel in his day. He's never gotten used to following others." His eyes brightened. "I may have to put him at the end of the line to teach him a lesson when we get down off these bluffs."

In addition to the steepness of the track, traversing back and forth through the sharp rocks jeopardized the precarious balance of the *haudaj* in which Amina rode. It swayed dangerously from side to side as the beast stepped carefully between rocks. Amina, her mouth dry with fear, remained wedged against the bar for the duration of the descent, her nails digging half-moons in the palms of her hands.

Contributing to her discomfort, Eman's old lead camel continued to press on hers, compounding the stress of the downward journey.

When the sun rose above them, Amina pulled her headscarf forward to shade her eyes. The jerking motion of the camel settled in her bones, making her wince. She was getting a headache and her buttocks were raw from the constant movement and friction.

It was mid-afternoon before Eman's string of camels reached the bottom of the escarpment. Hanna was still far behind.

They left the naked, rocky cliffs. The ground beneath them turned to gentle mounds of pebbled brown sand. Eman found a place to stop and rest the camels.

Amina stuck her head out of the cab and turned to look up at the track they had descended as the rest of the party made their way slowly down through the limestone rubble. When she caught sight of another camel with a *haudaj* coming into view, a smile of relief lit her face.

"You were worried about your companion?" Eman asked, as he held her camel's lead rope casually over a shoulder.

"Indeed. I'm glad she made it without a fall," Amina told him a bit defensively.

"It won't take as long to get to our meeting place," he said, moving forward. Amina waved to Hanna and they were off again.

As Amina's beast settled on more secure terrain, she noticed gray-green spiky plants sticking up from the wind-blown surface here and there. Their earthy, herbal smell caught in her nostrils. It was familiar. Her camel lowered his head as if he, too, was drawn to it.

"What is that plant, Eman?" Amina pointed to it.

"That one is *za'atar,* wild thyme."

The plant grew in abundance on either side of the track. It was a magnet for Amina's camel, drawing his head down as he tore off slender stalks to satisfy his appetite. With his large lower teeth, he masticated the twigs of thyme into slimy cuds, green saliva drooling from both corners of his mouth. Then he swallowed each cud, ready to bring one up at a moment's notice. Eman, sensing the animal's needs after the rugged descent, let him browse intermittently as they made their way down to the road that led to the Euphrates.

When they reached a series of dunes just off the main road, they found Sheikh Hassan waiting with Mustafa and the Moslawi traders. The sun cast mauve shadows across the landscape by the time they arrived.

"We will camp here for the night and make the crossing tomorrow," Hassan informed Eman. "The descent took longer than I thought it would."

Eman nodded, and led his string of camels to a spot where Amina could dismount. She was relieved. Every bone in her body ached. She could go no further, and cramps in her lower abdomen alerted her that her monthly flow might be imminent. As she waited, she looked anxiously for Hanna. She hadn't seen her since early morning.

Hanna looked flushed and disheveled when she arrived. She still gripped the front bar of her *haudaj.* When Salem halted his string of camels and Hanna dismounted, Amina could see that she was shaken. Her ashen face and anguished look told the story.

"Hanna. I'm so relieved to see you. Are you all right?"

"Yes. Now that we're not seesawing—it made me feel sick." Hanna adjusted herself, pulling her headscarf more tightly around her head and neck, as if to restore some of the dignity she had lost in the throes of descending the escarpment.

"What an awful trip. My camel slipped and Salem had to pull him up quickly to prevent him from falling. I thought I would be crushed . . . but the good Lord saved me."

"I'm glad it's over," Amina agreed. "It was scary. The news from the leader is that we'll spend the night here, before going on to the Euphrates tomorrow."

"What a relief. I hope Mustafa will give us a little water."

The next morning, the camel guides had already completed their prayers by the time Amina woke. She felt sticky between her thighs and took a folded rag from her bag and pushed it up between her legs to catch the blood, anchoring it in her drawers with two pins. It was the best she could do. She woke Hanna. They quickly packed up their things and had their tea. Amina heard Sheikh Hassan shouting orders. He beckoned to one of his assistants and introduced him to Mustafa.

Sheikh Hassan approached Amina and Hanna with Mustafa and a young Bedouin. "You two will go ahead with Mustafa and the traders to board the last morning ferry to the other side of the river," he told them. "In that way, you'll be spared the tedium of waiting for the entire caravan. My assistant, Asma," he introduced the Bedouin youth, "will be in charge."

Amina noticed that Asma had serious eyes, and they were the color of obsidian. He seemed about Amina and Hanna's age.

Asma turned to them and nodded slightly.

"I have your papers and the name of the inn where we are staying in Rahba," Mustafa told them. "We'll remain there for several days while the caravan takes on new provisions and exchanges some of the camels for others for the trip across the Syrian Desert. If we have time, we may visit Deir-ez-Zor. It's a thriving city just north of Rahba."

Sheikh Hassan cut him short here. "I must warn you, ladies. Rahba is a rough town of Bedouin traders, caravaneers, and thieves. Mustafa will escort you whenever you venture outside the inn." He nodded to Mustafa. "I will come for your group in three days."

Amina and Hanna mounted their camels and, with Eman and Salem leading the animals on foot, they left the rest of the caravan with Asma and Mustafa. Yousif Hamid and Jamal Obaid, the Moslawi traders, joined them on their way out to the main road that led to the river.

As they got closer to the Euphrates, the road became clogged with more and more camels, some ridden, others heavily laden with bags of winter wheat, bales of cotton and wool fleece. Still others carried large bundles full of red silk slippers and silk *keffiya* from Baghdad and Mosul, items much sought after in the Euphrates Valley and Damascus. Camel drivers jockeyed for position with donkeys pulling carts, and nomads driving bleeting herds of sheep and goats along the road. Bedouin tribesmen, dressed in flowing *djellaba*, ambled along each side of the road. There were few women to be seen, except for two carrying piles of sticks for their cooking fires on their heads. Dust, sheep urine, smoky fires, and sewage assailed Amina's nostrils. She took out a handkerchief and held it to her nose.

It took until mid-morning to reach the expansive, swollen Euphrates roaring its way down from the highlands in Turkey. A tributary, the Khabur, joined it just north of Rahba, adding to its volume. Then, as cliffs gave way to gentle hills and flatlands, the face of the river changed to one more placid. Amina saw a giant water wheel, made of wood, turning methodically, bringing power to turn the grinding stones used to crush barley in the mill next to it. Hanna pointed out smaller water wheels up and down the river.

Clusters of date palms rose, here and there, along the river's edge. Mustafa pointed out an unusual sandstone stele that came to a point at the top. It had arches around its exterior and stood above the palms, a symbol of a much earlier time.

Two fishermen, dressed in checked *keffiya* and long *djellaba* stood in a double-ended canoe. One put bait in a small woven fishtrap at the end of a line. Then the other man flung the trap out into water from the bow of the boat, where it sunk to catch fish. Other men tended to their fishing lines on shore. The river awed Amina with its many faces and activities.

"It's even larger than the Tigris," she shouted to Hanna.

Hanna nodded. "It makes me miss Mosul and Mama," her face filled with wistfulness.

"Me, too. But, cheer up, Hanna. We'll soon be in Rahba, a real town."

Amina looked northward and saw yellow bluffs coming down to the Euphrates' edge. But the terrain on either side of the river in front of them spread out until it lay almost flat like the palm of a hand. Further along it flowed between fingers of land and around small islands. It was broad here, less a menace than it was farther north. Irrigated *waddies* newly sown with rice seedlings hugged the edge of the river downstream. A quilt of brown, beige, and dove gray fields spread out behind them, interspersed with splashes of green where early vegetables had been planted. Reeds grew along the banks of the river in marshy places, giving shelter to ducks with bronze heads and teal green feathers that reminded Amina of those she had seen along the Tigris. An occasional gray-blue heron stood stoically in the marsh, waiting to spear a fish.

When they neared the ferry crossing, Amina noticed a huddle of beehive-shaped mud huts climbing up the slopes on either side of the road. The stench of sewage that ran in small streams between them was nauseating. She grimaced and held her breath, pulling up her scarf to cover her nose and wishing she had a sprig of mint.

When their party reached the ferry launch, she, Hanna and Mustafa dismounted. Eman and Salem carefully lowered the *haudaj* from the camels' backs, with the help of other handlers, to be loaded onto a barge from Rahba when it arrived. The two men led their beasts away to a worn piece of ground where other guides and their animals were gathered, waiting to make the river crossing.

Amina and Hanna carried their satchels down to the ferry landing to join others waiting at the top of a slope leading down to the water. Flat planks formed a walkway from the river's edge out to a floating platform where long dugout canoes, laden with bags of grain, spring vegetables and an assortment of items for sale, were tied up. From where they stood, Amina could see several sailing *dhows* and canoes zigzagging across the broad, muddy river.

"We're waiting for the ferry from Rahba to arrive," Mustafa explained. "It should be here soon."

"Is there a place where we can help ourselves while we wait?" Amina asked.

Mustafa looked flustered, then turned to Asma, Hassan's assistant, and spoke to him in rapid Arabic. He glanced toward the young women, then quickly shifted his eyes back to Mustafa and told him there was a small coffee shop nearby, but that the toilet was crude.

"Take them there," Mustafa ordered. "I'll wait with our belongings for the ferry."

By the time they got back to the ferry landing, a large boat, its wooden planks painted a dull red with a strip of blue running the length of each side and ending in flourishes at the upward curving bow, was tied to a large post on shore. A canvas awning covered the seating area of the boat, which consisted of rows of wooden seats. Asma, their guide, picked up the girls' satchels and led them and Mustafa down the slope to a small gangplank. It was no more than a foot wide and led to the ferry. Hanna seemed hesitant. Asma went up the plank first and turned around to give each girl a hand in entering on the aft deck. Amina lifted her skirt slightly and walked up quickly before she had time to lose her balance. Hanna took Asma's hand, and slowly put one foot in front of the other until she made it onto the deck. She giggled with relief at Amina, as they watched the others board. Once Mustafa and the two Moslawi traders had joined them, Asma led them forward, leaning down slightly to accommodate the low awning, to several rows of benches toward the front.

Amina saw a clutch of women who took up two rows of benches. They were shrouded in black *adowa,* with only their eyes showing. They chattered animatedly. One had a small boy with a shock of black hair and huge eyes who was standing in the middle of the aisle, staring at the strangers. He was snatched back quickly when Asma greeted the women and moved up the aisle. Asma put the girls' satchels down at one end of a row.

"You can sit here," he told Amina and Hanna, bowing.

The babble of voices behind them died to a whisper as the women watched like crows on a line as the outsiders settled into their seats. Mustafa and the other two men were directed to seats on the opposite side of the aisle.

Feeling the heat of the local women's gazes, Amina ignored them and turned to Hanna. "To tell the truth, I've been on a boat only once or twice. That was when I accompanied Father on a visit to a monastery outside Mosul. We had to cross a river to get there."

"I've never been on a boat," Hanna admitted. "I hope we'll be safe," she bit her lower lip, always a sign of Hanna's doubt about something.

"I think we'll be fine, as long as the ferry doesn't become overloaded." Amina looked around the boat's interior as she said it.

The aft part of the boat had a large compartment for storing boxes, parcels, and trunks. A sinewy Arab perched out on the aft end handled a long, upright paddle to steer it. Oarsmen were seated outside the passenger area, six to a side, each handling a long paddle. Amina didn't see the captain, but she heard his voice ordering the crew to pull up the small gangplank, and release the lines around the post on shore.

The din and chatter of the passengers quieted as they felt the sway of the ferry. A few of the women waved to well wishers on shore as the boat moved slowly out toward the expanse of water that marked the channel for the crossing.

"Are you sure it's safe?" Hanna asked Amina. Her features were gathered into a scowl. "I can't swim, you know," she said, eyeing the muddy water sliding over the oars.

"I should think so," Amina said and smiled to reassure Hanna.

The cluster of Bedouin women resumed their animated conversations as the ferry left behind the skiffs and inflated sheepskin rafts cluttering the river near shore and headed out toward deeper water. Their medley of voices came to Hanna.

"If they're not worried, I guess I shouldn't be either," she declared.

Amina squeezed her elbow to show her empathy.

"There is something familiar," Hanna pointed to a *kalak,* a raft made of inflated sheepskins lashed together in a rectangle. Wooden boxes were tied down in the middle to prevent them from shifting. A skinny boy sat on one of them, while another paddled the raft up river, staying close to the shore.

"I'm glad we're not traveling on that." Amina said.

"I am, too. But they are useful. I've seen them on the Tigris."

Amina was busy watching sailing *dhows* cutting across the river as they moved farther out.

Just then, a wave from a larger boat hit them, rocking the ferry.

Hanna froze and turned pale. She was silent, brooding, as her arms gripped her waist.

"Hanna. What's wrong?" Amina was frightened by the change in her.

"My stomach is hurting . . . a nasty taste in my throat." She clutched her neck.

"Oh Mother Mary. You need to . . ."

It was too late. Hanna leaned over, gagging, and with a great heave, vomited what was in her stomach at their feet. It formed a puddle of bile and stringy bread bits covered with mucus that caught on the edge of Hanna's skirt hem.

Amina's eyes opened wide. She quickly handed Hanna one of her large handkerchiefs.

Hanna began wiping her mouth and dress. "I wish we had some water."

"We should have thought of that before we got on the ferry." Amina was trying to control herself from gagging over the foul smell coming from the floor.

She felt someone poking her in the back. She turned abruptly to see one of the Bedouin women, her clear eyes showing empathy. Amina recognized her. She was the one who had yanked her son back from the aisle, a young woman like herself.

"Here, take this." She handed Amina a black cloth that came from a basket at her feet.

"*Shukran laki,*" Amina thanked her quickly. She dropped the rag over the puddle of vomit, and took her companion's hand, without saying anything.

As the ferry reached the midpoint in the river, Amina saw that the sun was descending into the west behind an uneven line of hills.

She noticed color coming back into Hanna's cheeks. Hanna had raised her head and was watching a *dhow* slip through the water. Though she still clutched her satchel, she seemed to be feeling better.

"I've never seen a boat that looks like that," Hanna motioned toward the *dhow.* "It's hard to believe that a large piece of cloth can keep it floating. The men who sail those things must be very clever."

Amina nodded, watching another *dhow* on the port side coming toward the ferry. It turned smoothly on a different tack just as Amina thought it might be in danger of running into them. Its destination seemed to be the sun, which now cast a yellow sheen on the water's surface. "Aren't they beautiful, Hanna? Look at the water—it's like melted gold."

Hanna smiled wanly.

Calls from oarsmen pulled the travelers out of their reverie. The ferry from Rahba, crammed with passengers, was passing them, drawing greeting shouts from the rowers on both boats and waves from a few passengers on their ferry. It was then that Amina saw the vague silhouette of a town backlit by the sun as they moved toward the far shore.

"It won't be long now before we're landing, Hanna. Look. You can just see the outline of Rahba in the distance."

Hanna shielded her eyes with her slim hand and looked ahead. She smiled back at Amina. "I never thought we'd reach there," she murmured, relieved.

Amina tried to make out the shapes of houses and buildings as Rahba came into view. What she saw in the fading sunlight were minarets. She picked out two mosques as the ferry made its way carefully into the town dock, where four dark-skinned, muscular Bedouins, wrapped in brown cloth from the waist down, waited to grab the lines to secure the ferry. Once they had landed, groups of passengers began standing up and collecting their baggage and baskets. As Amina stood, she felt herself swaying and had to plant her feet to keep from falling before retrieving her satchel.

She looked down at Hanna. "Be careful. It's a little rocky still."

They gathered their luggage and she and Hanna followed the group of local women, who were laughting and talking at once, up a small gangplank.

Amina found the woman who had given her the cloth and tried to offer her one of her handkerchiefs in return.

The young mother shook her head. "Have a safe journey." She smiled and hurried after the other Bedouin women, her son clinging to her hand.

Amina joined Hanna and the two traders from Mosul on the dock, where they waited for Mustafa to clear the Syrian border with their papers. He finally emerged, carrying one of his bags on his head. Amina stifled a giggle. He looked like a porter.

"A man from the inn is supposed to meet us at the top." Mustafa led them up the gangway to the crowded street in front of the quay where people were looking for porters and transport. "He should be here soon."

Amina heard a bedlam of sounds—men shouting, women greeting one another with laughter or tears, donkeys braying, a coffee seller with his large curved pot mingling through the crowd calling for customers, another vendor selling sweets. The river smells, slightly fishy and mud damp, mingled with the aromas of the street. It was a dusty town once you got away from the Euphrates. They waited nearly an hour before someone arrived.

Just as dusk was settling on the town, a dark Bedouin, dressed in ballooning trousers and a fez, arrived with a donkey-drawn cart that had KHAN DU ZOR written in large black letters on each side. Mustafa approached him quickly, giving the wooden cart a disapproving look. It had benches on each side, but not much room.

"Salaam alaykum. We're the passengers arrived from Mosul," he announced. "Are you sure this cart will hold all of us and our baggage as well?"

"Alaykum alsalaam. Welcome to Rahba." The man ignored Mustafa's question. "I am at your service, sahib."

He turned to the two young women. "Let me help you up." He put down a stool at the end of the cart for their use. Once they were in the cart, Amina and Hanna went to the front and sat down. The driver then helped Mustafa and the two Moslawi traders into the cart. He handed the bags and satchels up to the traders who put most of them under the benches. The rest remained at the end of the cart as the driver closed the rear panel on the luggage.

Getting up on a raised seat, the driver urged the donkey into action and soon they were threading their way through narrow streets bordered on each side by two-story adobe buildings with small balconies facing one another. Dim lights hovered in the upper stories as twilight faded to dark.

After a short bumpy ride, the cart came to a square and, circling it, drew up in front of a three-story building with sheltered balconies running across the front. It was the largest building on the street, but not nearly as grand as Amina's father's inn in Mosul.

They quickly exited the cart and went inside where hanging lanterns brightened the spacious reception area. The *khan's* manager, a rotund Arab with an oiled mustache and a glowing manner stepped forward to welcome them. Exhausted from the journey, the weary travelers collapsed into leatherback chairs. A servant arrived a few minutes later with tea.

All Amina could think of was a bath; she hadn't bathed in a week. The mint tea was welcome, but what she most wanted was to visit a *hammam,* a public bath, where she and Hanna might perform their ablutions among other women and revive themselves. Then she remembered that she still bled between her thighs. She would not be allowed to enter the *hammam* until the bleeding stopped. For the time being she would have to make do with whatever the inn offered.

CHAPTER 8

A Respite from the Journey

"I feel like a new person," Hanna beamed at Amina who was putting together her gritty travel clothes for the inn's laundry.

"I wish I had been able to go," Amina lamented. "You were lucky to find two women to accompany you. I had to cope with cleaning myself here. At least I've new clothes on. You better get your laundry ready. They are going to collect it at noon."

"I will." Hanna could see by the set of Amina's chin that her mistress was upset by not being able to go to the *hammam*. She quickly put the clothes she had worn the first week together and stuffed them in the laundry bag. She was relieved that she didn't have to do their laundry in Rahba. It left her feeling frivolous, to be without such duties.

Having donned clean, long-sleeved cotton dresses, and feeling languid and lazy after the constant push from Mosul, Amina and Hanna were glad to take their time before meeting Mustafa about their program at breakfast.

"I don't want to go anywhere today. I'd like to write a letter to Father and walk in the garden," Amina told Hanna as they descended the stairs.

"That would suit me. I need to do a few things of my own."

When they entered the inn's modest dining room, Mustafa was waiting for them. The trader stood up as the young ladies seated themselves across from him.

"You look rested this morning. What would you like with your tea?"

"Hummus and flat bread. And figs if they're ripe yet," Amina ventured.

"Hanna?"

"I'll just have bread with tea."

A servant approached dressed in a bright, full-sleeved white blouse with a red vest, black trousers and a red fez perched on his dark head. He took their order, but when it came to Amina's choice of fruit, he had disappointing news.

Mustafa turned to them. "I have business to do in preparation for the onward journey."

Amina nodded.

"Our next major stop will be Tudmor, the oasis town the Romans called Palmyra. We'll be there for four days. It is the halfway point between here and Damascus, and a busy town with much history. Egyptians, Romans and, later, the Ottomans competed with nomadic tribes for control over the City of Palms." He smiled, and paused to sip his tea. "Would you like to hear something about it?"

"Yes. Of course," Amina said eagerly.

"At one time, it was the center of the Tudmor Empire, an Arab emirate that stretched all the way from Egypt to the Syrian Desert. The empire was ruled, at its height, by a famous woman—Queen Zenobia."

"Who was she? I've never heard of her." Amina queried.

"She was the favorite consort of the Tudmor emperor. Zenobia had a son by him and after the emperor's death she moved to act as regent for her young son to ensure his right to inherit his father's crown once the boy came of age. The legal heir to the throne had died as a child. Zenobia's son was next in line."

Amina looked perplexed. "Did her son have a right to rule?"

"He was the emperor's son by Zenobia, even though she wasn't an official wife. Zenobia was a strong-willed woman and well organized. She was able to insist that her son be allowed to rule, with her as regent. That's how she became queen. She proved to be an able leader who raised an army against Tudmor's enemies, bringing them under her control. Later, she led her forces against the Romans to expel them from the region. The battle ended in the Emperor Aurelian's defeat." Mustafa stopped briefly to take another sip of tea.

"You can imagine that the emperor was furious when he heard that a woman at the head of an army had rousted his troops. Aurelian grew jealous of her power and raised a new force against her. She was captured and compelled to march through the streets of Tudmor in defeat. The Romans overran the city, renamed it Palmyra, and Queen Zenobia was thrown into prison for the remainder of her life."

"How sad," Amina looked downcast.

"What happened to her son?" Hanna asked.

"He turned out to be a weakling. And once the Romans conquered the region, they set out to build a city on the old ruins. They constructed a series of wells across the desert from Palmyra to the Euphrates to provide water for their caravans and armies. You will like visiting the town. There is much to see there."

Amina nodded. "I'm looking forward to seeing the place."

At that point the girls' tea arrived with the bread and hummus. Mustafa paused while they were served.

"The journey across the desert is not easy, but at least you'll have water available in many places. The Roman wells are still in use, those that have been maintained."

"Have you asked Sheikh Hassan about a night guard? My father would wish for nothing less, under the circumstances," Amina prompted.

"I will speak with a Bedouin chief about it today. I have also spoken with Jamal Obaid and Yousif Hamid, the Moslawi traders. They are as concerned about your wellbeing after the theft, as I am. They have offered to look out for you. Both are honorable men with families."

"I would like to see them while we're here in Rahba, so that Hanna and I become better acquainted with them."

"I will arrange it, *inshallah.* Perhaps an outing for tomorrow in which they join us."

"I'll mention the plans in the letter I'm writing to my father," Amina alerted him.

"I would be glad to see that a courier takes the letter." Mustafa leaned forward, as if to go. "Now, I have much to do, unless you wish me to escort you somewhere today."

"No, we'll rest at the inn today," Amina told her father's friend.

"Very well. I'll leave a message for you as to the time we'll meet tomorrow."

*   *   *

Amina and Hanna went up to their room.

"I think I will go down to the courtyard and do some sketching, if you don't need me," Hanna said.

"You brought a sketch pad with you? That's wonderful. I will stay here. I need to write a letter to Baba."

"A good idea. Give him my greetings." Hanna disappeared out the door.

Amina sat down at a small dressing table to write.

10th March, 1898, Rahba, Syria

Dearest Father,

We have arrived safely in the transit town of Rahba on the Euphrates. It took five days to get here. We camped the first and second nights, then slept in our haudaj the third night so we could be in Rahba by Friday, the Muslim Sabbath. Alas, it took longer to get down the steep bluffs we encountered before reaching the Euphrates Valley. We were too late to take the ferry to cross the river that day and were forced to spend another night camping before reaching the river the next day. The Euphrates River is very broad. It seems larger than the Tigris, with many gardens coming down to the water's edge. We also saw a number of waterwheels. On the river, people get around on kalak as they do on the Tigris.

Here, in Rahba, there are many Bedouins and some Arabs. We will
be staying here for three days.

There is something that I must inform you of. We have no
security guard. I thought Sahib Mustafa was providing one. During
our second night of camping, near the Sinjar Hills, we experienced
a theft that left both Hanna and me very frightened. In the middle
of the night, someone breached our tent and stole our waterbag.
We tried to call for help, but no one came to our rescue. Neither of
us was hurt, but we have lost our water. We hardly had enough to
get us across the Euphrates. After learning about the troubles the
good Montfort brothers had in the northern desert, I am eager to
make sure that we have a nightguard for the rest of our trip. I
spoke with Sahib Mustafa this morning and he has promised us
both a new waterbag and a guard before we leave Rahba. I hope a
courier gets this to you quickly so that you can contact Mustafa.
Please do not tell Mama about this incident as I am sure she will
faint.

Hanna and I are getting accustomed to the motion of the
camels. We find the haudaj comfortable, but lonely at times. We
entertain ourselves by singing and telling stories.

Give my love to Mama, hug Leila for me, and give the boys
my greetings.

Your obedient and loving daughter,
Amina Marie Rassam

Amina took her letter down to the innkeeper to inquire when a courier
might take it to Mosul. He told her one was leaving early the next morning.
Relieved, she left her letter with him.

*   *   *

A donkey brayed somewhere in the still morning air the next day, waking
Hanna. She got up, dressed quietly and slipped out the door. She heard noise
coming from the interior courtyard below and went down to see what it was all
about. When she got there she found traders busy opening double doors to rooms
where they had placed their goods for the night. The rooms had a slightly musty
odor.

Looking along the row, Hanna saw a large storage room filled with long
wrapped bales of fleece piled from floor to ceiling. She knew from listening to
the idle conversations of traders in the inn back in Mosul that the price for wool
and sheep had risen in the last decade, bringing handsome profits. She saw a
merchant about the age of Amina's father, taking stock of his bales. He wore a
fez and a long black muslin coat. He had a friendly smile and paternal manner,

as he greeted her. She returned his greeting, lowering her eyes discreetly, then asked him where he was taking his fleece.

"To Aleppo."

"Aleppo?" Her head came up. "That's a city we know. I am from Mosul. Both our cities trade in wool and cotton. We help each other with supplies."

"Ah ha. Did you know, young lady, that Aleppo is the greatest exporter of wool in Syria and the center of all sheep and fleece transactions here and in Egypt?"

"No." Hanna raised her eyebrows, looking at the stacks of fleece.

"Our merchants import sheep from as far away as Anatolia, Kurdistan and even your own Mosul province."

"That's quite a distance," Hanna said, as she ran her hand over a loose bale, fingering the soft fleece. It reminded her of home and the smell of wet wool.

"Our sheepskins and fleece are exported to France and England," the trader continued.

"I didn't know Aleppo was such a large center." Hanna kept her eyes on the bales.

"Of course. And now, as the sheep trade has become lucrative, the Bedouin are beginning to get into the business, selling sheep along with their camels. Some tribes have large herds, more than 5,000 sheep."

Hanna's eyes had begun straying to other storerooms, from which the smells of pistachios and pomegranates emanated. Uncomfortably aware that she was spending more time with this gentleman than propriety allowed, especially since she was unescorted, she said good-bye and hurried on. Traders had begun loitering in doorways to talk. Hanna saw a woman, slightly her elder, dressed in black but without a headscarf covering her dark hair. It hung in a braid down her back. She was leaning against a green door, looking at Hanna with disapproving eyes.

Hanna approached her with some hesitation and greeted her. She asked the woman where she had come from.

"From Sukhne. I'm here with my husband's family. We've brought wheat and pistachios to sell to the Bedouin in Rahba and Deir-ez-Zor."

"Do you get a good price for your wheat here?"

"I tell you," her voice dropped. "Since the Ottomans started encouraging the Bedouin to settle down and grow crops, we've seen the price of our grain drop. We don't get as much as we did for it. But we have to make a living." She lifted one generous black eyebrow, as if to emphasize the point.

Hanna smiled and nodded. She eyed the pistachios, suddenly feeling hungry.

"Where have you come from?"

"Mosul." Hanna looked up.

"That's a long way. What brings you here? You are not alone, are you?"

"No. I am accompanying my mistress to Damascus. She is having a rest from the road for a few days. Is Damascus far?"

"Yes. It willl take you many days. Does your mistress have business there?"

"No. She is traveling much further—to France."

The woman's eyebrows shot up. "Are you going all the way to France with her?"

"No. My mother is at home. I will leave her in Damascus and return to Mosul." Hanna shifted, suddenly feeling uneasy about her trip back to Mosul.

"You are a brave one. That's a long journey. I wish you well."

"And to you."

Hanna suddenly realized she had lost track of time. She went inside to find Amina. Her mistress was already seated in the dining room with Mustafa and the two Moslawi traders. Hanna slipped quietly into a seat, feeling uncomfortable as the others greeted her.

"Where have you been?" Amina whispered.

"I was walking in the courtyard."

Mustafa was outlining the program for the day, which included a visit to a local Bedouin trader. "He knows much about the history of the Euphrates Valley and the desert. An interesting man, he'll be our guide in Rahba. He has arranged for us to have lunch at a local restaurant. Afterwards, we'll walk down to the river to see the sights before returning to the inn."

"That sounds wonderful," Amina exclaimed.

"You've planned a grand outing," Jamal Obaid, the younger of the two traders agreed.

"Do not bring anything valuable with you, young ladies. As Sheikh Hassan warned, Rahba is a magnet for thieves, especially along the riverside. I've arranged for a donkey cart to take us to see my Bedouin friend. Be down at the reception desk at half past nine."

*　　*　　*

"Allow me to present Jada'an Fadil," Mustafa told his small group when they got to the trader's office. "He's the best *mutsellem el caravan,* supplier of caravans, in the area. His brother, Hajim, is sheikh of one of the largest tribes, the Feda'an. They winter in the Hamad, the desert region you will travel through. He can tell you much about the place." Mustafa then introduced his visitors to Fadil.

"Salaam alaykum," the man greeted them, nodding slightly.

Jada'an Fadil was a distinguished-looking man, slightly stooped with streaks of metal gray in his beard and the nose of a hawk. His piercing eyes missed nothing. He was lean as a timber and almost as tall as Mustafa, whose head had brushed the doorway coming in.

Mustafa told Amina that Fadil had agreed to secure a nightguard for them. Amina thanked him, relieved to hear the news, as was Hanna.

Fadil nodded. "Mustafa tells me you wish to learn something of the desert you are about to enter, and its people. Is that right?"

Amina and Hanna agreed.

"Sit down then, ladies. I'm sorry, gentlemen, there are not enough chairs."

Yousif Hamid set him at ease saying, "We've been on the road too long. It is good to stand for a change."

Hamid has a kind face, Amina mused, surprised she had not noticed it before.

"Well, let me begin by telling you something about the people who live and raise their children in the desert." Jada'an Fadil looked at Amina and Hanna.

"We camel herders are not one group, but many. One of the largest tribal alliances is the Anazeh, made up of the Assene, Roualla, Sba'a, and my own tribe, the Feda'an. We are like fingers on a hand, some larger than others, but when trouble comes we draw together into a fist to protect our tribes." He demonstrated, bringing his strong, weathered hand into a fist.

Amina was surprised to hear him mention the Anazeh—the tribe feared by caravaneers. "About forty years ago, the Roualla took over the southern part of the Palmyrene, and the Feda'an remained in the north. Between them were the Sba'a, a peace-loving people who live in Tudmor to this day.

"Another large alliance includes the tribes of Nedj, southwest of here. The third is the Shammar, who were pushed back to the northern steppe by the Feda'an. They winter in the Hamad. For a while, when Ibrahim Pasha's troops were posted in the desert, there was peace among the different groups, but when the Ottoman troops departed, the tribal wars over pasture, water, and animals broke out again. There was much looting and plunder. Rival tribes fought over villages and the people suffered; they could not keep up with the khuwwa, the protection money they had to pay to warring tribes. Many villagers migrated to Aleppo for safety."

"How many men could a tribal leader call to arms?" Jamal Obaid interrupted.

"It depended on the population. Sukhne had the largest population and could arm about four hundred men to defend the town." He stopped to light a cigarette and leaned back in his chair, inhaling, then blew the smoke skyward.

"The Ottomans made an effort to 'pacify' us," he continued, "by introducing farming in hopes that we would become *fellahin* and settle into the land. They sent cavalry forces on mules, carrying European rifles, to enforce their measures." He smiled with a twinge of irony at such folly.

At that point a servant came in with a tray of coffee and a plate of roasted pistachio nuts. As the man passed around small cups of coffee, Jada'an Fadil stopped and invited them to try the nuts. "They come from a plantation just east of Aleppo. It is famous for its pistachios."

The aroma of the warm, sweet-smelling nuts drew Amina. She helped herself to a handful as the servant served her coffee, then passed them to Hanna.

"These are delicious," Yousif Hamid said, putting a second nut between his teeth to break the hard shell."

"Now where was I?"

"You were telling us about the Ottoman's campaign to bring the Bedouins under their control," Mustafa said.

"Ah, yes," he nodded, after taking several sips of coffee. "A new administrative region was set up in the Euphrates Valley with its headquarters at Deir. But about twenty years ago, the Turks found their empire stretched in too many directions. They tried to appeal to our tribal *sheikhs,* to whom they'd given land, to become allies." He chuckled. "It did not please the *sheikhs."*

"They also tried to impose a military draft, but the tribes rejected it," Fadil frowned. "Most tribes were able to avoid it by disappearing into the mountains or moving to another area with their camel herds. Eight years ago, the Anazeh tribes emigrated toward Nedj to avoid being forced to serve the Ottomans. They are still on the move."

Amina recalled what the French brothers who visited Mosul had experienced at the hand of Anazeh raiders. Now, learning that they were on the run from the Ottoman troops, she saw that they were outcasts in their own land. "When did your tribe first get land?" She asked.

"My uncle, Sheikh Jada'an ibn Muha'id, who was the leader of all the Feda'an, received lands to farm from the Pasha some time ago. These included twenty villages. At that time, the Ottoman Pasha bestowed on him the title, *'Sheikh of the Desert.'*" The trader laughed.

Amina looked at him, unsure how to react. She bit into another nut.

"It was only the sheikhs' families, like young Mujhim, Jada'an's son, who have benefited. The Pasha saw to it that the sons of each *sheikh* were sent to Constantinople to be educated and learn Turkic ways. That's where Mujhim is now."

"How old is he?" Amina asked.

"Thirteen. He will one day be the *sheikh.* But the trouble with such an education is that the returning sons become used to city ways. It's hard for them to return to their herding life. They'd rather be in Deir or Aleppo than out in the desert."

He shifted and stood up. "That's enough for now. Let's go and have a look at the town, though it's a rough cut compared to Deir-ez-Zor."

The group walked through streets lined with shops and storehouses until they came to a small inn. "This is where we'll take lunch." Fadil stopped.

The party followed him in. Amina and Hanna excused themselves to wash before the meal. "That was interesting to learn something about the tribes," Amina said. "We think of the Bedouin as one people. But they are really many different groups."

"Even the Anazeh. I could never keep track of them all," Hanna said. "And to think that our guide is one of them." She shook her head as they made their way back to the group.

At the table, they found empty places across from the Moslawi traders and Mustafa. Their host had disappeared. Here in Rahba, unlike Mosul, men and women ate together, but on opposite sides. It was something Amina and Hanna would have to get used to.

"How did you find the morning's meeting with Fadil sahib?" Mustafa asked.

"A pleasure," Amina replied. "I had no idea the Bedouin were actually many tribes. I'm sorry to say, it's revealing of how little I know."

"You are not alone," Yousif Hamid told her. "Few of us understand them. To many people, they're mysterious and dangerous nomads. Yet without them, how would we get our trade goods across the deserts? We depend on them more than we're willing to admit."

"In what ways?" Amina took a piece of bread and dipped it into an eggplant dish.

"They are the men who provide us with the camels for the caravans. Some breed the animals for sale while others raise them for hire to caravan leaders who are responsible for organizing the trips. Some *mutsellem* specialize in supplying camels for specific types of traders, say in silk, wool, or spices. Others specialize in pilgrimages to and from Mecca. Some take groups of travelers from India, Europe and other places, though often travelers accompany other types of caravans, as you are doing."

"And they provide camel handlers and guides," Mustafa pointed out. "Without knowledge of the deserts and the various routes that cross them, one might become lost with little chance of survival. That has happened. Whole caravans have disappeared."

"What a horrifying thought," Amina cringed.

As if reading her mind, Hamid said, "In our case, you shouldn't worry. Sheikh Hassan is one of the best caravan leaders in the region. And he hires good men."

Mustafa was nodding.

After they had finished their lunch, Fadil appeared and asked if they would like to walk down to the river. "You'll see how the local women wash fleece to prepare it for shipping."

Hanna, who had been silent, suddenly came to life. "I'd like very much to see that. This morning I saw bales of fleece stored at the inn for transport."

"Indeed? Are you ready to go?" He turned to the rest of the group.

"By all means," Obaid said.

They followed Fadil through a series of arched passageways and came out on a slight rise above the river where they saw women, some in long dresses and others in carbon-black *adowa* waist deep in the water, washing long bundles of fleece. A rectangular fence with the shore side open, made of tree branches, was built out into the water, twenty meters from the shore. It marked the nearest group's wash station. Bales of fleece were piled up from the road down to the water's edge between each station, forming a makeshift fence. Women were spread out, some preparing fleece on shore while others bent to their washing in the river, fully clothed. Their children waded in the Euphrates or chased one another on shore. A few older ones helped their mothers.

"It's like a scene from the Bible," Amina observed. "Have you ever seen anything like it?" She turned to Hanna.

"Yes, in Mosul. They do the same thing in the Tigris. Haven't you noticed it?"

"Not that I remember." Amina felt suddenly deficient.

"On a few days, when my mother was released from her work at the inn, I'd go with her to a place where women washed fleece. My mother's sister was one of those who washed wool fleece for a merchant. Sometimes, we'd even help."

"I'm sure it's the case," interrupted Yousif Hamid, who had been listening. "I, too, have seen women washing fleece in the Tigris."

Hanna beamed, hearing Hamid. "At the end of the day," she continued, "we'd have a small picnic on the shore. That was the best part." A slight smile was playing on her lips.

Amina looked at her, awed. With a start, she realized that Hanna had hidden parts of her life that were unknown to her.

CHAPTER 9

Passage Into a Fickle Desert

Mustafa met Amina and Hanna in the reception area on the last morning in Rahba. He was talking with the *khanji,* the inn's owner, when they arrived. They waited for him to finish. Amina had had a restful night; she knew it might be her last for some time.

"Yes, ladies. Everything is settled. Eman has a new goatskin for you, and Jada'an Fadil found a trustworthy Feda'an to stand guard at night. His name is Ma'an. He will travel with us as far as Tudmor and will see to your bags during the journey.

"Amina, your father said you would spend a few days in the village of Ma'alula. Is that right? The village is a half-day's ride north of Damascus. It would be best if you visit Ma'alula on your way there."

"Yes. I want to visit the place. I'd like to stay at St. Serge Monastery for a couple of days while you make the arrangements for my transport from Damascus to Beirut."

"I will send a message to the Superior of St. Serge to expect you in four weeks' time."

"*Shukran.* A courier picked up my letter for my father yesterday. I told Father that you were arranging for a guard."

Mustafa seemed surprised, but nodded and helped Amina and Hanna into a donkey cart. The trio set off to meet Sheikh Hassan and his caravan just west of the town.

Having survived the first week of the journey, and ensconced in their *haudaj* again, Amina and Hanna were more aware of their surroundings than they had been when they left Mosul. The Euphrates valley was at their backs. They, now, traveled west toward a soaring wall of yellow sandstone cliffs. Amina could see the ruins of an ancient citadel clinging to one of the pinnacles.

"Is that a fortress up there, Eman?"

"It's one of many forts built by the Greeks or Romans. Very old."

The face of the escarpment appeared to be an impenetrable barrier, but as they neared its sheer walls, Amina saw what looked like a hidden gateway, a natural sandstone arch flying over a narrow entrance. It marked the beginning of the Syrian Desert, the desert that had haunted her dreams.

Amina was surprised and enchanted by the archway. "A secret passage," she called to Hanna, whose head was tilted back.

"Look, Amina. Swallows. They're flying in and out of caves up there."

Amina followed Hanna's gaze and saw the small birds flitting in agitated clouds among the cliffs. "I see them." But at that moment, her attention was drawn to a much larger bird swooping toward them. "Hanna, I think there's a hawk up there, or it might be an eagle." She pointed above the rock wall.

Eman turned back. "That's a golden eagle. You see them here in the desert. They are after the swallows."

"They don't kill them, do they?"

"They have to eat, just like us. When they can't find rabbits or mice, they go after other birds." Eman was on foot, leading Amina's camel and the others in his train into the passage that threaded its way between sheer taupe cliffs. It was darker and cooler here in the gorge.

Feeling a sudden chill, Amina pulled a cape around her shoulders. They were riding between rugged rock faces pockmarked with niches, crannies and caves, from which rock hydrax and an occasional fox appeared then darted away. A hush fell over the travelers, the very scale of the walls on either side reducing them to the size of ants.

Amina stared at the cliffs rising above her with awe, mingled with a touch of anxiety as she watched a loose rock tumble down an outcrop. *I hope nothing happens to us in here. If one of those boulders should . . . we'd be buried alive.* She crossed herself quickly for good measure, and tilted her head back to see a slice of cerulean sky. She took heart in the sunlight beginning to penetrate the vertical opening. Still, a dank smell clung to the canyon's walls.

The scent of dust from the track and camels' urine made her cough. She took hold of the scarf tied around her neck and pulled it up over her nose.

As the advancing column of camels and half a dozen horses moved along the track, Amina saw what looked like columbine clinging to a crevice in the rock wall, its red and pink flowers offering a bright spot in the bland, dun surface. She began looking for other signs of spring and saw cascades of tiny, white daisy-like flowers, fleabane, protruding from moist cracks here and there. Their ability to survive in such an environment amazed her.

Just then, she heard "A-MI-NA ... A-mi-na ... A-mi-na," echoing off nearby walls and looked ahead to see Yousif Hamid cupping his hands and calling her name to the canyon gods. She laughed, and joined in the fun, calling out "HAN-NA," hearing it echo back "Han-na ... Han-na." Soon everyone was doing it, leading to a cacophony of sounds.

It took them more than an hour to make their way through the gap. When they emerged on the other side, the sun was blinding. They clustered together, for a moment, getting used to the intense light. Amina saw that the landscape had changed; steep bluffs gave way to a broad plain, broken by occasional hills.

As they got closer to the mounds, Eman shouted up to Amina, "See those hills? They were *qasrs,* round huts made of stone where farmers used to store their crops. But once they were abandoned, the sands buried them."

"What a grueling force," Amina shouted back. *Not even granaries last for long here,* she thought, wondering about the farmers who had built them.

On they rode, over stony hard surfaces and salt-crusted sand, around tawny dunes and castle-like rocks that rose up from the desert floor. The caravan stopped early that day to let the animals graze on *za'atar,* the wild thyme, and *zizafun,* a type of herb that Eman explained to Amina was used for coughs and sore throats. The handlers took off the cumbersome *haudaj,* but left the other animals still burdened with their loads. They shooed them off to forage. The camels, loosely hobbled, quickly dispersed across the uneven terrain with mincing steps, while the tethered horses had to contend with grazing closer at hand.

In the meantime, the guides began the tedious task of bringing water up from a stone well that had led Sheikh Hassan to choose this spot for the night's campsite. One of the men unpacked a tent and got out a tent pole. He carried the pole over to the well and two handlers held it horizontally across the top of the well, while a third tied a rope to it in the middle with a leather bucket secured to the other end. The pole acted as a makeshift winch to bring up water for both animals and travelers.

Amina was curious about the operation and urged Hanna to come with her to watch the men and fill their canteens. Hanna joined her reluctantly, because she wanted to find a bushy spot in which to urinate and there were few such spots. Heading to the well, they met the two Moslawi traders, armed with an empty goatskin.

When the men saw the traders approaching, they stopped their work and poured a bucketful into the traders' goatskin. Jamal Obaid beckoned to the young women. "Bring your canteens."

Hanna took their two canteens to him, and he adroitly poured a stream of water into each with little lost to the desert.

Hanna thanked him and handed Amina her canteen.

Amina tipped hers up and took a thirsty gulp. "It's sweet. I didn't expect it would be.

"How far down does the well go?" Obaid asked one of the handlers.

"A hundred meters."

"A hundred meters? Did you hear that ladies? No wonder it tastes so good."

After quenching her thirst, Amina asked Yousif Hamid and Obaid if they would like to go for a walk. Both men agreed, but Hanna declined.

"I'd like to rest and make some drawings," she told Amina. The truth was she needed to be alone, free of her responsibilities as Amina's companion for a few hours. "I hope you don't mind."

"Of course not."

The two traders and Amina strolled out along the caravan road, away from the well and camp preparations, toward the sinking orb of the sun. A desert mouse skittered across the track in front of them. In the distance, Amina saw a band of deer-like animals springing across the desert.

Cupping her hand over her eyes, she watched them leaping in near unison.

"They're gazelle," Hamid told her. "We must have startled them." He turned to Obaid. "Maybe I should have brought my Winchester. They're tasty animals."

"By the time you fetched it, they'd be gone," Obaid laughed.

Amina pouted. The gazelle were so beautiful and free. Why not let them be?

"You don't like hunting?" Obaid said, reading her mind.

"I don't think I'd care for it. They're lovely to watch."

As they walked further, Amina began to see blue knobby spikes sticking up from gray-green plants. They looked like sage in bloom. She left the road to have a closer look and tore off a sprig of one, twisting it between her fingers and holding it to her nose. "It's sage," she called to the traders.

The clean, sharp pungency of the herb pleased her. She had seen it among a healer's dried herbs in Mosul, and growing in the inn's kitchen garden. Her mother used sage when she had a headache or cold. Its flowers signaled a change in the season, new growth. She put the twig in her pocket.

Further along, she found a low bush filled with long stems of delicate pink flowers, each with a yellow center. The blossoms reminded her of columbine, but the plant's leaves were thin, like spiders' legs. "I wonder what these are?" She turned to Hamid.

"That's what the Bedouin call *ahyet,*" he told her. "I can see you are intriqued by the desert's gifts."

"Yes, especially the plants' uses." Do you know what *ahyet* is used for?"

"I'm not sure. Maybe for coughs."

"It's pretty. I haven't seen it in Mosul."

They walked a little farther then turned back as the sun dipped behind the horizon. Chatting as they went, they were startled when a silver-tinged jackal burst from the bushes and, just as abruptly, vanished when it saw them in the road.

*　　*　　*

That night, Amina and Hanna met Ma'an for the first time. They found him standing in front of their tent when they arrived after supper. He spoke Arabic and introduced himself, telling them that Jada'an Fadil, the Feda'an trader in Rahba, had asked him to be their night watch.

Ma'an was a solid-looking man, sun-darkened with a broad forehead under a camelhair band that held his *keffiya* in place. His dress was simple, a striped *djellaba,* girded at the waist with a wide belt from which hung a long, curved knife in a sheath. He wore leather slippers, slightly turned up at the toes, in the Ottoman fashion. His sharp brown eyes appraised them as they drew near the tent. He greeted them cordially and stepped aside for them to enter.

"Ma'an makes me feel safer." Hanna set down the lantern between them in the tent.

"Yes. It's a relief to have him," Amina whispered, wiggling into her bedroll. She could hear the crunch of the guard's shoes as he made his circuit around their sleeping quarters. Then she heard a different sound. Their tent had been moved closer to Mustafa's and the other traders' tents for security, which meant they were nearer the beasts of burden.

"Do you hear that, Hanna?" she lay back and listened: The camels were chewing their cuds and groaning softly.

"Yes. It's ghastly. But I suppose we'll get used to it,"

Amina tried to relax. Just as she was about to fall asleep she heard a howl in the distance, and tensed. She heard it again. It sounded like a jackal. Another answered. She put a pillow over her head.

Hanna awoke. "Amina, do you hear them?" she whispered. "I pray they're not wolves. Let's hope the fire keeps them away."

Amina didn't answer.

Once Hanna realized that Amina was asleep, she turned over and closed her eyes again. *At least the camels are quiet now,* she thought sleepily.

*   *   *

The following morning, they left early to cross a broad plain before it heated up. It was the great Hamad, stretching all the way from the Bishari Hills east of Deir-ez-Zor to Jebel. According to Ma'an, they might run into the Feda'an tribe on its yearly migration from its winter quarters in the southern desert—where *wadis* began to dry up in late March—to the northern steppes of Syria where they grazed their camels and sheep flocks in the summer. It would take their own caravan all day to cross the high plain before they descended to a *wadi* that held the promise of water.

The plain was so vast that it was hard to know whether the hills shimmering on the distant horizon were real or just a mirage. The morning was clear, but by noon they felt the wind pick up. The air was hot and dry. The sky turned muddy gray.

The blustery wind increased. Coming out of the northwest, it picked up dust, swirling it into funnels that danced across the grimy plain ahead of them. It whistled around Amina's *haudaj* like an insistent child, pounding against the canvas. It blew sand into ridges that resembled frozen ocean waves.

The caravan was forced to slow down so it was barely moving against the onslaught of a blinding sandstorm. The guides, knowing the risks of becoming lost if they stopped, lowered their heads and pressed on.

The screeching wind whirled upwards, hitting Amina in the face, covering her with a layer of fine dust from the desert floor. It filled her nostrils so she could hardly breathe. She bit down on sand. It got in her eyes. She tried to draw the curtains across the front of the *haudaj*. It did little good. The restless gale lifted pebbles from the ground, hurling them against her camel's legs and flanks.

The angry force smelled of baked earth.

"Ouch!" Amina cried. Small stones nipped at her legs. She drew them into the cab and put her cape on, even though it made her feel hotter, then pulled up the scarf she wore bound around her neck to her eyes to protect her face from the stinging sand. *It feels like the desert has turned into an angry demon,* she muttered, feeling overwhelmed. She thought of Hanna. Where was she? She had lost track of her in the mounting storm.

The camels, she noticed, had closed their eyes and nostrils to slits. They plodded on, one foot after another. Amina felt a kernel of respect growing for them. *Camels are such dependable beasts,* she mused, *especially in the face of a storm like this.*

The wind whipped around the caravan. The atmosphere became heavy as the sky turned bruise-yellow with dust. Yet the guides and camels struggled on, heads bent low to the wind.

The air was so dense that Amina found it hard to see Eman walking ahead of her. She began to worry they might be lost. She recalled Mustafa telling them that the desert had swallowed whole caravans. She prayed: *Hail Mary, full of grace. I call on you in our hour of need to protect us as God protected Abraham and Moses in the desert . . . Please help Hanna, wherever she is. Let no harm come to her.*

The heat in the *haudaj* was oppressive. Her mouth felt gritty. Uncapping her canteen, Amina took a few sips of water and spit it out.

The gale continued to pick up speed. It tore open one of the panniers on a pack animal, scattering luggage. Amina was frightened that her *haudaj* might be ripped off her camel. It was like being in the middle of a swirling dust devil, with no way out.

Sheikh Hassan called a halt. Handlers ran to retrieve the boxes. The caravan slowed, then stopped. The horizon had disappeared: the edge of the plain was obscured by the sandstorm.

Sheikh Hassan ordered the guides and handlers, to pull the camels into a circle, with the Moslawi traders' horses and other mares in the center for protection. Amina could hear Eman yelling above the wind's howl, urging the frightened horses forward. She detected their anxious whinnies as the men led them, blindfolded, to the safe spot in the center. Eman waited, then coaxed Amina's camel into the ring. Amina could do nothing but stay in the middle of the chaos and pray.

At last, Eman came to her. He carefully coaxed the camel to his knees then edged Amina down from the *haudaj*. She hunkered down against the wind while Eman and Salem, who had appeared from nowhere, unfastened the straps of the *haudaj* and lowered it to the ground next to Amina's camel. "Get back inside before you are blown away," Eman ordered.

"Where is Hanna?" Amina screamed to Salem before she scrambled into the *haudaj*.

"She's safe." He pointed to Hanna's white camel in the dusty haze.

"Thank God. Bring her here, when you can, so we can be together." She wrapped a large cloth Eman gave her more tightly over her face to keep out the blowing sand.

Salem had lowered Hanna's camel to the ground and the two men were taking off the *haudaj* when Amina thought about Obaid and Hamid.

"Eman," she called. "If you see the traders from Mosul, ask them if they want to use Hanna's *haudaj*." They must be distressed with their horses hobbled and blindfolded in the center, and no shelter."

Eman nodded and disappeared like a ghost in the brown haze.

The wind whipped around Amina's *haudaj,* trying to find a way in. The shelter shook and swayed, threatening to topple over. Inside, Amina felt helpless, caught in the grasp of some catastrophic demon.

Finally, Hanna appeared. Her face was pinched with fear. She was engulfed in a black muslin cape. She crowded into the *haudaj* with Amina. They cried and hugged one another as if it was their last night together. Trying to shout over the whine of the sandstorm proved daunting.

Through the billowing curtains, Amina thought she saw the Moslawi traders sprint to Hanna's *haudaj*. "They made it," she yelled to Hanna, who shrugged and put a cupped hand to her ear.

Defeated by the effort to talk, Amina got out a backgammon board and a pair of dice. She shut the curtains and anchored them with her satchel and pillows. She leaned against the pillows while she and Hanna began to plot their moves.

The sandstorm raged on. There would be no chance of seeing the Feda'an that day.

CHAPTER 10

In Search of a Wadi

The next morning, the storm had spent itself, leaving a sparkling day. Hanna and Amina mounted their camels after a filling breakfast of warmed mare's milk, bread, goat cheese, and dates. The mare's milk was a treat from one of the traders' horses; she had foaled the previous night, on the tail of the sandstorm. The girls were eager to see the foal, but it would have to wait until they stopped. On they moved across the parched earth.

The caravan reached the far edge of the plain by mid-morning, having lost time in the face of the storm. Sheikh Hassan brought the horses to a standstill. He sent two of his most reliable guides and Ma'an to climb a nearby hill so they could scout the situation at a *wadi* below to identify any tribal groups that might be camped there. Obaid had binoculars and offered to accompany the search party.

Amina and Hanna dismounted to stretch their legs. They had chosen to sleep together in Amina's crowded *haudaj*, which did not help their dispositions. It had been the second night without much sleep. They strode off in different directions in search of places to relieve themselves. Hanna carried her sketchpad and canteen. Amina wandered off with a notebook, eager to make a list of the plants and their uses that she had encountered along the road. At the same time, she was feeling uncomfortably hot and sticky. She knew there was little chance of a wash unless they camped in the wadi that night. She took off her jacket and shook it hard to get rid of the last of the sand. After spreading it over a bush, she found a rock and sat down to make her list. *Let's see. Za'atar, an herb and fodder for camels . . . Zizafun, used for sore throats and coughs, especially when mixed with rose hips. Sage: used for congestion and headaches. Ahyet . . .* She stopped. She's forgotten its uses.

Resting her chin in her hand, she felt herself beginning to nod off. She got up and retrieved her jacket. *I must stay awake.* Walking back toward the track, she examined other plants. One resembled wild alfalfa. She picked a small piece and put it into the sleeve of her jacket to show Obaid when he returned. Another plant with gray-green leaves and small yellow button flowers drew her eye. She didn't recognize it, but took a sample. She wished the scouting party would come back. The heat was becoming unbearable.

When she returned to the meeting place, Eman and Salem approached her with a leather bag full of white, potato-sized roots. Eman held one up. *"Kemeyeh."* He saw her puzzled expression and handed her one.

"What is this? It feels like a mushroom and smells like one."

At that point, Yousif Hamid appeared. "They're truffles," he said. "They grow here in the spring. They have to be dug up, but they're quite tasty when cooked."

"What did you call it, Eman?"

He repeated the name. "It's a staple of the desert tribes."

"I'll have to add that to my list," she grinned, feeling the soft skin of the truffle.

Then she asked, "Do you know what has become of the mare and her foal? Hanna and I would dearly love to see them."

"The trader who owns the mare carried the foal on his horse and the mare followed, whinnying her distress. I will see where they are now. I'll let you know."

A few minutes later, Mustafa arrived. "So, Amina, you wish to see the new foal. She is with her mother, who is tethered near Sheikh Hassan's horse.

"Let me find Hanna." Amina ran off and, after several minutes, found her sketching a group of three camels.

Amina peered over her shoulder. "Why Hanna. I didn't know you had such talent."

Hanna put her arm over her sketchpad. "It's just a small thing. I find it relaxing to draw what I see on the journey. It will help me remember it after I get home."

"What a wonderful idea. I wish I could do as well." She paused as Hanna withdrew her arm from her drawing. "You are gifted, Hanna. Those look very much like our camels."

Hanna smiled modestly. Inwardly, she felt a glow; her efforts to draw were appreciated by her mistress. "What have you been doing?" she asked.

"I've been entering plants in my notebook. But the reason I came to find you is that Mustafa has come and he will show us the new foal. She is with her mother. Maybe you could draw them. Do you want to come?"

Hanna's eyes shone. "Of course." She closed her sketchpad and pocketing her pencil, got up and went with Amina to meet Mustafa.

He was where Amina had left him, talking to Eman. "At last. I was about to give you up," he scolded them. "Come with me."

Mustafa led them to a quiet spot where Sheikh Hassan's horse and the trader's mare were hobbled. The trader greeted them. The gangly foal stood close to her mother, viewing the approaching visitors with apprehension. She was rust brown with huge black eyes and long legs. Everything about her was harmonious, from her fine nose to her slim withers.

"She's so delicate. Truly beautiful," Amina breathed, with a sense of wonder over this new life.

"I've seen foals, but never one so perfect as this," Hanna said, her voice filled with awe. She stepped toward the foal, but the mare neighed, warning her to stop. Hanna backed up, and stood looking at the mother and foal. "She will be a prize one day."

"We must leave her, now, the trader said. "She has had enough excitement,"

"Thank you for letting us see her," Amina said. Then, turning to Mustafa, she added, "I will tell Father about the foal in my next letter."

At that moment, they heard whinnying from a distance, then general commotion as Obaid, Ma'an, and the guides returned from their reconnaissance. They gathered around Sheikh Hassan to give their report. Amina saw Ma'an gesturing with his arms, but she could not decipher what he was saying. It seemed as though everyone was talking at once. Finally, the group broke up and Obaid walked over to Yousif Hamid, who stood with Amina and Hanna.

"It is not as we had hoped. There's a large camp in the *wadi,* perhaps a thousand tents, and many camels and sheep. According to Ma'an, they are not Feda'an. They are Shammar, not a friendly tribe. Ma'an confirmed the tribe with my binoculars. He can tell by the shape of their tents and their lances thrust in the ground. We'll have to avoid the *wadi* and go on. Already, we're risking an attack by a *ghazul.*

"A what?" Amina stammered, alarmed.

"A raiding party, one looking for mares and camels."

Amina paled and looked at Hanna, whose face had suddenly closed tight.

"At times, there can be up to seventy men involved in a *ghazul.* It seems to be the way these desert tribes settle accounts," Obaid said. "One tribe raids another and carries off as many mares, camels, and sheep as they can. Then it's a matter of the offended tribe's *akhram,* its honor, to avenge the *ghazul* by organizing one of their own. It becomes a vicious cycle. In any case, we have to move quickly. We won't stop to camp tonight. It's a matter of urgency."

Amina was crestfallen. Another night in the *haudaj* was not what she and Hanna had envisioned. Moreover, the prospects of a real raid was terrifying.

Sheikh Hassan called for the chief *akam* to round up the other handlers and guides so they could be off the plain and on their way before the Shammar discovered them. A fury of activity ensued as the camels, which had been let out to forage with their packs on, were rounded up and brought back into line. The traders, including Mustafa, mounted their horses and moved to the front. Amina and Hanna followed on their camels.

It was a nerve-jarring descent from the plain, not so much for the terrain, which was a gentle slope, as for the knowledge that, at any time, they could be overtaken by Shammar raiders. Amina withdrew inside her *haudaj,* anxiety gripping her. She poured a little water from her canteen onto a corner of a handkerchief and wiped her hot, dusty face. She took a couple of sips, then nervously put it away. She knew Hanna was equally frightened. There was nothing to do but pray they escaped. She began murmuring a silent prayer for the caravan's protection until the rocking motion of the camel put her to sleep. Dusk was settling over the desert.

"*Khof!* . . . Danger!" Amina woke with a start, hearing the shout as the chief *akam,* mounted on a horse, galloped up the caravan line, yelling to the handlers, warning them of a *ghazul.* He urged the men to outrun the raiders. Amina felt her camel picking up speed and hung onto the front bar. It had turned dark while she slept.

Rifle shots rang in the distance. She clasped her hand to her throat, terrified.

Someone yelled, "The horses, the horses, look to the mares." It was Obaid.

The Moslawi traders raced forward, overtaking the lead camel, and gave the mares their heads, holding back nothing. The horses sped away.

The traders can escape the ghazul with their fast horses, Amina muttered to herself, *but what about my camel? And the others?*

More shouts and gun shots, then *"Le-le-le-le-le-le-le."* She heard men ululating in the distance. Where were they? She felt panic overtake her. She tried to hide in the pillows for fear the raiders might find her.

More shouting and gun shots. She had no idea where they were. She felt vulnerable in the *haudaj,* sure that they must be Shammar—they would know that women were hidden inside. She recalled the knife attack the second night and almost wet herself with fear. She and Hanna had been lucky then. But these were Shammar. They hated the Feda'an, Ma'an's tribe. She felt faint at the thought that she might be seized. And what about Hanna? She must be terrified. Where was Ma'an? In the anxiety of the moment, she'd forgotten about him. He should be protecting them. Where was he?

There was a surge in the caravan as it suddenly picked up speed. Amina's heart was in her throat. The frantic pace continued. She heard the pounding of horses' hooves and could smell the animals' fear as she was knocked about by her camel's frenzied galloping gait. She heard a camel scream. Had it been killed? The gun shots faded away.

Finally, after what seemed like a hideously long time, she felt the animal begin to slow down into a fast walk.

Eman called to reassure her the raiders were gone. They kept moving, but at a slower pace. Amina started crying with relief. She had been so tense that her shoulders and head ached. She began to relax her shoulders and unballed her tight fists. She was safe. They hadn't found her.

She heard the camels grunting as they moved along, but there was no way of knowing if any of the horses or camels had been killed or stolen until the caravan stopped. They had to keep going. She started worrying about Hanna, wondering if she was all right. She knew the caravan wouldn't stop until the leader saw dawn emerging. She'd have to wait.

It was difficult to find sleep; though her body was exhausted, it took a while for her frayed nerves to unwind.

*   *   *

A cold, gray fog clung to the desert. Amina awoke, feeling groggy. She peeked out behind the *haudaj's* curtain, wondering where they were. The caravan moved slowly now.

After what seemed like an interminable span of time, Sheikh Hassan called for a break. The guides and handlers tethered their camels while they went to see how many animals they had lost. Eman appeared and helped Amina off her mount. He told her that Mustafa was on his way to her. After yesterday's sandstorm, the chilly fog made her shiver. She walked around to warm herself. She didn't see Hanna's camel. It made her heart stop. Then she saw Mustafa.

"Have you seen Hanna?" she asked him, with panic rising in her voice.

"Yes. She had quite a scare, but she's fine now. I'll go get her."

"Mother Mary. What happened?"

"I'll let her tell you. She's your servant." He went off to get her.

How could he be so crass? He was being suspiciously secretive, she decided. *Did something happen to Hanna during the ghazul?*

When Hanna arrived, she looked distraught, as if she had been crying. Amina took her hands. They felt icy. Her eyes were red. She looked drained.

"Hanna. What happened?"

"When the *ghazul* came, I didn't know what to do. I heard the yelling and men shouting threats, then the *le-le-le-le.* Two men on horses, whose faces were wrapped except for their eyes, came up to Salem and tried to seize the lead rope of my camel. I heard them ask who was inside the *haudaj.* That terrified me, and I tried to put a blanket over myself to hide. They knocked Salem to the ground— I heard him cry out—then they grabbed the rope. I was petrified, thinking they'd killed him and were going to carry me away with the camel. I was afraid they might pull me out of the *haudaj* and abuse me, then kill me after taking my honor." Her lower lip trembled and she began crying with, breath-catching sobs.

Amina put her arms around her and hugged her tight, waiting for her tears to subside.

"It was Sheikh Hassan's assistant who saved me, the one who helped us get to the ferry," she said when she could speak again. "He saw what the men were doing and wheeled his camel around and attacked them with his lance. I heard fighting and grunts, but the raiders apparently didn't have lances or guns. That's what Salem told me after we stopped. They dropped the rope, and sped away on their horses."

"What a nightmare. How are you feeling, now?"

"Exhausted and a bit weak."

"I'm sorry. What about Salem? Is he safe?"

"Yes. He managed to get up and hide on the other side of the camels."

"That was clever." Amina looked around for Mustafa. When she saw him, she called him over. "What has become of the Moslawi traders? Did they manage to outrun the raiders last night?"

"They must have. They rode ahead, and Ma'an joined them."

"You mean Ma'an is not with us?" Hanna said.

"No. He was worried about his horse. He left because he wanted to save his mare. You've seen her; she's a beautiful black roan and he feared the Shammar might capture her."

Amina and Hanna looked at each other. "Wasn't he supposed to be protecting us as our guard?"

Mustafa started to explain, but he was interrupted by Sheikh Hassan's young assistant, Asma. "The Sheikh wishes to know how you are faring after the raid. He would like you ladies and Mustafa to take tea with him in his tent."

"Good morning, Asma," Amina said, ignoring Mustafa. "Hanna tells me you acted with great bravery last night. We are eternally in your debt."

Asma bowed to her. "It was my duty."

"Have the Moslawi traders returned? I understand they tried to outrun the Shammar."

"No. They went ahead with a guide to scout out a *wadi*. The horses must have water after last night's race. We were blessed to lose only one mare—*Hamdullah*, Praise God—but she was a valuable one, with a foal."

"Not the one who gave birth two nights ago?"

"Yes, that one. The foal was too small to keep up with the others and her mother turned back. The mare was caught with her foal."

"What horrible news! I can't believe they were captured," Amina said, helplessly. *How can such a miracle as the birth of a beautiful foal, be followed by such evil? It is too cruel.*

Hanna was equally upset. "It's not possible. We just saw them yesterday," she cried.

They clung to one another, in tears. The world had turned unexpectedly hostile.

Asma was troubled by their emotion. "A half dozen camels were carried off as well. It wasn't just the mare and her foal."

Hanna and Amina stared at him.

"The mare and her foal were valuable. It's true. But the camels are worth a great deal" he told them. "It's a loss we won't forget."

"I'm sure it must be difficult," Amina recovered, dabbing at her eyes.

"Will you take tea with the Sheikh?" He asked her.

"We should be happy to," she turned to Hanna, "if Ma'an agrees to accompany Mustafa and us."

"Your guard?" Asma looked surprised.

"Yes. He is a Feda'an and knows much about the desert that might be useful to your leader."

"I will convey your message to him." He turned and left.

Amina gave Hanna a conspiratorial look. "Even though Mustafa will be with us, we must have another escort, and Ma'an will do . . . *if* he has returned," she said. "Personally, I don't want to go, but we must not offend Sheikh Hassan."

Hanna agreed. "Who knows where Ma'an is."

Amina looked at Mustafa. "Would you see if Ma'an has returned?"

He nodded, looking sheepish, and disappeared.

After a cursory search, he returned. "I'm afraid your guard had gone with the traders."

Amina nodded and sent word to the sheikh that they were too upset by last night's *ghazul* to take tea. They asked Eman to get them some bread and dates to tide them over.

*   *   *

The sun was overhead by the time the *akam* returned with the Moslawi traders and Ma'an. The men looked spent. They had ridden at top speed for two hours, then, realizing they were far ahead of the caravan, reined in their horses. At Ma'an's urging, they had sought out a Feda'an whom he knew, to gather information about the Feda'an and the tribes that were camped in the wadis toward which the caravan was headed. The man stayed, part of the year, at a neglected Ottoman post where he was a translator for the remaining officer in charge.

"What did he find out?" Amina pressed.

"Ma'an learned that his tribe had reversed its usual migration pattern a month earlier, moving their camels and horses south, deeper into the Hamad, rather than north as they usually do. It was because the Pasha's troops were searching for young Feda'an to join their army. It's not the first time."

"It sounds as if we will not be meeting the Feda'an, after all."

"I'm afraid not. But we did find a *wadi* where Sba'a nomads are camped. They are allies of the Feda'an. Ma'an talked to their leader, who knows Jada'an Fadil. He told Ma'an that he is willing to give Sheikh Hassan permission to camp at the far end of the *wadi*. Of course, Hassan will have to pay some form of tribute—that's expected.

"What kind of tribute?" Amina asked.

"Most likely tobacco and sugar. But embroidered cloaks from Mosul also make handsome gifts. Mustafa may have a few to give away. Now, if we move quickly, we will be there before sunset."

"Hamdullah," Amina said under her breath.

*   *   *

They were on the move once more. Inside her *haudaj,* Hanna struggled to overcome the horror of the *ghazul.* She found her muscles still tight as springs, as if waiting for another attack. *Why had Ma'an left them when they desperately needed him? Was his horse more important than their safety?* The thought angered her. She hated the desert, now, resented its grasp over their lives. With a painful clarity, she recalled the comfort of the inn and her mother's warm kitchen. She gulped back tears thinking of the cozy spot where she used to sit, watching her mother roll out dough while she sang a favorite ditty. Hanna longed to be back there. *I wish Amina's father hadn't chosen me to accompany her. Why couldn't he have chosen another servant? Is it fate that I'm here? Or is it my destiny?* She pondered each, wondering if she would ever have control over her life. Then, feeling confused, she turned her thoughts to Amina: She had comforted her after the raid and listened to her fears when she most needed it. She could trust her. She was more than a mistress. She had become a true friend. Hanna sighed, and settled into her *haudaj's* cushions and fell into an exhausted sleep.

Rocking back and forth in her *haudaj,* Amina's thoughts turned to the future. She could not change the horror of the *ghazul.* What she had feared most in the desert—an attack—had happened. But she and Hanna had survived. We *survived,* she wanted to shout, feeling a sense of elation and wonder. Thank you, God. She made the sign of the cross, and was silent for a moment. Then, the expression of shock on Hanna's face after the attack, surfaced . . . How close she had come to losing her childhood friend. A chill gripped her. This journey was testing them. They depended on one another, now, despite their different ways. She thought about the many little things Hanna had done for her on the trip; making sure she had water, waking her in the morning, helping her with her boots, and just being there—a loyal companion, born of a lifetime together. Hanna meant more to her each day. She had crept into her heart.

Amina looked out to wave to Hanna, but the front curtains of her *haudaj* were closed. Disappointed, she retreated and her thoughts turned to the stolen mare and her foal. *That little foal was so vulnerable, even her mother could not protect her.* She ruminated over the mare's predicament. *Could she have left her foal behind?* The thought saddened her. *I guess I will never know the feeling of having to protect a child,* she acknowledged wistfully.

*   *   *

Traveling west, the landscape softened with a new green veneer. Heavy rains had fallen and the plain they now crossed was verdant with a carpet of emerald grass. Wildflowers had sprung up everywhere: pink flax, flame-red poppies, purple iris, and blankets of white and yellow chamomile in bloom.

Coming over a rise, Amina saw a dish-shaped valley below, a depression where water had collected from a spring in the limestone to form a *wadi* and fill several ponds. She was elated to see such riches after missing water for two days.

Looking more closely, she saw a sea of black tents set up at the far end of the *wadi* near the largest pond. In a cleared area, near the center of the camp, was a much larger tent with five poles holding it up instead of a single post. She could barely make out a collection of lances stuck in the ground in front of its entrance. It must be the Sba'a chief's tent. Farther away was a grassy pasture where hundreds of camels and sheep grazed. The horses—and there were more than fifty of them—were staked in a different spot, closer to the tents.

Ma'an came up on his handsome mare. "Ladies, the Sba'a have offered us their hospitality. This group is small compared with others we know, but the Sba'a are brothers. They are allies of the Feda'an. You will have nothing to fear tonight."

As they entered the *wadi,* a Sba'a welcoming party, made up of a dozen men, their horses decorated with colorful wool ribbons, raced up to honor Sheikh Hassan and his party with a *fantasia,* a mincing, prancing dance their horses performed for the visitors while the riders ululated. The horses, some black as ink, others beige or brown, were handsome animals with fine heads and strong legs.

"How wonderful," Amina exclaimed.

"It must take patience to train the horses to do that," Hanna smiled.

At the end, the caravan guides praised the display with their own ululations.

Ma'an appeared, ready to accompany Sheikh Hassan and Mustafa to the Sba'a leader's tent to pay their respects to the chief and give him gifts that Asma carried.

In the meantime, Amina and Hanna, overjoyed to be off their camels, went to fill their dry canteens. On the way down to the spring, which was partially hidden by rocks and ferns, Amina noticed cyclamen, like colorful stars, clinging to the stones.

Hanna perched on two rocks and motioned to Amina to pass her canteen. The exuberant spring splashed down in front of her. She took a handful of water and sipped it. "It is freezing, but sweet," she grinned, happy to forget last night's troubles.

Amina delighted in the burbling sound the water made as it fell over rocks and into a clear pool. She heard a frog croaking and smelled the wet moss that clung to the stones.

Having filled the canteens, Hanna looked around them to make sure there were no men hovering among the bushes. Amina saw what she was doing. "I think most of them have gone off to visit the Sba'a. We should be safe here."

Hanna helped Amina pull off her boots then took off hers. Raising their long skirts, they removed their stockings and put their feet in the water.

"Ouch. It's icy," Amina yelped, taking her feet out, then trying again.

Hanna stood up in the pool, lifted her skirt, and waded in a little deeper, despite the shocking temperature. The rocks were slippery. Letting go of her skirt, she waved her arms to balance herself and ended up toppling backwards into Amina's lap, splashing them both.

"Watch out, Hanna," Amina snorted. "We'll both end up in the pool."

They sat, piled up on the edge of the water, laughing uproariously. When they had caught their breath, they pulled back their headscarves and washed the grime from their faces, still giggling. Finally, they wiped their feet dry with their skirts. Hanna helped Amina with her boots, then put her own on, feeling a new sense of freedom and joy that made her want to dance.

Amina felt relief and contentment: they had survived the *ghazul* and it had brought Hanna closer to her. They had a reason to celebrate. She was glad they were alone, together.

As they hiked back up the trail, Amina smelled a familiar scent. "Look, Hanna. Spearmint." She picked a piece and sniffed it, then handed it to Hanna who smelled its clean essence with an exaggerated look of rapture, making Amina giggle.

"It's growing all along here. Let's pick some for tea tonight."

A little farther along the path, they recognized another familiar scent— oregano. Amina picked a few sprigs of it.

"I wish we had a sheep to slaughter for dinner," Hanna said. "We could have a rich meal of roasted lamb spiced with mint and oregano."

"Such dreams, Hanna. We'll be lucky to have bread and cheese."

*   *   *

That night, they sat on their own carpet near Mustafa and the Moslawi traders at the campfire. Asma appeared with an invitation they all heartily accepted. The Sba'a leader had sent Sheikh Hassan as a gift a young ram with a bulbous tail. The fatty tail was a particular delicacy among the nomads. The caravan leader lost no time in ordering the animal slaughtered. It was soon roasting over an open pit of hot coals. Amina and Hanna could smell the aroma of sizzling meat as they drank their mint tea. The men enjoyed the greasy tailpieces. Amina and Hanna were given small chunks of meat. Dinner was a banquet that put behind them the desert trials they had endured.

CHAPTER 11

Wolves and Truffles

The next morning was wet with fog in the *wadi*. Preparing to leave, Amina saw three Sba'a women, their hair in braids on either side of their faces, driving donkeys heavily burdened with firewood past their campsite. Looking over toward the Sba'a camp, she saw other women pulling down tents, rolling them up for loading. They, too, were on the move. Watching them work together at each task, she marveled at their cooperative spirit, so different from what she knew at home where servants handled the difficult work. She was glad that she and Hanna were coming to a more equitable companionship. She was learning that each of them had strengths and vulnerabilities.

The caravan left the *wadi* and headed west toward Esserieh and a row of hills that marked the halfway point between the Euphrates and Tudmor. A small tamarisk forest lay at the foot of the knolls, and the caravan stopped to collect wood for campfires. Amina thought she heard a magpie imitating the men's chatter as they fetched wood, and was not surprised when it flew out and landed on a nearby bush. One of the Moslawi traders shot a grouse, which ended up in a pot with truffles for dinner.

The desert here, though clothed in ephemeral spring blossoms, was bleak to the eye most of the year. Nonetheless, its light soil was perfect for truffles. Amina and Hanna saw men digging them out of the cracked earth and loading them into panniers on donkeys. When Sheikh Hassan stopped to purchase some, Amina learned that the nomads sliced and dried them on the tops of their tents. These men planned to sell their truffles in Suhkne.

The caravan traveled on, camping where they found a well, and occasionally pushing through the night. One day, they passed a derelict Ottoman guardhouse that had been burned down. Amina asked Eman about it.

"It was the Feda'an," he told her. "They don't like the Turks; the Ottomans think they own the desert. How can someone own a desert?"

The military posts they saw over the next several days were few and far between.

Camping one night in the shadow of a peach-brown ridge that resembled a man's knuckles, Amina discovered striated rocks that had been thrust up from the desert in another geological millennium. She walked over to examine them when a flash of brown and yellow caught her eye. A small bird, no larger than her hand, landed on a rock, then bounced to the ground at her feet. She was entranced. *How did it get here, in this desolate place?*

After a meal of rice, truffles and dates, Amina and Hanna retired to their tent before the moon rose. Amina bid Ma'an, on his nightly rounds, good-night. Just as she was falling asleep, she heard an ominous howling. Oow . . . oow . . . oow. Then an answer followed. It sounded louder than a jackal. Amina listened again, stupefied. Oow . . . oow.

A horse whinnied.

At that point, Yousif Hamid shouted to a handler, "Make sure our horses are secured close to our tent. I don't want them breaking away."

Amina could hear the mares' restless hooves pawing the ground.

Hanna awoke, startled by the noise. "What were those howls?" she asked.

"I don't know." Amina didn't want to frighten Hanna with anything after her experience during the *ghazul*. "Ma'an is out there," she said, her voice controlled, "and so is Hamid." She could hear Ma'an's restless footsteps and smell his heated intensity. It frightened her into silence.

Outside, Ma'an paced, then hearing the grunts and snarling, he yelled, "Build up the fire. It's a wolf."

More howls echoed, rolling over the empty desert.

Suddenly, the camp came to life.

"Get your rifle," Obaid barked.

"Bring my horse in, too, Hamid, sahib," Ma'an shouted.

"We'll tether him with ours," Obaid called.

"Hanna. Are you awake? You're so quiet." Amina lay frozen with fear. She could hear the agitated mares whinnying and blowing through their nostrils.

"How could I not be? I'm too afraid." Hanna shrunk into her quilt.

They heard more wolves howling around the edge of the camp. They sounded like camels when they growled, but were more fearsome.

Amina could see the light of the campfire as the *akam* threw more wood on it. It sparked and popped as the tamarisk logs caught fire and the flames rose. The fire smelled fragrant, but felt dangerous. No one was asleep.

The wolves continued to lurk around the camp. Amina could hear their whining above the sound of the roaring fire. Her heart pounded.

Suddenly, a zinging shot sliced through the air. Then another.

An anguished yowl followed.

"Did you get it?" Hamid shouted.

"I don't know. It disappeared. I can't see it anymore."

The wolves continued to pace along the edge of the campsite, emiting low grunts. Occasionally, a yelp sounded as the men continued to hunt down the beasts. The horses neighed, their nervous hooves scrapping against the ground outside the tents. Amina knew the men were standing guard to protect them and the camels, though the camel's height gave them an advantage.

As the night wore on, the wolves' cries became dimmer, as if they had moved away.

Amina spoke first. "I hope none of the horses suffered. Thank God, Ma'an is out there." Her teeth were chattering, from fear or cold, she couldn't be sure.

"Yes. It's good that Ma'an was there. This time," Hanna whispered, with an edge of bitterness.

"If the mares had been attacked, we would have heard it," she told Amina.

The horses continued to shift and mutter throughout the vigil.

"We're not going to get much sleep. It's almost morning." Hanna yawnd.

As dawn pushed aside the night, Amina heard the handlers saying their morning prayers. Their voices were reassuring. She fell asleep just as the sun was rising.

*   *   *

Buff-white cliffs rose from the desert in the distance. In their shadow lay the town of Suhkne, nestled against the face of a chalky slope that was part of the Uthahek hills. They spent one night here, in a small inn that belonged to a friend of Mustafa's. It was an uneventful night, except that Amina slept less well than she had expected: she had visitors in her straw mattress—*bed bugs.* She was awake turning and scratching half the night.

In the morning, she discovered that Hanna had been plagued with the same trouble.

*   *   *

The caravan left Suhkne before dawn to travel up a long valley hemmed in by cliffs to the east and lofty hills to the west. The winds had increased during the night. Fortunately for the camels, they were tail winds that failed to slow them down. By midday, the blustery weather had blown itself out. They reached the head of the valley, some eight kilometers away, where a small village hunkered at the bottom of a cliff. A spring nestled in the escarpment flowed downhill where it irrigated the villagers' barley fields. The caravan stopped to collect water from it, then moved on to camp in the desert to avoid thieves in the hills and to get a head start toward the oasis the Arabs called Tudmor.

They camped near a stream that night. "Isn't it lovely to hear the water and know it's close by?" Amina said to Hanna, who was busy setting out their quilts in the tent. She did not bother to answer.

Amina left the tent. She wandered off to hunt for new plants. "It is important not to let Hanna's little slights get the best of me," she told herself.

The sheikh's cook, who had secured two live chickens in Suhkne, slaughtered them and treated the travelers to a sumptuous meal. He invited Ma'an to join in the feast; he was leaving the caravan in Tudmor. Sitting across from Amina and Hanna, with the men, Amina noticed Ma'an's eyes drifting toward Hanna. *Could he be interested in her?* She knew Hanna was still angry with him for abandoning them during the *ghazul.*

Sheikh Hassan banged on a cup, which distracted Amina's musings.

"Before we reach Tudmor," he addressed the men, "I want to recognize someone who joined us late, but whom I've come to trust as a brother. Not only is he a worthy guard, but his skills as a scout have been a great service to me."

Amina glanced at Ma'an, who had lowered his *keffiya*-covered head.

"Ma'an, you leave a hole in our company," the caravan leader said. "But, *inshallah,* we will meet again. Are you sure I can't persuade you come to Damas with us?" He laughed, and hoisted a cup of locally brewed liquor. The Moslawi traders, Mustafa, and the *akam* joined him in the toast and drained their cups, smacking their lips afterwards.

Across from them, Amina and Hanna clapped discreetly and took up their mint tea.

Ma'an acknowledged the tribute with dignity, Amina noticed.

Hanna lowered her head, ignoring him.

*   *   *

It took less than a day to reach Tudmor. The camels and horses strained to get there, as if they smelled home. The Moslawi traders and Ma'an appeared briefly on their eager horses then passed out of sight as they raced toward the oasis town. Amina and Hanna had to be content with the pace of their camels.

They saw the City of Palms with its ancient citadel high on a bluff, just before the persistent sun began to sink behind it. Amina wondered at its beauty here in the midst of such a barren land. A magenta blaze washed across the promontory, softening the outlines of the fortress as they approached it. A hawk, in siloutte, circled lower into the shadow of the cliffs. It floated on air currents with an effortlessness that was spellbinding. Amina watched it glide down, with its brown wings spread, its angular head pointed toward an outcrop. It dove directly toward an unsuspecting rodent, grasping its struggling body in its talons as it flew up over the cliffs and disappeared into the distant haze.

Riding into Tudmor, on their way to the inn where they would spend several days, Amina was struck by the size of the gigantic Roman columns that still lined the stone streets on the outskirts of the town. Ruins of magnificent government buildings, public baths, and market centers constructed in the classical style fronted the main street of the ancient outpost. The Romans designed their public houses to last. They used rock, exploiting the labor of local tribesmen who hauled enormous granite boulders on sledges to the center of the town. Here, skilled craftsmen chiseled the stone into squares that fit snuggly together for walls. Amina had not imagined that such a city could be built. She felt the grandeur of ancient Palmyra and smelled the dust of its ruins as they made their way toward the center that had grown up around the old, historic part of the town.

With the exception of its colossal ruins, the town was an earth-brown collection of Sba'a adobes and Arab flat-roofed houses, several mosques, covered bazaars, and thriving outdoor markets that spanned whole blocks. Tudmor was still the crossroads where caravans from the north met those heading east or west. It was an easygoing town, partly due to its peace-loving inhabitants. At the same time, an overlay of hustle-and-bustle could be felt, stemming from the town's strategic position in the trans-desert trade. The Ottoman Empire had reinforced its position with a military garrison in the center. However, the empire was now spread so thin that the last vestiges of power were evaporating, its posts in the desert largely abandoned. In truth, by 1898, it was in the throes of decay, and the French and British were waiting in the wings to take the Ottoman's place.

The *khan* where Amina, Hanna, and the Moslawi traders were to stay was located adjacent to a date palm orchard, not far from the Temple of Baal. Once Amina and Hanna got to their room on the second floor, Amina ran to open the window. She looked out over the palm groves and the roof of a mosque toward the hills in the distance, just as lanterns began to flicker on like tiny fireflies across the town. Their magic wrapped around her like a silk cloak.

"I can't wait to go out tomorrow," she told Hanna, who had just arrived refreshed, with wet hair, from a bath. "I want to see the Temple of Baal most of all—that's where Queen Zenobia once worshipped," she smiled, remembering the story Mustafa had told them.

"It's quite decent," Hanna told Amina, referring to the bathing room as she rubbed her hair with a towel.

"My turn, then." Hanna had broken the spell.

Except for the occasional barking of wayward dogs, they slept like queens in their new surroundings.

CHAPTER 12

_____

Adventures in the City of Palms

Tudmor was a town like no other. It combined ruins as old as the Temple of Baal, raised three thousand years earlier to honor the god of the Sun and Fertility; roads and monuments built by the early Romans when these invaders conquered it in the fourth century, renaming it Palmyra; and ornate buildings from later Arab and Christian incursions. Most recently, the town had felt the neglect of the Ottoman Empire.

"I don't care if it pours or not," Amina told Hanna. "Hamid and Obaid have offered to be our guides, and Mustafa has agreed to the outing. I'm going. Are you ready, Hanna?"

She had woken early and seen heavy clouds hovering over the town.

"I'm a little tired this morning, Amina."

Amina's mouth formed into a thin line.

"And, there's our laundry to take care of," Hanna added, forgetting that Amina had handled it in Rabha. "Why don't you go with them? You can tell me about it later." The truth was she wanted to have the room to herself, without Amina's chatter.

Amina pouted. Then, after some minutes, she perked up. "All right. I'll see you for lunch."

She joined Hamid and Obaid in the lobby. They looked refreshed and had put on clean *djellaba*. She saw that Hamid had trimmed his beard. They both wore camel-skin slippers.

"Where would you like to go first?" Hamid asked, after Amina had explained that Hanna would not be accompanying them.

"To the Temple of Baal. We can walk to it, can't we?"

"Yes. It's not far."

As they ambled along the dusty road, Amina smelled roasting coffee. It reminded her of Mosul. Small stalls selling camel-leather bags, belts, and slippers lined the street at one end. The odor of the newly tanned leather wrinkled her nose. Bedouins used urine in the tanning process, and the cured leather had a rank smell worse than curdled milk.

Farther along, other shops boasted silver and tin lanterns, curved knives, and long lances; those specializing in the printed word featured the Qu'ran in Arabic and local languages; still others displayed *djellaba* and colorful capes hung on hangers to attract passersby. Taking a peek inside one shop, Amina saw rows of red and black silk slippers. The shopkeeper told her they came from Baghdad.

A skinny brown dog, his ribs showing and his head low, slunk by them as they approached a bakery stall where plate-sized rounds of hot bread sprinkled with cardamom seeds rested on a large tray. At the back of the shop, Amina could see their *taboon,* the oven where the flat bread was baked. A tantalizing aroma wafted out as one of the bakers removed a couple of steaming loaves.

"Do you mind if I stop to get one?" Amina couldn't resist.

"Why don't we stop on the way back?" Hamid suggested. "Unless you want to carry it to the ruins," he smiled playfully.

Amina noted the stall's location so she could return to it later.

As if reading her mind, one of the bakers handed her half a warm loaf and told her to tear off a piece.

She brightened, and ripped off a good-sized hunk. *"Shukran,"* she thanked him. "I'll be back later to buy a whole loaf."

The baker offered the bread to the two Moslawi traders. Obaid took a piece, but Hamid, the more fastidious of the two, declined.

Amina bit into the bread and closed her eyes, savoring the warm taste. She took another bite and put the rest in a handkerchief and stuffed it into a leather bag.

At last, they were climbing the steps to the central square where the spiritual life of the Tudmor had once flourished. They walked across the open court, lined on two sides by colonnades and shops. At the far end was what remained of the Temple of Baal, a work of art in bas-relief with two of its walls still standing and part of its ceiling intact. The temple was wrapped in colors of mustard and soft brick red. Parts of its original marble floors were still visible. Friezes of leaves and flowers around the tops of the walls and on the ceiling demonstrated the Tudmor rulers' love of nature. The temple's columns, some of which had fallen on their sides outside, bore bas-reliefs depicting the daily life of the ancient Tudmor, including a royal parade of camels and people dressed elaborately in many layers of clothing. Amina studied the scenes, feeling a connection with the original inhabitants after her journey across the desert. As they left the temple she learned from Hamid that the Tudmor nobles had buried their dead in family tombs, similar to Muslims.

Once the trio stepped into the central square again, Obaid led her to a huge, oblong granite rock, laid on its side. "This is where the priests of Baal made their sacrifices to the Sun God," he told her.

"What kind of sacrifices?"

"Both human and animal sacrifices, to appease Baal and bring fertility to the crops. The ancients believed that only in this way would they survive from season to season."

"What a dreadful practice!" Amina said. "This is how they lived? Sacrificing their own people?"

Obaid nodded solemnly. "Usually it was the youthful members who were chosen. It was considered an honor."

Amina recalled the nuns at her Dominican school in Mosul, citing the Old Testament warning that people should not make sacrifices to Baal. "Is this what Queen Zenobia was doing? Making sacrifices to Baal?"

Hamid spoke up. "Yes. Those ancient ones enjoyed a rich life. But they knew how fragile it was, especially here in the desert. They honored life in their celebrations and by offering sacrifices to appease Baal, whom they believed controlled their fate."

The trio walked to the eastern side of the square to take advantage of the shade the wall offered as the sun's heat intensified. Shops had been set up between the arches at its base with trinkets for tourists and items of antiquity. However, Amina was too disturbed by what she had just learned of the Tudmors to look at what was being offered. Her earlier fascination with the feisty warrior queen who had defeated the Romans had received a blow. That once courageous woman now seemed rapacious and cruel. Human sacrifice was abhorrent to her.

"I think I've seen enough for one morning," she told the Moslawi traders. "I feel a bit faint from the heat."

At the mention of heat, Obaid whipped out a parasol and opened it. "Try this."

Amina smiled, despite her mood, and thanked him.

As they prepared to walk back to the center of town, they saw young Bedouins leading camels, decorated with wool ribbons and fancy saddles, toward the entrance to the old Roman city. "Camel ride for the lady?" one of them called to Hamid.

Amina protested. "That's the last thing I need."

They walked along the stony Roman street, staying in the shade of the enormous columns until they came to the center of the town again.

Amina spied the bakery stall and stopped. "I would like to stop and buy a round of bread." She wanted to surprise Hanna with it.

"Of course," Hamid said.

She found the bakers had only two loaves left. She bought one. As she turned around, she glanced up the street and saw a young woman and a man walking together through the crowd coming in her direction.

She looked more closely. *Is that Hanna?* She stood for a moment and watched. *It is Hanna! Who is that man she's with?* Amina frowned and quickly backed into the shade of a stall selling lanterns to have a better look without being seen.

"Is something wrong?" Hamid asked.

"No, but I must return to the hotel right away."

CHAPTER 13

Hanna's Dilemma

After Amina had left that morning, Hanna put together the laundry and made sure someone came to fetch it. Then she got out her sketchpad and moved a chair to the window where she began recreating the scene below her. She drew in the tops of the palm trees, people walking on a road between mud walls that surrounded the palm groves on either side, four minarets, like graceful sand sculptures, poking above a sun-baked white mosque. She had been at it for a while when she realized she needed to get outside and stretch her legs. She knew it was unwise to venture out alone, but she felt she should see a bit more of Tudmor than their room. Grabbing her handbag, she felt around the bottom to make sure the small purse in which she carried her money was well buried.

Outside, she paused, unsure which direction to take. The smell of baking bread enticed her. She followed the scent around the corner to a busy bakery stall where she stood for some minutes watching two men toss rounds of dough in the air. Her mouth watered over the warm bread cooling on a large tray.

"Miss Hanna." She heard someone call her name and turned around to see Ma'an, the caravan night guard.

Surprised and still angry with him, Hanna chose to ignore him, unsure what to do.

"Miss Hanna?"

He had seen her. *What can I say to him?* She was so used to Amina taking the lead. "Yes, Ma'an," she said nervously, lowering her eyes to the bread.

"I didn't mean to disturb you. In fact, I came to buy several loaves for my mother. She's not well and is unable to bake these days."

"I'm sorry to hear it." Hanna twisted her handkerchief, looking at him sideways.

"Are you enjoying our town?"

"I haven't seen much of it yet." *I wish he would leave me alone.*

"You are not with your mistress?"

"No, she wanted to visit the Temple of Baal and other antiquities. I'm . . . I'm not so fond of such things."

"What kinds of sights interest you?"

Hanna felt irritated with his question, and remained silent.

He repeated his query, as if she hadn't heard.

"The *bazaar*," she finally said. "I love textiles and would like to see what Tudmor has to offer, especially in cotton and wool." Then, despite herself, she asked, "Do any of the shops sell brocades?"

Ma'an had begun to select bread rounds. "I'm not sure. The only way to find out is to visit the *bazaar*."

As he spoke, Hanna had watched him pick out two loaves, observing that he knew how to judge those that were well baked. She looked at the shape of his square hands as he felt a round—they showed competence. *I wish he had shown the kind of care he takes in choosing bread in guarding us the night of the ghazul,* she thought grumpily.

"If you're willing to have me as a guide," he said," I'll deliver this bread to my mother and then take you to the market." He paid the baker. "My mother's home is two blocks from here."

Hanna was disinclined to join him; it was unacceptable to be with a man without an escort, and she felt loath to encourage him. "I should go back to the hotel," she said.

Ma'an looked at her quizzically. "My brother will accompany us to the market, of course. We cannot go alone. I will deliver the bread to my mother then my brother Jamal and I will come to the hotel to get you."

She felt torn between propriety and her desire to visit the *bazaar*. "In that case, I accept your offer," she told him, primly. "I will meet you in the foyer in half an hour."

Ma'an took out a pocket watch to check the time. "I will see you at ten."

Hanna was impressed that he carried a watch; she had failed to notice it before. "I will be ready." She walked back quickly to the hotel, wondering why she had agreed to his offer. But she *did* want to visit the *bazaar*.

"This is my youngest brother Jamal," Ma'an introduced Hanna to a slim boy of about ten years. He will accompany us."

Hanna walked cautiously beside Ma'an, with Jamal trotting behind them. Ma'an graciously told her that he was taking the easiest route to the *bazaar*. She began to relax, and even enjoyed walking with him. He did most of the talking, while she glanced at his profile, from time to time, noticing his broad forehead and firm aquiline nose, his high cheekbones and deep-set eyes. His beard was well trimmed.

"I was born in this town," he told her. "My father was a horse breeder. He was known for the quality of his stock. He worked magic with mares, and they gave birth to jewels."

His expressive lips turned words in a way that made Hanna listen. Overall, his manner was not as insensitive as she had thought. She smiled to hear his banter as he led her through the Sunday market throngs, toward the part of the bazaar that specialized in textiles.

"*Salaam alaykum,*" he stopped to greet two men dressed in striped *djellaba*. They inquired about his recent travels, then greeted Jamal and asked about his mother. Hanna noticed that they studiously ignored her until Ma'an introduced her. "She has traveled all the way from Mosul, and is en route to Damas," he explained.

The two men, who looked to be Ma'an's age, nodded politely then went on their way.

"Those two men are Feda'an brothers. Our fathers were friends. They raised camels and horses together. But things are changing now."

"What do you mean, 'changing'?"

"More of our youth are turning to sheep rather than camel herding because it brings them better profits. Only in horse breeding do we continue to outdo the other tribes. Our fathers and grandfathers knew the secrets of breeding fast, strong horses and passed them on to us. We've improved on these skills to the point that even the Europeans are buying our fine Arabians. They pay a princely price for a good stud or brood mare."

"I noticed that the horse you rode in the caravan was, indeed, a fine mare. It is no wonder that you wanted to protect her, especially during that Shammar raid." Hanna stepped aside to let a coffee seller pass.

"Yes. She is my greatest treasure. But, in trying to save her that night, I'm afraid I neglected my duties as a guard. For that, there was no excuse." He looked at her gravely.

Hanna knew that he was trying to make amends for his negligence that night. Relieved, she accepted his explanation.

He smiled, sensing that her demeanor toward him was shifting to one more favorable.

"I was raised on a horse . . . from the time I could stand," he continued. A loaded donkey entered the narrow road and Ma'an stepped back, drawing Hanna with him. The smell of dung hung in the air. Jamal, who had stepped to the other side of the street when the donkey came, rejoined them, listening to his brother.

"My father used to hoist me up in front of him when he went riding or to check the herd," Ma'an continued. "He was a brilliant horseman. I vowed to follow his ways and learn the secrets of breeding superior stock. I am succeeding, with careful practice."

"Why did you agree to accompany us as a guard on the caravan, then?" Hanna was puzzled. "Or am I being too presumptuous in asking such a question?"

"Not at all. In truth, I needed a change from my many obligations at home. You see, my father died of tuberculosis some months ago, leaving my mother a widow.

"I am sorry to hear . . . of your father's passing. My own mother is a widow," Hanna said, feeling a sudden rush of empathy for him.

"There has been much for my brothers and me to take care of since his death."

At that point, a man with a tower of fezes balanced on one shoulder pushed through the crowd, separating them.

When they came back together Ma'an took up his story. "I was torn between my duties to my family and my desire to become a horse breeder. Jada'an Fadil, knowing of my dilemma, gave me an opportunity to earn some money and do a job requiring certain skills."

"What kind of skills?"

"He wanted a man who knew the terrain and tribes to protect two young women from Mosul who were part of a caravan crossing the desert." He smiled, teasingly, at her.

Feeling her neck redden, Hanna laughed. "And you were hired," she said.

"Jada'an Fadil knew of me through family ties. To tell the truth, I was eager to take the position, however temporary."

"Didn't it mean leaving behind your wife and children?" Hanna ventured.

Ma'an chuckled. "I have not seen fit to marry, yet. I need to build my horse-breeding venture before I take on such responsibilities."

"That seems wise," Hanna said, feeling a slight palpitation in hearing this news.

"We are at the textile section." He led her to a row of stalls, and stopped in front of one that displayed skeins of wool in a rainbow of colors piled in shelves on one side, and bolts of wool and cotton on the other. The front counters were festooned with bolts of pepper-red and purple silk threaded with silver and gold that came from as far away as India; green, blue and gray gingham from Germany; and hardy wools in earth tones from the mills of Manchester.

"Jamal," he called to his young brother, whose attention was riveted on a table of swords, "Stay with our visitor and assist her in any way you can while I go to meet a man about a halter." He turned to Hanna, "I'll return shortly to see how you're doing." He introduced Hanna to the stall's manager, who was small and wiry with a thin mustache. "You are in good hands."

"*Shukran,* Ma'an."

Hanna was mesmerized by the wealth of materials available in this desert town. It was nearly as impressive as the *suwayqa* in her neighborhood back in Mosul.

"Why don't you come in and take a seat, young lady. Can I bring you a cup of tea or coffee?" He pulled a leather stool out from behind the counter. "What about you, Jamal? Do you care for tea?"

"Yes, sahib."

Hanna sat down and rested her bag in her lap. "Tea would be fine for me, too."

"What sort of materials are you interested in? Perhaps something in silk to match your flawless complexion and lovely eyes?"

Hanna giggled to herself. *These men are the same everywhere.* "I was more inclined toward your cottons. Let's begin with those." She looked toward the rows of cotton bolts on the shelves. "Something in lavender or blue with a small design."

The man began pulling out great bolts unfolding a yard or so in front of her to show the material's weave and design. A skinny, barefoot young girl with dark eyes arrived with two glasses of tea on a tray and handed one to her and the other to Jamal, who was standing beside her.

Hanna took a sip. It smelled and tasted slightly of cloves. She went back to examining the materials spread out in front of her like a fan. None of them was pleasing—either the colors were too bold or the pattern was busy.

The bolts were gathered up as a woman dressed in a long *abaya* brought another pile and handed them to the manager without a word.

"Perhaps one of these."

Hanna smelled tobacco on his umber-stained hands as he unfolded the material. In contrast, the cotton had a new, fresh scent.

As he continued to unfold one bolt after another, she found nothing that interested her. "I was looking for something in a checked pattern, or diamonds."

"Ah, you want gingham." He grinned, and returned to the shelves.

He laid bolts of gingham in several colors in front of her and unfolded only one, a dark blue and white check.

"How much is this one?"

He told her and she gasped, dramatically. "But, surely, that is too much."

"Madam, this comes all the way from Europe. It is of very fine quality."

"I come from Mosul," Hanna countered. "And I know good cotton."

"How much do you think it's worth? Suggest a price."

Hanna countered with less than half the amount he had quoted.

The man shook his head. "That, young lady, is impossible. I could not operate a business with such low prices."

They bargained back and forth for a while. Finally, Hanna was able to get the cloth for a price she thought reasonable. She paid the shopkeeper and handed the bundle to Jamal to carry, proceeding to the next stall along the row.

She had always loved the exchanges that went with bargaining in the market. They pitted each person's wits against the other, yet they were accompanied by certain unwritten rules that each party respected, beginning with the merchant suggesting an outrageous price. The buyer then countered by cutting the amount in half. The seller responded with something in between his price and the counter offer, and so it went until they had reached an agreed upon price.

Talking with a Bedouin woman in another stall, Hanna asked where she might find brocades.

"Keep going—about four stalls along."

Hanna thanked her and hurried to the shop. She had lost track of the time and feared she had missed Ma'an. It was not hard to see the shop; it had a fine display of brocades. Sadly, the prices were much higher than she had anticipated. She dared not feel their quality for fear the shopkeeper, a robust Arab, might read her interest and begin pestering her to buy something. After pausing, she turned around with Jamal and headed back to the first stall where she saw Ma'an talking with the manager.

"I hope I didn't keep you," she said, breathlessly.

"It allowed me to find a new halter, a kind I've been searching for. Would you like to stop for a cup of tea or coffee?"

"What is the time now?"

"Nearly one."

'What? I should have come back sooner. My mistress will probably have returned. I must get back to the inn."

"Perhaps we can have a cup of tea later."

Hanna saw he was serious. "That would be a pleasure," she said, a smile escaping her lips, despite her intention to remain nonchalant.

They began walking back through the throng, when Ma'an asked, "What are your plans when you get to Damascus?"

"I'm not sure. I'll be staying at the inn of a friend of Amina's father while she is in Ma'alula visiting a convent."

"So, she is a Christian."

"Yes."

"And you?"

"I was raised in the Chaldean Church. But I am not so serious as my mistress. She is on her way to take her vows as a nun in France."

"In France? That's a great distance." He led her round a corner to a section of the market devoted to sweets: piles of crystal sugar in pyramids on colorful trays, baklava dripping in honey, and wrapped candies in bowls.

"I could never go that far," Hanna said, enjoying the tempting sweetness of the baklava as they passed. She noticed Jamal eyeing the wrapped sweets and offered to buy him one, but Ma'an discouraged her. "It is unnecessary," he said. "How did you come to know Mistress Rassam?"

"Her father owns an inn in Mosul. My mother is the cook there. My father died when I was only two. My mother was left a young widow. Rassam sahib took us under his wing. Amina and I grew up together."

"Being a widow is not easy. It was generous of Amina's father."

At that point Ma'an led them out of the market to the main road and back toward the inn. "Do you have relatives in Damascus?"

"None. I will stay at the inn for a fortnight then return to Mosul."

They were getting near the bakery when Ma'an noticed some slippers displayed in front of a shop. They hurried across the street to have a look.

"I would like to buy a round of bread for Mistress Rassam. Do you mind if I leave you here? The inn is near."

"If I may meet you and your mistress for tea at the hotel later."

"What hour did you have in mind?"

"When you hear the call for prayers before sunset."

Hanna smiled. "I will see if I can arrange it." She felt breathless.

They tipped their heads toward one another and parted.

CHAPTER 14

Frisson in the Journey

Amina had slipped back into the room just before Hanna. She was pacing the floor when she heard the key turn back and forth in the latch. She stopped.

"Who's there?" Her words had a sharp edge.

"Hanna." She let herself in, looked at Amina's dour expression, and handed her the round of bread she had bought. "Here. I know you like it."

Amina's eyes registered surprise. She hooted, despite her displeasure with Hanna's outing. "I cannot believe it." Pulling out the loaf she had bought, she thrust it into Hanna's hands. "I guess we had the same idea." They both burst into nervous laughter as they eyed one another warily.

"We won't go hungry." Hanna sat on her bed.

Amina came over and plopped down beside her. "Hanna, where have you been this morning? One can become lost here."

Hanna hesitated a moment, debating whether to tell the truth or weave a story.

"I was at the bakery around the corner, but I wanted to look at textiles." She paused. "I met, quite by chance, someone we know and he offered to show me the way to the *bazaar.*" She looked straight ahead, her eyes refusing to meet Amina's.

"Who is this 'someone'?"

"Ma'an, our caravan guard," Hanna told her. Glancing at Amina, and seeing her stern expression, she looked away.

"Hanna, I am surprised. I thought you were angry with him because he abandoned us during the *ghazul.* I don't understand this." She glanced at Hanna's stiff profile, her protruding lip. "We know the man little, other than what we've seen of him on the trip. What if Mustafa or Sheikh Hassan were to see you with him? Surely, you were not alone?" This imbroglio was something she had not anticipated. She felt tense, angry . . . and also scared. She was responsible for Hanna's wellbeing.

"Ma'an's brother was with us and there were always people around us— on the streets, in the *bazaar.* I learned more about him. He is not the man I thought he was earlier. Even Sheikh Hassan has grown to respect his talents." Her voice rose. "It is not as if I am a child!"

"No. Nor am I. But we need to take care—one never knows what webs men weave."

"With due respect, Mistress, I am well aware of such things and know how to act properly around the opposite sex," Hanna said icily.

Amina stopped, stunned by her response. She got up and strode toward the chair at the window and sat down heavily. She looked out across the palm trees to hide the tangled emotions she felt: rage, a sense of betrayal, and nagging fear.

Neither of them spoke.

"Hanna," she turned and saw her rigid expression.

Hanna did not respond.

"We have known each other all our lives. You were barely two years when I was born. You tried to help me up when I fell down the stairs and banged my head when I was barely three. We played together, making up stories. And when I was sent to school, I missed you because you were not there, next to me. I wanted you to go to school, too, but Father would not allow it. And that's why I always read my books to you. We've been like sisters." She stopped, waiting for Hanna to say something. But nothing came.

"On this journey, I've learned things about you I never realized before. You were braver than me when our waterskin was stolen. I will never forget your loyalty. I don't want the little time we have left together marred by . . . misunderstanding." Amina paused, trying to sort out the welter of feelings that had dropped to the pit of her stomach.

"What do you know of Ma'an, other than his bravery as a guard and his talents as a scout to the sheikh? Do you know anything of his family?" Her voice softened.

Hanna's rigid shoulders slowly dropped. She turned to Amina and began to tell her what she had learned about Ma'an's parents, his widowed mother, his father's work, and his own ambition to be a successful horse trader. As Amina listened and nodded her head, Hanna's enthusiasm in telling her about him increased. "He is not at all as I thought, Amina. He is a man of honor and ambition. And, his love of horses explains why he disappeared that night—to protect his mare. He apologized for his negligence to us."

"He does ride well," Amina acknowledged. "I saw how he cared for his horse. Do you remember that night the wolves came? He made sure his mare was safe." She stopped, pondering what she had observed. "Certainly, Sheikh Hassan has high regard for him."

"He's not a regular caravan guard," Hanna explained. "He took the position as a favor to Jada'an Fadil, the trader we met in Rahba."

Amina nodded. She noticed a new brightness in Hanna's voice as she spoke.

"He sounds like an ambitious man, from what you tell me." Amina paused to weigh her next question. "What are his . . . intentions toward you?"

"He certainly has none that I know of." Hanna scowled, looking at Amina, her chin set firmly. "He was only being helpful."

"He's not married?" Perhaps she was going too far, but she wanted to find out.

"No. He has too many family obligations just now," Hanna lowered her head then raised it. "Especially to his widowed mother."

"Do you care for him at all?"

Hanna squirmed uncomfortably. "I've had little time with him, as yet. He asked us to have tea with him later this afternoon. I will accept only if you join us."

Amina scanned Hanna's face. She could see she had gone far enough. "We're going to the Roman ruins this afternoon. If you are willing to come with the traders and me, I will happily join you and Ma'an for tea afterwards."

"He'll be coming to the inn before sunset."

"By then, we should have had enough walking . . . and enough of the ruins," Amina added. "Obaid and Hamid said they would come for me in an hour."

The two young women, carrying parasols to protect them from the midday heat, followed the Moslawi traders up the ancient boulevard on its uneven square stones, noting the shallow channel for rainwater and sewage the Romans had constructed down the middle. The Roman city was built on a grid; every edifice had its purpose but all led back to the main road. Many of the buildings fronting it were gone, but the partially restored columns remained.

Sitting down on the square base of one to rest, Amina marveled at its diameter and height. Erected in sections, one portion fit into the next, going up, with large stone pegs on the base fitting into snug holes in the next section to hold it, vertically, in place. "How did they ever manage to fit one on top of the other without them falling?"

"It took more than twenty men to lift each section to the next without toppling them. They used ropes and crude pulleys," Hamid explained.

Hanna's eyes strained to see the top of a column opposite them. She turned to the others. "I'm glad we live in modern times."

Amina could tell that her attention was not on the Roman ruins.

After two hours of meandering through the ruins, they had had enough, to say nothing of the patient traders; their legs were tired from traversing the uneven stones.

"Thank you for a grand tour," Amina told Hamid and Obaid, "but the heat has left me limp."

They returned to the inn.

Once inside the lobby, Amina glanced at Hanna, wondering if she should broach the question of inviting the Moslawi traders to join them for tea with Ma'an. Seeing that Hanna had already gone ahead to get their room key, she thanked the traders and freed them of their guide duties.

About the time they heard the muezzin's call for prayers, a sharp knock on the door came, startling Amina. "Yes?" She answered.

Hanna went to the door and opened it a crack to see a porter.

"A gentleman is waiting for you in the lobby."

"We'll be down in minutes." Hanna took a brush and ran it through her dark, wavy hair and took extra care to tie her headscarf neatly. She looked at her reflection in a long mirror. Her large, gray eyes sparkled, betraying the flutter she felt inside. She wished she had some kohl; it made her eyes look beautiful. She felt lucky to have clear skin and a trim waist. Smoothing down her full-length skirt, she asked Amina if she was ready.

Amina had been watching her. A pink flush had crept across Hanna's face that enhanced her comeliness. Amina was surprised she had failed to notice how pretty she was before. In truth, she had taken her for granted. A moment of sadness overcame her, observing Hanna. Was it because it reminded her that she would soon be leaving her once they got to Damascus? Or, was it because Hanna glowed with a special beauty that had surfaced with her new interest in Ma'an? *Feelings of infatuation for a man, she reminded herself, do not fit with my plans to become a Daughter of Wisdom.*

"Yes. Let's go meet Ma'an," she told Hanna. "You look lovely."

When they descended the winding stairs and came to the lobby, they saw him seated against a row of cushions. He got up quickly and came to greet them, first Amina, then Hanna. "How was your sight-seeing this afternoon, ladies? I ran into Obaid and Hamid just leaving. They said you were at the Roman ruins."

"We were," Amina said. "I found them overwhelming. To organize so many laborers in building such a city must have taken a mighty act of planning."

"And you, Hanna? Did you enjoy the sights?"

She blushed. "The ruins were quite . . . amazing. They thought of everything, even a way of disposing of their sewage."

Ma'an smiled. "A practical invention. Now, I have in mind a small coffee house—that also serves tea—a few blocks from here. I know the owner. If you're tired of walking, however, we can go to a place nearby."

Amina turned to Hanna to answer. It took her by surprise. She recovered. "I'd like to try the coffee house you suggested. Is that agreeable with you, Amina?"

Amina nodded. "We are in your hands, Ma'an."

He led them down the main road for a block then turned off onto a side street. They crossed several smaller ones and came to the coffee house. It sat on a corner with a handsome façade of shuttered balconies. Going inside, Ma'an hailed the owner and spoke to him quickly. The man led them through to a crowded courtyard filled with raised platforms with carpets and cushions where small groups of locals were gathered to trade news and gossip at the end of the day. He seated them at one overlooking a pond with a small fountain in the center. Amina saw carp swimming around lazily, and detected a slightly briny odor coming from the water. Large almond trees offered shade.

"A delightful setting," Amina said, sinking against a row of large cushions. Hanna collapsed next to her. Ma'an sat across from them.

A servant in a fez appeared. Ma'an ordered two teas and a coffee then turned to Amina.

"I understand you are traveling all the way to France, Mistress Rassam. That is quite a journey. Where will you embark from, once you get to the coast?"

"Beirut. A French steamship goes from Beirut to Marseille."

He was thoughtful. "It will be a very different trip from the one you've taken so far and, hopefully, much shorter. Let's see, from here, it should not take more than a week to ten days to get to Damascus, depending on the weather, then there is the trip over the mountains to the coast."

"I plan to stay in Ma'alula for two days. It's only a half-day's ride by donkey from Damascus, I've heard."

"Yes. That's about right . . . though I have never been there myself. Hanna tells me that you and she will be staying at an inn belonging to a friend of your father's, and that she will remain there while you are in Ma'alula. Do you know where it is located?"

"It is within walking distance of the Umayyad Mosque, I'm told."

"Ah, I know the area well. At one time, in the spot where the mosque compound is located, there was an early Christian monastery."

"How intriguing."

"The mosaic panels on the church walls are quite unique. Do you remember the name of the inn where you and Hanna will stay?"

"Not at the moment."

"I visit Damas quite often. It takes me four or five days to get there. It's much faster on a horse than a camel."

"That is quite a difference—half the time," Hanna spoke up.

"I should be there during the same week you are," he told her, then turned to Amina. "Perhaps I can show Hanna the Umayyad Mosque while you are in Ma'alula, that is, if it is agreeable to you."

Hanna looked quickly at Amina. "We should both love to see it," she said.

"Mustafa will be looking after Hanna while I am in Ma'alula. It would be a pity if she didn't see something of Damascus. Hamid and Obaid will also be there. You and the traders should take her to see the mosque, Ma'an. I will speak to Mustafa about it."

Hanna raised her eyebrows. *Is Amina allowing Ma'an to visit me?* She wondered.

"I would be delighted, and I'm sure the Moslawi traders will be available to accompany us," he smiled, pausing to look at Hanna.

The travelers spent three more days in Tudmor. During their time there, Ma'an managed to join their party on two other occasions. Amina could see the flowering of a friendship between him and Hanna. Hamid noticed it, too.

"I think Ma'an has taken a liking to your maidservant," he said the last day. "He is a decent man and an excellent horseman," the trader grinned.

"He seems honorable and has offered to escort her to see the sights in Damascus while I'm in Ma'alula. I was hoping you might go with them. What do you think, Hamid? I need the opinion of an older person, like you."

"You can trust the man. And, I can arrange to accompany them, take in a few sites."

"He has already suggested you might go with them to the Umayyad Mosque. That would ease my mind."

Amina wondered what Hanna's mother would say. The man was not a Christian. At the same time, he seemed respectful of those who did not share his beliefs in Allah. Her awareness of his good sense and sensibilities had grown over the last few days. She was beginning to see why Hanna was drawn to him. He was a practical man with worthy ambitions.

By the fifth day, the preparations for the final leg of the caravan had been completed. Ma'an came to the camel post to wish them well. His eyes were on Hanna as he promised to show her the sites when he arrived in Damascus. She kept her eyes lowered, but a smile broke as she acknowledged his words with a quick nod.

"This last part of the trip is the easiest," he told them. "It's a well-traveled route, and the Ottomans still control their garrisons between here and Damas."

"Thank you, Ma'an," Amina said, as she waited for Eman to lower her camel. "I look forward to seeing you in Damascus. I will be at the inn with Hanna for the last two days before my onward journey."

"I'll be interested in hearing about your visit to Ma'alula. Know that Hanna's honor is my interest."

Amina and Hanna mounted their camels as Ma'an waited to see them safely ensconced in their *haudaj*. He turned, and climbing on his horse, waved goodbye as their camels were led into the caravan.

*   *   *

After several days' travel, the caravan arrived at Ad Dmier, a thriving town northeast of Damascus. Amina was leaving the caravan, here, to visit Ma'alula. Mustafa had promised Zakariya that he would accompany her to the St. Gerge Convent, where he planned to entrust her to the convent's Superior. She and Hanna had a last night together, making plans about what they would do in Damascus. Then it was time to leave.

Amina hugged Hanna tightly. "Look to our baggage, and, dear girl, take care of yourself."

"I will," Hanna promised, releasing Amina's hand slowly. It would be strange not to have her mistress beside her.

Amina took her satchel and climbed aboard a donkey cart with Mustafa for her trip to Ma'alula. She was feeling a twinge of longing after saying good-bye to Hanna. At the same time, a kernel of nervous excitement had begun to grow about visiting the convent, despite her desire to become a Daughter of Wisdom in France. *What if I like what I see? Will I be persuaded to end my journey in Ma'alula, joining a different order?* The question nagged her as she and Mustafa left the caravan behind.

CHAPTER 15

Ma'alula—Between Two Worlds

Amina shaded her eyes and looked at the honeycomb of light-brown hovels nestled in the yellow escarpment. "I have never seen anything like this," she told Mustafa. "Villagers actually live here?"

The people of Ma'alula were cliff dwellers, and always had been. The village hugged the rock face, a collection of caves and sandstone hollows carved out of the crags. From a distance, the settlement blended into the chalky yellow precipice, impossible to see. It was only as the cart began to wind up the rocky track to the convent that she saw green vegetation in a ravine and the faint outline of the Convent of St. Gerge, which turned out to be a monastery, perched high on the bluffs. As they drew nearer she could pick out the rectangular shapes of pastel houses squeezed among the rubble of great boulders at the bottom of the escarpment.

A village of some 3,000 people, Ma'alula was one of the oldest ones in Syria; the population spoke Aramaic, the mother tongue of Jesus. Secreted in the folds and crevices of the cliffs, Ma'alula became a haven for Christians escaping the Roman Empire and Byzantine imperialists eager to conquer the strategic lands between Europe and Egypt. Early Greeks discovered the village bringing their own brand of Christianity, and stayed to found St. Gerge in the fourth century. Later intrusions by acquisitive Arabs, and then the Ottoman Turks, had little effect on the farmers and sheepherders who had lived there for centuries. Few Arabs settled in Ma'alula; those who did married Christian women and spoke their Aramaic language as well as their own. The Ottoman colonizers tolerated the town's Christians, preferring to concentrate their forces on the growing population of Damascus. By the end of the nineteenth century, fewer than a quarter of the people living in the village were Muslim. Children of both faiths grew up together and, if lucky, enjoyed a public education financed by the Ottoman state. Aramaic continued to be the village's primary language.

As the cart crested the top of the red plateau, Amina saw a panoramic view of the desert and valleys north of Damascus. The cart stopped before the dark wood doors of St. Gerge Monastery. A young priest in a black cassock came out to meet them, welcoming Amina in Aramaic and Mustafa in Arabic. "I am

Brother Elias. Welcome to St. Gerge," he smiled, revealing a gap between his two front teeth. "Father Simon is expecting you."

Amina responded in Syriac. It was closely related to Aramaic. After weeks in a foreign and often hostile desert, the familiar-sounding language moved her to tears. "I feel as if I'm coming home," she told Brother Elias.

He took her satchel, and led them down a few steps to a cloistered court-yard. Light filtered into the space from unseen windows on the second floor. Surrounded by walls of stone, the place had a cold, damp feeling with a smell of enduring mold, as if the desert air outside never quite penetrated it.

Mustafa told Brother Elias that he would not be staying, that he must be in Damascus by nightfall. "I am the agent of Zakariya Rassam of Mosul, who made the arrangements for his daughter to visit the convent. I think you received his letter."

"Yes. Father Simon has informed us of the request. But there is some confusion. St. Gerge is a monastery. There is a convent for women here, St. Tekla."

"Do not worry, though. The Superior has made arrangements for the girl to visit St. Tekla tomorrow," he said, when he saw Mustafa's expression.

"Thank you. I know you will look after Sahib Rassam's daughter. I will come back to get her in two days." He said good-bye to Amina, and took his leave.

After Mustafa had left, Brother Elias turned to Amina. "Before we go upstairs, would you like to visit the church? It's around the corner."

"Yes. I would."

"It was built in the fourth century." He led her into the darkened sanctuary. It was difficult to see at first, but Amina recognized the sharp fragrance of incense. Brother Elias lit a candle he carried and she saw that the space was smaller than she had expected with a dozen rows of wood benches on either side of the aisle. The nave was simple with lanterns hanging by chains from the ceiling. What drew Amina's attention were the paintings along the walls. Breathtaking and unique in their antiquity, they reminded her of the paintings in St. Peter's in Mosul.

Amina kneeled in the aisle. Crossing herself, she gave thanks to the Blessed Virgin for her safe arrival at the convent. She remembered to include her parents and family in the prayer, asking the Virgin to keep them safe. She ended with a plea for Hanna: "Watch over her, and grant her the wisdom to choose a path that is best for her."

When she got up, Brother Elias led her to the paintings. "They are quite rare," he said as he took her from one to another.

Some were exquisite in their detail. The brush strokes were in umber, reds, and blues, embellished by gold trim on the cloak of an apostle in one painting and on the halo surrounding Jesus in another. She preferred the ornate ones of the Virgin because she could see the care the artists had taken in rendering Mary sacred.

"I will come back to these. They are beautiful. But first I need to get settled."

"Let me take you upstairs then, and show you to your room. You can meet Father Simon afterwards."

They climbed stairs in a corner of the courtyard to an open balcony running around the perimeter of the second floor. Amina stopped and put her hand on the handsome, well-worn wood railing that protected them and gazed down on the gray, shadowed court below. It was warmer here and sunlight from high windows gave the residential quarters a cheerfulness missing from the ground floor. Brother Elias took her around to the opposite side of the balcony to a whitewashed room with wood paneling at the bottom and a tall window between two wood-frame beds. A small desk and simple bench completed the furnishings. The room smelled clean and slightly antiseptic.

"This is your room." Brother Elias put her satchel down on the oak bench, and told her where the washroom and toilet were.

Amina thanked him.

He disappeared when Amina half closed the door to her room. She saw a pristine-white towel on one of the beds. Delighted, she grabbed it and went to the washroom to get rid of the dirt after the morning's journey.

Shortly after returning to her room, she heard a knock.

"Father Simon will see you now," Brother Elias led her around to a small office where a lean cleric in an ink-black robe and a starched, white collar sat waiting for them at a low, round table. As he rose from his chair to greet Amina, she noticed that the Superior was slightly balding with a sallow complexion and sharp, penetrating eyes.

"God be with you," he said in a melodious voice. "I am glad you have arrived, at last. The post brought me a letter from Ahmad Mustafa and one from your father, informing me of your visit."

"I'm delighted to be here, Father. The journey across the desert was a long one."

"You are on a worthwhile mission; becoming a member of a religious order is a commitment that lasts a lifetime. You are most welcome at St. Gerge. We are here to serve you."

"Thank you. Being in a religious community for a few days will help me to see my calling more clearly. I feel I am turning a corner in my life, Father. The opportunity for prayer and solitude to reflect on the journey I have begun is welcome at this moment."

"I understand your intention is to join the Daughters of Wisdom in France. It is a worthy order, dedicated to working among the people. Would you like to visit this village to learn how someone like Brother Elias serves the villagers here?

"Nothing would please me more than accompanying Brother Elias on his visits."

"You can go with him this afternoon. You may even find what he does inspiring." His eyes twinkled. "We have made the arrangements for your visit to the Convent of St. Tekla. You will visit it tomorrow morning. It is small, but the nuns are very dedicated. You'll need a guide to find the place. It is hidden high in the cliffs."

Amina raised her eyebrows. She was about to ask Father Simon where it was located, but held her tongue, deciding it was better to wait and see.

After a simple lunch in the dining hall, Amina exchanged her black head-scarf for a silk one with tiny roses. She put on her walking shoes, and joined Brother Elias for the outing to the village.

They did not take the main road. Instead, he led her down a circuitous route to a series of connected tunnels and narrow, twisted passageways that linked various parts of Ma'alula but were invisible from the road. Homes, some consisting of two or three small rooms, were caves or had been carved out of sandstone on either side of a tunnel. A few were graced with wood doors, but most had a curtain across the entrance, giving little privacy or protection from the damp climate.

Curious young children, clothed in worn, mis-matched trousers and sweaters, collected in dark corners to watch Amina pass by. She greeted them in their language and they smiled back shyly, then faded into secret niches or ran ahead of her and Brother Elias to the next stop.

"I must look in on Leila Wehbe, a widow who is ailing with gout. Part of our mission is to look after the sick and lonely. Her home is near. Do you mind if we stop there?"

"Not at all."

They walked along an uneven passageway and turned an abrupt corner where Brother Elias stopped. He called out to let the woman know he'd arrived. Her home was a cave with a small, whitewashed sitting room at the front. When the cleric and Amina entered, they found the debilitated lady dozing on a thin, straw mattress on the floor. There was little furniture in the place other than a cupboard and chair. Brother Elias knelt and spoke to the woman, telling her he had brought a visitor. With some difficulty, she rose groggily and stood on arthritic legs that showed below her long, heavy black skirt. Her weathered feet were bare. She took a brown headscarf and tied it around the black cap that covered her forehead so that none of her hair showed.

As she stood, Amina saw that she was not quite five feet tall. Her wizened face reminded her of a wrinkled apple. She eyed Amina out of deep-set blue eyes as Brother Elias made the introductions.

"She is very old," Brother Elias said. "She's lived through most of this century."

When Amina smiled in admiration, Leila grinned broadly, revealing that most of her teeth were gone. Taking off her headscarf and black cap, she turned her head to reveal a long, thick white braid that fell below her waist.

Amina smiled and said with a sense of wonder, "I hope I live to be so old. You have seen much more than I have. It humbles me."

The woman chortled, then winced and sat down on the pallet to cover her hair and braid again. "Where does she come from?" she asked Brother Elias, looking at Amina.

"Mosul, in Mesopotamia."

The woman's eyes grew wide. "Why is she here?"

"She is on her way to France, to become a nun."

The old lady smiled, looking pleased with her visitor, but said no more.

Amina backed away as Brother Elias again knelt down and talked to her softly, pulling out a small can. He opened it to show her a concoction of local roots and dried pulverized bark. "Tell your granddaughter to boil this with water, then drink it as a tea. It should help quiet your joint pains." He put the container with the powdered mixture on the chair so she could see where it was.

"Thank you, Father," she said in a quaking voice. "Sophia will come this morning. I'll see that she makes it."

"You can let me know if it helps when I come back in two days."

The woman nodded her head and lay back to rest.

Amina followed Brother Elias out and down through another tunnel, stopping at two more cave homes to give comfort and advice. They finally emerged from the tunnel into the afternoon sunlight and began ascending stairs that led toward another hidden passageway. Traversing the cliffs they resurfaced back at the monastery just as the sun was beginning to set in a rosy glow.

"I'm left speechless by your healing work," Amina told Brother Elias as they came into St. Gerge's courtyard. "I feel sad that I can't stay here longer to learn from you. I became interested in medicinal plants and their uses, while we were in the desert. I collected a few samples. I wish I knew more."

"It takes time to learn these things. Maybe you will have an opportunity when you get to France. Right now, though, if you want to visit the church again, you should go immediately, before prayers."

"In that case, I'll see you tomorrow."

* * *

The next morning, a plump young nun with rosy cheeks wearing a black habit and serviceable black oxfords came to St. Gerge, looking for their visitor.

Father Simon took Amina down to the courtyard to meet her. "This is Sister Rebeka from St. Tekla. She will take you to the convent. You can visit with the nuns and the Superior and learn about their work. Its founder, who came from southern Anatolia, is a village saint. Sister Rebeka will tell you her story." He grinned at the little nun.

Sister Rebeka was about Amina's age and height, barely five feet tall. She had an engaging smile with dimples. Her brown eyes shone with good humor. Amina liked her at once.

"I understand you are interested in taking the vows of a nun," she queried Amina as they left St. Gerge and began winding down through the tunnels and narrow streets.

"Yes, that's right. I am on my way to France, to take the vows of the Daughters of Wisdom. Have you heard of them?"

"No. But their name is an interesting one. How did you learn about the order?

"Through two French Monfort brothers who visited Mosul last year. They inspired me to follow the path of consecration. Theirs is a missionary order."

"I see. Let me begin by telling you about our founder, St. Tekla. She was a disciple of St. Paul and adopted his religion. Her parents, however, were pagans who tried to stop her from following her new faith. They, and other villagers, persecuted her so that she was forced to escape from the southern Ottoman region to this area. When she got to Ma'alula, she found her way blocked by a sheer mountain. She knelt down and prayed for help. The boulders parted, revealing a canyon with cliffs as red as bricks on either side. A stream flowed down the center, covering her feet. That was the miracle that brought us St. Tekla who founded of our convent."

"That's an inspiring story. She was a brave girl to leave her home and travel here." Amina stopped to look up at steps leading to a steep ascent. "What work do the nuns of your order engage in?" She followed Sister Rebeka up the steps.

"Work of the soul. We are a contemplative order. We seek consecration through prayer. Some of the nuns teach in the village mission school. But most of us prefer a life of quietude and prayer." Sister Rebeka stopped to catch her breath. "We are almost there." She pointed up to a rock overhang above them. "The convent is hidden in a cleft of the canyon wall..Few people other than the villagers and some Christians outside know that it is even here."

As they hiked up around a bend, Amina saw an open archway over a ledge cut in the mountain face. A gnarled tree's twisted branches protruded out over a rock wall that ran the diameter of the veranda. Diamond-shaped leaves clustered at the ends of branches forming splashes of green against the brown trunk.

Ascending the last of the stone steps to the open courtyard—a long veranda that fronted the convent—Amina saw that the tree she had seen below grew out of a protected spot under the eave of the rock ledge. The archway framing one part of the airy convent was built of rectangular sandstone blocks. The same kind of stones had been used in the front of a building tucked back into the recess of the cliff. The amazing improbability of this secluded spot high up in the rock wall, safe from mauraders, left Amina speechless.

As Sister Rebeka led her across the stone veranda, Amina noticed paintings of the Virgin and various saints on the outside walls of the building. Nearing the opposite side of the long, open ledge, she saw steps leading to an open sanctuary protected by a wrought iron fence. Behind it, she could see relics displayed in the niche of a huge, brown stone that seemed to have been there for years. It appeared to be the altar. She could see several nuns in prayer while others moved about slowly behind the lacey fence. There were no candles, but morning sunlight poured through from a crevice high in the cave wall, giving the space a mystical sheen.

Sister Rebeka rang a small bell and a nun came and unlocked the gate so they could enter. Amina felt herself pulled in several directions as they walked silently across the stone floor. Her eyes rested on the simple rock alter and the gold-painted crucifix that nestled in it. She marveled at the elegance of the sanctuary and, at the same time, its simplicity and openness to the elements. There appeared to be no benches. The nuns worshipped on their knees or standing before the central altar. And when they finished, they had the whole valley to gaze on from their aerie among the cliffs. *What an unusual setting for a convent,* Amina mused.

"This is a place that certainly inspires contemplation . . . and communion with God," she told Sister Rebeka.

"Yes, I feel fortunate to have ended up here. Let me inform the Mother Superior that you have arrived."

Amina nodded and Sister Rebeka glided across the smooth, worn floor and disappeared behind a door at the back of the ledge. Amina wondered how many nuns lived here and how often they visited the village below them. The place seemed so remote, as if St. Tekla's devotees preferred not to mingle with the larger world.

At that moment, Sister Rebeka returned with the Superior following her.

"We are blessed to see you, Amina Rassam," the Mother Superior told her. "We welcome your visit and hope that we can assist you in your spiritual journey." The woman standing before her in a coal-black habit, white coif, and dark veil, spoke with a gentle lilt, but her eyes and posture suggested to Amina that she had great strength. "The decision to join an order is not always easy. It is a life commitment."

"Thank you, Mother Superior. It has been some time since I left my home in Mosul and the road has been difficult. My mind was made up to join an order in France, but learning about your order and seeing your convent now raises certain questions. If you have time, I seek your wisdom in these matters," she gave a sidelong, uneasy glance toward Sister Rebeka.

"Of course, these affairs deserve our loving attention." The Superior turned to Sister Rebeka. "You are excused now. I will take Amina to my office."

The young nun curtsied and disappeared through a recessed doorway.

"The view of the village and valley below is inspiring," Amina said to cover her uneasiness.

"We are blessed with God's beauty around us here." She led Amina to a small room off the front of the cave building. It was whitewashed and spotless with a wood desk, chair, and bookcases filled with liturgical literature, much of it in Aramaic. A hand-carved crucifix hung from the wall behind the desk and a small painting of the Virgin was on another wall. Several chairs were clustered around a table in a corner. The door was open to let in the light from outside. "Come, let's sit here," the Superior said, pulling out a chair from the table.

Amina sat down.

"Would you like a cup of tea or coffee?"

"Thank you. It is not necessary."

"Then, tell me, what brings you here to St. Gerge and our convent?"

"I wanted to see a Christian community in Syria and my father knew about St. Gerge in Ma'alula. My intention is to spend a few days here. I want to make sure that my decision to join an order in France is the right one."

Amina proceeded to tell the Superior about the circumstances of her decision to become a *Fille de la Sagesse,* and the importance of the Virgin in her choice of the order. "There are no convents in Mosul, only monasteries," she finished. "So, going to France seemed the best solution."

The woman listened quietly, asking questions from time to time.

"Now, staying in St. Gerge and visiting St. Tekla, I am troubled. Have I made the right choice? Perhaps taking vows in a place like St. Tekla might better serve God's will."

"What is it that draws you to the Daughters of Wisdom, my child?"

"The order encourages a mystical union with the Virgin Mary, and through her to God and his will on earth. Its members are committed to a vow of poverty and to working among the lame, the infirm, and the destitute. I want to follow that path."

"That is a noble endeavor," the Mother Superior said. "St. Tekla's Convent takes girls from local villages, but others come from as far away as Athens or Beirut. We do not do missionary work. Ours is a contemplative life of prayer and devotion to God. Only a few of the nuns have sought teaching. It is a refuge for young women who want to pursue the spiritual life in a remote, quiet environment." The Superior looked at Amina pointedly.

"I understand," she responded. "When I was traveling through the desert, I began noticing plants, and learned that some have medicinal uses. When I arrived at St. Gerge, I went into the village with Brother Elias and observed him using mixtures of ground herbs and bark to reduce pain, to help people. That was yesterday—I cannot believe it was only yesterday. I would like to learn more about healing. His work impressed me very much."

"Yes, it has great value and may be something you are able to pursue by joining the Daughters of Wisdom. Now tell me, do you think your father might be upset if you were to stay in Syria instead of going on to France?"

"France still seems to be a far-away place. I had no idea the journey would be so long and difficult." Amina paused. "I suppose my father would be unhappy. But he might be relieved."

"What fears do you have about making the rest of this journey?"

"I know I have come only part way. I still have to travel over the Mt. Lebanon mountains, down to Beirut. My father's friend is making the arrangements on my behalf, but I have no idea with whom I will travel. And then there's the boat trip across the Mediterranean to Marseille. I can't even imagine what kind of a journey that will be." She struggled not to break down.

"Will someone from the mother house be meeting you in Marseille?"

"Yes. It it is all arranged." Stunned for a moment, Amina realized that her destiny was set. She could not stop here, however inviting it seemed. She must go on.

"I have been so confused since I left Brother Elias last night. I guess my fears of the journey ahead haven't helped. Until yesterday, I had a companion, a dear servant whom I grew up with, to accompany me. I will see her in Damascus, but from then on, I will truly be alone. At times, it scares me." Amina looked down to hide her tears, embarrassed.

"Look how far you've come already, child. You are more than halfway there. Do not be afraid to seek God's help for the rest of your journey."

Amina looked up hesitantly. "Thank you, Mother Superior," she said, wiping away her tears. " I will follow your advice and pray."

The supervisor sent word to Sister Rebeka, who came to take Amina on a short tour of the convent, then accompanied her back to St. Gerge.

That evening, after vespers, Amina spent an hour in St. Gerge chapel. When she emerged, she felt a new resolve for the next leg of her journey.

CHAPTER 16

Damascus Interlude

"Ma'an has been a faithful guide," Hanna told Amina. "He has taken me every-where. Did you know this is the oldest inhabited city in the world? People have lived here forever."

"I had no idea Damascus was so ancient. It sounds as if you've been enjoying yourself."

Hanna nodded. "How was your stay in Ma'alula? Did you enjoy the convent?"

"St. Gerge is beautiful. It's high on a bluff. But the Convent of St. Tekla is the one that astounded me. It's dug into the cliff face, on a large ledge. The view is magnificent. But the convent is very remote. It's not a place I could remain for long."

"Do they really speak Aramaic? That is what Ma'an told me."

"Yes. I liked the village. I felt as if I were back in Mosul."

"Incredible. But you didn't want to stay?"

"No. My destiny lies in France. I'm hoping to learn something about the uses of herbal medicines at the Convent of St. Laurent, so that I can help people in need."

"That's a noble idea, Amina." She looked at her wistfully. "We have only one more day together before you leave. Damascus is a grand city, much larger than Mosul. You don't have much time, but we could visit the Umayyad Mosque. We can walk to it and, inside, there's a surprise that will delight you. Would you like to see it?" Hanna could hardly contain her enthusiasm.

"Of course. You make it sound mysterious. Let's go, now."

"Bring your slippers; you will need them for the mosque. It is huge and quite beautiful."

They walked through cobblestone streets. They reminded Amina of their neighborhood in Mosul: the smell of coffee brewing; cardamom and clove spices wafting through the throngs of people crowding the streets; a merchant trying to attract buyers to a shipment of fancy chairs from Europe; and, from a fruit stand, the fragrance of fresh strawberries. Cosmopolitan in its ways, Damascus was an invigorating city. It radiated charm, power, and commerce.

Horse-drawn cabs and donkeys plied the busy streets. The city even had a street-car imported from France. It was an exciting place that left Amina breathless after the quietness of Ma'alula.

"We're here," Hanna told Amina, as they faced a formidable white wall, broken by a single entrance. They walked through the alabaster-adorned archway and came into an enormous courtyard, set in white marble. It was filled with people. Buildings surrounded it on all sides. The mosque took up one side and an ancient church and monastery sat at the far end.

"You see, at one time the Christians were here, even before the Muslims," Hanna told her.

"I'd forgotten." Amina looked toward the mosaic-adorned church.

Sitting on a bench, the girls changed into their slippers, then walked across the marble square toward an open pavilion in the middle. It was equipped with spigots and troughs for ablutions around its exterior. Muslim men, dressed in *djellaba,* followed by their wives and children, gathered in front of rows of low faucets to wash before they entered the mosque.

Amina watched with amusement as a small dark-haired child struggled to wash one of her stubby feet under a steady trickle of water while she clung to the spigot for balance, then switched to the other foot. She wore an expression of utter concentration. Amina glanced about for a parent and saw none. It was hard to tell if the child was completing her ablution or merely playing with the water.

"I wonder where her mother is?" she asked Hanna, who was watching the child, too.

Hanna shrugged. "Probably in the mosque."

At that moment, an older girl, wearing loose trousers and a long shirt, ran up to the child. She grabbed her by the hand and dragged her toward the mosque.

Seeing the two disappear, Hanna led Amina to a marble walk in front of the mosque where women, dressed from head to toe in black *abaya,* were walking in twos and threes around the perimeter of the courtyard. They joined them in their perambulations. "The mosque has a crypt inside," Hanna told Amina as they strolled past. "They told me it holds the head of St. John the Baptist. But you really can't see much. The crypt is protected by a fence. Do you want to go inside?"

"I don't think so, if we can't see the saint. Let's continue. I want to see the church."

As she and Hanna approached the end of the courtyard, Amina saw large Turkish carpets spread out on the marble courtyard in front of a beautiful, but modest, church where groups of women had settled with their infants and toddlers to enjoy the morning sun. Children played hide-and-seek around marble columns under the portico of the ancient building. The side of the church was embellished with mosaic panels. They covered the entire wall and depicted the daily life of the early Christians in Damascus, including a deer hunt.

"Those are the most exquisite panels I have ever seen," Amina said.

"This is the surprise." Hanna said. "Aren't these brilliant?"

"Yes," was all Amina could say. She went up to look at one panel, running her hand across the rough surface, and found that tiny squares of colored glass no more than a half inch, some in gold, had transformed the wall into an intricate picture—a lush environment full of flora and fauna. Stepping back to look at the scene again, it stunned her to realize that these ancient lands must have been, at one time, much greener than they were now. It made her wish she had been alive in those ancient times to experience such abundance.

"You're going to get a crick in your neck from gazing up like that," Hanna said.

Amina turned around and smiled, thoughtfully. "Wouldn't it be wonderful to have lived then? Look how beautiful the landscape was."

"Like a Garden of Eden," Hanna mused. "But they had their problems, too. It didn't last forever."

"That's true." Amina suddenly became aware that they were in a courtyard filled, mainly, with Muslims—Arabs and Ottoman Turks. She knew that Christianity had co-existed with Islam for centuries here, with Damascus being home to many churches as well as mosques. But, being a member of a Christian minority in a Muslim compound that had swallowed a Christian church left her feeling uncomfortable. She frowned. "Let's go now," she told Hanna, looking for the exit. "The church is lovely. I've seen enough."

                              *   *   *

When they got back to the inn and were in the privacy of their room, Amina said to Hanna, "It's as if the Christians were stamped out, except for the shell of their church. Why didn't they leave the church and monastery and build the mosque somewhere else?"

"I guess they wanted to push them aside," Hanna said. "It continues to happen. Ma'an told me about an attack on Christians by Muslims in a good neighborhood here. It happened only thirty years ago. Homes were ransacked and destroyed. More than a thousand people were killed," she paused. "And this, despite the Ottoman Pasha's policy of religious tolerance."

"How awful! It doesn't make me want to stay in Damascus for long. Who were the culprits?"

"Sunni artisans and shopkeepers. Apparently, they felt squeezed by a flood of Europeans and Turkish merchants arriving in the city. Many Christians fled, seeking refuge with Maronite Christians farther west."

Amina nodded her head. "Ma'an sounds like a tolerant man," she said.

"He is." Hanna was quiet for a moment.

"Did you enjoy your time with him?"

Hanna blushed. "I did. He knows so much. He was lucky to receive an education. Not every Bedouin does. And he has applied himself."

"That speaks well for him," she said, then turned to something that had been needling her since they returned to the inn.

"Mustafa tells me he made arrangements for you to return to Mosul on Sheikh Hassan's caravan. I'm glad to know that you are well taken care of."

Hanna looked at Amina with a clouded expression, as if she wanted to say something, but wasn't sure how to begin.

"Ma'an has asked me to join him on his return to Tudmor," she blurted out.

"What?" Amina's eyes widened. She scrutinized Hanna's face and saw that she was serious.

"He wants to teach me how to ride a horse so I can accompany him. I know women in Mosul don't ride horses much," she hurried on. "But he convinced me that it is more comfortable and a faster way to travel than by camel. I must admit that I would like to learn how to ride. I think I would enjoy it."

"But Hanna . . . "

"It's the modern way of traveling, even for women. Ma'an told me that European women have been riding horses for centuries and so have Bedouin women, though they don't reveal it to outsiders."

"That may be true, but it's not the point. Your mother expects you to return with Mustafa on Sheikh Hassan's caravan in six weeks. And, it is not wise for you to travel with a man you know little."

Hanna looked down, fumbling with her hankerchief in distress.

"While in Damascus," she raised her head, "Ma'an met a Sba'a family from Tudmor who came here for a wedding. They asked if they could accompany him on the journey back—for security's sake. He agreed to take them. Ma'an promised me that I will be well chaperoned as the party includes both the man's wife and his mother, as well as other family members."

"Ma'an thinks of everything," Amina chuckled. "But what about Sheikh Hassan's caravan?"

"I could join it in Tudmor. We will be getting there a whole week before it arrives from Damascus."

"I see." Amina paused to consider what she'd heard.

"Hanna. I know you have enjoyed your time with Ma'an, but I think Father, and your mother, would not approve of your joining a man whom you have only recently met on a caravan, regardless of the circumstances. I cannot allow it . . . I'm sorry. You must return to Mosul under the protection of Mustafa with Sheikh Hassan's caravan."

Hanna got up and strode across the room to a window that overlooked the city, turning her back on Amina. "If that's your decision, I have no choice but to comply. I will let Ma'an know," she said, without turning around.

Late in the afternoon, Mustafa arrived at the inn with Yousif Hamid. Amina was overjoyed to see them, especially Yousif Hamid. He had become a trusted friend. They went into a coffee shop to talk about her travel arrangements. Amina did not mention her talk with Hanna. She was still upset by it.

"A family of Maronite Christians who are visiting Damascus for a child's baptism are returning to Beirut in two days' time," Mustafa told her. "I talked with their leader about you and your desire to become a nun, and the need for you to get to Beruit so you can travel to Marseille. He was touched to hear your story and has agreed to take you in his party. They will be traveling by donkey. The road over the mountains is tortuous. It will take about six days."

"*Shukran*. It is more than I hoped for. To be traveling with fellow Christians will be a comfort."

"I've made arrangements for your trunks to be delivered to Josef Khoury, the family's leader, for loading. I will be unable to escort you to the meeting place, but Hamid will come for you at dawn on Thursday and will accompany you to Al Umawiyeen Square. That is where you will meet the Khoury party. From there you will travel west to Masnaa, then northwest into Mount Lebanon,* and through the mountains to the coast."

Amina turned to Hamid. "That is most generous of you, Hamid sahib. I hope this won't be an inconvenience."

"Not at all," the man replied. "I'm sure Mustafa would do the same for one of my daughters."

Mustafa nodded. "I would."

"I want to confirm that you have made arrangements for Hanna to return to Mosul with you on Sheikh Hassan's caravan, Mustafa. When will it be leaving?"

"Tomorrow, at midday. The Sheikh has completed his business."

"Will there be any women travelers in your party to keep Hanna company?"

"Yes. A family going to Baghdad will be in our party for most of the journey."

Amina smiled. "That is good news. Now, I must talk to Hanna."

Amina could not wait to tell Hanna about the travel plans. She flew up to their room, but found it empty. *Where could she be?*

She rushed down the three flights of stairs to the reception area and looked around. Walking toward a lounge at the back, she spied a corner where low seats with cushions provided a haven from the bustle of crowds. Ma'an, Obaid, and Hanna were gathered there. Amina rushed up to them, eager to share the news about her onward journey, then hesitated as they looked up and saw her. The two men quickly got to their feet.

"How was your meeting with Mustafa and Hamid?" Obaid asked.

---

*The Ottoman rulers and Europeans referred to what is present-day Lebanon as Mount Lebanon; it was an integral part of Syria in the late nineteenth century.

"Pleasant. I am much relieved to know the travel arrangements."

"Please join us," Ma'an offered her a place next to Hanna, who looked contrite, or so it seemed to Amina.

"What is the news of your trip to Beriut?" Ma'an queried.

"I will leave in two days with a party of Christians who are returning to Beirut after visting relatives here."

"That's splendid," Ma'an grinned. "You will be in good hands, *inshallah.*"

They laughed at his choice of words.

"And Sheikh Hassan's caravan will leave tomorrow."

The men nodded.

During the exchange, Hanna had been silent. Now, she spoke up. "I know you must feel relieved that you've settled the matter of your journey."

"Yes." Amina smiled and turned to Ma'an. "And what of your plans for returning to Tudmor?"

Ma'an glanced quickly at Hanna. "I will be leaving tomorrow," he told her.

Obaid interrupted. "Ma'an and I were just talking about his return trip to Tudmor. It would be faster than going with Sheikh Hassan's caravan and I have completed my business here. I was thinking of joining his party."

Ma'an explained to Amina that he also had a family in his group.

That Obaid might be traveling with Ma'an rather than waiting for Hamid puzzled Amina, but she put it to the back of her mind.

*   *   *

"She's gone," Amina cried. Hanna was not in her bed. Amina looked for her clothes on the chair, and her satchel. They were missing. She had awoken a little after dawn. Now, she felt a mounting constriction in her throat. She raced around the room. *Could someone have kidnapped her without my hearing?* She put the thought out of her mind. *If she left of her own accord, she'd been as silent as a cat.* That thought nagged at Amina: It smelled like betrayal.

She sat down on the bed and put her head in her hands, feeling chilled and anxious. What could have become of her companion? It was not like her to leave without notice. She dressed quickly and went down to the reception desk. An aging Bedouin sat behind it.

"Have you seen the girl who is traveling with me? We stay together in the same room."

"What does she look like?"

"Medium height. Gray eyes. Wearing a headscarf. About my age," Amina shot back.

The old man clutched his chin for a moment.

"A man came to fetch a girl like the one you describe early this morning, before dawn. She had a satchel with her."

"Oh, dear God."

Amina raced up the stairs. Her stomach was in an uproar. *What am I going to do?"*

She didn't know where Mustafa stayed in Damascus. Nor Ma'an. *I will wait until one of the Moslawi traders rises,* she pondered her options. *They will help me.*

When Hamid came down for tea with Obaid, Amina was relieved to see both of them.

"Hanna's disappeared!" She broke into tears. "Obaid, what do you know? I'm glad you did not go with Ma'an, but you must know something."

"I decided to wait until Hamid has seen you safely on your way, tomorrow," Obaid said. "I know nothing about Hanna's whereabouts. I saw that Ma'an and she were becoming friendly. Do you suspect she might have gone with him?"

"She wanted to. I told her she should return to Mosul with Mustafa, as planned. She was very upset at first. But, then, she seemed to accept it. She didn't say anything about it again. Do you know where Ma'an stays in Damascus?

"No. We usually meet him at the inn,' Obaid told her.

"This is scandalous," Hamid said. "We need to inform Mustafa as soon as possible."

There was nothing Amina could do. She felt better knowing that Hamid shared her feelings. If Hanna had left with Ma'an, they would be several hours on the road by now. "Can I count on you two to find Mustafa and inform him of this . . . deplorable situation?"

"We will do our best," Hamid said.

Amina returned to her room, her chin set, and began packing for the trip to Beirut with a vengeance that bordered on the obsessive: it helped to keep her frayed nerves off Hanna. Afterwards, she sat down to write her father.

12th May, 1898, Damascus

Dear Baba,

I have reached Damascus safely. I spent a short time in Ma'alula at the St. Gerge Monastery and visited the St. Tekla Convent. The Convent is very isolated.

It is on a remote ledge in the cliffs. The nuns of St. Tekla are devoted to prayer and contemplation. I feel my own destiny lies in working among the destitute. I accompanied Brother Elias of St. Gerge on his rounds in the village. He administers to the sick. I was impressed with his healing skills. I think this is my path, to learn about medicines so that I can be a healing sister. I will continue to France, Baba.

I have shocking news to report. Hanna has vanished. I fear she may have left Damascus this morning with a small caravan headed for Tudmor that was led by our guard Ma'an, instead of remaining here to join Mustafa on Sheikh Hassan's return caravan to Mosul. I have not seen Mustafa today. When I do, I will alert him to Hanna's disappearance. I will leave the matter in his hands.

I leave for Beirut early tomorrow with a Maronite Christian family. We should arrive there early next week. Mustafa booked space for me on a ship to Marseille.

Please do not trouble Hanna's mother about her disappearance. I'm sure Mustafa will contact you as soon as he knows something about her.

I won't write again until I reach the Mother House in St. Laurent.

Your loving daughter,
Amina

* * *

Amina dressed quickly to meet Hamid the next morning. She felt her lips trembling when she looked around the room and thought of Hanna. *I must look ahead,* she told herself. *It's the only way I can make the journey to Beruit.* She hurried down the stairs to meet Hamid.

They were late. She and Hamid had been waiting for more than an hour for the Khoury family to arrive. It was enough time to reflect on Hanna's decision to leave. Amina felt miserable. It was as if some part of her was missing. She prayed, hoping that Hanna was safe.

An uneasy feeling grew in the pit of her stomach as they waited. She began pacing back and forth at the departure point to keep her mind off her worries. Hamid tried to calm her—the family had been held up, the early-morning roads were congested. It helped little.

Just when she was about to give up, a group of travelers on donkeys arrived, led by a gray-bearded gentleman with a moon-shaped face and eyes the color of cobalt. He wore a black cap that resembled a fez and a striped shirt with full sleeves and trousers. His legs hung down on either side of the donkey he rode. Roughly twenty people accompanied him with several small children riding with their parents. Five donkeys carrying the luggage brought up the rear.

The leader got off his mule as Hamid approached him. They had a halting conversation in Arabic. At last, Hamid called to Amina and introduced her to Josef Khoury, who greeted her in Syriac, much to her surprise. He held the reins of a riderless donkey and gestured for her to get on. She mounted quickly, with Hamid's help. She could tell the man was in a hurry to leave.

Amina waved to Hamid as their party turned west toward the mountains. She felt wretched about Hanna. It was a catastrophe she hadn't foreseen. Yet, she had to move on. She felt both sad and angry. It nagged her like a burr for the whole of her journey across Mt. Lebanon.

CHAPTER 17

Beirut Briefly

"Bonjoir, Mademoiselle Rassam?" A Frenchman, who was somewhat of a dandy, greeted Amina at a crossroads east of Beirut. It was where she was parting company with the Khoury family. They were turning south toward their village. It had taken the group six days, going up over mountains dotted with small villages, running steams, and cedar trees, to reach the outskirts of the bustling city.

Amina hugged the Khoury women good-bye and gave her thanks to their father, as she watched her luggage transferred from a couple of the pack animals to a donkey cart that the Frenchman had brought from Beirut. The man introduced himself as a representative of the French shipping firm that owned the steamship Amina was to board for Marseille.

"I am here to take you to a delightful little inn," he explained, once the Khourys had left. "It is near the Bay of Beirut. Your steamer is scheduled to leave tomorrow."

Amina was surprised to hear she was leaving so soon. At the same time, coming into a new city—one perched on a sea front—took her mind off Hanna. She smelled the brininess of the Mediterranean and felt a cooling breeze on her face before they reached their destination.

A small inn tucked between square, limestone buildings on a bluff overlooking the turquoise Mediterranean beckoned Amina. She was thrilled to see its location. The ship's agent helped her down and then asked her which of her *portmanteau* she wished to take up to her room for the night. The rest of her luggage, he explained, would be taken to the shipping office until the next day when it would be transferred to the ship.

"I will take the satchel and a small bag and leave the larger ones with you." She thanked him and asked if he could arrange for a guide to show her a little of Beirut. "I need to do a bit of walking after being on a donkey all morning."

"We will consult the concierge," he said, leading her up the marble steps to the inn's foyer. "I will arrange it while you're getting settled in your room. *Bientot.*"

Amina followed a porter who carried her bags up a narrow staircase to a series of rooms that faced west, toward the sea. He pushed the door open to one. It felt and smelled stuffy. Putting Amina's bags on a low bench, he went to the French windows overlooking the bay and threw them open to let in the sea breeze. Amina gave him a few coins for his efforts and then scurried to the windows. It was her first time to gaze on any body of water larger than the Euphrates. She felt the gentle wind on her cheeks as the smell of the sea wafted up to her.

The rugged limestone coast below the cliffs dropped quickly to restless, gray-green surf that threw itself against the rocks with such constancy that Amina found it unsettling. A white brackish spume had collected on the surface of the water near the darkened rocks. Looking up the coast she saw that the sea had carved a hole through the base of a yellow bluff that stuck out into the bay. The waves had worn down the limestone to form swirls of rock in some places. The view and the tangy odor of the bay held Amina captive for several minutes until she heard a tapping on her door and a porter beckoned her to come downstairs.

The shipping agent had returned. "Mademoiselle, a guide will meet you here, in the foyer, as soon as you are ready," he said with a flourish. "Monsieur Selem is an excellent guide. He will take you to see the attractions around the inn and then to walk along the promenade. There, you will have a fine view of the bay. Do you wish to take lunch before you go?"

"Merci, Monsieur. No. It will not be necessary. Let me freshen up and I will return promptly."

Monsieur Selem, the guide, turned out to be a middle-aged gentleman who explained right away that he, too, was a Christian. When they left the inn, she discovered that Beirut was a beautiful city full of winding streets and hills. Small Maronite churches, Muslim mosques, and Jewish synagogues crowded up against one another on old coblestone streets. The place had the same assortment of shops and the savory aroma of spices as the Chaldean quarter back in Mosul. It made her wish she had more time in Beirut. All roads, she soon discovered, led back to the Mediterranean coast.

Amina was entranced by the promenade that bordered the rocky shore where the sea breezes brought relief from the steamy climate. As she walked along it with the guide he described the life of the ancient sea-faring people, the Phoenicans. "Their trading ships plied the Mediterranean for many years," he told her.

She thought about the sailboats she had seen when they crossed the Euphrates, and that reminded her of Hanna's misery. She was left with a feeling of regret that she and Hanna had parted so abruptly in Damascus after all their trials of the desert crossing. Had she forced Hanna into Ma'an's arms by her obstinance?

As the guide unfurled a litany of Beirut's blessings, Amina's attention turned to the sea. It was so much larger than she had expected. She watched a ship on the horizon, marveling that she would soon be on one. It excited her. At the same time, it unnerved her to think that she might be out there, far away from land. And, she didn't know how to swim. Her attention returned to Beirut's bay, which was crowded with ships and fishing boats. It gave her a sense of comfort.

A European couple, holding hands, brought her back to the promenade. *I wonder if people do that in France? It's so . . . embarrassing,* she thought. *No one in Mosul would ever be caught doing that!* She noticed that the people strolling the promenade came from many places, according to their dress and appearance: some men wore turbans or *keffiya* with long *djellaba,* other men sported Turkic trousers and fezzes and, still others wore European styles. The few local women on the streets had on black *abaya* or long skirts with head-scarves in a variety of colors.

The city's flowers, bougainvillea and oleanders blooming in profusion along the promenade, cascaded down the hills in shades of magenta, orange, rose-red and bright pink. They amazed Amina with their flamboyance. Outdoor coffee shops and restaurants sprinkled along the way gave passersby a chance to quench their thirst and feed their appetites while enjoying the views of the bay and the sounds of the surf below. Amina and her guide stopped at a café for coffee.

Beirut was a noisy city, alive with the music and arts of many ethnic groups. People from various regions seemed to co-exist here without friction—so different from Damascus. Amina wished she had more than a night here to explore the city's hidden secrets.

While she and Monsieur Selem sat watching the brilliant orb of the sun drop into a gold-plaited sea, a sense of longing gripped Amina. *Not only am I leaving behind this magical city, but the land of my people—my mother who nurtured me and my father who always listened to me, my whole family—and dear Hanna, wherever she is. Will I ever see them again?*

She stood up abruptly. "Please take me back to the inn," she told Monsieur Selem, her voice shaking. The next day she would begin a sea journey that she could not even begin to imagine. It was almost too much to bear.

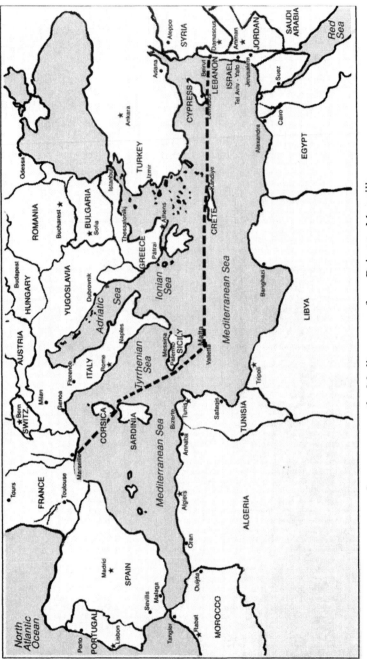

Journey across the Mediterranean from Beirut to Marseille.

CHAPTER 18

A Rough Crossing to Marseille

"Mademoiselle, the ship has arrived and is being loaded. It leaves at 13:30, just after lunch. If you have anything you need to take care of, do it now," the shipping agent told Amina the next morning.

"I have a letter I'd like sent with a courier to Mosul. Can I give it to you?" It was important to Amina that her father heard that she had arrived safely in Beirut and was leaving for Marseille this very day.

"The hotel will see that it is dispatched," he nodded toward the concierge. "I will come back for you in two hours. We must be at the wharf an hour before the *Meridien* sets sail."

"Isn't it a steamship?" Amina asked feeling confused by the agent's last words.

"*Oui.* You'll see." He paused. "Ah, Mademoiselle, 'set sail' is a nautical term. We use it for all ships when they are to depart. I'll be here for you at noon."

When they arrived at the port where the *Meridien* was docked, Amina gazed at the ship, dumbstruck. It was much larger than she anticipated, long and sleek and painted red at the waterline with a blue stripe above it. The upper part was stark white. Its name was emblazoned on the side. She counted three black smoke stacks on top. The tricolor French flag flew fore and aft.

The wharf was alive with stevedores, their bare backs glistening with sweat as they hauled crates and boxes up a narrow ladder to be stored in the ship's hold. A cacophony of languages exploded that sounded like a dockside opera as the men shouted to one another.

Along the quay were street sellers offering last minute treasures from the Orient; sheepskins and silks, knives and daggers, silver coffee urns, and snacks for the journey—oranges and nuts, spicy rice dishes, roasted lamb on wooden skewers, and teas of all kinds. Passengers, their families, and wellwishers gathered at the bottom of a huge wooden gangplank that ran from the dock up to the ship's deck. People crowded toward it.

Amina heard the searing blast of a deep horn from somewhere on the ship as a steward came down the gangway and removed the chain barrier at the bottom, hooking it to a post.

"Time to board," the *Meridien* agent told Amina, taking her smaller bag over one shoulder and offering her his arm. She took it and pressed forward with the rest of the passengers, eager to board. A kernel of nervous excitement was growing in the lower part of her stomach.

Once they reached the lower deck, the agent took out a plan of the ship to locate her cabin. "Let's see," he paused. "You are on this side—we call it the starboard side—toward the front. Come with me."

Amina followed him, dutifully, along a narrow passage with a row of small white doors facing out to sea. Each had a number on it. A guardrail ran the length of the ship on the outside. The agent came to a door near the end of the row and unlocked it with a key. Holding the door open for Amina, he said, "Madamoiselle, your cabin."

Amina entered and dropped her satchel. The room was tiny. A bunk took up half the cabin. She was drawn to the lower bunk and stooped to pick up her satchel. She put it on top of the tightly made bed. As she did so, she noticed a long net slung above it on the wall. The agent handed her the small bag he was carrying, and retreated to the doorway.

"Will anyone be sharing the cabin with me?"

"Not that I know of. It is booked in your name for the duration of the trip," the agent said.

Amina nodded, relieved.

"However, sometimes things change in the course of a journey. Yours is a second-class cabin. It's hard to tell," the man shrugged. "The toilet is forward, just the other side of the end cabin, and the bath is near it. Is there anything you need at the moment?"

"Nothing," Amina said softly, feeling overwhelmed.

"In that case, let me tell you something about the ship's itinerary," he continued. "You will be making a short stop later today in Cyprus. It's an island off the coast. The ship will stop to take on a few passengers and fuel. But, you will not be able to get off. There is unrest between the Greek Cypriots and the Turks there. It's not safe."

"Oh, dear. What is the cause of the problem?"

"The Greeks are trying to break away from the British, who took Cyprus from the Ottomans twenty years ago. Turkish Cypriots, who settled the island when it was under Ottoman rule, want the island partitioned between the Greeks and the Turks to protect their own interests."

"It sounds complicated," Amina interrupted. "I will gladly stay on board."

"That is best. Once the *Meridien* leaves Cyprus," he contined, "it will go on to Crete. It arrives there tomorrow morning. You will have a chance to leave the ship for a few hours' stroll. From there you will sail to Malta off the coast of North Africa. It has an interesting history; it was settled by Jesuit Knights

Hospitalers in the sixteenth century and has seen both French and British occupiers since then."

Amina was about to ask about the Jesuit Knights, but saw from the expression on the agent's face that he wanted to complete the itinerary.

"The ship will turn north from Malta, past the large islands of Sicily and Sardinia, and then head for Marseille. It will take about a week, depending on the weather."

Amina nodded silently. To her, it seemed a jumble of places with exotic names she could not keep straight. She thanked him.

Another sharp blast of the ship's horn sounded somewhere above them. Amina covered her ears.

"That's the warning for visitors to leave before the gangplank is taken away. Here is the key to your cabin. Keep it with you at all times. You might want to go out on deck to see the *Meridien's* departure from Beirut. It is always exciting to watch a steamer depart from the wharf," he smiled.

"I wish you a pleasant journey, Mademoiselle Rassam." He bowed from the waist, as she nodded, then turned and retreated along the passage, leaving Amina to her new, condensed surroundings.

"At least it will be more comfortable than sleeping in a *haudaj*," she said out loud, laughing. She took the key and, locking her cabin, went back to where they had boarded. She made for the ship's crowded rail, squeezing between other passengers just in time to see the massive lines that held the *Meridien* to the wharf being removed.

From the deck, she watched wellwishers below wave to loved ones as the ship slowly moved away from the dock. She wished she had someone there to see her off. Clinging to the rail to keep her balance, the wharf and the figures on it began to recede in the distance until they blended into the arms of Beirut's harbor. Finally, with the liner's steam engines pumping somewhere below, they were on their way out of the bay, heading into a sea that Amina had only read about in books.

Her legs adjusted to the ship's motion as it plowed through gentle swells while she clung to the rail. The day was placid with lazy cumulus clouds treading across a perfect blue sky. Sea gulls followed the steamer for a while then turned away finding nothing to their liking. Farther out, an occasional frigate bird swooped close. At one point, Amina saw a sleek black shape burst from the surface of the water, its stubby nose pointing up as it arched and splashed down again. She watched it dive, its tail fin disappearing last.

"What is that?" she asked a steward who was dressed in a crisp, white uniform. He was about her age. She pointed to a trail of bubbles on the water's surface.

"Probably, a dolphin. There will be more," he said, standing next to her at the rail. "Sometimes we get several following alongside on a clear day like this. I relish the sight of them. They seem so free, as if they haven't a worry in the world." He turned to her, his unusually green eyes full of enjoyment. "Oh, *par-

don moi, Mademoiselle. I didn't introduce myself. Anton Lepage, at your service. I am the steward for this section."

Amina smiled to hear him suddenly remember his official role. "They are extraordinary animals," she said, catching sight of a trio of dolphins surfacing, leaping above the water with abandon then disappearing. "I am Mademoselle Rassam."

"I detect a slight accent in your French, Mademoseille. Where are you from?"

"Mosul, in Mesopotamia," she said hastily, not wanting to get into an explanation of her journey. "Now, I need to return to my cabin."

"Of course, Mademoseille. Coffee and tea will be served in the dining room shortly and dinner is at seven. *Bientot.*"

Amina felt herself redden as she turned back to her cabin. She might have been a little abrupt, but meeting a man alone was still new to her and this one, with his clear, green eyes—something rarely seen in Mesopotamia—was a steward, after all. Yet he was young, and not unattractive. She put the key in the door and, struggling a bit, opened it.

Unbuckling her satchel, she took some of her things out and began putting them into the small hammock on the wall above her bunk. It calmed her and gave her a feeling of being more settled. Knowing that she had a cabin to retreat to on this sea voyage was a comfort. She lay down and closed her eyes, letting the fleeting scenes of her departure from Beirut surface, then retreat, as she dozed.

A series of horn blasts startled her awake. She heard the ship's engines' change and felt the *Meridien* slowing down. They must be coming into the next port.

Amina got up sleepily and put her hand to her forehead. Her headscarf had slipped off. She retrieved it and quickly pulled it back over her head, then went out to find the toilet and washroom. The toilet was nearby. She disappeared into it, then ducked into the washroom just as she heard the steward calling, "Lemassol . . . Lemassol. We are arriving in the port of Lemassol. Onward passengers please remain on board."

Dabbing her eyes with water helped Amina wake up. She looked critically at herself in a mirror inserted above the sink. Her puffy eyes had gray crescents under them. She frowned and tightened her headscarf and secured the ends around her neck. Just then, she felt a sudden jolt that caused her to lose her balance. She picked herself up, and felt yet another bump and grasped the sink to steady herself.

Alarmed, she hastily left the washroom and ran to the rail to see what was happening. The steamship had reversed direction and backed into a berth at the dock. They had arrived in Cyprus. Local Cypriots and a few travelers were milling about on the wharf while stevedores heaved loads of fuel coal aboard the *Meridien.*

Looking around, Amina overheard a passenger say they had arrived in Akrotiri Bay. Lemassol clung to the water's edge, its harbor providing a haven for a cluster of ships, some with sails. Fishing fleets were beginning to return with the day's catch. Behind the town, low hills shimmered in the late afternoon light. Many of them were planted in wine grapes, their robust vines twined in chartreuse braids running across the contours of the land. Terraced ridges were planted in barley and tobacco. Closer to the town, she saw orange groves, their trees' dark leaves protecting the growing fruit from the vicious June sun. In other places, she spied silvery olive trees. A soft cooling breeze blew in from the sea as Amina's attention turned to the activity on the wharf.

Now that the *Meridien* was tied to the dock and felt more secure, she decided to take a stroll around the deck. She wanted to locate the dining room. Going forward, she discovered rows of benches filled with passengers enjoying the late afternoon air, some conversing animatedly in French and others in languages her ear did not recognize. An aging woman in black with two grown men, perhaps her sons, sat together, their heads bobbing as they talked. Several merchants huddled on one bench discussing their affairs. On another, a mother struggled to keep her three small children close to her while her husband wandered off to inspect the ship.

Amina continued her circuit of the steamer, but did not find the dining room. Crossing over to the other side, she saw more fishing boats returning to the bay, their hulls deep in the water with the loads they carried. She watched them for a while, then sought out a steward and asked him where the dining room was.

"It is upstairs, Madam. Would you like me to show you?"

"Yes. If you don't mind."

She followed the man up a steep stairway, making sure she raised her long skirt so it did not become tangled in the metal rungs. When they got to the upper deck, she found it was more spacious than the lower one. This must be where the first-class passengers stay, she decided.

"Come this way. The dining room is behind us," the steward led her to a set of double doors, painted white like all the others on the ship. "This is where you will be dining this evening. The staff is busy with preparations so I cannot take you inside. The doors open at 16:45, a little before seven. Tables are assigned. I will be on duty this evening. Look for me if you have trouble locating your table."

"*Merci, Monsieur,*" Amina thanked him and went over to the rail to see what the bay looked like from this elevated vantage. The sight of the water far below made her queasy. She retreated to the stairway and, descending it, hurried back to her cabin to put on a fresh dress for dinner.

That evening, returning to the dining room, she found herself seated with other second-class passengers. They included an elderly French couple returning from a visit to their son who worked in Beirut, two young Lebanese men from a French shipping company who were on their way to Marseille to learn the business, and a middle-aged woman with her gray hair piled on her head. She had lively, expressive eyes, and turned out to be a teacher. Amina took a seat next to her.

"I am Madam Michaud," the woman introduced herself. She told Amina that she had taught at a mission school in Mt. Lebanon for nearly ten years. But her father had recently fallen gravely ill and she was returning to France to care for him. "I will miss Beirut," she said. "I found it an entertaining city with much to do. But duty calls and I must return home to Lyon to care for poor Papa."

"I would do the same for my Father," Amina said, introducing herself. Thinking of Baba now—his ready smile and deep-set eyes that could see right through her, and even his rough beard—left her with a longing to see him, to feel his arms around her.

"Tell me about yourself, Mademoiselle Rassam. You seem an adventuresome young woman." Amina was about to give her the abridged account of her spiritual quest when a waiter arrived and put steaming bowls of lentil soup in front of them. The diversion was welcome; it took Amina's thoughts off her father, and with a mouth full of soup, it was difficult to say much about her journey. It could wait.

Savory roast lamb and potatoes with green beans followed the soup. Some of the guests took sweets for dessert, but Amina was not one of them. She waited for the rest to finish, then bid them good-night. As she prepared to walk back to her cabin, Madam Michaud stopped her. "Would you like to take coffee out on the deck? Perhaps we will see the moon rise over the bay; it is such a pleasant evening."

"I would, but I'm afraid I might not find my way back to my cabin when it gets dark."

"Where is it located?"

"On the starboard side of the ship, one deck down."

"We must be near one another. My cabin is number 48. What is yours?"

Amina looked at her key. "52."

"We are in the same section. I can accompany you to your cabin after our coffee and go on to my own." Madam Michaud smiled.

"Then I'll join you for coffee," Amina said. "But I prefer tea."

Once they found seats, Madam Michaud called a steward and arranged for their hot drinks.

They fell into silence as they watched the sun sink into the liquid horizon, leaving a wash of bright orange, pink and lavender reflected in the water. Amina sighed, relishing the beauty. It gave her a sense of peace.

The ship's horn sounded. There was a shudder as the *Meridien* began moving away from the dock and into the bay. They passed a lighthouse, whose eyes winked at Amina in the waning light. "What is that for?" She pointed.

"To alert ships to the entrance of the harbor. Soon we will be passing Cape Gata, the last point on Cyprus. Then, while we are sleeping, the *Meridien* will carry us to Crete. The locals call it Kriti. There's not much to see between here and there. Just the sea."

A waiter arrived with their hot drinks as dusk began falling like a cloak over the ship. Amina sipped her tea and listened intently to her new companion as she described how she came to be in Beirut. Her story was not unlike Amina's own. They both had left home, in part to escape marriages that promised to suffocate them.

By the time they finished their coffee, darkness had settled on the ship. Looking up at the sky, Amina saw pinpoints of light emerging here and there. The two women made their way to the stairs and descended to the lower deck. "I think I will stop at the washroom first," Amina told Madam Michaud. "I look forward to seeing you tomorrow. *Bonsoir.*"

"Don't forget to look for the moon," the teacher said. "The sky is clear."

* * *

The following morning Amina went up to breakfast, hoping to see Madam Michaud again. But she was nowhere around. Amina was not eager to talk to the two shipping apprentices, so she finished quickly and returned to the lower deck and the forward rail. In the distance she saw a hint of land coming into view.

"Bonjour, Mademoiselle Rassam."

Madam Michaud had come up behind her. She stood, straining to see ahead.

"I looked for you at breakfast."

"I was lazy this morning," the older woman grinned. "We are nearing *Kriti.* Look." She pointed to a barren island coming into view off the northern tip of Crete. "You see that island?"

"Oui."

"It is a leper colony. A sad place."

Amina had heard of lepers, but never seen one. "Are they confined there?"

"Yes. It is a very contagious, disfiguring disease. Poor things. There are missionaries who live on the island and care for them. They are true saints. It won't be long before we are in *Megalo Kastro,* Big Castle, as the Greeks like to call it. Its official Ottoman name is *Kandiye.* It is the major port in the north, but Hania, on the western side, is also well known."

Amina nodded, as they steamed toward the large island.

"The political situation has left things very much up in the air here. Last year, the Greeks on the island revolted against Ottoman rule. The Sultan called on the Great Powers for help to put it down. Britain persuaded the others that it could offer stability if Crete came under its rule as a British Mandate. The Ottoman Sultan has resisted, but he has little choice."

"Will it be safe for us to get off in Kandiye, then?" Amina said.

"Yes. Things are calmer than they were last year."

As the *Meridien* approached the harbor, Amina saw that it was crowded with ships. There seemed to be a narrow channel for them to get into the actual port.

"Much of the harbor has become filled with silt. The Ottomans have not kept it dredged, as they should have. A French trader in Beirut told me that smaller ships have been diverted to Hania. We are lucky to get in."

Amina watched the *Meridien* follow others in a queue through the channel until they arrived at the wharf. She saw a bustle of activity as they docked and the gangway was swung into place. Large, stone warehouses ran along the wharves. The island looked mountainous and wore a green mantle at this time of year.

"What kinds of things does Crete grow?"

"Many. The people raise sheep and goats. Their meat, skins, and fleece, especially the sheep's, are sold locally and exported abroad. They grow all kinds of fruit—oranges, lemons, guavas, plums, and grapes for wine and for eating. But they export most of their winegrapes to Europe. Grapes are one of France's main imports from Kriti. They also grow olives and produce olive oil."

"That is similar to Mt. Lebanon," Amina interrupted.

"True, but Kriti also is known for its artichokes, tomatoes, squash, and other vegetables. The island has a temperate climate, so the growing season is almost year-round. You'll see people selling red clay pottery today. They make huge jugs and other vessels for wine, water, and for curing olives."

Madam Michaud's account made Amina hungry. "Do you think we'll be able to get something to eat once we're off the boat?"

"Of course. There are usually so many vendors crowding around the passengers as they get off that it is hard to get through. Stick close to me. My favorite food is *dolmades* stuffed with savory rice and peppers. Also, the stuffed zucchini are tasty. The island is blessed with many herbs so the food is well spiced."

"You are tempting me," Amina said, grinning. "Let's go forward so we can be among the first off the ship."

Once they stepped onto the dock, Amina and Madam Michaud were besieged by vendors. One was selling *loofa* for the skin made from dried squash, and sea sponges, others held up knives and daggers with ram's horn handles. Crafters of leather goods and metal bells were among the hawkers. Then, there were the vendors selling mouth-watering kebabs on skewers, dolmades and spicy fried squid and octopus. Amina savored the aromas. *This is enough to tempt even the most tempermental palate,* she mused.

Madam Michaud was adroit in keeping the hawkers at bay, except for an old woman selling dolmades and stuffed zucchini. She had singled her out in the crush of eager vendors. The teacher approached her and bought several dolmades and stuffed zucchini for each of them, and a small helping of calamari for herself. The two women took their treasures up to a clump of rocks away from the wharf and sat down to watch fishing boats navigate the harbor while they ate their lunch. "What we need, now, is some wine," Madame Michaud declared. "I will be right back."

As she disappeared, Amina looked at the array of finger foods her companion had accumulated. The dolmades and zucchini looked tempting, but the fried squid—she could leave that. Seafood with tentacles and eyes didn't appeal to her.

Madam Michaud returned with a bottle of *retsina*. "This is the specialty of the island. You must try some. The man was good enough to uncork the bottle and provide us with two small glasses." She took them out of her bag. They were carefully wrapped in brown paper, along with two hand-painted dishes she had also purchased.

Amina laughed, seeing her pull one thing out after another like a magician.

They found a couple of rocks with flat surfaces and perched on top of them with their feast. Amina served the food while Madam Michaud poured the wine. Seeing that Amina had put no calamari on her plate, the teacher scolded her. "How will you learn about new flavors unless you try a little," she offered some calamari to her.

Amina pursed her lips.

"If you are going to live in France, you will not escape being introduced to a host of gourmet dishes. Leave yourself open to trying them."

Amina nodded and put one miniature, fried squid on her plate, looking at it with skeptical distaste.

Her companion poured a little *retsina* into a glass. "Here. Try this with it."

Amina had never drunk alcohol and she was not sure she wanted to try now. After savoring the dolmades and one zucchini, she took a bite of the squid. It was chewy. She took a quick sip of *retsina*. It tasted bitter and burned a little going down. She grimaced and finished it, then took another bite of calamari, holding her breath.

Madam Michaud started to refill her glass, but Amina put her hand up to ward off the drink. She held the squid between her fingers and gulped it down. She changed her mind about the wine; she needed something to wash away the taste.

They finished their picnic and watched boats arriving with their afternoon catches. Fishermen unloaded bass, perch, octopus, lobster, and shellfish of all kinds. The briny, piscine smells coming from the wharf were new to Amina.

Madam Michaud put the remainder of the *retsina* back in her bag along with the glasses and plates, and they took a walk along the quay. Looking up at the houses clinging to the steep hills, Amina saw geraniums and bougainvillea in shades that reflected the color of the island's red earth and the pinks and purples of its grapes. It reminded her of Beirut.

By the time they got back to the ship, most of the other passengers had already boarded. Amina thanked Madam Michaud. "The lunch was so ample I think I will forego dinner tonight."

The teacher raised her eyebrows. Then, seeing that Amina was serious, she told her to rest well, and climbed the stairs to the upper deck.

Amina continued on to the toilet and washroom then backtracked to her cabin and, letting herself in, collapsed on the bed feeling light headed. She felt the ship lurch as it left the wharf. They were underway. She could hear the turbines as the *Meridien* headed out of the harbor. Malta was their next stop.

She lit the lantern and tried to read, but her head was beginning to spin. So was her stomach. She tried to ignore the queasiness. It was aggrevated by the motion of the ship as it reached open waters. Amina got up and felt worse. She lay down again. The nauseous feeling persisted. She was afraid she might be sick right there if she did not reach the toilet. Hurrying along the deck, she noticed steel gray clouds moving eastward at a rapid clip. A chilly wind hit her. It seemed a storm was bearing down on them.

The ship plowed through curls of white spray as the front coming in from the west churned the sea. The steamer's rolling motion did nothing to settle Amina's stomach. She barely reached the toilet room before she vomited much of her lunch into the toilet bowl. Feeling weak, she did her best to pump the toilet dry. It was a mess. The stench was overpowering. She had to get out, but felt weak on her feet.

Struggling, she made it to the rail and threw up again over the side of the ship, into the wind. Vomit blew back onto her, splattering her face. *"Mon Dieu,"* she cried helplessly. Horrified, she took out a handkerchief and wiped her face, keeping her eyes on the quickly disappearing lights of the harbor rather than looking ahead into the darkness of the sea.

Could it be that squid I ate for lunch? She tried to hold onto the rail and keep her feet planted on the deck. *I must get back to my cabin and lie down. Or I may faint right here.* She clutched the rail in desperation, but felt herself sinking.

A light suddenly shone in her eyes. "Mademoiselle Rassam, are you all right?" It was Anton Lepage, the green-eyed steward she had met the first day.

"No. I'm afraid I ate something that didn't agree with me. I need to get back to my cabin."

"What a pity. Yes, of course." He gagged at the smell then quickly recovered. "Let me help you to your cabin. You shouldn't be on deck in this condition."

Amina had no recourse but to take his arm as he held her up and dragged her slowly back to her cabin.

At the door she stopped. The door was unlocked. She had forgotten to lock it in her haste. "Can you get a pail in case I am sick?" She was embarrassed to ask.

"I'll bring you a bucket. Isn't Madam Michaud an acquaintance of yours? I saw the two of you leaving the ship together today."

"Please. Could you send for her?"

"Yes. And I'll give her the pail. You had best lie down, Mademoiselle. Your palor is not good."

After she closed the door, Amina loosened her skirt, letting it fall to the floor and crawled into bed feeling as though she wanted to die with the cramps that grabbed her now.

A sharp knock and Madam Michaud's voice gave her the strength to answer. "Come in."

Madam Michaud held a lantern. She put it close to Amina's face, then hung it on a hook. "*Mon petite,* you look positively gray. And to tell the truth, you don't smell so sweet, either. Where do you keep your nightclothes? Let me bathe you with the water I've brought in this pail. The steward gave me an empty bucket, too."

Amina motioned to the near end of the hammock above her.

Madam Michaud rummaged around and found a nightdress. She took off Amina's headscarf and, dipping a cloth in the water, washed the girl's wan face. Then she helped her to a sitting position so she could take off her blouse and chemise. The teacher gently washed Amina's neck, chest and back before putting the gown over her head.

Amina could sit up no longer. She fell back, weak and listless, while Madam Michaud gently pulled the nightdress down over the rest of her body.

The woman gave her a small glass of water to rinse her mouth.

"I am putting the bucket next to your bed in case you need to use it," she told Amina, who nodded weakly. "I will check on you after I return from dinner. May I take your key to let myself in?"

"*Oui. Merci,*" Amina stammered.

"Try to sleep."

But Amina did not sleep. She tried to relax her body to the motion of the ship as it battled the storm. She dozed for a few minutes, but then whatever was nagging her innards grabbed her again. Pulling back her hair, she leaned over the side of the bunk and threw up again and again. Her belly ached from the effort. And so did her head.

She thought of Hanna and her nausea on the ferry crossing the Euphrates. She commiserated with her even more now that she was feeling so awful. The memory of Hanna brought tears of agony and remorse. Their paths had diverged with some acrimony. She did not know if she would ever see her again. Amina wiped her eyes on the sheet covering her, feeling miserable. Then the boat rolled again and she was thrown to the side as another wave of nausea engulfed her. She struggled not to be sick, but barely managed to get her head over the side as another stream of vomit missed the bucket, this time.

Spent, she lay back. After a few minutes, she heard a knock and the door opening. "It is me, Jenne Michaud." The teacher shrugged out of her yellow rain slicker and, putting it on a hook, went to Amina. "*Mon Dieu, Mademoiselle.* You are still throwing up? This is not good." She eyed the foul-smelling mess on the floor near the pail and gagged. "Let me call someone to clean up."

Madam Michaud retreated from the cabin and Amina heard her calling a steward. The woman came back inside. "Someone is coming with a mop." She looked at Amina's pale, anguished face and said with determination, "It is time to get a doctor. You will become dehydrated at this rate."

Amina could only guess at what she meant, but was relieved that someone was taking charge.

"The conversation at dinner was all about the growing storm, " the teacher said briskly to take Amina's mind off her condition. "The captain told us it came from the coast of Tunisia and is heading right toward us. We are too far along to turn back. He thinks the *Meridien* can ride it out. But we may be in for some rough seas. He urged us to take extra caution when out on the decks as the rain has made them slippery. We have been advised to stay inside. I guess that won't be a problem for you," she smiled ruefully.

Amina listened to the worrisome news, but felt too weak to respond.

A knock on the door brought a teenage boy who entered with a mop and pail and cleaned up the floor without looking at Amina, who had pulled the sheet over her head and turned away. He took Amina's bucket and returned with a clean one.

After he left, Madam Michaud said matter-of-factly. "I will stay with you for a while in case you need anything. I sent for the doctor. He should be here soon." She sat down on a stool in the corner of the cabin and got out her knitting.

Amina dozed, listening to the soft click of Madam's needles. But she soon woke feeling queasy again. She vomited into the pail and fell back, spent.

Madam Michaud went to her. She put a cool, wet compress on her forehead and, looking at her watch, saw that it was after midnight. Where was the ship's doctor? She took Amina's canteen from her satchel and poured a cup of water for the girl. Taking it to Amina, she put her hand behind her neck and raised her head.

Amina tried to take a couple of sips of water, but it was an effort. Her eyes barely focused. She was exhausted.

The woman poured the rest into the pail and sat down again, dozing when the roll of the ship did not threaten to send her across the cabin.

Amina vomited again, but little came up. It was almost a reflex action.

Madam Michaud changed the compress and smoothed the girl's long hair. She saw weak light coming from under the door and realized it must be morning. The doctor still had not appeared. She looked at her watch. The hands pointed to eight-thirty. She went to the door, hanging on to furniture as the ship rolled.

Outside, the sky was a dark, metallic gray. Rain pelted down on the deck beyond the covered walkway. She looked for a steward. None. She ducked back in and saw that Amina had fallen asleep. She put on her yellow slicker.

The teacher slid out of the cabin, locking it, and moved carefully along the deck to search for the doctor. When she ran into the ship's purser, quite by chance, she told him about Amina's illness. "I sent for the doctor last night and

I still haven't seen him. Can you please find him and see that he goes immediately to Cabin 52? I will meet him there. I know it would be upsetting to the captain to have a death on the *Meridien* that could have been avoided," she challenged him.

"Madam. I will take it as my personal duty to see that the doctor is there before the half hour." The purser turned on his heels and disappeared.

Madam Michaud returned to her vigil in Amina's room.

Fifteen minutes later, an insistant knock on the door aroused Amina. She saw Madam Michaud answer it. A round man with spectacles and a receding hairline, dressed in a white coat, entered. He carried the tools of his profession in a black, slightly worn, leather bag. He approached Amina.

"Mademoiselle," he took her limp wrist to check her pulse, "I understand that you are not feeling well and have lost much of what you ate yesterday."

Amina looked up with a blank expression, her eyes dull. "I have not kept . . . anything down. I feel weak," she struggled to answer him.

The doctor took out a thermometer, shook it, and stuck it under her tongue.

"Perhaps a touch of sea sickness? This storm has not made for a pleasant journey."

Amina could not answer and closed her eyes so she did not have to look at him.

When he removed the thermometer, she told him her aches and nausea had begun before the storm overtook them.

"Umm." The doctor read the thermometer. "You do have a fever.

What did you eat yesterday, before you were sick?

Amina thought for a moment. She told him what she had eaten for lunch, including the squid, but did not mention the *retsina*.

"It could be the squid; it may not agree with you. Or you might have a case of flu with such a fever. We're seeing too much of it these days."

Amina was not sure what he meant. He made her sit up, and placing a cold stethoscope against her chest, he listened in his ear pieces, then moved it to another spot and finally to her back, asking her to breathe deeply. The whole process was humiliating—having a stranger, especially a man, examine her like this.

"I will send a pot of ginger tea down to your room, Mademoiselle. Drink as much of it as you can and keep drinking it over the next three days. It will help settle your stomach. Are you having trouble with your bowels?"

"No." Amina was emphatic. She reclined again, facing the wall rather than endure further embarrassment.

"If the stomach cramps continue, let me know. I will give you something for them."

That was the last she saw of the ship's doctor, but her troubles did not end.

*   *   *

When they got to Valletta, the main port on the island of Malta, Amina was too weak to get out of bed. Madam Michaud made sure that she had ginger tea and brought a few biscuits to tempt her, but Amina had no appetite.

The teacher entertained her with stories of Malta, beginning by telling her that it was actually three islands, including a small one, Comino, between Malta and Gozo, the larger islands. "The Maltese, being islanders, are known for their skills as shipbuilders," she told Amina. "They are excellent craftsmen."

"What about the Knights Hospitalers of St. John?" Amina asked weakly.

"They were a Jesuit Order. They came after the Arabs and the Spanish, in the sixteenth century. The Knights Hospitalers did much for the islands, even setting up a School of Anatomy and Surgery at the Sacred Infirmary, their hospital in Valletta. The order owned many properties, but when Napoleon's army invaded the islands on his way to Egypt, he had the Knights expelled and took their lands. The Maltese people were shocked and angered. They rose in revolt against French occupation. The French were forced to surrender when the British stepped in and took over the islands the next year. Malta became the headquarters of the British Mediterranean fleet. The opening of the Suez Canal solidified Malta's strategic position."

"I had no idea it was so important. I wish I felt well enough to go ashore," Amina said.

"I will be your eyes," Madame Michaud teased. "And I better get ready if I'm to have any time on land. Try to get some rest. I'll stop in when I get back."

"*Merci*, Madam. You have saved me."

"Poo, poo. That's nonsense. You're nowhere near death."

* * *

For the next three days, Amina teetered between feeling slightly better and feeling horrible. She began to be plagued by diarrhea. It only added to her feeling of desperation. She drank more ginger tea in hopes of flushing the demons out, but spent half her time running to the toilet. At times, she felt as though she would die before they reached Marseille.

Two days before they were to leave the ship, she began to improve. Her fever had broken and the cramps and diarrhea subsided. She longed for a bath, but settled for a thorough wash.

Throughout her ordeal, Madame Michaud had been a vigilant friend, retrieving little things Amina wanted, helping her out of bed when she needed it, and bringing her tasty morsels from the dining table to tempt her. Amina had little appetite, except for clear soups. The teacher, by cajoling a waiter into bringing her soups from the kitchen, made sure that Amina got the nutrients she needed.

Amina had missed seeing much on the Mediterranean. But she was on her feet again and moving about by the time they reached Marseille. What she saw from the *Meridien* as they came into the harbor was a bustling port and a gracious city with abroad boulevards. Amina had expected a town.

"Marseille is bigger than I thought it would be," she told Madame Michaud.

When the *Meridien* tied up at the wharf that afternoon, it was teeming with people, many heading toward the ship to greet the arrivals.

Amina kissed Madame Michaud on both cheeks. "You have been my guardian angel. I might not have survived the trip without your care. I hope we will meet again some day."

"Enjoy your time at the convent in St. Laurent, Amina. I will pray for you," she hugged Amina. "And now we must say, *adieu*. I have a train to catch." The woman released her and hurried toward the gangway.

Amina scanned the faces on the wharf below, hoping that one of them belonged to Mother Marie Patrice, the Superior of the Convent of St.-Laurent-sur-Sevre where she was to spend the next year, taking her vows as a *Fille de la Sagesse*. Beyond that, Amina had no idea where her journey would take her.

PART II

Sister Marie Reine de Jesus

CHAPTER 19

My Rebirth as a Daughter of Wisdom

Journal, 25th October 1904, The Mother House

Finding time to write in this journal that Mother Patrice awarded me after my final vows has not been easy. We were called back to the Mother House from our various institutions—mine being the Institute for Deaf-Mute Girls and the hospital in Toulouse where I worked as a pharmacologist—two weeks ago to prepare for missionary work in Africa. Our days have been filled with learning new skills; the importance of boiling water daily, the use of mosquito nets, and the care of wounds. Our evenings are devoted to prayer and contemplation. We leave St. Laurent for Marseille in two days. I made a promise to myself to put down my memories of becoming a Daughter of Wisdom before we embark on our new journey. Mother Patrice, the Superior of our order helped me through the transition with love and patience.

When I first arrived in Marseille, I recall feeling overwhelmed as the ship tied up to the dock. Marseille was much bigger than I had expected. I felt out of place and frightened. Then I saw Mother Marie Patrice in the crowd on the dock, standing erect in an ash-gray habit. She was tall and proud in a square white headdress and veil. She gazed up, as if trying to spot me. I waved, but was lost in the crowd at the railing. I looked at her closely. She seemed to wear a mantle of tranquility despite the confusion on the wharf. Her stillness, her self-possession strengthened me after my ordeal on the *Meridien.*

When I left the ship, I went straight to her. She welcomed me with open arms. She asked about my journey then told me we were meeting another girl at the train station who also was entering the convent.

'From there,' I recall her telling me, 'we will take a train to St.-Laurent-sur-Sevre. That is where our Mother House is located.'

The news that we would be traveling by train excited me. I'd never been on one. Mother Patrice explained that the town of St. Laurent was in the Loire valley, northwest of Marseille. It would take more than a day to get there.

We met Suzette, who was waiting for us with an older brother, at the station. She was dressed in a green frock and wore a small hat. She looked hesitant, though it seemed she was trying to put on a brave face. The three of us boarded the train and found our seats. Once I got used to the gentle rocking of the train, I fell to sleeping. I was still weak. A fog of fatigue and disorientation had overtaken me. What I remember most about that train trip was feeling relieved to be traveling under the protection of Mother Patrice and having another girl my age there, though she was as shy as I was. I found it was not easy to converse with them in French. I tried hard to follow their conversations, but the language sounded different from the French I'd learned in Mosul. The effort tired me.

Looking back, that trip has faded in my mind. In contrast, my memories of the transfomation I underwent when we got to the *Filles de la Sagesse* Mother House are still vivid, even though much has happened since then. To think that we are in a new millennium—the twentieth century—makes me realize how much I have changed. I am a new person.

It seems an eon ago that I shed my worldly garb, including my clothes and much of my hair (which was cut short) when I entered the Mother House. I donned the plain white shift of a *Filles de la Sagesse* postulate, the first stage of taking our vows. I remained at the Mother House for a year, until I took my first Profession of Obedience to work among the poor and physically afflicted. That first year, I have to admit, was not easy. Initially, there were the changes of dress and diet to get used to, and I found the Rules of our Order a challenge, especially the Rule of Silence. We were taught to open drawers, windows and doors without any noise, and to maintain silence both within our cells and in the corridors. I missed the sounds of voices talking and the laughter that I took for granted in the inn and on the streets of Mosul. I missed my family and Hanna, although Baba wrote that she had gone with Ma'an to Tudmor and that the two of them had continued on to Mosul to meet Hanna's mother and him. Baba revealed that he liked Ma'an, despite his initial misgivings; he seemed honest and hardworking. When Ma'an finally got up the courage to ask for Hanna's hand in marriage, Baba and her mother, after a month's time, gave their approval. Hanna and Ma'an were married soon thereafter. I was miserable knowing that I was to miss Hanna's wedding. I also felt unbearably alone, especially when a letter arrived from Baba, full of news of the family and home.

Here, at the Mother House, I was forced to wash my face and hands in a basin of ice-cold water as winter arrived. It left me perennially chilled. This place is much colder than Mosul. The dull-gray, musty stone of the convent seems to resist the warmth of fires in mid-winter. I constantly shivered during my ablutions that first year.

With persistence, I learned to keep petty complaints to myself. At times, suffering seemed to be the price of sanctity in our religious community. But all that is behind me. Joys and sorrows now remain unspoken, tucked away in my heart, including the knowledge that I will never see my dear little sister again. A letter from Baba, last year, brought the heartbreaking news that Leila's life was taken in an epidemic of measles. It is hard to believe she is gone, my only sister. It grieves me that she was taken so young. Leila resides among the Angels now. I have come to accept what God has shown me.

After six months in the convent, I donned the pale shift and starched white veil of a novice. Each stage of my spiritual training led to the next and prepared me for taking the final vow of Perpetual Profession and my commitment to work with the maimed, blind and deaf. I now wear the gray habit of the *Filles de la Sagesse*. It has full, wide sleeves and a plain bodice (flat as a shield) that covers my bound chest and is buttoned at the upper corners to a white blouse underneath. The long-sleeved blouse is simple with a pointed collar. The crucifix around my neck hangs down and nestles in the bodice, reminding me of my vows. The veil and *bandeau* we wear are quite different from those of other Orders I have seen here in France. The *bandeau* is white and heavily starched. We tie it across our foreheads and around the back to form a high bridge that looks like an arch or the lower part of an "H." It stands above our heads to form a square, cloth *coiffe*. The veil, equally pristine and bleached, reminds me of a long headscarf and drops from each corner of the *coiffe* to shield the sides of our faces, then flairs out over our shoulders.

The bodice of our habit is tight, but the skirt is loose and comfortable to fit the needs of our work. For me, our garments of faith are both a blessing and a burden, the latter because each of us is responsible for keeping her own clean and starched. The starching, especially, is messy and distasteful, partly because of the smell. But, I remind myself that it is part of doing God's work.

I am no longer Amina Rassam. That girl is gone. At times I miss her and the joyful life she had. In taking my sacred vows, I have emerged a new woman. I am now *Soeur Marie-Reine de Jesus*. I feel the change both inside and out. The texture of my skin is different, perhaps because of the environment. I move more slowly with less fuss. I feel a new sense of confidence and serenity. The seed of stillness within me, growing out of the ritual of contemplation I've learned, has become my strength. In practising spiritual solitude, I feel communion with our Blessed Virgin and with God. I am ready to undertake the mission that the Community of Mary has set before me.

*   *   *

Sister Marie-Reine closed the first entry of her journal, and took up a sheet of paper from her desk to write a letter to Hanna. She had written her twice from France, but had never received a reply. Sister Marie suspected the reason she had heard nothing was because Hanna lacked writing skills and Ma'an was too preoccupied to write for her. Now that she was leaving for a new, untried part of the world, Sister Marie felt compelled to write one last time, even though she knew she might not receive an answer in Africa.

25 October, 1904

Dearest Hanna,

It has been too long since I last wrote. My negligence is partly because I have not heard from you and Ma'an, and also because the last two years have been filled with work outside the convent. My training at the Institute for Deaf-Mutes, and also at a hospital in Toulouse where I was under the tutelage of a Dr. Villiard learning healing practices, kept me busy.

I hope you and Ma'an are well and that the hot weather is behind you. I was relieved to hear from Father of his pleasure in meeting Ma'an, and that he had given Ma'an his blessing for your marriage. I hope your mother has come to some peace with your decision. The last letter I had from Father—his letters come only every six months or so—brought the news that you had given birth to a son. How wonderful. He must be two years by now. What do you call him? How I would love to see him.

My heart aches knowing that our lives, once so intertwined, have taken very different paths with little prospect of our seeing one another again. I had hoped that I might return to a mission near Mosul. Alas, fate and duty have prevented my returning home.

I am leaving the Mother House in France to work in a mission station in Africa started by the Montfort Brothers. Do you remember those two Frenchmen that visited us at the inn? The mission is called Nzama and is located in southern Africa. Three other sisters from our Order will accompany me to that far-away place. It is no longer safe for us to remain here in France. A horrid wave of anti-Catholicism is sweeping across this land. I am in God's hands.

If you have someone who can write, I would welcome news of you and your family. Father will have my postal address at the new mission.

You will always be in my prayers.

Faithfully yours,
Sister Marie-Reine de Jesus (Amina)

*   *   *

The Daughters of Wisdom's exodus from France in the early twentieth century was not without cause. The French government had closed a number of the order's institutions, including schools for the deaf and blind. More closures were threatened. It was not the first time that the Filles de la Sagesse had experienced religious bigotry.

In 1794, during the French revolution leading up to the Republic, twenty-six Daughters of Wisdom sisters were forcefully removed from the convent in St. Laurent and were shackled, two by two, as criminals and marched through the streets of the village while people spat on them and threw rocks. One sister was hacked to death, another slain in her sickbed and her corpse dragged through the streets, while others were thrown into a prison in Nantes, where eight died of starvation. Two sisters met their fates at the guillotine in the same city. A sister was put to death in Coron and two others massacred at Longeron. In Poitiers, where the founder of the order had worked in a hospital, three sisters were exhibited in a public square with a sign hung over them reading, "Harborers of Fanatic Priests," referring to the Montfort Order. When nurses were needed to care for wounded and ill soldiers in a hospital in Brest, seventy imprisoned sisters were sent there. They were the first of many orders affected by the revolutionary zeal sweeping republican France and were unable to resume their religious lives until 1800.

Under Napoleon, the Daughters of Wisdom recovered most of their former houses, were granted 30,000 francs for building new schools and convents, and were paid an annuity of 12,000 francs by the French government until 1848. The membership in the order grew from 260 in 1800 to 1,500 in the mid-nineteenth century.

Sister Marie-Reine and her colleagues were aware of the order's precarious history. When anti-clericism again flaired in the early twentieth century, the Filles de la Sagesse's opportunities in France shriveled once more, and Sister Marie set out on a new journey.

*   *   *

Journal, 26th October, 1904

We are forced to leave France. Anti-Catholicism is setting fire to this country. The mounting opposition to the Church by the State, using new anti-clerical laws, has prompted the closure of our schools and persuaded our spiritual leaders in the Montfort Order that we will better serve our Lord by working elsewhere. Missions are opening in South America, North America (among the Red Indians) and in Africa where the need is greatest. Father Lhoumeau, the Superior General, informed us that, four years ago, Montfort brothers began building a mission in the Shire valley of Nyasaland. They are bringing light and learning to that part of southern Africa. But, they desperately need sisters to help.

When Mother Patrice asked if any of us was willing to serve God in this new mission, I volunteered, along with three other sisters. Mother Patrice was eager that I join the group. 'Your knowledge of medicine and pharmacology will help in the work of the Nzama Mission,' she told me.

I was full of remorse and disappointment knowing that my work in France was coming to an end. I never expected that I would be leaving Europe and heading to an unknown continent. I thought I might return to Mosul, but it seems that the political situation at home is precarious. The Ottoman leaders are weak and the competition between France and Britain grows worse. I feel a sense of helplessness knowing that my reunion with my dear family must be postponed. It appears that my destiny is to serve elsewhere. Returning to the Mother House from Toulouse helped: with time for contemplation and prayer I have come to realize that the opportunity to serve in Africa may bear fruit.

I will write about the ceremony blessing our journey tomorrow when I am less tired.

*   *   *

27th October

I am scribbling on a train. It is taking us in the opposite direction from which I came five years ago—back to Marseille to board a ship that will take us to southern Africa. The train's motion doesn't make for easy writing, but I have a quiet moment. My head is swirling with new impressions and I do not want to entrust them to mere memory.

Mother Patrice is coming with us to Marseille. She wants to make sure that our ship, the *Kronpritz*, is docked there. She told us that she would accompany us onto the boat to help her 'daughters,' as she calls us, get settled before we depart.

Yesterday, the bells of St. Laurent rang out through the town announcing the departure ceremony convened on our behalf. Father Lhoumeau, assisted by Fathers Bourdieu and Ricard, officiated at the Benediction of the Blessed Sacrament. Sister Helene led the four of us to the foot of the altar for the blessing. Many came to the service. It helped to strengthen my resolve for the journey ahead. The convent community bid us adieu with some fanfare and great warmth, ending with evening prayers for our safe passage.

The other sisters accompanying me on this journey are Sister Lucie Marie, Sister Therese, and Sister Elaine de St. Pierre. Srs. Therese and Elaine are younger than I am. Sister Lucie is slightly older. All are French citizens. I am the only foreigner. Sister Therese is the tallest of us, with gray eyes that match her habit. She has a lovely smile, but I know her little. She was in the group of postulates ahead of me.

Sister Elaine comes from Brittany. She has warm, brown eyes set close together, and a small mouth that breaks into a smile when she sees children. She adores them and worked in a school for the blind during her training. She is a lively person and will be a fine teacher.

Sister Lucie has eyes the color of desert sage and a very straight nose and pleasant disposition. She seems a steady person, someone I would go to. We've been told that we are 'plowing new ground,' being the first Catholic sisters to be stationed in this part of Africa.

We left from St. Laurent at four o'clock this morning. I am feeling *trez fatigue*. I will rest now as we are getting off at Chatillon to visit the shrine of Our Lady of the Sacred Heart in Niort later this afternoon. We'll spend the night at a convent there and travel on to Marseille tomorrow.

28th October

Our visit to the shrine was inspiring and staying in the convent reminded me of my travels in Mt. Lebanon, where we also spent nights in convents. While on the train Mother Patrice told us that she has decided to dedicate the first house of the mission at Nzama to the Blessed Virgin. It will be known as the Immaculate Conception, and is where we sisters will live. We all agreed enthusiastically with her decision.

Today, we reach Marseille. We will visit the shrine of Our Lady of Perpetual Help this evening. We need all the help we can get for this undertaking! It will be our last night in France. I am feeling sad, knowing that my ties with the Mother House are coming to an end. I'm also uneasy about getting on a ship again. My illness last time nearly killed me. None of my companions has ever been on a ship, so I must keep my personal fears to myself.

29 October, Marseille

We got up early and arrived at the dock where the *Kronprinz* was tied up. It is a huge German liner, about 160 meters [500 feet] long, according to the captain, Herr Stahl. Mother Patrice led us to our cabin. I was surprised to find it much larger than the one I had on the steamer from Beirut. It has two ample bunks and all four of us will be together. What a happy surprise.

Lunch was served in our cabin and we had a merry time with Mother Superior keeping us busy with questions to divert our thoughts from the journey. At four in the afternoon, music came through loud speakers, announcing our departure. Our hearts were heavy as we said good-bye to our benefactor. She remained on the dock watching us, and waved vigorously as the ship pulled away from the wharf until neither her white *coiffe,* nor ours, were visible to the other. Back in our cabin, Sister Therese said, 'I am going to miss Mother Patrice. She is so dependable.' We all agreed. Then, a moment of silence overtook us, as we looked around the cabin, undecided about where to sleep.

'I will take an upper bunk,' I offered, having had a lower one on the *Meridien.* Sister Lucie admitted to being afraid of having to climb a ladder. She took the bunk underneath me. Sister Therese ended up on top of the other bunk, so we are eye-to-eye. As we began unpacking a few things to put in our hammocks, there was much lively—do I dare say nervous—chatter. Then the ship lurched. It brought a few shreaks from my cabin sisters as we made our way out of the harbor. We are heading toward Italy, where we will make a stop in Naples.

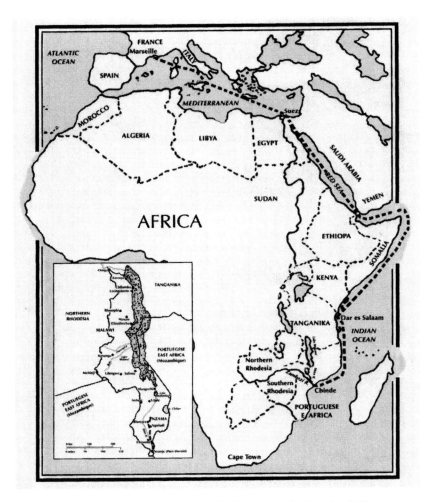

The journey from Marseille to Chinde and up the Zambezi River.

CHAPTER 20

Life Aboard the Kronprinz

Journal, 31st October

I've been too occupied with my companions and the activities on board to
write in my journal. But tonight the *Kronprinz* arrived in Naples. We will be
here until tomorrow evening. For dinner we had fish because we were fasting
for All Hallow's Eve. Others had meat.

This ship has many more passengers than I found on the *Meridien*.
Yesterday, we met a tall, blue-eyed German nun in a pitch-black habit. Her
name is Sister Agnes von Frankenberg, though she pronounced 'sister' as
'*schwester*,' the German word for *soeur*. She comes from Freiburg. I guess she
saw my puzzled look because she said, 'It's in southern Germany, near the
Black Forest.' Sister Therese seemed to know where it was. To me, it meant
nothing. Sister Agnes does speak some French. She told us that she is on her
way to Tanganika. She will leave us at Dar es-salaam. There is much need of
missionaries there, she explained, as the Africans are either Mohammedans or
'heathens.' I guess she meant non-believers. That there are Mohammedans in
Africa surprised me. Father Lhoumeau did not tell us this. I wonder if they
speak Arabic? I thought Sister Agnes brave to be traveling alone, but she said
that a group of Germans were traveling to Dar es-Salaam together. I guess she
will not be lonely, after all.

1st November, All Souls' Day

We left Naples at nine in the evening with a full load of passengers. We attended Mass for All Souls' Day at a cathedral in Naples and came back to the ship
for dinner. It was a feast honoring this blessed day. Upon returning to our
cabin afterwards, we found four passenger lists shoved under the door. The list
is like a program with a drawing on the front cover of the *Kronprinz,* with
black smoke pouring out of its smokestack. You can just see the two decks and
tall masts on either side. Captain Stahl's name is printed underneath the ship.

Inside we found the passengers listed by destinations. I quickly found 'the Four Sisters,' as we are being called on board. We are listed individually under *Chinde*. It is the eighth port out of fourteen before the *Kronprinz* reaches *Capstadt* (Cape Town) in South Africa. I am listed as 'Schwester Marie Reine de Jesus.' In addition to our small group, there are five other passengers disembarking at *Chinde*—all men. But in Dar es-salaam, eighteen passengers are leaving us, including Sister Agnes. One of them is listed as the Government Secretary, H. Vollmering. He must be important. The Germans seem to have a keen interest in Tanganika. Among the German passengers is a doctor. I would like to meet him and learn of his work.

When I finished looking through the passengers' names, I turned to the back and on it was the ship's staff. We have five officers aboard. One of them has an English name, 'Adams,' but the rest are German. There are six machinists to handle the turbines and engines down below, but only one doctor. For this size liner, I am surprised they have only one. But we do have the German doctor aboard, in case he is needed. Two waiters staff the dining room, one German and an assistant who must be English, from the looks of his name. Last listed are three stewards and two stewardesses. This is an improvement from my last voyage. It is reassuring to see two *fraulein* listed among the staff after the problems I had on the *Meridien*.

We had quite an exchange in our cabin as we went through the passenger list. Sister Therese noticed that in Portuguese East Africa [Mozambique] only men are disembarking at Quelimane and Beira. Then Sister Lucie pointed out that we are the only women disembarking at Chinde. This is where we leave to travel up the Zambezi River to Nyasaland.

'Are there no missions in Chinde? The Portuguese are Catholics like us.' Sister Therese sounded indignant. To be truthful, none of us has any idea what to expect when we get to Chinde. For now, we just have to take each day as a blessing.

2nd November

We were told that, at midnight, the ship passed through the Straits of Messina. It separates the tip of Italy from the island of Sicily. We bypassed Malta and traveled southeast toward Port Said, Egypt. So far, the weather has been fair. But last night, when I climbed into my bunk, I said a special prayer asking the Blessed Virgin to protect us from any storm we encounter crossing the Mediterranean. I cannot forget that awful sea voyage five years ago.

4th November

The weather is cooler now and we wear our wool capes when we're outside on deck. Fortunately, it has not clouded over yet. Perhaps it is the size of this ship, but I don't feel the motion of the sea as much as I did on the *Meridien*. Every morning after breakfast, which we have in our cabin, we take a stroll, walking two by two, around the deck. We have not seen many fish or porpoises, but we saw a whale spouting off in the distance this morning. Overhead, the last of the migratory birds are making their way from Europe across the Mediterranean to Africa for the winter. Yesterday, we saw a great V-shaped formation of geese and, today, cranes. There are also dark clouds of small birds swinging back and forth above us. They seem to come in the afternoon. And, of course, seagulls, and a few pelicans, their necks hunched into their wings, flying along on the air currents.

As we walked the deck, I learned from Sister Elaine her reason for joining the *Filles de la Sagesse.* Her mother had died when she was ten, and life was very hard taking care of three younger siblings. Her father was no help. He was often away and when he did return home, she smelled alcohol on him, and knew to stay out of his way because it made him surly. Two years later, he remarried. His new wife was quite a bit younger than her mother. She had a child, a nasty four-year-old daughter who fought with Sister Elaine's siblings. Shortly after the marriage, the woman began to make demands on her that were overly burdensome: making Sister Elaine fetch water from the village well and wash the children's clothes without help. The woman's exchanges with her sounded acrimonious and cruel. She knew that her stepmother resented her. Withdrawing into herself, she begged her father to allow her to enter a convent. She was fifteen. He finally agreed and sent his daughter to the Mother House in St. Laurent six months later. Sister Elaine was afraid that the Mother Superior might treat her differently because of her impoverished background, but she didn't. 'Leaving home and going to the convent was my salvation,' she told me.

Hearing Sister Elaine's story made me feel sad. No wonder she has such affection for children—she knows what it is to be mistreated. It makes me realize how lucky I am to have such a generous father and a family who loves me. I miss them terribly sometimes.

*   *   *

At this point, Sister Marie shut her journal, ready for bed. Sister Therese had been watching her from her bunk.

"You are better than I am at writing in your journal," she said. "Are you doing it every night?"

"No. It's not always possible with all there is happening on this ship. But I do want to put down my thoughts about this journey. It is not very often four sisters go off to Africa together," she said, smiling.

"That's true. Do you mind if I turn down the lantern? I'm sleepy."

"Not at all." Sister Marie turned onto her stomach and pulled up the wool blanket.

"Good-night," Sister Therese said."I wish I wrote more easily." She yawned.

"Write everyday," Sister Marie said softly. "No one is going to see your journal. Remember what Mother Patrice told us? It is for your eyes only. Good-night."

"I will try," her cabinmate said snuffing out the lantern on the post next to her.

While they slept, the Kronprintz stopped in Port Said at two in the morning to let off twenty passengers and take on fuel. They were on their way to the Suez Canal. It would take them to the Gulf of Aden, and then to the Indian Ocean.

*   *   *

Journal, 6th November, Suez Canal

The weather has suddenly changed and become hotter. We have been traveling through the Suez Canal this morning. It links the Mediterrean with the Red Sea. The climate below decks is quite temperate, but if we go up on top, it is blistering. The sun's heat reflects off the water and onto the white deck, right into my eyes. We stayed on the lower deck and watched a ship ahead of us in the canal. It seemed to be carrying cargo. No passengers appeared on deck. After lunch, we had a stroll, then settled down to read. Sister Elaine is devouring Dickens' "Tale of Two Cities." I must read it after she is through.

8th November

New territory. Today we saw date palms and some small mud-hut villages with people riding donkeys or walking along dirt tracks, a Biblical scene. Now, there is nothing but sand and endless brown desert on both sides. It reminds me of places in the Syrian Desert—a wasteland from a distance. Even the Red Sea, which Moses once parted to lead his people to safety, shimmers with heat as the ship moves through it. I wish we could see the Nile River from here, but it is too far away. There is hardly a bird in the air it is so hot.

Sometimes, I've seen tall, dark-skinned men, with little on but a cloth over their private parts, walking along a beach. I finally asked one of the stewards who they were. He squinted toward the coast and told me they are *Nuer*, part of a nomadic group that wanders the dry lands and pans in search of water for their cattle. I asked him what a 'pan' was. He told me it is a depression in the earth where rain water once collected, but has since dried up. I nodded and am putting it down so I won't forget.

10th November

I have learned something more about Sister Therese in the last few days. She comes from a small village outside Paris. She is the fourth of six daughters and was called Nanette. Her parents had two sons, but one died shortly after his birth. Her father has a small farm with a dairy. They barely make enough to sustain themselves. Both of her oldest sisters married before they were seventeen years. A sister, Monique, slightly older than Sister Therese, with a pretty face and a cheerful disposition, caught the eye of a tailor. He was ten years her senior. Monique had other ideas than becoming a tailor's wife. She wanted to go to Paris. The story sounds familiar: it reminds me of when my parents wanted me to marry someone, but I had already decided to join the Daughters of Wisdom. Monique was forced to accept the man's proposal and they were married the following year. She often returned home, complaining that her husband was beating her. It was not a happy marriage, even after her sister produced a son.

It was at this point that Nanette decided to join an order. Knowing that she was not nearly as comely as Monique, she approached her mother and told her she had received a message from the Blessed Virgin that she should join the *Filles de la Sagesse.* She had heard about the order from the family's priest. Nanette sought the man's support and he approached her father. The priest told him that he would write to the Mother Superior on Nanette's behalf, and would help raise money for a small dowry. He was persuasive in convincing Nanette's father that if she entered a convent it would 'take one more daughter off his hands.' Those are Sister Therese's very words! Her father quickly agreed. That is how she came to be at the convent in St. Laurent a year before I arrived.

I saw her once when she returned to take her final Vows of Profession, before I left the Mother House for Toulouse. The Government closed the school in Rennes where Sister Therese was teaching. She was forced to return to St. Laurent. I found her at the convent when I returned in September. She readily agreed to become part of the group going to the mission in Nzama because, as she told me, 'I have teaching skills and I see no other alternative.'

It is amazing to me how the four of us, each with our own story, have managed to come together on a ship bound for a place that is hard to imagine.

*   *   *

For the next few days, the Kronprinz made its way down along the coast of North Africa, passing an island called Harmil that signaled their arrival at the Dahlak Archipelago, a cluster of islands off the coast of Ethiopia in the Red Sea. Ethiopia was a country unique in that part of the world in 1904. It was a kingdom ruled by an Amharic-speaking nobleman, Menelik. He traced his linguistic roots to an ancient biblical language, Ge'ez, and his lineage back to the Queen of Sheba. Largely Coptic Christian, Ethiopia had never been conquered by a European nation, unlike the territories that surrounded it. Although Egypt was under Great Britain's control and the Sudan had been passed between France and Britain like a football, Ethiopia remained independent, protected by her formidable highlands and a strong ruler.

As the Kronprintz passed an island off its port side, it shifted toward Bab-al-Madab, the Gates of Tears, named for its treacherously narrow straits that caused more than one ship to crash against the rocks and sink. The passage connected the Red Sea with the Gulf of Aden. It would take six more days for the Kronprintz to clear the Gulf of Aden and make its way around the Horn of Africa to the Indian Ocean. Its first stop along the lengthy African coast was Kilindini.

*   *   *

Journal, 13th November

This last week has seemed endless. As we headed east in the Gulf of Aden, then south around the Horn, the climate became warmer and warmer. We have seen long fishing boats, carved from large hollowed-out logs, plying the waters off the coast. Black-skinned fishermen stand up in these dugouts and pole them while they are close to the shore. They use paddles farther out. The boats are quite large. One was filled with about twenty men and approached the ship. The Africans started scanning the *Kronprintz's* steep hull, talking wildly to one another. It was hard to hear what they said; it sounded like excited gibberish to me. The ship's loudspeaker suddenly sounded with a voice warning us to ignore the circling dugouts and go below. A knowledgeable German, who'd stood with us watching the dugouts, told us that the men might be pirates. 'They are not unknown in this part the Indian Ocean,' he said.

Looking at the small boats, it was hard to see how the men could board a ship of this size—rather like a mackerel trying to attack a whale. Just then, a stewardess came up and told us to go below, warning that sometimes the pirates take women. We hid our laughter and went down to our cabin, where we all began talking at once. 'What are we supposed to do? Hide under our bunks?' Sister Elaine asked in jest, her eyes shining.

'We wouldn't all fit,' Sister Therese grinned. 'How can men on such small crafts possibly hoist themselves up to a ship like the *Kronprintz?*'

I agreed. The whole thing seemed preposterous.

But Sister Lucie looked thoughtful. When she finally spoke, we all paid attention because she's the oldest among us and, probably, the most sensible. 'The fishermen might have ladders hidden in their long dugouts that they lashed together so they can mount a ship,' she said. Then she pointed out that they could move quickly and quietly with great stealth, carrying knives and small cutlasses in their mouths. 'Maybe they are just pretending to be fishermen.'

This silenced the rest of us.

'If none of the ship's staff detected their movements,' Sister Lucie finished, 'they could be on board before anyone knew it. And, where would we go?' She let her words sink in then told us she had heard about such assaults on ships on the Atlantic side of Africa.

I stared at her with some disbelief, but then recalled the tribal attack Hanna and I had experienced in the Syrian Desert. I told them about it.

'Whether on land or sea,' I whispered, 'desperate men will come up with fantastical plans.' I looked at Sister Therese, whose gray eyes were beginning to cloud.

Sister Elaine got up and went to our door, which we'd left ajar to let in air. She shut and locked it, even though it made the cabin hotter than it already was. She turned around with a satisfied expression, her mouth a thin line.

'We might as well relax until we hear from the captain,' she said.

With that, we took up our fans and put them to use cooling our faces as we exchanged ideas about what we would do if pirates really did board the *Kronprintz*. With our ears tuned to every noise outside, we rested on our beds, so as not to raise our body heat. I decided to write in my journal.

Later in the day

I must confess that the rest of the afternoon passed uneventfully. We emerged from our cabin just before dinner and made our way to the dining room. Sister Agnes von Frankenburg and Herr Dr. Hans Boehme, the doctor in her party, joined us for the evening meal. He is a stylish man with a well-trimed beard and penetrating brown eyes. He seems to be in his thirties, neither young nor old. He confessed that he has not yet married because he is too busy 'seeing the world.' That comment peaked my curiosity and I asked about his plans in Africa. He told me that he has worked in Tanganika previously. He is returning to Dar es-Salaam to be the official doctor-in-residence for the German community at the Government compound. It seems that several officers are taking their children with them and they want their little ones cared for by German medical staff. I was disappointed that he is not a missionary doctor, but enjoyed talking with him, nevertheless. None of us mentioned the pirates.

15th November

Today we crossed the Equator amidst much excitement. All the passengers
came up to the top deck and the captain opened a bottle of French champagne
with a loud pop. The cork shot over the side of the ship. We toasted to our having arrived at the Southern Hemisphere. I had never stopped to think about what
it would mean to be in a different hemisphere. For people living on the Equator,
Dr. Boehme explained, the sun rises and sets at the same time everyday. He told
us that the Swahili-speaking people living along the coast tell time by the position of the sun in the sky. What they do when it rains, I'm not sure. And it does
rain, as we discovered when we awoke this morning. The decks are still wet
and a bit slippery. Yet there is little respite from the sultry heat. If anything, it
has become more humid. We changed to the cotton habits that Mother Patrice
insisted we take with us. And we are still dripping. It is a bit cooler in our
cabin, but not much.

 Tomorrow, we arrive at Kilindini. I looked at the passenger list and it
seems, from their names, that the ten men disembarking are all British. Among
them are Lord D. Clifford and a Sir Evan James. I wonder if they could be
royalty? Also, something I had not noted before: there are three doctors leaving us in Kilindini. It is too late to meet them and they probably speak only
English, in any case.

 Hopefully we will have a chance to get off the ship and walk for a bit. It
is our first port in Africa and I am anxious to see how the place looks.

16th November, Kilindini

We steamed down the coast and landed at Kilindini in the early afternoon. It is
a small port and village squeezed between coconut plantations. We were
allowed to disembark for two hours while the ship took on provisions. Africans
had gathered in an open space for what looked like a *bazaar.* I could see, while
going down the gangway, pyramids of fruits and vegetables set out on flour
sacks on the ground. The scent of cloves, cumin and curry reminded me of the
markets at home. And there were rows of baskets filled with grains, rice, and
beans. I heard sheep and goats bleating somewhere and smelled their urine. In
the background I spied small open shops selling all kinds of goods. The bazaar
was full of color and vitality, a joyful surprise.

 Once on firm ground, we created quite a stir among the local villagers
who had gathered in front of the market to watch the *Kronprintz* land at the
wharf. The women covered their heads, and some wore long black *adowa.*
Most are Mohammedans, according to Dr. Boehme, who accompanied us on
shore.

 'They have never seen people like you,' he told us, 'and probably think
you four Sisters are some kind of enormous birds with your tall, white headdresses,' he teased us. In fact, the Africans ran away when they first saw us.

Then they wandered back slowly to have a look, the men wrapping their long, colorful cloths more tightly around their dark waists and the women staring at us out of eyes hidden deep in their shadowed faces. They were somber as they silently appraised us from a distance. Dr. Boehme, who seems to know a little of their language, stepped forward and explained to the Africans who we were and where we were going. They nodded their heads and the oldest man among them went over to the women and explained, I guess, that we were religious sisters on our way to Chinde. A couple of the women opened their mouths, laughing and revealing rows of beautiful white teeth. This was my first introduction to Africans—mahogany dark skin and very white teeth, women dressed in *adowa* that reminded me of Arab women in my own town of Mosul.

17th November

Early this morning we passed the busy port of Mombasa. The sun was just beginning to illuminate the town's rust-colored slave fort built by the Portuguese on a prominent bluff overlooking the harbor. I could see, as well, minarets in the rosy distance. The fort was where slaves captured inland by Swahili raiders were held before being transported across the Indian Ocean to the Seychelles Islands or north to the Arabian Peninsula, according to Dr. Boehme. He has become our resident specialist on African history, a very learned man.

The coastline here is lush with flora and fauna of all kinds. We can hear monkeys chattering and yelling to each other in the coconut and macademia nut trees. We also caught sight of baboons on shore, running and chasing each other.

As we traveled south of Mombasa, a group of women, some with children, came down to the shore to collect small crabs. They brought gourds to put them in. Forming lines along the beach, they bent over from the waist as one and began digging into the sand where holes appeared, dumping handfuls of crabs into gourds, all the while singing a wonderfully engaging song as they dug, lifted, and threw the crabs into a gourd in one fluid motion. I must not forget this scene. Even the children helped, running down to the shore with empty gourds when their mothers needed them.

It is Saturday, and both the passengers and crew have been considerate of our needs as a religious group, making space for us to hold prayer services when the spirit moves. Sister Lucie has made arrangements for us to use a reception room tonight, for a prayer service that she will lead. Other passengers may join us.

18th November, Dar es-salaam

We arrived in Dar es-salaam at two o'clock this afternoon. It is a city of white-washed walls, low square houses, and minarets. After saying good-bye to Sister Agnes and Dr. Boehme, who were disembarking here, we went ashore to visit a Benedictine Convent where we were to stay the night. A man from the convent had been sent to fetch us with a cart. The slow ride through the town was hot and dusty, with many Africans crowding the narrow roads.

While at the convent, the four of us took the opportunity of going to confession, something we had not done since leaving the Mother House.

It has given me, as well as my companions, great comfort to be in a religious community again. We have been living in crowded quarters on the ship and, at times, I feel a tension (that I think the others share) in being so close. I have to admit that I was short tempered with Sister Elaine yesterday. She kept asking aimless questions that none of us could answer and I finally asked her to be silent.

19th November, Dar es-Salaam

This morning, at the convent, we got up early to be at the church by six o'clock for Mass and Holy Communion. Afterwards, we made our way back to the ship, which was scheduled to depart at noon. We had barely settled in our cabin when someone knocked on the door. It was a steward informing us that we would be arriving in Port Mocambo the following morning and that dinner would be served at the usual hour. I was happy to hear the news as it gives me a chance to rest and write after our visit to the convent.

20th November, Port Mocambo

We arrived here at ten in the morning, after a breakfast of rolls, fresh fruit, and coffee. I am learning to enjoy coffee—served with a good dollop of cream. Port Mocambo is not nearly as large as Dar es-salaam, but it is where we shall disembark to sleep in a hospital run by the Congregation of St. Joseph of Cluny. Before we left, Mother Patrice told us that she had written ahead to Mother Marie Antoinette, the Superior of the hospital, who agreed to host us while we are here.

21st November

Our stay at the hospital was most interesting. Mother Marie Antoinette, an energetic woman despite her years, met us at the entrance and led us to a small house behind the hospital that serves as her residence. We left our satchels there, and after a steaming cup of coffee with freshly roasted cashew nuts, which I found delicious, she took us on a tour of the hospital. It is newly white washed and very clean, with the same smells of disinfectant and ill bodies that I remembered from the hospital in Toulouse. The hospital here is modest with only four wards: one for expectant mothers and their newborn infants, another for patients with malaria and other non-communicable diseases, and a third ward for children. The fourth ward is set slightly apart from the others; it serves patients with communicable diseases such as tuberculosis, influenza, and sexually transmitted diseases, such as syphilis.

A small outpatient clinic at the front of the hospital had a long line of mostly women with babies and young children snaking its way out the double doors and onto the thin lawn, where some women had spread colorful cloths and were sitting on them to wait their turn. Mother Superior explained that the hospital does not provide food for the patients. She told us that the patients' families usually come once or twice a day to cook for them. We did see small groups of women cooking over outdoor fires near the hospital.

I asked Mother Marie where most of the patients came from. She explained that since St. Joseph's Hospital is the only one in the area, to get to it many people have to walk from villages a far distance away, carrying their sick children on their backs or, if it is an ill or injured adult, on the back of a bicycle. Few have access to a donkey or a cart. She told the story of a father who had bicycled ten kilometers with a child who was suffering from malaria, only to find that by the time he reached the clinic, his son was so weak that he died within the hour. Life seems very fragile here.

Sister Elaine wanted to know about other children's diseases. Malaria, diarrhea, parasites and kwashiorkor are the major child killers, the Mother Superior told us. She explained that kwashiorkor is extreme malnutrition. It attacks children during the 'hunger season' when the crops are finished, or during a drought. She also told us that some children are afflicted with elephantiasis, a disease caused by a worm that produces an enlargement and thickening of the tissues in a limb. In children, it most often affects the legs. Sometimes one or both legs swell to double or triple their size and are very painful to walk on. This news horrified me. I had seen some parasites among the deaf girls at the Institute, also influenza and whooping cough. But these diseases are of a totally different nature. It is overwhelming. Do they exist elsewhere in southern Africa? What will I find when we get to the Nzama mission?

CHAPTER 21

The Zambezi Meets the Shire River

23rd November, Chinde

We are here—at the port of Chinde, our final destination on the coast. The place looked somnolent when we arrived, steeped in the mid-afternoon heat. The harbor turned out to be on the north side of a delta formed by the Zambezi River's flow into the Indian Ocean. The town of Chinde, where we are spending three nights, is on the south side. We had to transfer to another boat to get here.

We packed our satchels, eager to leave the *Kronprinz*. However, just before we were to disembark, the ship's purser approached us to collect 250 *francs* extra for our 'excessive' luggage. What an outrage! Sister Lucie, who has a finely tuned sense of justice, took the matter to the captain, a man who understood a little French. After some discussion, a list of our luggage that we had given to the purser was produced, and the 250 *francs* was waived. So, in the end, justice was served.

Having arrived at the mouth of the Zambezi, a smaller ship, the *Cadet,* pulled up along side the *Kronprinz*. First the luggage, and then seventeen passengers had to be transferred by basket to the *Cadet.* I wondered how we were going to get into those large, woven containers with our bulky habits. We four were assigned to the last two. We paired up and I shared one with Sister Lucie. We carefully raised our skirts and got into one of the baskets, our hearts thumping. Then the crew lowered the basket, with us shaking inside, to the deck of the *Cadet.* It must have been quite a sight watching us get in and out of the baskets in our ungainly garb. The remaining passengers on the *Kronprinz* gathered to watch us leave and wish us well.

Soon after we extricated ourselves from the baskets, we were on our way to Chinde town. Whenever the boat stopped at a dock along the river it was surrounded by small dugouts, handled by Africans. On one of them we saw two white men pointing at us. They turned out to be Comta, a Portuguese, and the flotilla agent. The latter man took care of our luggage to see that it arrived at the French hotel where we are staying two nights. Chinde doesn't have much to offer other than its location at the entrance of the Zambezi River. But it is good to be on land again.

26th November, Chinde

We are bored. Having arrived at the hotel two days ago, we've seen everything there is to see in this small waterfront town. And the heat is oppressive. The hotel is clean and comfortable with a view of the river. We certainly can't complain about the price: It is only 50 *francs* a day, everything included. But the climate is like being under a blanket of steam and the mosquitos are ferocious, especially in the early evening. Between the fetid smells drifting up from the river and the mosquitos we must keep our windows closed. We are forced to stay inside and have spent much of the time knitting or playing cards.

Sister Lucie, who is a dedicated reader, has been engrossed in a Dickens novel, newly translated into French, about a young girl whose mother abandons her. Sister Lucie entertained us by reading some passages last night. But it upset Sister Elaine, who burst into tears, upon hearing of the girl's sad life. Perhaps it reminded her of her own early years when she was mistreated by her father and stepmother. Sister Therese gathered Sister Elaine into her arms and held her. 'That was a horrid time,' she told our youngest member. 'But we are far away from England. And look what an elegant room we have here in Africa,' she chided. Her words seemed to raise Sister Elaine's spirits.

To tell the truth, although we are treated like princesses by the hotel staff, we are fed up with this rough and tumble town. We are eager to leave and begin our journey up the Zambezi.

27th November, On the Zambezi River

At one o'clock yesterday, under a blazing sun, we left the hotel and ventured down to the shore where the *Kind,* a side-wheel steamer, was waiting to take us up the Zambezi. From there, we go north up a smaller river, the Shire. Our final destination is a village in the bush.

When we boarded the *Kind,* we found it filled with dark-skinned Africans who seemed more interested in us than their work of loading the boat. A peculiar attraction, we found, is our knitting. The boatmen have become so engrossed in our hand movements that it appears they want to learn how to knit stockings, too!

We are the only passengers aboard. The captain and the mechanic, both Englishmen, take their meals with us and study French, even while we eat, to better understand us. They have done everything they can to be entertaining. When a bird or an animal appears on the river, they call us to see it. Today, Sunday, the captain put on steam to try and catch up with a herd of gazelle on shore. Sadly, we were unable to overtake them, but it reminded me of the ones

I'd seen in the Syrian Desert on the caravan. How long ago it seems. Further up river, we saw amazing creatures: hippopotamuses with big heads, half submerged, looking drowsy. Two of them opened their huge, pink mouths to reveal menacing teeth, then disappeared under the murky water's surface. Alligators were less shy—they didn't even move from the muddy riverbank when they heard the noise of the steamer. But, when the captain's gunshot rang out, they quickly paddled into the water. Now, I know we have entered Africa.

We've seen birds of every size in the most beautiful array of colors. Some seem to be parrots, but others I don't recognize. When we stopped at Schoupanga, despite the midday heat, the captain decided to take us to see two Jesuit Fathers, who had heard of our existence. First, we had to get into small dugouts. It was difficult to enter them with the weight of our long habits and the boats tipping back and forth. Sister Elaine nearly lost her balance, but the captain's mate caught her arm in time. The heat was oppressive. We had to walk up the bank and follow a path to get to the Jesuit mission. When we reached it, we found a collection of huts, one larger than the others. The two Fathers welcomed us with broad grins and related, with some humor, that they were jealous of the Montfort Brothers because, for eight years, they had requested nuns to join them at their station without success. We took coffee with them and to please us at the end of our short visit, they accompanied us to the river and filled our boats with bananas, cabbages, and French potatoes. We thanked them profusely and waved our good-byes as we headed back to the *Kind*. I felt a bit sorry for them. It must be very lonely where they are, with little outside contact except for the occasional traveler from the river. Yet the Jesuit Fathers seemed cheerful, so their spiritual work must be satisfying.

29th November

Despite a storm, heat, and mosquitos, we have managed to enjoy the journey up the Zambezi the last three days. We have seen not only animals, but a few grass-thatched villages, with African men setting traps for fishing in the river, and in shallower parts, women washing cotton wraps while their children run along the shore to see us. A few stared at us and then ran away screaming. A fisherman waved, but most seemed occupied with their labors.

Today, we reached a place where the water is no longer deep enough for the *Kind* to go farther. Tomorrow, we will have to leave and continue our journey in a smaller boat. We have no choice. Let us thank the Star of the Seas for having protected us thus far. Blessed is she, that none of us have come down with fevers or other ailments. I know that the Africans aboard will miss seeing and hearing our knitting needles at work.

30th November, Villebocage

When we arrived at Villebocage, yesterday, two boats awaited us. Each had a cabin in the middle and looked like a small houseboat. Rather than separate, Sister Lucie suggested we settle in one of the boats and put our luggage in the other—a practical solution. The four of us had to squeeze into the tiny cabin. It is about three meters square [less than 10 feet square]. There are only two wood benches on either side for sitting on. We put our trunks and most of our valises into the cabin of the other boat. Each boat is steered by a pilot with ten rowers, five to a side, doing the hard work. There are two cooks to serve our meals, one having been sent by the Montfort brothers from Chiromo. This one knows a little English, which, of course, we don't understand, so he rides on the luggage boat most of the time.

1st December, 1904

Having come this far, we are now surrounded by Africans. I find them to be quite docile and very respectful toward us. When they start to argue with each other, we scold them in French (which, of course, they don't understand). But they get the point of our gestures and immediately return to their tasks in silence. Since they eat only once a day, they spend most of their time rowing, except when they pull up to the shore and one member of the team lights a pipe and they pass it around amongst themselves for a few minutes. I have no idea what they are smoking. It doesn't smell like anything my father used. This stop seems to serve as their break. Their perseverance is admirable. I have never seen such dedicated workers.

When we are hungry, we motion to the cooks. The boats pull up on shore, and one of the cooks leaps out, barely touching the water, and runs up the bank to find firewood while the other one kills and plucks a chicken produced from somewhere. One man makes a fire in between three rocks and fries potatoes in a pan over it. The other heats water for tea in a pot before making chicken stew. They are very clever the way they cook over the fire, handling the blackened pots by their edges with their bare fingertips, without using potholders. The meals are simple, but delicious. What worries us, though, is the use of river water for cooking. Not only do thousands of Africans, not counting hippopotamuses and other animals, bathe in this river, the same water is used for drinking and cooking! Even though we are suffering from heat and fever, we have no choice but to drink the water despite its bad taste and filthiness. I pray none of us becomes ill from it.

The days are fine, with good weather now, but the nights are long. In the evenings, the pilots take our boats part way up on shore, tying the lines to a bush or rock on the riverbank while they spend the night in neighboring grass-thatched huts, leaving us alone on these small boats. It doesn't seem fair. The four of us have to lie down, as best as we can, on the two benches, end to end.

I sleep fairly well, though the 'bed' is hard. But the others have gotten little sleep the last two nights. Sister Lucie confided that she couldn't even close her eyes because every noise coming from the bank of the river leaves her rigid with fear. Is that a monkey or a leopard? I have heard howling and grunts, too. But what can we do?

'I try to pretend that everything is fine so as not to worry Srs. Elaine and Therese,' Sister Lucie told me. 'But what if a hippopotamus should come out of the water and bump the boat while we are sleeping and knock it over?' I didn't want to think about this. I tried to get Sister Lucie to put her imagination to rest, and to pray for courage. Giving her this advice calmed my own jitters. Surviving a wolf attack in the Syrian Desert left me feeling stronger, in ways that can be dangerous for others as well as myself. I took the vow of humility, to recognize my weaknesses along with my strengths. The two become intertwined at times like this. I must to pray for God's understanding and mercy.

2nd December

We arrived at Port Herald late this afternoon. It is the point on the Zambezi where the Shire River joins it from the north. We stopped for a half hour, which afforded the Africans up on the riverbank, a view of us. At least 200 of them squatted along the river, watching us with open mouths. It made me feel ridiculous. A kind of Indian/mulatto came aboard and told us in French that the next day, at this time, we would be in Chiromo, our destination. We hugged each other for joy at this news. But he turned out to be wrong: we found out that it is a 17-hour trip when the water is sufficiently high to go by boat; that is, when there has been sufficient rain in the northern mountains to fill the Shire river.

3rd December

Our boats stopped for the night a little beyond Port Herald. The next morning, at five AM, our pilots (guides) tried to move up the Shire, but the river was shallow and the two boats got stuck in the muddy sand. The rowers took advantage of the situation. They swam and had fun while we waited for more water in the river. When we saw our boats were beginning to float on the water, we scolded the men and told them we wanted to sleep in Chiromo, so they went back to their posts. They rowed viegorously the rest of the day, much to our relief. At sunset, I thought we might be reaching Chiromo, but the pilot told us that we still had a seven-hour ride ahead. We were furious. Then it started to rain and we were forced to retreat to the cabin, which by now, smelled damp and moldy.

Despite a night as dark as a tunnel, the African rowers continued their work, all the while singing to keep up their spirits. From time to time the boats got stuck in reeds or on sand banks. Then, the poor men had to get into the murky water and pull the boat out, turn it around, and feel their way in the dark water in order to make progress before encountering other obstacles. At one point, we heard a terrifying scream from one of the Africans and the boat seemed to lose headway. There was a great commotion outside. The agonized scream continued, causing us to nearly faint. I worried that one of them in the water might have met with a ravenous, unseen river creature. To counter such thoughts, I took up my knitting. We were all knitting now, trying to remain calm. The shouting and screaming persisted until the boat bumped against the shore. I was so distraught I wanted to go out and see what had happened, despite the rain.

'You might be in the way, if it is an accident,' Sister Lucie told me.

'But if someone is hurt, I might be able to help,' I pleaded.

'It's dark and wet out there. You could slip on the deck and fall into the river. You'd best stay inside, ' Sister Therese pointed out.

The sisters persuaded me to stay in our cabin. We began to pray while we waited to hear what had happened. After what seemed like an eternity, the cries stopped and the boat began to move again. The pilot came to report that one of the men had stumbled on a submerged alligator. The angry creature had attacked him. The man had lost most of his leg. He was bleeding badly. Two of the other rowers had carried him, half delirious, to a nearby hut. There was not much they could do for him tonight. A family in the hut and others who had heard the man's agonized cries, promised to watch over him while a boy ran to the village for a doctor.

I felt sick. The man would surely die. And, yet, there was not much I could do under the circumstances. We all fell to praying for the rower's deliverance and our own safety.

A little while later, we heard what turned out to be a monkey screeching in the dark. We could hardly breathe for the terror the sound brought to our hearts. Then we heard what sounded like grunting laughter in the distance. The pilot knocked on the door, making us jump. He told us that what we heard was a hyena, and that it was far away in the bush.

On the shore, we could see not a single house, hut, or light, now. And none of the men had a lantern. No one said a word, though each of us struggled with our own nightmares. Not one of us slept. The cabin became a place of silence, except for the sound of our knitting needles.

At one o'clock in the morning, the pilot knocked on the door's window and announced that we had reached Chiromo. The cook, who came from this place, arrived to ask us if we would like to push on to the mission station. *At such an hour?* It was unthinkable. We had had enough harrowing experiences for one night! Sister Lucie told him we would stay on board. We remained in our cabin, sitting on those hard benches, to wait for daylight. To their credit, the rowers stayed at their posts, unwilling to leave the boat before we did. They were subdued after the attack on their fellow oarsman.

Someone knocked loudly on the cabin door, startling us. Then, an unfamiliar male voice said in French, 'So, dear Sisters, what are you doing here? Do you plan to spend the night on the boat?'

Those words, so like our brothers of the Montfort Order, delighted us. They reassured us that, indeed, a member of the Montfort community had arrived to rescue us. We all began to shout at once through the door, Sister Elaine and Sister Therese bursting into tears of relief. We emerged from the cabin and saw, among the Africans with him, Father Winnen, a tall, robust man in a cleric's frock. We mistook him for the Father Prefect. Later, we found that he was the Superior of Nzama Mission, our final destination. He spoke to us in French and alternately to the Africans waiting on shore in a language we didn't understand—a moment of hearty confusion. I told him about the vicious attack on the rower. It was uppermost in my mind. I feared the man would not live through the night. Father Winnen was upset with the news and promised to talk to the crew.

Despite the tragedy, our joy at seeing such a fine man after the terrifying journey up the river lifted our spirits. We followed him to Chiromo Mission, where he had been waiting for *four* days for us to arrive! Many Africans followed with our luggage, including the trunks.

When we got to the mission, Father Winnen wanted to have supper prepared for us as we had hardly eaten that day. But so great was our relief in being in a mission, and it was so late, that food was our last thought. Moreover, we didn't want to disturb the other two Fathers at the mission who were asleep. Actually, Father Pinot, hearing the commotion, did get up to greet us briefly, but then disappeared.

Finally, at 2:30 in the morning, we were told that our bedrooms were ready. Father Winnen had given up his room for us. His large bed had been divided in two with a mosquito net for each half. Sister Therese and I slept there. It was hard to sleep—I kept hearing the cries of that poor man and visualizing his demise. Exhaustion finally caught up with me and I slept. The next morning, when the other two sisters saw that we had shared a bed, they had a good laugh.

In order not to shock the English in residence, who never travel on Sundays, we spent the next day in Chiromo. Father Winnen's African companions came to greet us, one at a time. I noticed a big difference between these Africans and others we had met earlier. These were converts with respectful manners and pleasant faces. Several of them wore metal medallions from St. Laurent around their necks or at their belts. Some had sewn them to their caps to show their intentions. I was glad we had a day here to rest and meet other converts.

*   *   *

The four sisters had reached a stage in their journey where they could no longer travel by water. Chiromo, nestled in a broad, fertile valley surrounded by lush mountains, drew its source of life from the Shire River as it meandered through the valley and from the mountain streams close by. Africans (specifically, Mang'anja) at the mission caught fish that ended up on the plates of the Fathers, and in their own pots. As the river periodically flooded and then receded, it left a rich, black covering of alluvial soil on its banks that the Mang'anja, who lived here, put to good use. They formed rows of raised mounds with their short wooden hoes in which they planted sorghum, maize, and beans. When the river's waters receded after a flood, they collected salt from nearby pans to trade to their neighbors and grew vegetables in gardens adjacent to the river's banks. In the lush mountains surrounding the valley, men hunted game and women collected berries and nuts, and dug for mushrooms. By 1904, they had already come into contact with Uzungu—*white men from South Africa, Portuguese East Africa, and Europe—who had come looking for fertile land and minerals to exploit. Missionaries, both Anglicans from England and Scottish Presbyterians were settling in the highlands. It was only recently that French Catholic Fathers had begun to settle in the lower Shire valley.*

By the time the Daughters of Wisdom arrived in what is now Malawi, a railway had been constructed by British engineers with the help of local labor. It connected the Shire valley to a new commercial center in Blantyre. However, mission stations were still few and far between. To get from Chiromo to Nzama mission, a distance of over 250 miles, it was necessary for the four sisters to go on foot or by machila. This conveyance consisted of a canvas hammock suspended from two long bamboo poles that were carried by four African porters, one at each corner—their shoulders bore the brunt of the weight. The machila was already known in Europe. Explorers penetrating tropical areas in Asia and Latin America, as well as in Africa, had used it. The Montfort missionaries, knowing of the machila, recommended to the Superior of the Filles de la Sagesse *in France that the four sisters bring hammocks produced in Europe with them. The Africans would provide the bamboo poles and labor.*

For the overland journey from Chiromo to Nzama the village chief of Nzama recruited two hundred Mang'anja men to carry the four sisters and their luggage to the new mission. They had arrived in Chiromo fifteen days before the Sisters and had been waiting for them ever since.

Sister Marie-Reine in front of her *machila* before entering lion country.

CHAPTER 22

Through Lion Country

Journal, 5th December, Chiromo

At one o'clock in the afternoon, we left Chiromo and began our overland journey to the mission in Nzama. Fair skies brightened our departure. It took us some time to figure out how to get into the *maquila* without ending up on our sides or heads, at the same time keeping our habits and *coiffes [square cloth headdresses]* in order. I was not at all enthusiastic about riding in such a contraption. I offered to walk. Both Father Winnen and the Africans insisted that it was much safer for me to be carried, making reference to poisonous snakes, scorpions, and large ants with fearful jaws that bite, leaving a stinging venom and their heads embedded in a person's skin.

I needed no more convincing. I also recalled that, after all, I had spent six weeks in a *haudaj* in the Syrian Desert, which, I must admit, offered more room than the *maquila*. At least the weather blessed us with sunshine.

We traveled through a palm forest this afternoon. We were told it was infested with lions. The day before, Africans had killed two lions outside Chiromo village because a child had recently been attacked and dragged off by a lioness. No one had seen her or the lioness since. It was not a story to settle the nerves. I was glad we were traveling in a large group.

We arrived at a camping place in the bush at about six in the evening. Instead of lions, we found three caravan groups already camped there. In the middle, two tents had been set up, facing each other. About twenty fires lit the camp to keep the animals away. We joined other travelers for meals and Father Winnen entertained us with stories. After dinner, we four retreated to one of the tents to sleep on folding camp beds. The sound of roaring lions—their growls like the echo of hollow drums—kept us awake until it started raining hard, causing another sort of unpleasantness. We heard no more lions, but water leaked into our tent and softened our previously starched *coiffes*. It drenched our clothes and bedding. It was a most miserable night!

6th December, Mt. Thyolo *[pronounced Cho-lo]*

We got up early and were on the track by six o'clock, reaching the foot of
Thyolo Mountain about nine. It was pouring rain by then and we were glad we
had put on our wool capes with the hoods. The path up was steep and very
slippery. The bearers were not able to make the climb with their heavy loads,
so we climbed out of our *machilas.* Using the poles as walking sticks against
the slick mud, we were able to get about half way up the mountain. It was not
easy. We constantly felt our shoes slipping on the mud. It was only our poles
that kept us from sliding back down. The rain didn't help. The steady downpour continued for more than an hour. When it let up a bit, we stopped for a
brief rest. I looked back across the valley and saw green ridges and peaks poking up above a sea of fog, but nothing more. Then something purple and white
on a bush caught my eye next to the track. It was a delicate flower hanging
from a stem, with beads of rain clinging to it. And there were others. I pointed
it out to Father Winnen and asked him what it was. 'An orchid,' he said.
'There are many wild orchids in these mountains.' I was enchanted; I had no
idea that we would find such flowers in this remote land. The other sisters
gathered around to see it. Its fragile beauty gave us a lift.

    None of us complained as we climbed slowly up the track again. We
kept going for several hours. Finally, when we could go no farther, the bearers,
out of pity for us, once again hoisted our *machila* up onto their shoulders and
the climb continued.

    At two o'clock, we reached a timber cabin used by the British Railway
Club. Father Winnen told us it was an official rest place for railway workers.
Inside, we found a large table and six beds in three rooms. The only guests we
had were rats. After the trek in the rain, we could have not wished for anything
better. The poor Africans huddled against trees outside, using some of the luggage as shelter.

7th December, To Nguludi

At four in the morning a whistle sounded, thanks to Father Winnen. It woke
the entire group. Without having had any breakfast, and in complete silence,
the Africans took up their loads and were off again. I heard them singing.
Their cheerful fortitude amazed me.

    An hour later, we climbed back into our *machilas.* We were on our way
to Father Prezeau's residence in Nguludi. The road was a good one and the
Africans' pace increased because they knew we were in reach of the mission.
An hour later, the singing became louder as more Africans joined the caravan.
The bearers started running and, as a result, we were splattered with red mud
being flung up into the *machilas.* Even the square shape of our *coiffes* had dis-
appeared with the rain and the ride. Finally, at 11:00 we arrived at the Shire
Prefecture where Father Prezeau, a lean, angular man with slim hands and

busy eyes, waited with Father Gachassin and Brother Cleopha to welcome us on the veranda of his house. I was so shaken up in the *machila* by the porters' running that when we stopped and I got out and tried to walk over to the veranda, I must have looked like a drunkard. Our once white veils and blouses were rust colored from the mud. Only our gray habits identified us as *Filles de la Sagesse.*

We found a sizable group of Africans at Nguludi Mission who were there to meet us, including several women. They had come from Nzama mission to cheer us on. Among the gathering was the Chief of Nzama village, a stout man dressed in a rust-colored toga who used a beautifully carved walking stick to support himself. His name was very long and difficult to remember. Through Father Winnen, he told us that he wanted to come to Chiromo to welcome us. However, the Father Prefect had told him to stay in Nzama, jokingly telling him that he was too fat to carry a *machila*. Instead, he came to Nguludi. He had been waiting here for over ten days for us to arrive. The chief admitted that he was responsible for keeping an eye on the porters and for any damage or accidents that might come to us, or our luggage. The Father was pleased with the chief's work and gave him a gift of a large umbrella and fan that he accepted with dignity then turned over to an assistant to carry. Afterwards, the chief raised his hand to us, as if to bless us on our safe arrival. We sisters were touched and slightly amused.

8th December, Nguludi

The Father Prefect set up two tables in the dining room. We were pleased with the arrangement: it made us feel like part of the mission family. The practice was continued for the rest of our stay in Nguludi. That evening, we prepared the chapel for a special benediction: we placed a table in front of the altar to serve as a pedestal for our statue of Mary Immaculate and the solemn feast of the Immaculate Conception. It was the first benediction at the mission. We were glad to be part of it.

9th December

Frs. Prezeau and Winnen left early with Srs. Lucie and Therese to go to Blantyre to present the sisters and their credentials to the British government authorities and to buy some household necessities. When we saw them again, they related they'd completed their tasks and had had dinner with a Mr. Greffines and his wife. They returned to the mission just before dark. In the meantime, Sister Elaine and I had a chance to do some laundry. When the Africans saw our intentions, they insisted on taking over. We thanked them, and enjoyed a nice stroll around the grounds during which we talked about our trip up the Zambezi and what a nightmare the Shire River had been. We heard giggles behind us and, turning around, found a group of children in scant clothing following us, apparently fascinated by the two strangers and their unintelligible conversation. It was a beautiful day and the blue-green mountains to the east were sparklingly clear. I could see and smell smoke coming from fires set in the foothills and wondered about their purpose. I also noticed that Mt. Thyolo, which we had climbed three days earlier, was among the smaller peaks around. Tomorrow, Sunday, we will spend the whole day in Nguludi. We hope that by Monday, our baggage will have arrived so that we can continue our journey.

13th December, To Nzama

A group of porters, hungry and tired, arrived with our baggage this morning. Father Winnen, who seems to be on good terms with them, noted that the men had lost weight. It must have been a difficult trip. We checked our trunks and found that everything was there, except for the cask of white wine. It was completely empty. I was relieved to find that the medicines and bandages I had packed were still there. I asked about the man who had been attacked by the alligator. The Africans hung their heads, saying nothing. They had given me the answer. I vowed to offer a prayer for the brave man and his family. He had lost his life in service to us.

17th December

Under the protection of St. Lucie (whose feast day it was) we climbed back into our *machilas,* eager to reach Nzama. The luggage carriers went first, then our four *machilas.* Father Winnen led the caravan and the Father Prefect brought up the rear. After a half hour, we found that the bamboo poles for the hammocks were useless. Sister Lucie's were so badly bent by the weight that we had to stop. While the carriers repaired hers, the rest of us went on and arrived about three o'clock at the house of Mr. Brackenridge just north of Blantyre. Father Prezeau stayed back with Sister Lucie. They were to have lunch with a magistrate in Blantyre, and join us later. We are staying at the Brackenridge home tonight.

18th December

After Blantyre, we saw no more European houses. We continued through the bush and finally pitched our tents among the African porters who were quite amazed to see the Daughters of Wisdom putting up their own tents amongst them.

The third night we camped in an African [Mang'anja] village where we easily got acquainted with the women, despite language barriers. They have sweet dispositions and are very hard working. Most of them wore cloths wrapped around their waists that covered everything but their bare feet. Their hair was either shorn or they wore a colorful headscarf. Their houses are made of brick-red mud and wattle with grass-thatched roofs. Father Prefect talked to the women and we went inside one of their homes where we found a fireplace dug in the center, stools, and a couple of chairs. What impressed me, though, was how they stored grains and other foods in large, round woven baskets, each with a lid of woven grass. I also noticed a large gourd used for water. There were many children of various ages running around. Some of the smallest ran inside their houses or crouched behind their mothers in fear when they saw us, which amused their mothers and the men, including the Fathers.

The distance between the mission in Nguludi and the new one in Nzama is 50 leagues [about 175 miles]. The journey took us five days. On the fourth day, two Africans, who had been sent by Father Cadoret from Nzama, arrived with fresh provisions. We were getting tired and hungry by then and were elated to see them. We even had real French bread, which delighted the French sisters.

On the fifth day, we awoke to rain and fog. It enveloped us all morning and dampened our mood as we rode toward Nzama. Around midday, it began to clear and on a hillside we saw two European-style brick buildings. The carriers began shouting, 'Nzama, Nzama!' Africans from Nzama came toward us, one of them carrying a bottle of milk. It had been sent ahead by one of the Fathers from Nzama, Father Deau. We got down from our *machilas* and gulped it up. After a five-hour trek, it was refreshing. Then we heard shouting and singing in the road ahead, and suddenly Father Deau, a florid, jolly man, appeared with a group of African men and women, shouting, singing, and ululating. The nearer they came, the louder the singing. They accompanied us all the way to our new home.

As we drew nearer, the two houses we'd seen earlier became more visable. One was larger and a bit higher on the hill than the other. Father Deau told us that the Fathers lived in the larger one. The one lower down, which looked like a small chalet, turned out to be ours.

When we finally arrived at the mission, we were so grateful to be there that the first thing we did was to visit the chapel. The oratory turned out to be too small to hold all four of us Sisters, as well as the Fathers, and we spilled out into the sanctuary. The Africans filled the catechumen room at the back of the chapel. We sang the Magnificat after completing prayers to give thanks for our safe arrival.

Afterwards, we went to the dining room in the Fathers' house where eight places had been set at a long table. Father Deau had killed an éland, an animal like a large antelope with straight, spiraled horns and a hump at his shoulders. The meat of the beast had been roasted and was served with rice and all kinds of sauces. The aromas of the feast were intoxicating. I was famished by then and enjoyed the meal immensely. After dinner, the Fathers took us to our new home. The Father Prefect, Father Prezeau, assembled us for a blessing of our new house, which had already been dedicated to our Sacred Mother with the name 'Immaculate Conception.' Afterwards, the Fathers retreated and left us in peace.

Mother Patrice would be amazed to see how spacious and clean our house is. It has nine rooms that are well designed. We could easily have six or seven sisters here. A veranda runs around two sides of the house, to protect us from the sun. The views of the surrounding hills and valley are beautiful. At last, we are in our new home. And, having written so much, I am ready to retire.

Settling into Nzama. Sister Marie-Reine is in front row, far left.

CHAPTER 23

Settling Into Nzama

Journal, 20th December, Nzama Mission

Our first Sunday here, and it is overcast and pouring. The rain is as cold as it is in France this time of year. For the last three days we have continued to have our meals with the Fathers. It is not something we anticipated. Although we feared offending them, we finally got up the courage to ask to have our meals separately, in our own house. Julius and Govan prepared breakfast for us this morning in the refectory. Two girls, Mangira and Maesi, who are catechumens preparing for baptism, washed the dishes. Being Sunday, Mass was held. But no one came. The weather is too cold.

The rain is continuous with a fierce, driving wind. We are constantly shivering. Reflecting on the climate of the past few weeks, we have gone from very hot, humid weather on the coast and up the Zambezi to freezing weather here in Nzama. We are inside, now, huddled over a small fire in the refectory, reading, writing and knitting. None of us says what she is thinking—that this is not the weather we had expected. We were told that it is summer in the Southern Hemisphere this time of year and we would find the weather warm and comfortable, without the need for heavy wraps.

In unpacking a crate today, we found that the butter, chocolate, and cookies of all kinds survived the journey in good shape, much to our relief. They had been put into the crate with ice, and I guess they were buried deep enough in the ship to stay cool, so that the overland journey from Chiromo to Nzama had not affected them. Out of the twelve apples we packed, half were rotten. We took the seeds out of the rotten ones and washed them for planting later. As for the other six apples, we gave them to the Fathers, who feasted on them. We were still grieving over the empty cask of white wine, but discovered the barrel of red wine we'd brought intact and untouched. Since the Fathers had run out of wine to make the Sacrament, this new source prompted Father Winnen to exclaim, 'Our prayers have been answered,' which amused us. Some things we thought we had brought—vestments and ornaments for the chapel—seem to have disappered since we left Nguludi. No use in fretting about it; we were bound to lose something on that rough trip to Nzama.

23rd December

The last few days have been spent unpacking our trunks and sorting out our belongings. Each of us has chosen a room. Mine has a window with a view down the valley. All the rooms have a bed with a wood frame and stuffed mattress, a desk and chair. I am glad that Mother Patrice advised us to bring our own linens and towels from the Mother House. The toilet and bath are at the end of the hall. They are as clean as the rest of the house.

It looks as though Mangira and Maesi will be doing the work of keeping things neat and tidy. Mangira is tall with a broad, smooth face as if melted chocolate were poured over a mold. Her black eyes are set far apart and her flat nose flairs out to balance senuous, full lips below. She wears her hair very short against her scalp. It emphazises her 'widow's peak,' though she's no widow. She has a quiet dignity that I like. Of the two girls, Mangira is the shyer one. Maesi is petite and a lighter brown than Mangira. She also wears her hair cropped short. Perhaps it is easier to keep clean this way. She is blessed with a perfect oval face, delicate, expressive eyes, and a small, straight nose. What caught my attention most was her beautiful smile—it revealed very straight, pearl-like teeth. She appears to be the more lively one, often giggling as they scrub our clothes together. Both wear colorful cotton wraps around their hips that fall to their ankles. They have spent the last two days washing the rusty mud out of our habits and coiffes. Bless them; it is tedious work. They told us the water comes from a nearby river. It must be fetched and carried back in large pails on their heads, then heated in a metal cauldron over an outdoor fire before the girls can begin scrubbing the clothes in large pots. The two of them are very serious about their work. And with four sisters they are going to be kept busy. I saw yesterday that they use rags to mop the floors. It means that they spend a great deal of time bent over from the waist to accomplish this task. It would give me a backache. I thank the Blessed Virgin (and Father Winnen) for the girls' capable presence in our house.

Christmas is only two days off. It hardly seems possible. I wonder what kind of celebration we will have? Today, we four enjoyed breakfast together and were about to have a meeting to decide how we should divide the household responsibilities, when Fr. Deau called us to come and see the temporary altar they had set up in our chapel. Father Prefect is going to celebrate the first Mass in it at 5:30 tomorrow morning. With a bath and a clean habit and coiffe, I will be ready for it. I wonder if any of the Africans will come?

24th December

It is late, but I want to put down what I have just seen—a Christmas Eve celebration to honor our arrival that I will never forget. About 400 Africans, whom
Father Winnen told us are *Mang'anja,* came with drums, wood flutes and voices to sing and dance in the Fathers' courtyard tonight. A fire had been lit there
for the occasion. Chairs were brought out for the Fathers and for us, with
woven mats spread on the ground around the edge of the courtyard for the
Africans. One of the chief's assistants brought an intricately carved chair for
him to sit in, and several of the older men brought small stools. The villagers
arrived in costumes, one that looked like a large moa and another like a serpent, made out of raffia. The Serpent snaked and danced around the circle,
jumping and kicking with many legs sticking out below. The costume was very
clever with large eyes and a wide-open mouth. Chief Njobvuyalema of Nzama
gave a speech in Chimang'anja, the local language, welcoming us. It was
translated by Father Winnen. The chief praised us for coming so far to bring
light to his people. He also said he was happy to see four sisters as women are
very important in their culture. Then several women came forward with baskets of bananas, mangos, and avocados for us. We responded, thanking them
and expressing our joy at being here to share Christmas with them. The
women trilled [ululated] after hearing the translation, and invited us to join
them in dancing. We declined with excuses of fatigue, though with our tall
headdresses shaking—which must have looked like costumes to the villagers—we would have added something unique.

The people danced most of the night, with Chief Njobvuyalema being
the liveliest dancer of all. We sisters finally retired to our house just after midnight. I could still hear the villagers singing and shuffling, and smell the
pinewood fire well after retiring.

One thing I know now is that if I am to work here, I must learn the language.

25th December, CHRISTMAS

Today Father Winnen said three Masses in our chapel, assisted by Fathers
Cadoret and Deau. The Africans came, dressed in their best clothes, and
squeezed into the catechumen room to hear Mass. The men sang with the
Fathers and the women sang with us. To see them with their catechism books
was a special pleasure. The women showed us their books, each one opening
hers to the first page so we might write her name there.

After Mass, Father Prezeau sent for us and we went with the Fathers to
visit the closest Mang'anja villages. In the first one, we found the women
preparing a Christmas feast. An outdoor cooking fire had been lit in the courtyard, where a huge pot of stew was slowly bubbling. It smelled delicious, like
the meals we had on the caravan in Syria, with a combination of grains, rice,

and onions mixed with the smoky flavor of the fire. In another pot on the ground, a thick, hot gruel of what looked like cornmeal was emitting bursts of steam as a thin, walnut-skinned woman stirred it with great energy. She was so intent on her task that she hardly looked up when we came through to greet people. When I asked what it was, Father Winnen told us it was *nsima,* their staple. I looked puzzled and he explained that the gruel is beaten rapidly while still hot until it becomes thick. It sets for a few minutes and when solid is cut into pieces. It is served with every meal. The Africans take a small hunk of *nsima* in one hand, usually the right one, and roll it into a ball then make a dent in it with their thumb to form a sort of spoon to scoop up stew or relish, much as we might dip bread in a sauce, a very clever idea.

No exchange of presents takes place here, as in France. Feasting and dancing occupy the converts on Christmas. Only a few Mang'anja have become Christians: many are still pagans with their own beliefs. Others are Mohammedans.

After greeting people in the village, we went to see the Fathers' first house, where they lived before their mission house was built. It is made of wood and mud, and is still standing, but is no longer used. We looked inside. It was a dark place with an earthen floor. We felt sad knowing they had to live in such a place for eight months.

On our way back to the mission, we stopped in the chief's village to pay our respects. When we got there, Chief Njobvuyalema's wives were outside his large house sitting on woven grass mats on the ground talking quietly and playing with their youngest children. Nothing we could see set them apart from the other women, either in dress or manner. The way they sat reminded me of village women at home in Mesopotamia, except that there, women usually sit on carpets. I could see that the wives and other women were trying not to stare at us, especially at the white coiffes on our heads. One of them had a small child who appeared to have a fever. She spoke to Father Winnen, apparently asking for help. He turned to me, having heard from Sister Lucie that I am a pharmacologist. I crouched down to the child and put my hand across his brow, with Father Winnen explaining what I was doing. His little forehead was hot and his eyes listless. I told his worried mother that I was at a loss because I hadn't brought my medicine bag with me. But I recommended that she try and get his fever down by wrapping him in cold towels or cloths. I promised to come the next day with my kit. It is hard to watch a child suffering.

When we returned to the mission, we had two more Christmas Masses and then a feast of our own. Just before Vespers, Father Prezeau baptized an eleven-month-old mulatto child that had arrived on the doorstep of the mission unannounced one day. To baptize this child on Christmas Day seemed fitting. Father Winnen told us that a Protestant family had brought the child to the mission and had left him in a basket in front of the door of the Fathers' house. A few coins were tucked into the basket. He guessed that whoever had given up the baby wanted the Fathers to raise him as a Catholic. Father Prezeau asked Father Winnen to serve as the child's godfather, a role the Father said he was proud to fill. The ceremony was beautiful and especially meaningful as it coincided with our Lord Jesus Christ's birth. Now, as I write this, I'm beginning to wonder who will really raise the child, surely not the Fathers. Nine other children from the villages will be baptized in January, we were told. The little girls will be named after us, the boys after the Fathers.

Having unpacked our trunks, we got out a box of children's clothes we had brought from France, thinking they would be welcome. But the Fathers, and the Africans, told us they prefer *chitenje* [plain cotton cloth] rather than European clothing with buttons and sleeves and trousers to figure out. However, it did please them to get pearls and copper buttons; they like to use them as decorations with their *chitenje.*

27th December

Father Prezeau returned to Nguludi today, with a group of Africans from his mission who had accompanied us to Nzama to help with the luggage. He is a fine Prefect and we feel reassured that someone so dedicated to his work is not too far away.

It seems that all of us are suffering from fever. It may be a consequence of having been subjected to extremes in the weather the past two weeks and because fatigue has finally caught up with us. I have tried to keep going, but today, at the other Sisters' urging, I am spending the day resting. At least I know what medicines to take for the fever. To keep busy, we are learning the local language. Father Winnen gave us some notebooks with phrases and Mangira and Maesi are providing informal lessons while we mend the garments of the Fathers, who are busy building the kitchen for our house. In a few months time the Fathers will go to the Prefecture in Nguludi to help build a house like ours for that mission. It seems they are as occupied with hammers, wood, and cement as they are with saving souls.

I returned to the chief's village yesterday, to see if the sick child was any better and to give him a little medicine that might bring the fever down. Father Winnen accompanied me, and acted as translator. We arrived in the mid-afternoon. Father told me the women would have returned from their farms by then. We first went to Chief Njobvuyalema's house, but he was not there, having gone to another village on business. His first wife, who is the oldest of the three, offered to take us to the home of the mother with the sick child. The first wife's name is Chilembe, but the Mang'anja villagers call her *Mai* [Mother of] Ng'ambi, for her first-born child, who is a girl. Mai Ng'ambi has a weathered face. Her scalp is shaved except for a few gray hairs showing around her ears. Long earlobes set her apart from the other two wives who seem to be in their child-bearing years. The youngest wife is quite pretty, with large eyes and a pert nose.

We walked about a half-kilometer to another compound, a homestead with three houses and two smaller huts. A boy greeted Father Winnen and took us to the home of the ailing child. Father Winnen called, *'Odi,'* and stood before the doorway, waiting. I thought this unusual. But, he explained that it was common practice to let people know someone had arrived since few houses have doors. The mother came and curtsied, then invited us in, smiling shyly at me. It was dark inside; only a table with an unlit lantern on it was visible at first. There was one chair, which she offered to Father Winnen. He sat down and inquired about the boy.

A stream of words came from the woman, few of which I understood. She was very animated and looked from me to the child, whom I finally realized was lying on a mat against a wall, covered by a dirty *chitenje* cloth. Father Winnen told me that she had taken my advice and bathed her child in cool water. It seemed to help, but now he had loose stools. I put my medical bag on the table and asked her to light the lantern so I could have a better look at the boy.

She lit it and walked over to her son's mat and knelt down and motioned me to come over. The child, who appeared to be about four-years-old, stirred. Rather than try to put a thermometer in his mouth, which might have frightened him and broken the thermometer, I knelt down and held his wrist, then put my hand on his forehead. He was quiet, but his eyes spoke of fear. I asked Father Winnen to explain to him what I was doing. Father came over and stood behind me, while I talked to the child in soothing tones, telling him that if he drank a lot of the medicine tea I was leaving with his mother, and continued to rest, he should feel better soon. I smiled to reassure him and got up slowly and turned to his mother. I explained that I was leaving six white tablets for the fever along with shreaded, dried ginger from which she was to make tea for him. I gave her directions for giving the boy the medicine and stressed that she must make sure the water was boiled for at least five minutes before she made the tea.

Father Winnen had duly translated all this, pointing to the tablets and the tea. But he abruptly stopped and said to me, 'How is she going to know what minutes are? These people do not have watches nor do they really understand time, except as the sun rises and sets and the seasons change.'

I blushed. 'Tell her to put the water on the fire and, when it is bubbling hard, to let it continue until she sees that some of it has boiled away. Then she should take it off the fire and make the tea.' I explained that she could save the boiled water that she didn't use for cooking.

As Father Winnen translated this, the mother nodded her head and looked at me, then smiled. *'Zikomo,'* she said. *Zikomo kwan mbili.'* I knew she was thanking me.

On the way back to the mission, Father Winnen asked me how I had come to be a pharmacist. I told him the story of my interest in medicinal plants, beginning in the Syrian Desert. And how, when I completed my Profession, I had been sent to a hospital to learn more about healing practices and pharmacology. Working with a doctor in Toulouse and then applying what I learned to take care of the deaf and dumb girls at the Institute strengthened my conviction that healing is what I wanted to do.

'We are blessed to have you, Sister Marie-Reine. You are greatly needed here.'

I thanked him, but told him I still had much to learn.

Later, I thought about time; the way we measure it, and how we come to depend on our timepieces. But if Africans don't have watches, I must adjust and learn how to prescribe medicines that use a different method of keeping track of time. Their lives are more like the way the nomads in the Syrian desert live, using their own sense of time: internal clocks adjusted to their ritual of prayers and the needs of their camels.

31st December

As a New Year's gift the Fathers brought us one new bed, so that we now have five in the house. We are still too tired from our journey and the Christmas festivities to celebrate, except with a Mass. But I am feeling that this mission is truly my new home. The end of 1904 brought us to this place after two long months of travel. Now, 1905 marks the beginning of our new life in southern Africa.

CHAPTER 24

Trial and Error

Journal, 16th January 1905

I have been neglecting this journal, but my work is becoming more important. I am still struggling to learn the Mang'anja language. I do like the sound of it even thought it is not easy. Yesterday, Mangira, the older of the two girls who help us, had difficulty hiding her amusement over the way I pronounced certain words in her mother tongue. When I asked her to correct me, she hesitated, becoming shy. Later, I learned from Father Winnen that the reason she acted in such a manner is because of the difference between our ages: here, young people and children are expected to be respectful and subservient to older people, even a few years older.

I have become concerned about the small boy to whom I gave medicine two weeks ago. I want to see if he is any better. The Fathers are too busy with construction work to accompany me to the village. I asked the other sisters if any of them would like to go with me. Srs. Elaine and Therese declined, saying they were busy working on plans for a school at the mission. Sister Lucie—bless her—told me she would be happy to go that afternoon. I like her cheerful practicality.

The weather had cleared, turning dry and crisp. Sister Lucie and I put on our cloaks. I took my medicine kit, and we set out. I remembered the route to the chief's village and from there I felt sure I would recognize the track to the homestead where the mother and her children live. As we walked along, I noticed a trail of mango pits, yellow and stringy, dropped here and there on the edge of the burnt-orange road. Looking around, I didn't see anyone sucking the fruit. Then I looked up and found dark-leafed trees hovering above us on either side of the road. I knew they were mango trees, but larger than the ones in Mosul. I stopped to look for mangos in the nearest tree, and was not disappointed. Egg-shaped fruits hung down from the branches like green ornaments, but they were too high to reach. Sister Lucie followed my gaze and, I'm sure, was wondering why I was craning my neck.

'It must be mango season,' I said happily, pointing to the large lemon-colored pits along the road. Just then we heard the most awful ruckus in the tree—a wild screeching, followed by great commotion in the green canopy above us. Suddenly, a gray monkey with a frightened expression and a mouth full of dripping mango burst through the leafy cover, bouncing from one branch to another, a second monkey chasing her. They made a terrible racket. The first monkey dropped her fruit and it fell with a thud right in front of us. It happened so quickly we were speechless.

Sister Lucie looked over at me and began laughing, pointing to my head. I realized I had raised my medicine kit to protect myself from being hit. I lowered it somewhat sheepishly.

'What did you think you were doing? Protecting your coiffe from the mangos or the flying monkeys?' Sister Lucie grinned.

'I didn't see the monkeys. I like mangos and was trying to figure out how we could get some down, but I was interrupted by those rambunctious thieves.'

'I know less about mangos than either you or the monkeys, it seems,' Sister Lucie said. 'I've never tasted one.'

'Really? You are in for a treat. They are the most succulent fruit. It looks like we'll have plenty of them here in Nzama.'

At that point two African men, in trousers and jackets, appeared from the other direction. We nodded politely, but did not attempt to greet them. Then a small group of women, some with babies tied firmly to their backs, came toward us in the distance. When they got closer and saw us, they gawked at us—two oddly dressed *Uzungu* [European] women. I quieted my unsteady nerves and said brightly, *'Moni. Mwle bwanji?'*

The village women, who were dressed in a rainbow of bright *chitenje,* curtsied slightly to us. A couple of them covered their mouths, as if to suppress a giggle. Finally an older woman answered, *'Ndili bwino,'* and stopped to greet us, extending her hand to shake mine. She wanted to know where we came from.

'The mission. Do you know Father Winnen?' I asked.

'Aie, Yes.' The woman still had hold of my hand and was shaking it gently up and down.

'It is beyond Nzama village.' I felt pleased that I had gotten this much out without stumbling. Sister Lucie was silent, listening to me.

'Where are you going?' the woman asked me. Her high cheekbones, flat face, and yellow-brown skin set her apart from her companions. She also was less shy than the others. She finally dropped my hand.

'A *nyumba ya Mai* . . . ,' I stuttered. I had forgotten the boy's mother's name. *Mother-of-whom?* I was thinking desperately. *'Mai ya Chuge,'* I burst out.

'I know her.' The woman turned to the others and they responded with nods, or 'Yes, we know her.'

'She is married to the son of my husband's sister,' the woman said, then introduced herself. 'You do not have far to go.' She shook each of our hands, as did the other women, and they moved off down the road while I tried to figure out what her relationship was to the woman we were on our way to meet.

'*Trez bon.* You did well,' Sister Lucie told me excitedly. 'You are a far better linguist than I am.'

'When we practice together at the mission, it is easier because we can stop and correct one another,' I reminded her. 'But I got a little flustered knowing that I was speaking to a woman who has grown up with the language. Also, I'm still wondering how she is related to Mai Chuge.'

'Umm. It sounds like she might be a grown niece of some sort. We should visit the villages more often to practice the language and learn about their family relationships.'

'It will be your turn to do the greeting the next time we see someone,' I told her playfully. But we didn't see anyone else until we reached Chief Njobvuyalema's village where we greeted a couple of women in the courtyard. They pointed us in the direction of the track that led to Mai Chuge's homestead. As we neared it, I saw cirrus clouds scudding across the mountain peaks and smelled cooking fires nearby.

'*Odi,*' I called as we entered the compound, just as I'd seen Father Winnen do.

No one answered, so I tried again, more loudly, '*O-di.*'

A boy about nine years of age appeared, shadowed in the dark doorway. His bare rounded chest revealed the outline of his ribs. He wore a pair of shorts that needed mending and was barefoot. The children have little to wear.

I introduced myself and told him we were here to visit his mother and to find out how his little brother was feeling. I explained that I had left medicine for him the last time I visited. 'I don't remember seeing you then. This is Sister Lucie. We stay at Nzama Mission.'

The boy's eyes moved from his feet to us, especially to our coiffes. It looked as if he was trying to decide if our headdresses were real or not. 'My mother is not here.'

I was disappointed. 'If she is away,' I told him, 'we won't stay. It might be some time before she returns. Is your small brother, the one called Chuge, better?'

The boy smiled, then his face took on a puzzled expression. 'Chuge? I am Chuge. The brother who was sick is Bembo.' He looked down as if to cover his amusement.

'Oh. I didn't know. Your mother told me to call her *Mai Chuge,* and I thought that she was referring to your brother. Are you the oldest?'

'Yes, Madam. That is why my mother is Mai Chuge.'

'I see. Is Bembo any better?'

'Yes.'

While this conversation was unraveling, a small group of adults with children had siddled up to stare at us.

Sister Lucie turned around and saw them before I did. She began greeting some of them with *'Moni. Mwle bwanji,'* extending her hand in greeting.

I smiled, watching her, then remembered the purpose of my call.

A talkative woman, overhearing our exchange, said she recognized me from my last visit. She told me that Bembo had recovered. 'We are most grateful to you, Sister. Mai Chuge's boy is well. The reason you do not find him here is that he is with his mother. They have gone to Anyani village to visit her brother. But, if you have time, I have a child who is ill. I would take her to the clinic, but it is too far.'

I nodded and followed the woman to her house, carrying my medicine bag. Entering the dark house, I stood for a moment adjusting my eyes to the poor light. I saw a thin girl of about twelve years, lying on a pallet looking feverish, her body shivering intermittently.

'How long has she been like this?' I asked, squatting down next to the pallet. From what I could see, I suspected malaria. The disease is rampant here in the rainy season, according to Father Winnen. Using my best efforts, I spoke softly to the girl in her language to reassure her and put my hand on her forehead. She was burning with fever. I took her pulse and lifted one of her eyelids to look at the whites of her eyes, which were shot through with red vessels. She began moaning and talking incoherently.

'She has malaria. Have you seen a doctor?'

"No. We took her to the *sinyanga*. We thought someone might have bewitched her. There are those who envy her because she is clever.'

'The *sinyanga*?'

'Yes. He lives in a homestead nearby.'

'Did it help? Who is this *sinyanga*?'

'A healer. He uses our traditional medicine. We had to give him a goat when he came to treat this daughter of mine.'

'I see. And the goat?'

'It was for his work of healing, using his medicines.'

'Is there any way I might meet this *sinyanga*?' I knew it was a bold question, but I wanted to find out.

'You would have to ask Chief Njobvuyalema,' she told me.

'Let me leave some tablets for your daughter. Hopefully, they will help. Keep her warm while the chills last, then wash her in cool water to lower her fever.'

On the way back to the mission Sr. Lucie and I didn't say a word for a while because I was digesting what I had been told. Finally, she said, 'I can see that you have the gift of healing, Sister Marie. Soon, the word will spread. But the woman told you she sought the advice of another person. Who is this person?'

'A *sinyanga*. a healer who uses traditional methods. I think it is important that I meet this person before I go much further. I have no idea what a *sinyanga* uses in the way of medicines, where they come from, or how he prepares and administers them. Some must be taken from plants or roots,' I told her. 'Until I learn about his ways, and the people come to know me better, I should be careful. I could get into trouble.'

'What kind of trouble? You trained in European pharmacology and medical treatments. Surely, French medicine is far better than any kind of primitive healing.'

'That may be true. The woman said she thought her daughter was bewitched, and that is why she took her to the *sinyanga*. Witchcraft is beyond my skills.'

'Bewitched?' That sounds like something out of medieval times.'

'It seems the Africans have their own beliefs about illness and health. I need to be cautious and not give out medicines until I learn more about those beliefs.'

'That seems best,' Sister Lucie agreed. 'None of the rest of us has the kind of medical knowledge you do,' she reminded me.

We arrived home in time for Vespers and I prayed for the courage to trust what I do not know. I must listen carefully and respect what local people have to teach me.

Tonight, as I write this, I'm not so sure that the kind of training I have will be of help to these villagers. What I learned from Dr. Villiard about diseases and healing was scientific, but many of the drugs we use are derived from plants; look at ginger, and also at spireas, which comes from the rose family. Perhaps there are plants here that are used to treat the villagers' illnesses and maladies. I must find out. First, though, I need to gain the trust of Chief Njobvuyalema, so that he will allow me to visit this *sinyanga*.

23rd April, Nzama Mission

Over the past months I have treated several cases of diarrhea, which is rampant due to the lack of sanitation and clean drinking water. I am doing my best to educate the women about the importance of boiling the water they bring home from the river. It is an uphill trek. They tell me they are so busy cultivating their crops, looking for firewood, tending to their children's needs, that they have no time for boiling water. Part of the problem is that they do not SEE the bacteria and microbes I tell them are in the water. In their minds what they do not see, does not exit. If only I had a microscope, I could show them. But would they believe those wiggling things actually have the power to make them ill? Another problem lies in the muddy water bordered by reeds along the river. It is a perfect place for bilharzia-bearing snails. It is hard for mothers and their children to make a connection between the blood they find in their urine and those small snails in the river. But when the disease takes over their bodies, it leads to death.

Each new day brings challenges to test my skills. Yesterday, a woman in great distress arrived at the mission from Anyani village and pleaded with me to help her daughter who had been in labor for two days. I have refrained from offering my services unless someone calls me and Mai Kamu's anguish touched me. I had no recourse but to go. I put on my cloak because it was raining and followed her to their compound. It was her daughter's first baby.

When we got there, she led me to a hut where her pregnant daughter sat on a stool, her legs spread wide. Her head rested against a solid-looking, older woman sitting behind her. She looked exhausted. Her eyes were closed. A soft, woven mat had been spread on the ground where the baby would be delivered. The expectant mother looked anemic, spent. Several women were in the hut to assist with the birth, including a gray-haired grandmother, whom I was told was the midwife. Mai Kamu's laboring daughter began groaning in pain. I told Mai Kamu to boil water in a big pot and to bring it to the hut.

In the meantime, I paid my respects to the midwife and asked her about the woman's condition. She told me that the baby's feet were about to come out first. She had tried to turn the baby around, without success. I suggested that if we worked together, we might be able to shift the position of the baby. She looked at my garb and youth, and hesitated. I asked if it would be possible for me to inspect the baby's progress. The midwife seemed nearly as tired and upset as the mother. She quickly agreed.

Several women in the room moved to allow me to kneel down in front of the laboring woman's spread legs. It looked as if her water had broken, but that the vaginal canal was not responding to the mother's efforts to bear down. I could see the curled-up feet of the baby, and, from checking her outside, could tell the baby's head was still at the top of the womb.

At that moment the hot water arrived. I asked Mai Kamu to pour some in a bucket so I could wash my hands. I felt I was being examined as the other women in the hut watched carefully. I rolled up my sleeves and scrubbed my arms to my elbows. I rinsed and shook off the excess water. If I could get the midwife to work on the position of the baby from the outside—I felt the firm, round shape of the head and showed her how it was tilted up, explaining that we needed to turn the baby around—I would reach my hands up into her womb and turn the baby around so that the head came out first. It was tricky and not without risk, as the child had already dropped. I had assisted in such a procedure only once in the hospital in France. If the placenta broke loose, I would have a crisis on my hands. I held my breath and watched the midwife begin to apply pressure to rotate the unborn child from the outside. I grasped hold of the feet and small legs.

I tried once to turn the baby, with the poor mother biting down on her teeth and then screaming in pain. Afraid that we might fail a second time, I asked for the blessings of our Virgin to assist me, and with renewed courage, shifted the body of the baby as the midwife pushed gently from the outside. Suddenly, I saw a dark head in the birth canal. I asked the weakened mother to push one last time. She seemed to gather strength and grunted, bearing down hard for several minutes until the baby's head and body slid out, covered with blood, into the waiting hands of her grandmother. It was a girl, a blessing to the Mang'anja. The mother's perineum had torn, and I dug into my medicine kit for gauze pads to stop the bleeding. After the bloody placenta was expulsed into a large gourd, the midwife handed it to another woman who quickly took it outside and buried it away from the hut. I cut the baby's umbilical cord and tied it off, then took out my sterilized needle and thread from a packet and began suturing up the worst of the tears in the mother's perineum, as the mid-wife stood by to assist. I hadn't seen any visible damage to the cervix, and prayed that the woman's strength would carry her through.

Every woman in the birth hut seemed to know what to do. Two women, who stopped to scrub their hands the way they had seen me do, washed the curley-haired infant in a half pot while the midwife took a clean cloth and bound up the mother's womb. Her mother helped her to a pallet where she lay down, exhausted by her ordeal. I heard the baby's protests over her first bath, a reassuring sound, and saw her mother's quiet joy when she was put down on the woman's chest. After I washed my arms and hands, and pulled down my blouse sleeves, I picked up my cloak and put it on. I could hear several women outside the hut ululating to announce the news of the baby girl's arrival. It brought joy to my tired spirits.

A sister of the new mother escorted me home. 'Without you, I don't think my sister would have remained among us,' she told me solemnly. 'We were very frightened. We praise God for your good work. You will always be welcome as a friend in our village.'

I was so exhausted after I returned from Anyani late in the afternoon that I barely got through Vespers. I thanked God for giving me the strength to carry out such a difficult delivery. Then I collapsed and slept right through morning prayers. The sisters did not disturb me.

*   *   *

Sister Marie's visits to the villages increased, despite her reluctance to practice her healing arts unless someone called for her. Before long, word of her skills spread and, at times, when she visited a village she found a clutch of peo-ple waiting to see her. Some mothers came with infections or stomach ailments themselves, others with sick children. In addition to diarrhea and malaria, chron-ic coughing due to respiratory diseases, headaches, stomach disorders, and worms plagued the villagers. She treated the coughing with lemon juice mixed with honey harvested from hives hanging in nearby trees. She felt sure that there must be other remedies that were known locally. The supply of medicines she had brought with her was dwindling. Shipments from France were few and far between. This predicament strengthened her resolve to visit the sinyanga.

A local healing plant, *mfutsa (Vernonia adoensis)*, used by village women.

CHAPTER 25

Contentious Questions

"Why do you want to visit the *sinyanga?*" Chief Njobvuyalema stood up to his full height, his jet-black eyes like small coals boring into Sister Marie.

"I have been here over a year," she said humbly, "and every few months I have asked to meet the healer. You have discouraged me from doing so. I have explained why I wish to see him; that I may run out of medicines. It is important that I learn how to use local resources. This is why I need to see the *sinyanga*."

"Sister Marie, I have explained to you that the *sinyanga's* knowledge is his to keep. It is something handed down from father to son, mother to daughter or granddaughter, based on experience. It takes years to learn the skills of a healer, not a few months."

"I respect this. I understand," Sister Marie said, bowing her head. "I am not expecting to learn anything quickly. It takes time, perseverence." She stopped to weigh her next words.

"Chief Njobvuyalema, you are revered by your people, and I honor you for your wisdom and generosity. I have nowhere to go," she spread her hands wide in supplication. "I will spend all the years it takes to learn what the *sinyanga* is willing to teach me. In turn, I will share my healing secrets with him." She looked across the fields of sorghum newly planted, finding hope in the green shoots beginning to sprout.

The chief took his eyes off the bold young woman, and thought about her recurring request. She showed obstinancy, but she was respectful.

"You have learned to speak our language almost like a Mang'anja," he said slowly. "That is good. And the women speak well of your work."

Sister Marie lowered her head, again, resisting the urge to drop to her knees. Her heart was fluttering wildly. She felt a shift, like a gentle wind, in the chief.

"Perhaps you will benefit from learning something of our traditional ways. Let me think on it. I will visit the *sinyanga* and find out if he is willing to see you. It will depend on him."

Sister Marie raised her head to read his face. He seemed resolved.

"Zikomo kwan bili. I will be ready when you call for me." She curtsied low and backed away from him as she had seen the younger women do in his village.

But, he hadn't called her. In the meantime, two years had slipped by. She tried to maintain a measure of equanimity about the situation, filling her days with visits to villagers who wanted her services. She also began to learn from women who were willing to share with her, about healing plants.

*   *   *

Sister Marie's journal, 8th January 1908

Today, I visited Mai Chinsapo, the woman in Anyani village whose daughter I helped deliver the first year I was here. Chinsapo is nearly four years now and she has a year-old brother, who is called Kuti. Chinsapo was a gift—a gift from God, working through me. Her parents became catechumens after her birth. They attend Mass at the mission on most Sundays. When Chinsapo was baptized, they asked me to be one of her godmothers, and gave her my name. She is Marie Chinsapo, but I still call her Chinsapo.

Two of the women at Anyani village have been helpful in telling me about the plants they use to control or cure certain diseases. One of the plants is called *libare*. Its scientific name is *Pyrenacantha kaurabassana,* according to Father Winnen, who looked it up in a botany book on herbal plants. It comes from a bush with light green leaves that feel like velvet, and has red berries at certain times of the year. Mai Jere showed me the bush. It is the plant's tubers that the women use. They dig them up, dry them, and mash them into a powder, then mix the powder with boiling water and give it to people with high fevers. It is also used as a soaking solution for children with fevers. Mai Jere then showed me a vine that climbs on trees. The people call it *chilambe* (*Cissampelos mucronata* is its scientific name). They pound its leaves and put them in boiling water and drink the liquid to stop diarrhea. Sometimes it works, sometimes it doesn't, she said. When it does not work, she goes to the clinic. But it is far away. The clinic is one that the British started near Malembe.

18th March 1908

It has been a long time since I last heard word from Chief Njobvuyalema about seeing the *sinyanga*. He informed me, through Father Winnen, that the healer was still not ready: I needed to work in the villages a while longer. This news was not welcome. I felt as if the healer was pushing me away. I suspected he didn't want to see me at all. I have been patient. But, this time I wanted to march over to the *sinyanga's* village and confront him. Instead, I went into the chapel and prayed to the Virgin for fortitude and good will. A space began opening inside me. Compassion for the *sinyanga* filled it and swelled like a billowing cloud. I couldn't contain the feeling. It leaped from me to the *sinyanga* in his village, surrounding us in warmth. This is what had been missing—my love and compassion for a fellow healer. I had been so intent on getting the knowledge I needed to be effective here, that blinders prevented me from reaching out, through prayer, to the *sinyanga*. He had become an obstacle rather than someone to revere for his accrued knowledge. I vowed to change this. I also must write Father.

*   *   *

20th March 1908

Dear Baba,

I have been neglectful in writing this past year. I am unaware if you have written to me, the mails to this part of Africa being unreliable. I've had no letters since 1907. How are Mother and Dina? My brothers must be as tall as you are by now. Are any of them attending university? What do you hear from Hanna and Ma'an? I have missed news of them since arriving in Africa.

Your last letter, dated 29th February 1907, didn't refer to them. I know they returned to Tudmor after their first child was a year old and that another was born there. Does Ma'am write to you? I wonder how his horse breeding goes.

I feel sad knowing that they have faded from my life.

My healing work in the villages has increased with the long rains at this time of year. I am well, but one or another of the Sisters in our mission seems to be down with a fever in this dank weather, due to influenza or malaria. The latter is a curse, but with the medicines I brought from France we have managed until now. We are running out. I hope to work with a local healer to learn of the native medicines he uses. So far, he has resisted seeing me. Regardless, some of the kind village women are teaching me about local remedies.

Please give Mother my love, and write when you can.

Your loving daughter,
Amina (Sister Marie-Reine)

*   *   *

Journal, 20th December 1908

The wind is howling outside, blowing leaves and loose branches against the house. It has turned unseasonably cold. Rain threatens. It's hard to believe that four years have passed since we arrived here. I've ignored writing in my journal for the last several months because there hasn't been much to write about; only a few cold, dry months with little rain. Being farmers, the villagers worry about rain. Every year they burn their fields after the harvest to send smoke up to the thunderclouds. It's to encourage them to release the rain, so new seeds will grow. 'Sometimes, we make an offering to *Napolo,* the Serpent who lives on top of the mountain where the rain comes from,' one of the women told me. 'When all else fails,' she said, 'the chief calls a rainmaker to peform a ritual offering in hopes of bringing rain.' Let's hope the rain comes soon.

Today, Sister Lucie came to me with a letter she has written to our Superior, Mother Patrice, in France. It tells about our work at the mission and how Srs. Elaine and Therese have started an outdoor school here. I've copied it into my journal because it reminds me of our progress, even if my own work has been stymied.

19th December 1908

Dear Mother Patrice,

Greetings from Nzama Mission. We are growing. Our school is becoming part of the compound. It rests against one of the outside walls of our house. We have painted the wall black to serve as a rough chalkboard. The roof is thatched grass that hangs down on three sides. It shelters the teachers and the students from the hot sun and cold rain. The school has no walls at this point. Posts support the roof at the outside corners. Eventually we hope to have fired brick walls, God willing.

The first two years the children had nothing but grass mats to sit on. Now they have wooden benches, thanks to the Fathers. Srs. Elaine and Therese are able to hold two classes in the school. Sometimes, when the weather is fine, they take their classes outdoors under an avocado tree.

I thought Sister Lucie was through when she looked up from reading her letter. I told her I liked it. 'They have raised a school from dust, truly they have,' I added.

'But you haven't heard what I've written about you, Sister. Let me continue.'

The medicine we brought is nearly finished, and we have received only two shipments from home. In spite of this, Sister Marie-Reine is the greatest pharmacologist in the country. She is becoming known throughout the villages.

The people's growing trust in her is shown by the willingness of some women to share their secret remedies with her. She is helping people in the communities to survive. She also serves our own health needs. The number of converts is growing because of it. Is there anything you can do to urge the Order to send the much needed medical supplies we requested?

Yours very truly,

Sister Lucie
Nzama Mission

Sister Lucie folded her letter. 'You have made a difference in the villagers' lives, Sister Marie,' she told me.'Mother Patrice will be pleased.'

I told her that her description was very generous, and that it left out her own role in assisting me: 'The way you calm the fears of young children when I treat them and keep the mothers occupied while I tend to their families. Your constancy is a great source of comfort to me.'

It is true. Sister Lucie has become my dearest friend, someone I can talk to and whom I trust to keep confidences. When I was distraught over what to do about the *sinyanga* she listened to my concerns and helped to settle my mind. She is the one who suggested that I not wait for the *sinyanga* and, instead, approach the village women about their knowledge and use of medicinal plants.

Sister Lucie and I come from similar kinds of families. We were both sent to Dominican schools, but she is better at mathematics than I am. Even Father Winnen has come to appreciate her skills and has set her to record keeping. She is a gifted sister.

*   *   *

8th March 1909

Three days ago there was an emergency in Anyani village. Mai Chinsapo called for me because a child had fallen into a cooking fire and half her body was burned. I put burn ointment and bandages in my medicine kit and went straight away. When I got to the village, I could hear the child screaming from one of the huts. Mai Chinsapo met me and explained that the little girl was barely three years. She was playing near her mother's cooking fire with another child when she lost her balance and fell against one of the stones of the fireplace and toppled into the fire.

When I saw the child, I was horrified. Half of her face had been burned away, leaving the pink underskin partially covered by the charred epidermis. Fortunately, only the eyelashes of her right eye had been singed. The rest of her body, from shoulder to thigh, and down her right leg was terribly burned. The smell of her charred skin still clung to her body. She was crying in agony on a pallet with her distraught parents looking over her. When her mother tried to touch the little girl, she screamed louder. I asked what her name was. Her mother told me 'Makina.'

I noticed that Makina was wearing nothing. It meant that there were no clothes to be cut away, but her tender skin was sticking to the *chitenge* she was lying on. I squatted down at the edge of the pallet with my medicine kit, and began taking out the burn ointment, a salve, and sterile bandages, all the while talking softly to the child. I asked *Mai* Makina, the mother, to hold her on her good side, so that I could clean away dirt and ashes that had gotten lodged in around the charred skin and apply the ointment. At first the child wiggled and protested in her mother's arms, then as I began singing while cleaning her with the burn ointment, her voice became a whimper, and she sniffed up air in the wake of her crying spell.

Her mother soothed Makina as I worked. I began with her head and moved slowly down to her shoulder and burned stomach, applying burn ointment and salve. Then I moved to her thigh, leg and foot. She must have fallen head first, as her foot had the least damage from burns. I worked for nearly two hours, painstakingly covering each part of her burned body. At times, Makina cried out when I reached a particularly tender spot, but otherwise her large eyes remained glazed with the shock of the accident and she relaxed into her mother's arms.

I put special bandages I had brought from France on her face to keep her from scratching at the burned skin as it healed, and did likewise along her shoulder and stomach, which were raw. I did not have enough bandages for her leg, and told Mai Makina to make sure she lay on her good side, so that the other side would heal. I suggested she use several clean *chitenje*, rolled up, to keep the child propped in that position, and told her I would come back in three days. Mai Makina seemed nearly as shocked and dazed by the accident as her small daughter. Seeing this, I turned to the child's father and her uncle standing nearby. I asked if the family had other children. I was concerned that Makina's siblings might become curious and want to touch her. The child needed to be kept quiet if she was to heal.

The uncle shook his head. 'She is the firstborn.'

'Do not, under any circumstances,' I told the father, 'let other children into your house to see her. She should not be disturbed if her skin is to heal and grow back.'

'Will it ever come back?' he asked.

'A new layer of skin will grow in place of the burned parts of her body. But it takes time for it to form and it will only happen if she stays quiet on a clean bed and is not disturbed. Make sure you change the *chitenge* under her everyday and replace it with a new one,' I told both parents.

They nodded their heads solemnly, thanked me, and gave me a large papaya.

Mai Chinsapo peeked in to see how the child was and greeted the parents and uncle. She told me she was going to her gardens to work for a while.

The uncle escorted me to the edge of the village, carrying my medicine bag, then insisted on accompanying me all the way to the mission. 'Makina is a clan daughter and a first child,' he said. 'Her health and wellbeing are my responsibility, as much as her mother's. I will look in on her everyday.' He handed me back the medicine kit as we parted.

I realized, later, that what he said made sense: Here, children are born into their mother's clan, whether girls or boys, and they take their mother's clan name and become members of that kin group rather than the father's. The tie between a woman and her brother is generally stronger than between a husband and wife, I've observed. I have been told that a maternal uncle's word, especially the senior uncle's, is more important than a father's word in raising the children. It is the reverse of the custom in Mosul or in France.

10th March 1909

I went back to Anyani village to look at Makina and to change her bandages today. It was my second visit after the accident. I also hoped to see Mai Jere, one of the two older women who had begun educating me about local medicines.

The little girl was slightly better, though her mother told me that it had been difficult keeping her immobile. I took a small rag doll I'd brought from France and gave it to Makina. Her right eye was partially under the bandage, but her left eye lit up with interest as she took the doll from me and looked at it then showed it to her mother. I spent over an hour taking off the bandages, putting more ointment and salve on the burned parts of her body, and applying the last of my French bandages. All the while her mother was very careful in holding her so I could do my work.

Afterwards, I went to Mai Jere's house and she welcomed me with a customary curtsy, and invited me in for tea. She explained that she had not gone to her farm that morning because she was suffering from aches in her legs; the damp weather didn't help. She asked about Makina's burns and I told her it would take time for the skin to heal. She was sympathic and wanted to know what I had used on the child's body. I explained to her what I had done.

'What do people use here for burns?' I asked.

'There is not much that works. A child as badly burned as Makina might have died. I'm glad you taught Mai Makina how to care for the child while she recovers.'

Then we began talking about medicinal plants. Mai Jere told me that there is another plant, besides *libare*, that they use for diarrhea. It is called *mfutsa (Vernonia adoensis),* according to Father Winnen's book. Its leaves have pricky edges, like holly in France. She collects the leaves, washes and pulverizes them, then mixes them with *chilambe (Cissampelos mucronata)* to make a tea. 'It reduces the chances of diarrhea reoccurring,' she said.

I am now making a list of these plants and their scientific names for my future use, but I still think that better sanitation and boiling water would help in preventing diarrhea all together.

I stopped to see Mai Chinsapo, who was coming from her farm with her son tied to her back and a load of pidgeon peas in a basket balanced on her head. She swung the basket down and put it on the narrow clay veranda that runs around her house. 'Sister Marie,' she hugged me, 'we are always glad to see you. I have some news for you.'

'What is it?'

'We want to give you a Mang'anja name because you are one of us now, and with this new healing, we have decided to call you *'Mai Moto.'*

'Mother-of-Fire? But why?'

'Because nothing stops you, not even a cooking fire, in healing us. Fire can also heal. That is why we light fires in our fields after harvesting the crops. The charcoal feeds the soil and the smoke of the fires brings down rain to water the new seeds we plant. We think of you as a fire healer. Also, you have a lively character.' She smiled mischievously.

I laughed at this. 'I see.' I told her. I felt honored to receive a Mang'anja name. It will be easier for them to say than Sister Marie.

When I arrived back at the mission, I wanted to tell Sister Lucie about my new name, but the grim expression on her face stopped me. 'I have some bad news,' she told me. 'Sister Elaine is leaving us.' I stared back at her in disbelief. Sister Elaine had said nothing to me about being unhappy or dissatisfied.

Sister Lucie asked me to come to her room, and there she told me the story. Sister Elaine, who is very fair skinned, has had trouble adjusting to the fierce sunlight and hot climate of this country. But that is only part of it. Apparently, the lack of privacy she experiences, especially as a teacher in the community, is something she has never become accustomed to. She enjoys teaching, but wants to return to a more contemplative life.

'Sister Elaine has written to the Father Prefect in Nguludi and to the Montfort Superior in St. Laurent, asking to be transferred back to France *within the year,*' Sister Lucie completed her story, emphasizing the last part.

This is a setback for the mission, especially for Sister Therese who will have to carry the full burden of running the school and teaching without assistance, except for occasional help from Sister Lucie as she has time. The Order must find and send us a replacement.

I asked Sister Lucie if she thought my talking with Sister Elaine might persuade her to stay. She said, no, that her mind was made up. 'Neither Sister Therese nor Father Winnen has been able to dissuade her,' she said.
'Hopefully, the *Filles de la Sagesse* will send more sisters by September.'

We have been promised as much, and they are desperately needed as our work expands. Already the school has grown to four classes, with another one planned. My work and that of the other Sisters, grows every day.

The only good news I received when I returned to the mission after visiting the burned child was a message from Chief Nyobvuyalema telling me that the *sinyanga* had sent word that he is ready to see me. I should feel overjoyed, but it has been so long since I made the request that I had nearly forgotten about it. And the news of Sister Elaine's decision has left me feeling dispirited.

Chilambe (Cissampelos mucronata) pounded leaves used in tea to cure diarrhea.

CHAPTER 26

A Visit to the Sinyanga

"You must come with me, Sister Lucie. I need someone to take notes so I can keep track of the plants while the *sinyanga* tells me about them. It is too hard to both listen and write in my notebook," Sister Marie said. "And I will be going from his place to another village some distance away to see a new patient."

"What village?"

"Mangochi. It is on Lake Malawi. The chief there has sent for me. His wife is seriously ill and he wants me to diagnose her condition. Father Winnen said he would escort me. He knows the way. But I will need your help. I have no idea of the gravity of her situation. It would be a chance to see more of this country, too."

Sister Lucie hesitated. She did not feel up to such a trip, having felt a little tired lately, and she had the mission birth records to bring up to date as well as other nagging duties. At the same time, Sister Marie had become her closest friend, and her skills as a healer constantly amazed her.

"You know I need an assistant, as well as your companionship for the journey. It will take us over a day to get to Mangochi village," Sister Marie pressed. "You must come, dear friend." If she were honest with herself, her sense of propriety instilled in her from her upbringing in Mosul left her with an uncomfortable feeling about traveling alone with a man, even a religious Father.

"All right," Sister Lucie sighed. "You have convinced me."

"*Zikomo,* Sister," she smiled, and hugged her. "Knowing that you are going gives me peace of mind. Father Winnen will meet us at the *sinyanga's* village. It's on the way to Machinga, where we will spend the night at a mission before going on to Mangochi. So, pack a bag. We will be away for three days."

"Three days?" Sister Lucie's eyebrows shot up.

"We'll spend two nights in Mangochi and leave before dawn to return to Nzama the next day."

"How will we travel? Not by those dreadful *machilas,* I hope."

"No. I've spoken to Father Winnen about using the mission's donkey cart. We can walk to the healer's place, and Father Winnen will bring the cart there."

"What time will we leave tomorrow?"

"By six. A boy from Chief Njobvuyalema's village is coming to the mission to be our guide to the *sinyanga's* house," she finished. "I'm exhausted. I need to pack my satchel."

Sister Lucie nodded and they hugged each other good night.

After packing, Sister Marie bathed, not knowing what the facilities would be in Machinga or Mangochi. Afterward, she lay down, feeling clean and drowsy. But sleep would not come. Her mind was preoccupied with the seriousness of treating an important chief's wife.

*   *   *

Journal, 11th March 1909, Machinga Mission

The first leg of our journey was tiring. I am glad that Father Winnen agreed to use the donkey and cart. Without it, the trip would have been long and tedious. My companions have retired, but I'm staying up to write about my visit to the *sinyanga.*

He turned out to be a rather ordinary-looking man, except for his long, coiled hair, which was turning gray. I expected him to be wearing a leopard skin, but he wore trousers with a brown toga over them. He lives in a small, very dark hut at the edge of the village. I suggested we go outside and sit on mats. He brought one out, along with two stools, one for himself. I gestured to Sister Lucie to take the other stool, so she could write on her lap. I spread a *chitenje* cloth over the mat and sat on it, right below the healer. It surprised him. I waited for him to speak.

'How long have you been at Nzama?' he asked.

I told him over four years.

He nodded, then asked, 'How did you come to speak our language?'

"Practice. And working in the villages,' I told him.

'Where is your mother's home?" I thought this an odd question. Then he remarked, 'You are browner than most Europeans.'

I smiled at his boldness and told him, 'Mesopotamia.'

He looked blank.

When I began to fidget, he turned to the subject of our mutual interest. I began by asking him about *mfutsa (Vernonia adoensis).* I'd heard about it from the women in Anyani. I wanted to compare his uses of the plant with theirs.

'I use *mfutsa* to cure men's infertility,' he said, looking me straight in the eye.

I have to admit that I was not prepared for this and hid my discomfort by asking him how he prepares the medicine.

'I take the roots of *mfutsa* and slice them, then bind them with fibers from the plant. Next, I slaughter a chicken and take its neck and cook it with the roots and a little salt. I boil some *nsima* [maizemeal] separately and, when it is thick as a paste, I smear it on the neck as a covering. The root juice is absorbed by the neck and *nsima*. The man who has the problem eats the neck and drinks the soup for several days. After some time, he is able to make his wife pregnant.'

I didn't know whether he was pulling my leg, or neck, but found his explanation quite amusing. Who knows, it may work. And, it's a good excuse for having a chicken feast. I'm sure the *sinyanga* enjoys eating the other parts of the bird. I asked him if he used this medicine for women's infertility.

'It doesn't work for them,' he said.

Another plant he told me about is *nanyimbo*. The name refers to a tree whose large roots he uses. (I will have to look up its scientific name later). It grows in places where people have planted crops. The villagers don't disturb the tree until it 'dries.' I asked him what he meant by 'dried.' He said, 'The tree has died.'

'What happens if a person cuts down the tree before it dries?'

'That person will feel back pain because he caused pain to the tree,' he replied.

I was taken by his explanation that a human being suffers when he hurts, or kills a tree. How often are we held responsible for what we do to plants and trees in the interests of man?

The *sinyanga* related that *nanyimbo* has three medicinal uses: 1. for curing swollen glands, especially the gonads; 2. for treating rheumatism; and 3. for curing gonorrhea. I wanted to ask how the villagers came to be infected with gonorrhea, but thought better of it.

For swollen glands he said: 'Take the roots of the plant and pound and grind them when they are fresh and put them in a half gourd with hot water. Mix this with *phala* (an infant food made of mashed bananas and maizemeal).' He advises the patient to take the mixure for two days, or until he feels better. He also told me that sometimes, if it is a stubborn case, he puts a piece of the root on the fire and grinds it up with charcoal. He applies the paste to the affected areas by putting it into four cuts in the skin he has made, two in front of the gonads and two in back. I winced inwardly at the thought of this, but tried to act as if it were of little consequence.

For rheumatism: He uses a similar method, using cuts.

For gonorrhea, 'especially if there is pus,' he said, he uses the same method. However, he makes cuts only if he sees blood in the infection. If the mixture fails as a cure, he uses the milk [latex] of a banana plant's fruit and mixes it with water and boils it. The person takes it for several days. (How does this cure gonorrhea? I was beginning to have doubts.)

He went on to explain that he uses the roots and leaves of *chisoso,* which he showed me, to cure asthma and other breathing problems. He pounds the stringy roots and leaves together, then puts them in a pot, adding salt and hot water. He gives this concoction to his patient. If the person is not better in two days, he repeats the medicine.

A second use of *chisoso* is for snakebites. He chops up the roots and gives them to the bitten person to eat. He also uses a vine to tie a tourniquet above the affected area to stop the poison from spreading while the family takes the patient to the nearest hospital. 'Snakes are a serious menace,' he said. 'We take care in looking for them on the paths and roads we travel.'

He did not have to convince me. I told him I'd seen a black mamba once on the track from Nzama to Anyani, and had given it wide berth.

He responded by telling me about a man in Nzama who had lost an arm due to a snake that had bitten him on the hand when he was a child. 'In order to save him,' he explained, 'they had had to chop off his arm above here.'' He made a chopping motion above the elbow. 'It was a lesson to the children in the village.'

The *sinyanga* handed me a plant called *chilambe* with twisted, brown roots about the width of a man's thumb. He said he scrapes the outer skin and slices the root into pieces that he puts in a cup of hot water as medicine. It makes a very bitter tea, but helps to cure stomach pains and diarrhea. He told me if the diarrhea is serious, he administers the medicine three times a day for two days. He was very specific.

Finally, he explained that the root of *libare (Pyrenacantha kaurabassana)* which I learned about from Mai Jere, has several uses. When I asked what the root looks like, he said a 'large bulb.' He went inside his house and got one to show me. It is white and covered by a brown skin with pimples. He removes the skin. To me it looks like a large celery root. It has many uses: curing stomach aches, hemorrhoids and, when mixed with other ingredients, such as the bark of the *nkuyu* (a wild fig) and the roots of *mwanda wampo* and *cucumis,* serves as a cure for women's recovery after childbirth. This peaked my curiosity. I need to find out more about this mixture.

I was so fascinated by what I was learning that I hardly heard the donkey cart approach where we were sitting. The time had tumbled away from me. Father Winnen was ready to take us to Machinga mission.

'Zikomo kwan mbili,' I thanked the *sinyanga,* and from my bag took a wool sweater I had recently finished knitting and gave it to him.

'Zikomo, Mai Moto,' he said, looking pleased.

Having Sister Lucie along was a great help. She took down all the details. One thing I didn't think to ask is what he uses for a cure when someone comes to him who has been betwitched by another person. I guess I will have to ask the village women about this.

And now I must sleep. Tomorrow is another full day to get to Mangochi.

12th March 1909, Machinga

When we awakened this morning I heard the mournful call to prayers of a *muezzin* somewhere near the mission. It took me back to my childhood in

Mosul and during our caravan trip across Syria when the camel handlers said
their prayers. It seems there are more Mohammedans here than in Nzama's villages, though they are there, too.

Machinga is a dry place. The mission's buildings are made of fired
bricks and are quite handsome. There is a small garden with flowers, but the
compound itself is dusty. Both Sister Lucie and I were happy to get back in the
cart and be on our way to the lake, where we hoped it would be cooler. Father
Winnen told us that Mangochi village sits at the southern end of Lake Malawi.
The people are mainly Yao with some Mang'anja. Their religion is Islam, he
told us.

The journey from Machinga to Mangochi took nearly the whole day. If I
try to describe the scenery we saw on our way, I will never finish, so I'll be
brief. It was rather dry and flat in some places with tall, brown grass. We saw
gazelle bounding through the brush and several elephants emerging from a
wooded area. They are enormous creatures, larger than I expected, with wrinkled gray hides, very large ears that they use to fan themselves and, of course,
long trunks and tusks that I would not want to see up close. There were two
babies in the group and they kept running to keep up with their mothers. I felt
sorry for them.

Villages we passed were hidden in the bush, with only their thatched
conical roofs showing. Some clung to the roadside, with a few *ndukas* [shops]
lined up for business. We saw a string of women carrying bundles of firewood
on their heads, walking on the side of the road. A few men straggled along,
too, with hoes or *pangas* [machetes]. Their fields and gardens seem to be away
from the main road. We stopped at one *nduka,* where a few people had gathered to buy matches, kerosene and sodas, and to trade stories. We bought
sodas. Father Winnen talked to the local men, but Sister Lucie and I, seeing
them staring at our attire, hurriedly got back into the cart after visiting a fly-
infested latrine.

Mangochi Village at last!

The heat and humidity became oppressive and the land turned greener as we
got closer to Lake Malawi this afternoon. Coming down a winding hill, we
saw it, like a blue snake shimmering in the distance. The sun was beginning to
sink behind us spreading swaths of orange on the lake's surface. By then, all
we wanted to do was to reach Mangochi village before dark. Father Winnen
put the whip to the donkey to hasten its pace, causing us a bumpy ride. As we
neared the lake, we smelled the salty odor of fish being dried somewhere. It
mingled with the scent of cooking fires. We slowed down when the minarets of
the village came into view. At sunset, Mangochi was bathed in a wash of yel-

low and flamingo pink. Its beauty captivated me almost to tears. I thanked our Heavenly Father for our safe arrival.

We made our way down the main street, where *ndukas* and tea shops, some in bright colors, hugged both sides of the dusty street. Father Winnen turned the cart onto a side road. People hurried past on their way to their homes carrying forgotten items for the night's meal, while the muezzin's call to prayer echoed across the village. At the end of the road, we found ourselves in front of the chief's compound, a collection of thatched-roof round houses, with one of them noticeably larger than the rest. They were constructed of brick with a layer of pale clay on the outside. It gave them a whitewashed look. Very neat. Raised granaries, like miniature houses, peeked out from behind the houses here and there.

The compound was alive with elders, naked children, fat chickens, and a couple of goats. The enticing aroma of cooking fires and roasting meat beckoned us. Sister Lucie and I got out of the cart with our bags while Father Winnen went to the largest house in the village to find the chief.

A tall, rather handsome man in an ochre brown toga came across the courtyard with the Father. 'This is Chief Nyala,' he introduced us. 'He has been looking for us since mid-afternoon.

Sister Lucie and I curtsied briefly, unsure what the custom was in this area.

'We are honored by your visit,' the chief said graciously, looking from Sister Lucie to me. 'Your reputation as a healer has preceded you, Sister Marie. I have a brother who is married to a woman who comes from a village near Anyani and he told me how you saved the life of a newborn child and her mother.'

I felt myself begin to redden and lowered my head quickly.

'You must be tired from the journey.' He called to a young girl with a *chitenje* wrapped around her. It dropped from her budding breasts to her ankles. Her eyes dominated her nut-brown face. They were enormous and luminous like stones in water. She dropped to her knees in front of the chief, her head bowed.

'Take these visitors to your auntie's house,' he told her, motioning toward our satchels on the ground. The girl got up and gave us an uncertain smile, then picked up our bags. We followed her to a house that was some distance from the chief's.

A lithe, sinewy woman with slim, capable hands and toughened feet that looked as if they knew every furrow in her garden, met us at the entrance of the house. She welcomed us with a deep curtsy then introduced herself as Lenika Chitendze. She told us she is called Mai Samidi, for her oldest son, and we could call her that, too.

We nodded.

'My sister is the mother of Chief Nyala's Big Wife.'

I wasn't sure what the term 'Big Wife' meant. Was the woman large in size? Or was she the chief's first and, therefore, most revered wife? It was confusing. I had never heard Chief Njobvuyalema's first wife referred to as his 'Big Wife.' (Later, I learned that it was a term reserved for a first wife, who usually has the most status among co-wives.)

'What is the name of Chief Nyala's first wife?' I asked.

'Her name is Tjele, but we call her Mai Abdullah. She is the daughter of my sister, Zione Makaika.'

My head was spinning with all the names.

She asked us if we would like *chai*.

'Aye. Zikomo,' I said tiredly, with Sister Lucie echoing. Somewhere I could smell groundnuts roasting. Their tempting fragrance was making my stomach growl. As it happened, they came with the tea. Mai Samidi told us they were from her garden.

After we finished our tea and had gobbled up some of the groundnuts, she told us that we would be staying in her house during our visit. 'I am going to sleep at our mother's compound. It is not far from here. Please feel at home. The girl has brought water for bathing. It is in this large pot.' She pointed to a clay pot near the door. 'If you need anything, call her. She is Fania.' With that, Mai Samidi tightened her *chitenje* and threw another one around her shoulders, picked up a basket and balanced it on her head, and off she went.

Sister Lucie and I looked at each other and barely smothered our laughter. We both felt overwhelmed by the woman, her generosity, and all the names.

Fania, who had disappeared, returned to tell us that the chief was expecting us for supper. By then, darkness had fallen over the compound and lamps shone dimly from other houses. We asked Fania-of-the-beautiful-eyes for a lantern and she fetched one from a shelf in the wall and lit it for us, waiting expectantly. We realized she wanted us to accompany her to the chief's house. Sister Lucie took the lantern from her and we followed the girl to Chief Nyala's large abode. It had an earthen clay veranda that ran around the outside where several young boys were gathered. They suddenly stopped talking when we appeared. I greeted them. They answered politely and began to move away as we entered.

The chief's tall house was divided into several compartments with a large sitting room for visitors at the front and rooms going off on both sides. A large drum had been set up like a table in the middle of the room and four wooden bowls and spoons were set out on it. Four chairs had been drawn up to it. I could smell the flavors of a goat stew wafting in from the outside kitchen.

Chief Nyala, dressed in a clean, beautifully decorated rust toga, welcomed us and offered us seats at the drum. Father Winnen came out of one of the side rooms and he and Chief Nyala joined us at the table, which surprised me. I thought we might be eating separately—women and men—a practice I had seen in other African homes. A young man came in with a basin of water and a cloth and, beginning with the chief, offered it for hand washing. I was impressed. The chief has the gentile qualities of a well-to-do merchant, more so than Chief Njobvuyalema.

The meal of goat stew and rice with greens and other relishes was satisfying. As always, *nsima* accompanied the dinner, but enough other dishes filled the table so that I didn't have to eat it for a change. I find it heavy and filling with not much flavor. There was little conversation during the meal. The men concentrated on the food, and we followed suit. At the end, when tea was served, Chief Nyala began to tell me about his ailing wife.

She had borne a son, Abdullah, in their first years of marriage. The boy was now ten. His birth was followed by a miscarriage. She managed to have two daughters in a row after that, but had been unable to bear a child since then. As a result, Chief Nyala had taken a second wife three years earlier. She had recently given birth to twins. Shortly afterwards, Mai Abdullah became pregnant, much to the surprise of everyone. She went into labor early and gave birth to a stillborn son. There were complications. The chief was distraught, thinking he might lose her.

'This woman is like gold to me. She must get well.' he said, with real feeling. 'However,' he cautioned, 'I have another problem. It involves Mai Abdullah's mothers.'

It seems that Mai Abdullah's mother and her aunt, the one in whose house we were to spend the night, recommended that the chief call a *sinyanga* to divine the source of her illness and produce a remedy. They suspected that the second wife had bewitched Mai Abdullah and that only a *sinyanga* could cure her. Chief Nyala was opposed to the idea. Nonetheless, because he is a Mohammedan, as is his wife, he did not want one of the male doctors at the British clinic to come and examine her. He had heard about me from a relative and contacted Father Winnen, whom he had met in Zomba, a market center. 'The good Father promised to bring you to Mangochi as soon as he could,' the chief concluded his story. 'I know that the hour is late, but would you mind looking at her tonight?' he turned to me.

I was totally unprepared for such a request and turned to Sister Lucie.

CHAPTER 27

Bad Blood

13th March 1909, Mangochi

Even though I didn't want to see the chief's wife last night, Sister Lucie prompted me to do it. When she heard Chief Nyala's request and saw the look of hesitation on my face, she said, 'I'll get your medicine kit, Sister Marie.'

When she returned with my black bag, the three of us walked across the compound to a house that was larger than the one in which we were spending the night, but smaller than the chief's. Sister Lucie carried the lantern.

The chief called, *'O-di,'* somewhat softly.

A woman answered, and came to the doorway. She was a solid-looking Mang'anja with a smile that revealed prominent teeth. The chief introduced her as another auntie of his sick wife. The woman ducked out of the sitting room after we arrived, saying something I didn't hear to the chief as she left.

Chief Nyala's face clouded. He explained that he wanted to go in first and tell his wife that the 'Medicine Sister' had arrived.

'Tell her that *Mai Moto* has come,' I told him. 'It is what the villagers in Nzama call me. Also, let her know that Sister Lucie is with me.'

'I see,' he said, looking a little perplexed. He disappeared into a room next to the sitting area.

A few minutes later he emerged. 'You can go in. I will wait outside.'

I went into the room with my medical kit and adjusting my eyes to the darkness, told Sister Lucie to come in, too, with the lantern.

The woman I saw lying on a large pallet, was wan, but startlingly beautiful. She was not much older than we are—possibly in her mid-thirties—with smooth ebony skin that hugged the contours of her face. Her hair was cut close to her scalp. It emphasized her high cheekbones and the line of her fine nose. Her eyes tilted up slightly at the corners. She opened them to look at us and focused on me as I knelt down next to her with my medical bag. From the appearance of her eyes and pallor, I suspected she might be anemic. She had lost blood at the time of the stillbirth.

I surveyed her more closely. Her breathing was shallow, but normal. I began talking to her gently, telling her not to speak unless she wanted to tell me something.

She nodded.

I took her limp wrist and held it to take her pulse. It was weak.

A *chitenje* and a wool blanket covered her flaccid body. Sister Lucie put down the lantern next to me and backed away to sit on a stool. I opened the kit, took out my stethoscope and explained what it is used for. Warming it up in my lap, I gently lowered the *chitenje* covering her and glanced at her breasts resting like two dark eggs on her chest. I put the stethoscope up against the left one and listened, then shifted it to another spot. I found nothing abnormal: there were no lung problems. I felt down around her stomach for changes in her internal organs that might have been caused by the recent birth. Finally, I asked her to tell me about the blood she had lost after the birth and if it was still flowing. She nodded and told me there had been much blood after the child's delivery. At that point, she looked away as if mentioning the stillborn was too painful for her.

I thought for a few minutes, going through various illnesses I had learned about at the hospital in Toulouse. The main problem was the loss of blood. I explained this to her and told her that she should begin taking foods, like meats and soups with spinach greens, that would help to strengthen her blood, and to drink soups as much as she could. 'Most important,' I said. 'You must rest. You should do no work for a while.' I felt sure her anemic condition was the cause of her fatigue and weakness.

'You do not think someone has bewitched me?' she asked.

I was taken aback, but did not ask her why she thought such a thing.

'No. The problem is in your blood,' I told her. 'You lost a lot during the birth and your red blood cells are low. You must eat things that make your blood strong.' I emphasized, again, how crucial rest was for her recovery.

Her head dropped back and a slight smile played at the edges of her mouth. '*Zikomo*, Mai Moto,' she sounded relieved. 'You see, I thought I was being punished,' she said slowly, 'giving birth to a dead child. Then, when I continued to bleed, the feeling that someone was putting a curse on my body overcame me. I have felt tired all the time and thought there was no hope for my life.'

'There is hope,' I told her emphatically. 'I will tell the chief what I have told you, especially about the foods you should eat and the importance of rest to your healing. He is very worried about your health and wants you to get better. You must not fail him,' I said softly.

I knew then that I didn't want this beautiful woman to end up in a hospital having to get a transfusion. It is still a risky procedure in Europe, let alone in an African village. I had heard, while working at the hospital in France, that a European physician discovered in 1900, that human beings have three different blood types. The transfer of blood from one person to another was tried in France just before I left for Africa. It was a success, but matching donors and patients for a blood transfer is still new. Who knows if the British physicians in Blantyre are capable of carrying out such a procedure. I hoped that rest and the right food would bring Mai Abdullah back to health.

Chief Nyala arose when I emerged from Mai Abdullah's room. I explained the situation and the foods she should be fed over the next few months to build up her blood and stamina. I told him how critical rest was and that anemia caused her fatigue. I promised him that Sister Lucie and I would look after her the next day and make sure she was getting the proper foods. He nodded slowly and escorted us to Mai Samidi's house, thanking me and bidding us a restful sleep.

I've finally finished this report on Mai Abdullah. It is later than I expected. Sister Lucie is asleep. I've been writing this under the cover of my mosquito net. Father Winnen warned us that we would need our nets at the lake. He was right. We covered our beds with them tonight, but I still hear a mosquito's nervous buzz outside mine. I don't even want to put my arm out to turn off the lantern, for fear of getting bitten. Malaria is a serious problem here. We can't be too careful.

I pray that Mai Abdullah will be better by tomorrow.

14th March 1909

Yesterday, Sister Lucie and I took turns caring for our patient and making sure she got the foods she needs. Mai Abdullah's mother and aunties began cooking up great steaming pots of lamb stew—that smelled delicious—and preparing chicken soup with what looked like wild spinach and carrots. Nothing more was said about their daughter being bewitched.

By the end of the day, when I last visited her, Mai Abdullah looked much improved and her color was better. I'm not sure whether the feeding program I prescribed or the relief of learning that she is not bewitched is responsible. What matters is that her appetite has increased. With dignity, she thanked me and told me that I 'shouldn't be a stranger,' as she put it. 'We need someone with *Uzungu* knowledge to visit our village from time to time. You will always be welcome here.'

'I will come back,' I promised. "You have God to thank, *Mashallah.*'

Her large eyes registered surprise. 'You speak Arabic? The language of the mosque?'

'Yes. I come from a country where many people speak it.'

'Which one?' she looked at me. 'In Africa?'

'No. I come from Mesopotamia, north of Arabia.'

'That must be far away. I have never heard of it. I hope you will return so I can learn about your country and you can teach me Arabic.'

I promised her I would.

16th March, Nzama Mission

Our last night in Chief Nyala's compound was a stifling one. As we began
packing, I realized I hadn't seen the chief's second wife. She must have stayed
away when she saw us, wondering what we were doing with Mai Abdullah.
The young mother has her arms full with small twins to care for. I didn't
believe for a moment that she was capable of witchcraft. Such a thing would
have brought havoc to Chief Nyala's compound. I said as much to Sister Lucie
and asked her what she thought.

'Witchcraft had nothing to do with her illness,' she said emphatically. 'It
was a medical problem.' She put a night shirt in her satchel.

'The chief appears to love and respect Mai Abdullah,' I added. 'He told
me that out of respect for him, she became a Mohammedan when they married
and he, in turn, promised her that their children would belong to her
Mang'anja clan rather than his own clan. He seems to be a sensible man, don't
you think?'

She nodded. 'He does, and a highly respected chief.'

'But there is something that bothers me,' I continued, watching Sister
Lucie fold a blouse to pack.

'What is that?'

'It is the amount of influence Mai Abdullah's mothers—her own mother
and her aunties—have in family decisions.'

'At least they live in a different village,' Sister Lucie pointed out. 'I
think Mai Samidi has a particular interest in Mai Abdullah. Do you suppose
she is her godmother?'

'I doubt it. They are not Christians. Her son's name, Samidi, is
Mohammedan.'

Sister Lucie stopped packing and looked at me with those penetrating
eyes of hers. 'I suppose you're right. But, things would be so much easier for
them if they were all Christians, as we are in France.' She said it with such
conviction, tinged with an edge of condescension, that it caught me by surprise.

'Sister, you forget that I am not French,' I told her quickly, feeling
annoyed. Sometimes it seems that the French think they are the best people in
the world, and everyone should do as they do. 'And in France things have not
been so peaceful between Christians,' I added. 'Look at the way the
Government closed our schools and good works five years ago.'

Sister Lucie lowered her head, embarrassed. In order to smooth the
waters, I reminded her that I was raised as a Christian, and added, 'I will
remain a Christian until Our Lord decides to take me, regardless of where I
am.'

She looked up and, barely hiding a smile, said, 'That is a relief. It would
be difficult not to be a Christian in the *Fille de la Sagesse.*'

'Touche,' I laughed. 'Do you think it was a twist of fate that a Christian like me, from a Mohammedan country, ended up in a place like this where many people believe in Allah and the Qu'ran?' I pushed my dirty blouse and stockings down in my satchel.

She chuckled. 'Now, that is ironic. Do you suppose our Blessed Savior is testing you?'

I looked up. 'Perhaps. The world is a strange place. I heard in a recent letter from my Father that the Ottoman Turks have been waging a campaign against the Armenians, especially the Christians, forcing them to leave their homes and villages in Turkey, and killing thousands of them. I am glad I'm not in Mosul right now. I fear for my family and other Christians living there,' I admitted for the first time.

She came over and gently put her hand on my shoulder. 'I'm so sorry, Sister. I had no idea. I guess the best we can do is to concentrate on saving the lives and souls of people here since we can't be everywhere.'

I nodded, knowing she was right. Mosul has become too dangerous, despite my desire to return home. I must trust God to look after my family while I am doing my work here.

I took my cloak, folded it and lay it on top of the other things in my satchel, but there was one thing Sister Lucie and I left out—our mosquito nets. We still needed them.

After we crawled under our nets and lay down for the night, I could hear a persistent little whining outside the net, adding to my misery in trying to sleep in the oppressive heat.

I was glad we left Mangochi, even though I enjoyed the chief's hospitality and had made a new friend in Mai Abdullah.

I knew I would see her again.

CHAPTER 28

The Fragility of Living

"I feel as if I have been gone for a week, even though it was only three days," Sister Lucie said with a sigh.

"I know you have much on your mind, Sister. Thank you for going with me to Mangochi. Your help was invaluable," Sister Marie replied. She knew that the trip had caused her friend to fall behind in her administrative duties, including the entries she made in the mission record of new births, baptisms, and confirmations. It was a task that Father Winnen had recently turned over to her.

"There are three requests for burial services from our congregants," Sister Lucie told her. "They want the services to be conducted in their homesteads. I must make the arrangements and ask one of the Fathers to officiate." When she was not teaching or working on the mission's records, Sister Lucie visited the surrounding villages to collect information about changes in their populations and attend to the congregants' needs.

"I've noticed that it's the young men, and a few women, who adopt our faith, rather than the old people," she said. "They stick to their African beliefs or Mohammedanism."

"You do your best, Sister. Let me know when I can assist you," Sister Marie told her, feeling guilty about having taken her friend away from the mission at such a busy time.

Sister Marie's visits to Nzama village and Anyani increased. She was not always successful in her healing practices, especially in curing tropical diseases. Elephantiasis, for one, was a pernicious disease that afflicted adults and children alike. The only way to prevent it was if the people stayed out of the stagnant water in the reeds that clung to the banks of the river and took their water from places where it flowed more freely. But going into deeper places brought other risks, especially of a submerged alligator or of being swept away by the current. The women preferred using water close to shore for drinking, bathing, and washing their chitenje. As a result, some of them (and their children) came into contact with elephantiasis-bearing snails. Sister Marie would see those bur-

dened with the disease dragging a grossly enlarged leg along side their normal one. It was a visual reminder of the limitations in her practice.

Malaria was another challenge. It swept through the villages during the short rains, beginning in October, and throughout the long rains that lasted, off and on, until June. She lacked sufficient medicine to treat everyone who was ill and concentrated on helping mothers and children, leaving the men to the sinyanga. The old healer made much of Sister Marie's shortcomings, especially her lack of ready cures for common diseases that plagued the villagers, such as throat and lung infections, and malaria.

Since arriving five years earlier, Sister Marie had seen malaria come and go, taking some lives, leaving others weakened by it, and missing others all together. It puzzled her. So far, none of the Sisters or Brothers at the mission had had a serious case. However, a few months after she and Sister Lucie returned from Mangochi Village, Sister Lucie came down with a raging fever.

It appeared, at first, to be flu with a headache and chills. However, when Sister Lucie's fever soared and she called for more blankets, Sister Marie realized that it was the dreaded scourge and began mixing what she had left of the special powder from France into liquids that she forced her friend to drink. Sister Lucie became delirious, writhing and calling out gibberish, and occasionally a man's name that Sister Marie had never heard her mention.

Frightened by the woman's condition, Sister Marie cut back her visits to the villages and turned her full attention to her closest friend—they could not lose her from the mission. She had become a key to its smooth operation.

For days, Sister Marie alternated between bathing the woman's frail body with cold water and piling on more blankets when she called for them. Sister Lucie's lips were dry and her teeth chattered constantly. She was nauseous and, except for an occasional sip of soup and the tea laced with cinchona that she was forced to drink, she turned away from all food. Nothing seemed to assuage the demons that had taken possession of her body. Sister Marie was alternately frantic and fatigued in trying to care for her. She was unaware that help was on the way from an unlikely source.

Journal, 20th May, 1909

Today, I had a surprise. A visitor came to the mission and called out, '*Odi, Odi,*' to see if anyone was here. When I heard his voice, I went out to the yard and was flabbergasted to see a knarled old man with long locks standing there. I knew in an instant who it was—the *sinyanga* from Chirombe, whom Sister Lucie and I met on the way to Mangochi. I felt a white heat surround me in seeing him. It was as if he had appeared by divine intervention.

I barely managed to stammer out, '*Ho-di. Mwle bwanji?*' But I had the good sense to follow it with the usual litany of questions about his health, that of his family, and his village.

The *sinyanga* told me that he was well, that most of his family was as expected in this season of short rains, that his village was blessing the downpour, and the women were cultivating the new crops they had planted. The matter-of-fact way he gave me this news brought me down to earth. I told him about Sister Lucie's grave condition.

He nodded solemnly. He told me he'd learned of her malaria from villagers in Anyani. 'They told me she is very sick,' he said. 'That is why I am here. I have brought special *ndugu* medicine to lower her fever. It should help.'

I hesitated, fearing his concoction might adversely affect Sister Lucie, making her even worse. It might even kill her, in her weak condition.

'That is very kind of you,' I told him. 'Why don't you sit in this chair. You should have a cup of tea after walking all this way. I will see that you get it right now.'

On my way to the kitchen to prepare the tea, I stopped, and from a pocket in my habit, took out my notebook of healing herbs that included the ones the *sinyanga* had shared. I scanned the list quickly and did not see the one he had brought among them. But he had been generous with his knowledge and I didn't want to offend him by refusing his medicine.

I found Maesi in the kitchen and asked the girl to fix a cup of tea for the visitor, while I ran to consult Father Winnen.

I found him in his workshop. His gray head was bent over a small table that he was in the process of sanding. 'May I interrupt you, Father? I am in a quandary,' I said, out of breath.

'Of course, Sister.' He straightened up. 'What seems to be the problem?'

'It's about Sister Lucie—you know how ill she is,' I blurted out.

He nodded, calmly put down the sand paper and wiped his hands on a dirty cloth. 'We are all worried about Sister Lucie. She is in our prayers everytime we say Mass,' he told me. Furrows suddenly appeared in his broad brow, and he asked, 'Is she worse? If so, we should send for a doctor from Blantyre.'

I told him she is still very feverish and is vomiting now, despite the cinchona medicine I gave her. 'And I have run out of that,' I added. 'But the *sinyanga* from Chirombe village has just arrived with some bush medicine that he says will ease her fever.' I looked at Father Winnen to see his reaction. 'What do you think, Father? Should I let him treat her?'

He looked grave, and said, 'This, indeed, is a dilemma. I'm not sure Sister Lucie will benefit from the medicine . . . and it could do harm.' He stopped. 'But, again, we might find a new local cure for the disease.' He scratched the stubble on his chin. 'You certainly don't want to offend the man. He is highly regarded in the villages and was generous in sharing his knowledge of healing substances with you.'

'Yes. I thought about this,' I told him. 'And that is why I don't know what to do.'

'I have an idea,' Father Winnen brightened. 'Why don't you ask him to leave a little of his medicine for you to give to Sister Lucie. Then bring it to me and I will take a dose similar to the one he prescribes for our patient tonight, and if I feel no ill effects, we can give it to Sister Lucie tomorrow.'

I was aghast at the suggestion. 'Are you sure you want to do this?'

'A man with the strength of an ox like me?' He even grinned.

'You are a generous man, Father Winnen. What a splendid idea. I will explain to the healer that I welcome his medicine, but as Sister Lucie's mission doctor I would like to administer the dose to her.'

'That sounds like a wise approach. When he is gone, bring the mixture to me.'

I assured Father Winnen that I would, then returned to the courtyard where I found the *sinyanga* enjoying his tea with great slurping sounds.

I sat down with him and Maesi brought me a cup. When we had both finished, I broached the subject to him. 'I am much obliged that you thought to come and bring some of your special medicine for Sister Lucie,' I told him. 'You are a gifted man, as I learned when we visited you in Chirombe. We are honored by your visit. Sister Lucie had a fitful night and I do not want to disturb her. She needs to sleep. Is it possible for you leave the medicine with me, and tell me the correct dosage so that I can give it to her later when she wakes?'

'I can wait until she wakes,' the *sinyanga* told me, looking at me quizzically.

'But you are such a busy man. We can't keep you from other patients who might need you. Have you visited Anyani village yet? There is malaria there, too. They will need you.'

The *sinyanga* pondered my suggestion for a few moments while he gazed off at the distant mountains and I held my breath.

'Yes. This is the season of colds and malaria,' he said, with a hint of irritation that made me uneasy. Then he stood up abruptly. 'It keeps us moving.' He reached into the recesses of his toga and pulled out a skin pouch, made from the hide of a gazelle. He sat down again. The pouch was about the size of a large man's hand and was drawn tight at the top with a thin leather thong. I wanted to know it contents, but kept quiet. He asked Maesi, who was retrieving the used tea cups, to bring him a clean one.

The girl curtsied low and disappeared into the kitchen with the tray.

'Is there much malaria in your village?' I asked. I was not sure why he wanted a cup. Perhaps he was going to insist on treating Sister Lucie.

'Not as much as there is here and in Anyani,' he replied affably. 'We get less rain. It is drier down there.'

'We have had good rains so far this year, haven't we?' I knew I was searching for conversation to calm my sense of foreboding.

'It depends on where you are. You are close to the mountain here, so you get more rain. But you also get malaria more often.' Then we were both silent.

Maesi returned with the cup and, going down on her knees in front of the *sinyanga,* she handed it to him on the palm of her hand as if it was a sacred gift.

The healer took it and put it on the small table where the tea tray had rested, as Maesi disappeared. He took up the pouch and opened it carefully.

'Would you like a spoon?' I asked, full of curiosity.

'No. That won't be necessary.' Slowly, from the pouch in his lap he drew a small packet, about the size of an avocado pit, wrapped in thin cloth and tied with thread. He handed it to me.

It fit like an egg in the palm of my hand and was very light. 'What is it?' I finally asked.

'It is a mixture of two things, one a root and the other the bark of a tree. I grind them together to make a powder. Take half of it and put it into the bottom of the cup and mix it with boiling water. It will taste bitter, but it will lower the fever and calm the nausea.

I wanted to ask him for the names of the root and the bark, but I felt he might object. Part of being a medicine man, or a pharmacist, for that matter, is knowing the medicinal properties of various plants and how to use them, a knowledge that is known only to practioners. Although, the *sinyanga* had been generous in sharing what he knew when I visited him, now, he had become more reticent and protective of it. I thanked him for the medicine packet and accompanied him part way down the path that led to Anyani.

Returning to the mission, I took the cup with the packet directly to Father Winnen and explained the directions for taking the medicine, emphasizing that he should use only half the powder in boiled water.

Father Winnen, the gentle giant, looked down at me and listened intently to the instructions with just a ghost of a smile. I wasn't sure what it meant.

'This will be an interesting experiment—and I do like experiments,' he told me, his blue eyes twinkling. 'If I'm not dead in the morning, you will know it is all right to give some to Sister Lucie.'

'Father, how can you say such a thing?'

His eyes creased and he broke into laughter. 'Don't forget to come and see how I am first thing in the morning—after prayers, of course.'

'I will pray for you tonight,' I assured him. 'And you'll see me tomorrow,' I added. 'Now I must be off to care for Sister Lucie. I do wish she could keep food down.'

I hate to admit that I was up much of the night, worrying about Father Winnen. I was glad to have a patient to look after. It helped keep my mind off him, while I emptied Sister Lucie's bedpan and changed her compresses. I finally fell asleep in a chair just as the first doves began cooing from the mission's roof to waken others of their kind.

The chapel bell ringing insistently is what woke me several hours later. It startled me out of a troubled dream. Morning prayers were beginning. I looked at Sister Lucie under a mound of quilts and saw that she was still shivering and feverish. Her pale face was squeezed in pain, so I wet a cloth with cold water and pressed it to her forehead. I felt helpless, wishing I could do more for her. I was frightened that she would succumb to the fever before we could save her. Looking out the window at the first blush of dawn creeping over the mountains, I suddenly remembered Father Winnen. Oh, Lord. Is he all right? I worried. What if the *sinynaga's* medicine harmed him? What if he . . . ?

I threw on my cloak and dashed to the chapel. If Father Winnen was there, it was a sign that he had survived. If he wasn't, I thought, God help us. I tiptoed into the back of the chapel, adjusting my eyes to the dim light of the candles, and looked down the aisle to see if I could find him at the front of the sanctuary. He was not there. I froze, and fell on my knees and began praying.

'Please, dear Lord, have mercy. Protect Father Winnen from any evil that might have done him harm. He is the heart and soul of this mission. I don't know what we would do if he was to be taken from us.' I felt tears stinging my cheeks and wiped them away on the sleeve of my habit. Getting up, I crossed myself again, and, at that very moment, the side door to the sacristy opened and I saw someone approaching the altar. His even walk was familiar, but it was his tall stature and the shape of his robust profile that gave him away. 'Praise God,' I shouted, without realizing it at the time, and raised my hands to heaven in thanks.

I wanted to stay for the service, but I knew my place was at the side of my friend.

An hour later, Father Winnen appeared at the door of Sister Lucie's room. I'd heard him and opened it, then tiptoed out to meet him in the hallway. 'I saw you in the chapel this morning and knew you were saved. How did you find the bush medicine? Did you like it?'

'Not much, but I did take it,' he said. 'And, it doesn't seem to have affected me one way or the other. Rather disappointing, if you must know,' he grinned. 'I feel about the same, with a slight headache from the weather's dampness. But nothing more.' He paused and looked down at me, thoughtfully.

'Sister Marie, I have known Monsieur Kwafulu, the healer, for some time now,' he explained. 'I respect what he does for the people. He is a traditional healer, so he knows things that the British doctors in Blantyre don't have a clue about. Sometimes a villager will feel out of sorts and his problem begins to affect others in the community. When that occurs, he goes to the *sinyanga* for help to bring him back in harmony with the people. Kwafulu also helps someone who feels they might be the object of witchcraft by finding out who the culprit was, and what it was about the targeted person's behavior that caused the curse, or magic, in the first place. From there, Kwafulu recommends steps to be taken to counter the effects of the curse so the person can return to normal. He also has reliable cures for certain ailments and infections that he learned from his uncle, who was also a *sinyanga.* You have to respect the man. He is highly regarded in the villages. I don't know what this medicine I took was, but it certainly won't hurt Sister Lucie.'

It was almost a soliloquy. I was humbled by the wisdom of his words. 'Your observations are reassuring, Father. This may have been a test for me, to see if I am willing to open my mind to local ways of healing.'

'I know it is not easy, coming from a background in French medicine and pharmacology. But you were right to seek him out, as long as you respect the man's skills and knowledge. He is a healer like you. Be willing to share your knowledge with him, too.'

'I will, Father,' I promised. 'Did you bring the packet of medicine?'

He nodded, and from his pocket took it and handed it to me. 'Remember, half the packet,' he grinned. 'At least for now.'

'Thank-you. I'll have Maesi boil the water right away.' His words gave me new courage.

                                    *   *   *

Ten days into Sister Lucie's ordeal, Sister Marie gave her the last of the medicine that the sinyanga had brought, including a second packet he had left when he returned from Anyani on his way to his village.

Two mornings later, Sister Marie entered her patient's room and found her awake and resting. Her fever had broken. Sister Marie was ecstatic. She attributed it to the sinyanga's medicine.

Journal, 30th March

It worked! The traditional healer's medicine worked. 'You owe your life to the sinyanga,' I told Sister Lucie. 'He heard you were terribly sick with malaria and came with local medicine. I have to admit I was relieved to find it worked. You see, Sister, I had run out of what I brought from France. What a miracle it was.'

Sister Lucie smiled wanly at the time, but soon after, her color began to return. We knew then that she would recover.

I had to insist that she rest, however. I feared she might get up too soon and have a relapse. Then, a few days later, when she was beginning to regain her health, she said, quite suddenly, 'You know, Sister. I don't remember a thing. How ill was I?'

I told her she had a very high fever, with spells of delirium. 'I'm glad that you are beginning to come back to us.'

'How do you think I came down with malaria?' She wanted to know.

I told her she might have been bitten when we were at the lake several months earlier. Or it could have happened here, even though our mosquito nets are supposed to keep out the little bloodsuckers.

Then Sister Lucie asked me a strange question: 'Was there anyone else in here besides you?' I guess I looked puzzled because she went on and said, 'In a dream, I saw another sister come in to pray over me. Did I just dream it?'

'No,' I assured her. 'Sisters Elaine and Therese each came to see you, especially in the evenings after prayers.' I told her we had all been praying for her, including the Fathers, the students who come to the mission, and their parents. 'Some of the villagers have even left small gifts for you,' I concluded.

'That explains it. I thought I heard Sister Therese praying one night, but my head was such a muddle, I wasn't sure.'

That gave me a chance to ask her about something that had been bothering me. 'I am curious, Sister,' I began carefully. 'In your delirium, you mentioned a man's name—a Herbert—or something like that. Is that the name of your father?'

Sister Lucie looked surprised and turned away from me. She shook her head. 'No. He was a dear friend,' she mumbled. I told her not to give it a thought, to rest. But, it did make me wonder if she had ever had a beau in her life before she became a nun.

I also realized that Sister Lucie was still not herself. She was very weak.

CHAPTER 29

Shortages in the Mission

Journal, 15th September 1909

I don't know how we are going to manage. Sister Elaine left yesterday. Despite a letter that I wrote to Mother Patrice telling her of Sister Lucie's illness, and reminding her of our request for more Sisters and the need to replenish our supplies, we have had no word from her or the Superior of the Community of Mary.

The Fathers, assisted by us, performed a special service in the chapel for Sister Elaine's leavetaking. Fathers Deau and Cadoret will accompany her all the way to Chinde, to make sure that she gets on the ship taking her back to France. Afterwards, they will load new provisions on a smaller boat and make the return trip to Nzama. With good luck, Sr. Elaine should be back in St. Laurent by Christmas. We will miss her good humor and her sweet ways with the children. I know that Sister Therese will feel her absence most of all.

21st October, 1909

I have returned to Mangochi village twice since I saw Mai Abdullah last March. I found her completedly recovered by May. I went during the cold season this last time and she took me to her gardens and showed me where her cassava, pumpkins, onions and carrots were coming up. Her groundnut vines were also spreading their dark leaves across the raised beds. Cultivating begins here in November and December to catch the short rains, with the longer rains blessing the crops later.

I have come to like and respect Mai Abdullah immensely. She is an intelligent woman who cares about the wellbeing of her family and her village. She wants me to find a teacher, so that she can set up a school for girls in the village to teach them numbers as well as reading and writing, 'similar to what the boys get in the mosque school,' she told me, with a smile. 'With more and more British settlers arriving,' she continued, 'we must see that the children know how to figure numbers and read in order not to be cheated.'

Neither she nor the chief trusts the British, who have stayed mainly in the Shire Highlands and the north, but now are beginning to spread toward the lake. I would like to get down to Mangochi every few months to see how their plans are progressing. If only I had some help, another pharmacist to work with me, I would be able to serve more people.

12th November

I have been fortunate in my health, but Sister Therese had a miserable chest infection with a cough last month. I'm sure the cold weather didn't help. The change forced us into our gray wool habits, though we don't wear them much anymore. Mother Superior was right when she insisted that we take cotton habits to Africa.

We now depend on two new girls, Esmie and Scolla, to do our laundry and cleaning. Mangira and Maesi have left. According to their custom, they went for *Chinamwali,* the coming-of-age rite, in late October and returned to their villages to help their mothers, and to marry in the next year or so.

Chinamwali, I learned from Mai Chinsapo, is like a special girls' school that prepares them for becoming women. It is a combination of learning about homestead chores, instruction about sexual matters, including what to do when a girl first sees blood and needs to remove herself from others during menstruation, and how to behave properly around young men, so she 'doesn't get a baby before she is married,' as Mai Chinsapo put it. The rituals last for about six days. The girls, their women relatives, and other young women who are their sponsors, remove themselves from the village to a secluded place for the lessons, and events that include singing instructive songs and dancing. At the end of the teachings, the girls are taken to the river and cleansed by their older sponsors.

Afterwards, they return to their village in a queue, with women singing and ululating to announce their arrival. The whole village—men, women and children—come out to welcome them back. The celebration ends with a feast. *Chinamwali* seems very different from the way young Catholic girls go through catechism and prepare for their first communion. I guess each one serves its own purpose.

Of the two new girls helping us now, I like Esmie, especially, because she has a quick mind and is eager to learn. She is nine years old, her mother thinks; she was born before we arrived and it is only recently that we have encouraged the villagers to register the births of their children at the mission. In any case, it was Esmie's mother who gave her to us. The woman has eight other children and she told me that working for us at the mission would be good for her daughter because she will learn new things, especially how to read and write. I hope so. I would like her to go to the school in the mornings, after she has finished with some of the chores. I will have to talk to the other Sisters about Esmie's education.

Scolla doesn't seem to have the same interest in school or learning.

25th December, 1909 CHRISTMAS

We have been here for five years. Last night, the villagers treated us to another celebration, complete with the masks, the serpent, dancing and singing. This year-end festival is the way we keep track of our time here. We miss Sister Elaine, but a letter from the Superior arrived last week, telling us that the Order is sending two more sisters and a Mother Superior to take care of administrative duties next month. This is a huge relief because, frankly, one or the other of us has been down with something the past three months, so that only two of us are able to carry out our duties. Fortunately, our school is closed for a month for the holidays, so that Sister Therese can help with other things, such as preparing the rooms for our new arrivals.

Part of what convinced the Montford Brothers' Superior was hearing a firsthand account of our daily lives and services from Sister Elaine when she arrived at the convent. Mother Patrice related that Sister Elaine was exhausted from her journey, but was well and happy to be back in France. She will assume a new position at the Mother House in January, as an assistant to Mother Patrice. Her responsibilities will include training and orientation of teaching sisters who plan to work in Africa. 'Her knowledge of how to go about setting up a school and working with African students will be especially useful,' the Mother Superior wrote. What a wonderful solution! Sister Elaine will have a chance to share her new skills.

On this day of our Lord, Jesus' birth, I made two special prayers during the first Mass. One was for my family at home—that they escape the crises of an uncertain future left by a decaying Ottoman Empire. The other is for Sister Lucie. She has not been well. I fear that the malaria we thought she was over may have returned. How I wish the Sisters from the Mother House would arrive with the new supply of cinchona powder I asked Mother Patrice to send us. I can only pray for a miracle, not only for our sakes, but because Sister Lucie truly wants to stay in Africa where she feels she is most useful. In this, we are kindred spirits.

I have grown to love these hard-working people, and the hills, mountains and rivers that surround us. I enjoy my healing work. Returning to Mosul is out of the question, and settling in France does not appeal to me. I like our home here, the Immaculate Conception. It honors the Mother of all *Fille de la Sagesse.* And the religious community nourishes my spiritual needs. Sister Lucie's wisdom and humor are part of the joy I feel in this place.

6th January, 1910

Yesterday, a dark shadow fell on my life. I feel a heavy fog smothering me, twisting around my heart. After caring for Sister Lucie all these days between Christmas and New Year's, hoping and praying that she would vanquish the disease once more, she succumbed last night, quietly, almost as if she was tiptoeing away.

Her strength ebbed like an outgoing tide. The fever never left her. She was caught in a vice of aches, nausea and pain. It was awful to see her ashen, wasted body barely hanging on, and not being able to do something. Father Winnen came and suggested I call the *sinyanga*. I sent an urgent message to Kwafulu, just as 1910 broke open, and prayed that he might, again, carry a miracle. But by the time he arrived, Father Winnen was giving our beloved sister the last rites as Sister Therese and I gathered at her bedside with the Fathers, weeping and sighing. She left us like a morning star slipping over the horizon. I still cannot believe this sweet companion has been taken from us. I am left numb, unchanged.

Oh, Lord. Why did you take her from us when we most needed her?

10th January

The last two days I feel I've been in a shroud, not a habit. I can't quite bring myself to acknowledge the passing of this humble sister. I still feel her presence. Sister Therese helped me wash and prepare her for her next journey, while the Fathers made a simple wood coffin to hold her. Earlier they had consecrated a plot of land for the mission's cemetery, and yesterday we held her funeral followed by the burial rites. There were just those of us from the mission, Chief Njobvulemba, and some of the villagers who walked from the chapel with us to our sister's final resting place. I hardly remember what Fathers Winnen and Deau said as they lowered the coffin into the ground. Nor do I remember the meager words that I said as I poured a shovel of dirt onto her casket. Words are so inadequate now.

12th January

A special Mass was held for Sister Lucie yesterday. Father Winnen officiated and Sister Therese and I each had a role. Two of the older village boys, who have gone through the catechism, were acolytes. Many people crowded into the chapel, with more standing on the stone steps and outside in front, to pay their respects. The Africans were distraught. They had grown to respect and cherish Sister Lucie's gentle ways and many of them were in attendance. Their caring touched me deeply. Two village women told me how Sister Lucie had brought food to them after each of them had given birth to a child. The chief spoke of her patience in collecting information for birth records and other documents.

I know that it will take time for me to adjust to not having Sister Lucie next door, to take a walk with her, and assist me in my healing work. I remember when we visited Mai Abdullah for the first time and I was afraid of making a diagnosis that might be wrong, and how Sister Lucie's presence had a calming effect that gave me the courage to treat the woman. And now, she is gone.

18th January

I have been struggling with the burden I feel now that two of our Sisters have left us. Where are the new Sisters and the Mother Superior we were promised? It remains to be seen when they will arrive.

Each morning I get up and dress only to remember that I cannot go into Sister Lucie's room to see if she is ready for breakfast. Her room is empty now.

Last night, watching the firey sun dip behind the distant mountains, I realized that if I am to do God's work, I must pick myself up and go back to the villages. Even though I failed to save the life of this dear friend, in my grief I cannot abandon the Africans for whom death is a daily occurrence. Help me, God, to set aside my grief and carry on.

I cannot bring Sister Lucie back. But as I go about my work she will be with me, a constant companion—always.

*   *   *

26th January

Today I heard someone calling, 'Mai Moto, Mai Moto. Come quickly, the Sisters are here!' It was Mai Chinsapo with Mai Jere and some of the other women who had gone to Nguludi to meet the new arrivals from France and escort them to the mission. The Anyani women were ululating now as they paraded ahead of three *machilas,* singing and dancing up the road. I stood on the veranda of the Immaculate Conception House and watched their progress as they wound up the knoll. Sister Therese hurried around from the school to join me.

'Are those *machilas* I see?' she asked with a lilt.

'They could be,' I smiled mischievously. "I never let myself believe they would come. And now, here they are. Mother Patrice kept her word after all."

The Nzama Mission and Chief Njobvuyalema had been alerted by the Father Prefect in Nguludi that the sisters and Mother Clarise were on their way. Even then, it was hard to know when the trio would get there. The party accompanying them was smaller this time because the aging chief waited at Nzama village rather than going to Nguludi to greet them.

When the machilas *stopped, three women, their distinctive white coiffes bobbing as they extricated themselves from the hammocks, stood unsteadily. One of them was taller by a head than the other two. She stretched up to her full height and began talking to her companions, who appeared to be younger.*

Sister Therese looked at Sister Marie and giggled. "Do you remember how glad we were to get out of those things?"

"Yes. And how filthy we were, covered with red mud."

"The tall one must be Mother Clarise, don't you think?"

"I do. She will, no doubt, take us all in hand."

"It's a new day. I hope both sisters are teachers, and that the Mother Superior is as kind as Mother Patrice, *Mai Moto.*"

Sister Marie smiled hearing Sister Therese use the Mang'anja name the village women had given her. It gave her a feeling of warmth and substance, knowing that she had found a place in their hearts.

ACKNOWLEDGMENTS

People on four continents made this book possible. For historical documents on the Ottoman Empire in 19th century Mesopotamia and Syria, I am indebted to Sami Moubayed, Abdel Karim Rafeq, and the staff of the *Institut Francais d'Arabes du Proche-Orient* in Damascus, Syria. It specializes in Ottoman history. For a sense of historic Mosul, and for keeping my Iraqi Arabic correct, Sadek and Gail Mosawy were helpful, and sent me historic photographs of Mosul to draw on. In addition, two Iraqi couples from Mosul whom I met in a bazaar in Aleppo, Syria gave me a rare picture of their city and alerted me to the connection between Aleppo and Mosul which were once sister cities, both trading in textiles and sheep.

For the section on the caravan across the Syrian Desert, I drew on the descriptions of Anne Blunt in *Bedouin Tribes of the Euphrates* (1879), George von Siemens' *The Syrian Land* (1900), interviews with Bedouin camel caravaneers in Palmyra in 2006, and my own research in Syria. In addition, I took an extended camel caravan trip in Morocco and a shorter one in Jordan to get a feel for desert travel. Francoise Metral's paper *"Changements dans les routes el les flux commerciaux du desert syrien 1870-1920"* was particularly useful and included two maps of 19th century caravan routes across Syria, one of which I used.

For the chapter on Ma'alula, Maha al Haj, the curator of the museum in St. Serge Convent, acted as my guide and translator for interviews with villagers.

Sister Lise Therrien, the archivist for the *Filles de la Sagesse* in Rome, shared a wealth of information on her order and sent me journal entries and old photos of four sisters, one from Mesopotamia, who had traveled in 1904 from the Mother House to Marseille where they left for southern Africa. Father Mower of Maine also was helpful in providing context.

I am solely responsible for the settings, history, and language in Malawi having lived there for three years while teaching at the university. It is where I found the footnote that inspired this adventure. Thanks to all the generous people who read drafts of this book, including Sadek and Gail Mosawy, Jacqueline Michaud, J. Traub, Dana Leman, Jane Parsons, the Deer Isle Writers Group, Maureen Farr, who designed the maps, and Valerie Gazaui for the cover.